DAUGHTERS of ODUMA

DAUGHTERS of ODUMA

Moses Ose Utomi

atheneum New York London Toronto Sydney New Delhi

atheneum
An imprint of Simon & Schuster Children's Publishing Division
1230 Avenue of the Americas, New York, New York 10020
This book is a work of fiction. Any references to historical events, real people, or real places are used fictitiously. Other names, characters, places, and events are products of the author's imagination, and any resemblance to actual events or places or persons, living or dead, is entirely coincidental.

Interior design by Irene Metaxatos
The text for this book was set in Modum.
Manufactured in the United States of America
First Edition
10 9 8 7 6 5 4 3 2 1
Library of Congress Cataloging-in-Publication Data
Names: Utomi, Moses Ose, author.
Title: Daughters of Oduma / Moses Ose Utomi.
Description: First edition. | New York : Atheneum Books for Young Readers, [2023] | Audience: Ages 12 and Up. | Summary: Sixteen-year-old Dirt, a retired elite female fighter, must enter the South God Bow tournament to protect her found family of younger sisters and their beloved Mud Fam.
Identifiers: LCCN 2022016508 | ISBN 9781665918138 (hardcover) | ISBN 9781665918152 (ebook)
Subjects: CYAC: Hand-to-hand fighting—Fiction. | Contests—Fiction. | Black people—Fiction. | Feminism—Fiction. | Africa—Fiction. | Fantasy. | Fantasy fiction. lcgft | Novels. lcgft | BISAC: YOUNG ADULT FICTION / Fantasy / General | YOUNG ADULT FICTION / Girls & Women
Classification: LCC PZ7.1.U88 Dau 2023 | DDC [Fic]—dc23
LC record available at https://lccn.loc.gov/2022016508

To my sister,
Ijenerumhen Joy Utomi,
who was blessed with the skin
of the gods

And to my niece,
Elysia Ijenerumhen Utomi,
the First of the First

Na North
Na West
Na East
Na Isle
Na South
Na Vine
Na River
Grand Temple
Na Creek
Na Mud
Antie Yaya's
Na Rock
Na Sand
N
W
E
S

DAUGHTERS *of* ODUMA

1

The Mud Fam

SIS DIRT, the Second of the Mud Fam, stood on the edge of the jungle, staring down the narrow path. Heavy fig and yaro tree branches dangled over it. Drooping vine bridges spanned its scant width, easy crossing for the snakes and gekko. The path was near invisible if a girl didn't know where to look.

But Dirt had known the path her whole life, knew it better than any girl alive. She wasn't there to learn its winding curves.

She was waiting for her sisters.

They were out on their morning run, the start of every Bower's day. For the younger girls, the morning run helped build the endurance, strength, and discipline they'd need for Bowing competition. For the older girls who were already competing, the run gave them a chance to prepare their mind for a day of hard training.

A small part of Dirt missed it. Those jaunts through the jungle had made up much of her early life. But those years were behind her. Now she was an elder, more suited to a day of tea and sitting than one of runs and hard training. She was almost seventeen, after all.

Dirt heard her sisters before she saw them, their footfalls echoing through the bush as they rounded the bend and jogged into camp. Swoo was first, of course. Even in training, she needed to win. Despite the long run, her half-length top only had a few dark drops of sweat. Her pants, baggy around the thighs and cinched at midcalf, had none. What would have been a workout for some was barely a warm-up for Swoo.

"Na good day, Sis Dirt," she said, still jogging in place.

"Na good day, NoBe Swoo. Where are na Bibi?"

Swoo shrugged. "Too slow." She drew her handaxe from her waistband and squared off with an imaginary foe. The handaxe was for chopping wood, but Swoo used it mainly to practice chopping enemies. "But I say to them, 'Any Bibi too slow will feed na jungle cat.' So they will hurry."

Dirt suppressed her irritation. It was Swoo's duty to watch over the young ones. A Fam was only a Fam if each sister played her role.

"While we wait for na Bibi," Dirt said, "your Sis Dirt wants tea." She gave Swoo a flat look.

Swoo scowled, then went to get the requested tea, mumbling under her breath.

Dirt turned back to watch for the younger sisters, but called out over her shoulder, "I cannot hear you, NoBe Swoo."

"Your tea is coming," Swoo said sweetly before adding, in a lower voice, "you shabby goat."

Dirt ignored her. Swoo lacked the size and fat a Bower at her level should have, but she more than made up for those in other areas. She was as unbearably confident as a Flagga boy, tenacious as a starving street dog, faster than any other NoBe and half of the Sis. She'd finished the season with five wins in a row and, with her exciting Bowing style, flashy dance skills, and fashionable haircut—shaved on both sides with a high strip of tight curls leading back to a fluffy bun—had become a fan favorite.

And she knew it. Her ego was growing faster than her belly.

Any other day, Dirt would have disciplined her. But today, peace was more important than pride. If Dirt had to swallow one to keep the other, then so be it.

Soon the Bibi came huffing out of the jungle. With her long strides, seven-year-old Nana led the way. She was the skinniest Bower that Dirt had ever seen, but her body was tall and strong, and she had a quick mind for technique. Little Snore, straggling behind, was the opposite. Short, more round than long, and with plenty of good child fat left on her bones, the four-year-old had the look of a future champion, but the mind and mood of a very sleepy mamba. When she was awake, she was tireless and always plotting trouble.

When she was awake.

"Sis Dirt!" Nana said. "Na good day!" She was missing a lower tooth, knocked out in yesterday's training. The gap only made her smile more endearing.

"Na good day, Sis Dirr," Snore said with theatrical exhaustion. She collapsed onto her back, swinging her arms and legs in the dirt like she was splashing in a puddle. "Sis Dirr, I am tired."

"Up, up," Dirt said. "You are home. Na training must begin."

They groaned their disagreement.

The Mud camp lay in a muddy clearing amid the South's untamed jungles. In the rear corner was the Mud Fam's sleep hut, a driftwood shack bound by twine. Beside it lay the garden, which was half for crops—peppers, tea leaves, various fruits and vegetables—and half for chickens. In the center was the fighting ring, essential to any Bower camp. It was five strides in every direction, filled a finger deep with golden sand, and enclosed by a ring of canvas sandbags that divided it from the muddy grass of the rest of the Mud camp.

As Dirt ordered the Bibi into the ring to begin the day's training, Swoo returned with the tea and an eye roll, offering both to Dirt before sitting over by the sleep hut to watch.

"Time to train, Swoo," Dirt said. She could ignore the eye roll, but she couldn't ignore the break from routine.

"Why train with na Bibi? I am no longer NoBe."

It was somewhat true. Swoo would be a Sis next season and no longer compete as a NoBe. But the next season hadn't started yet, and the girl needed to show some humility.

Dirt wanted to say something sharp, but she looked over at the sleep hut, where Sis Webba slumbered, and thought better of it.

Peace, not pride, she said to herself. *Peace, not pride.*

So instead she turned back to the Bibi.

"Stand strong!" Dirt boomed. The Bibi hurried into their Bowing stances, feet shoulder width apart, one in front and one behind. They bent their knees just slightly, hands up, upper bodies loose. When they were in position, she began the Bowing sequence. "Slap na water!"

The two Bibi did as told, rolling their shoulders, palms reaching out and smacking down atop an invisible waterline.

"Ride na wind!"

They crouched low and surged forward, so close to the ground that each girl's rear leg dragged through the sand before she hopped back to her feet.

"Trap na fire!"

They smacked palm against palm and tightened their grips around the waist of an imaginary enemy.

"And Bow to na earth!" Dirt finished.

They were supposed to bend forward or backward or rotate sideways, bodies arcing like the unique swoops of narrow tree trunks.

But they were young.

Nana, indecisive as ever, couldn't commit to any direction. So she did all of them, wobbling around like a palm in a monsoon. Completely ineffective.

For Little Snore, it was playtime. She fell forward, flat on her face. Her coughed giggle dispersed the sand around her mouth.

As the Second of the Mud, it was Dirt's responsibility to train the Bibi and NoBe. She had to teach them not just the rules and traditions of Bower life, but also the fighting art of Bowing. She had learned long ago that she didn't have the spirit for competition, but she knew the craft of Bowing well and had made herself into the best trainer she could be.

"Breathe easy, Nana," Dirt said in a low voice. As usual, Nana was stiff. Even though she'd done the sequence a thousand times, her shoulders were tight with worry.

Nana let out a long exhale, the way Dirt had taught her years ago.

"Snore, up, up!" The youngest Mud sister stood back up and fell into her Bowing stance.

Once the Bibi were settled, Dirt continued. "Again!" she growled.

Even as the Bibi flopped through their techniques, Dirt felt a warm pride watching her sisters train. Ever since she was a

Bibi, she'd dreamed of being the First of a mighty Fam, one with hundreds of sisters and a camp large enough for them all. She'd dreamed of walking among the ranks of her sisters as they trained, fixing their technique, adjusting their posture, giving a word of encouragement here and a reprimanding look there. Though she would never be a champion Bower herself, she could still experience the glory of victory through her Fam. That would be her legacy.

Her dream still eluded her. She wasn't a First, she was a Second. And the Mud Fam didn't have hundreds of sisters, it had five. But every tree started with a seed, and with water and sun and a little bit of–

"Chaaaiii," Swoo exclaimed, watching the Bibi with mock disgust. "You Bow like sicksick dogs." She hopped to her feet and headed for the ring. "I will show you."

Snore laughed at Swoo's criticism and barked like a dog. Nana, however, stared hard at the floor as if she'd been scolded. She was a sensitive girl; Dirt often had to protect her against Swoo's flippant tongue.

Dirt felt a flame of anger starting to burn within her. Only Swoo ever made her that angry.

"NoBe Swoo, sit dow–" Dirt began, but Swoo was already going through the whole sequence.

She Slapped quickly, then glided low and cat-quick in a Ride, her favorite technique. She was one of the best Riders in the whole South, even when compared to full Sis. That was where her name had come from. The crowds that watched her fights loved to shout "SWOOOO" like the sound of rushing wind as she Rode.

Swoo snapped up to her feet, arms forming a tight Trap. Without slowing, she moved right into a flashy Back Bow, bending backward at the hip, far enough to threaten gravity, but not far enough to drive her head into the sand. Her Bowing technique was still years away from the level of the South's elite Bowers, but it wasn't bad for a NoBe.

Snore's tiny hands broke into applause as Swoo finished. "Chaaaiii," she cooed as Swoo flexed her muscles and soaked up the admiration.

Any other day, Dirt would have given Swoo such a tongue-lashing the arrogant girl wouldn't be able to look Dirt in the eye for a half moon.

But not today. She couldn't risk a loud argument.

"Your toes," she said.

Swoo raised an eyebrow.

"When you Bow," Dirt explained, "you must rise on your toes." She stretched her back nonchalantly, wincing at the small, satisfying pops.

Swoo rolled her eyes. "Sis Dirt, this is training." She did the whole sequence again, faster. Dirt grunted at the increasingly sloppy technique, but she envied the youthful athleticism. "Training is not fighting."

"Train bad, fight bad," Dirt said.

"Train fast, fight faster," Swoo countered, still battling the air.

Dirt looked to the Bibi. "Give Swoo no mind. There is much she does not know."

Swoo smirked. "Eh heh, and what do you know, eh? Do you fight?"

The mood shifted, as if a pebble had struck and sent a ripple through the camp. The Bibi's eyes slid from Dirt to Swoo and back.

"Na Sis knows many things, *NoBe* Swoo," Dirt said.

"Then come and show me," Swoo retorted. She stepped toward Dirt, competitive thirst in her eyes. "Teach me, wisewise Sis Dirt."

"Chaaaiii," cooed Nana and Snore.

Dirt sipped her tea, maintaining her calm. "How can I teach one who knows all? Go and sit."

But Swoo didn't move. She stayed in the ring, her face a mask of stubbornness tinged with curiosity.

Dirt understood what was happening. NoBe were young, strong, eager to prove themselves. The only reason they didn't challenge Sis more often was out of respect, not humility. And Dirt was old and out of shape, her belly shrinking, arms skinnying. Even in her prime, she'd been a notoriously terrible competitor. In a fight, the best Bowers were able to clear their minds and focus on battle, but Dirt's mind would get overwhelmed by her opponent's moves, the crowd's reaction, her sisters' encouragement, and, mostly, her own doubts. She was the only Sis in all the South who didn't actually compete.

In short, she was a perfect target for an overeager NoBe. To Swoo, Dirt wasn't a threat, she was a trophy.

But the only thing worse for Dirt than having her weak body and rusty Bowing skills exposed by a NoBe would be ignoring the challenge altogether. The Bibi would never respect her again if she backed down.

"You breezy, Sis Dirt?" Swoo goaded, delight in her eyes. "You breezy to Bow with Swoo, eh?"

So Dirt did what had to be done.

"I see you wish to learn," Dirt said. She hiked her baggy pants up at the waist, slid the cinched legs above her knees. "Then come. I will teach."

2

Bowing Lesson

DIRT AND SWOO stared at each other from across the ring.

All around them, the camp was still. The trees were quiet. The birds and monkeys, normally so restless, settled in to watch the fight below. A delicate breeze rolled through, just enough to tussle Dirt's short, already-tussled hair.

Nana let out a concerned groan. "Sis Webba!" she shouted, speeding off toward the sleep hut.

"Mama Eghi's teeth . . . ," Dirt swore. "Nana!" she hissed, but the younger girl was already going through the sleep hut door.

Just like that, all the care Dirt had taken to not wake Webba was wasted. But if she chased after Nana now, Dirt knew it would only look like she was trying to avoid the fight. Swoo would never let her hear the end of it.

She would settle this problem with Swoo, apologize to Webba, then discipline Nana appropriately.

Other than the creatures of the jungle, Little Snore was their only spectator. The youngest Mud sister found a good angle outside the ring and plopped down to watch.

Swoo fell into her Bowing stance. She was heavier on her front foot than most, a common trait among Riders. It allowed for a quicker burst toward the opponent. Dirt could remember the exact lesson, years before, when she'd taught Swoo that stance.

Then Swoo started Slapping, her shoulders rolling, hands outstretching and touching down on the air at shoulder height before retracting. She was gauging distance with caution and precision, like a snake's tongue tasting the air.

It was at that moment that Dirt realized exactly how much of a fool she was. Swoo was five years her junior, a competitive Bower approaching her prime; Dirt was an aging, long-retired coach. Swoo was already making all the calculations a fighter had to make, ready to capitalize on any error Dirt made; Dirt was still standing with her arms at her side, watching the younger girl advance. Swoo was one of the best NoBe in the South, lean muscle and a small but firm belly; Dirt was the only Sis in the entire Isle who didn't compete, with a great belly that was soft and sagging.

Dirt wasn't just going to lose. She was going to be humiliated.

"You ready, Sis Dirt?"

Na Gods forgive my proud head, Dirt thought.

Swoo Rode in hard, springing forward and low, arms outstretched. The speed of it froze Dirt in place, too quick for her to react, but Swoo must have thought it was some sort of trap. She stopped mid-Ride, springing away and to the side, well beyond Dirt's reach.

Dirt finally raised her arms and began Slapping. Offensively, a good Slapper could quickly push an opponent out of the ring for an easy win. Defensively, a good Slapper could keep an opponent away for as long as she wanted. In her youth, Dirt had been as good a Slapper as Swoo was a Rider.

In her youth.

But at sixteen, she wasn't young anymore, and before she could find a rhythm, Swoo was Riding in again. Dirt Slapped twice, landing glancing blows on each of Swoo's shoulders, but Swoo blew through them as if they were no more than mosquito bites. Her arms wrapped just under Dirt's armpits, around her back. She felt Swoo's palms clasp together, locking her in place. Trapped.

"Sis Diiirt," Swoo crooned into her ear.

Dirt was already breathing heavy. "Eh?"

"You ready, eh?"

That was when the real struggle began. Trapping was the most exhausting part of Bowing. It was a fight to break the opponent's grip and establish one's own. It involved prying fingers off, wrenching limbs askew, jutting hips out of reach in a struggle for superior position. Swoo's Trapping technique wasn't the best, but she was relentless, and far stronger than she looked. It took all of Dirt's strength and balance to break grip after grip, and soon her muscles became too tired to break them. All she could do was fight to keep her balance as Swoo dragged her around the ring, setting up what would surely be a painful and demoralizing Bow.

As her strength ebbed away from her, Dirt began to remember. The speed of the fight. The tug and pull, the shifts in weight, the moments of gulped breaths before the struggle resumed. The rhythm. You could always hear music when Bowing, even if none was playing. It was the music of the dust swirling beneath the feet, the music of the pounding heart, the music of the opponent's Slaps and Rides.

Swoo fought like a drum circle, fury from every direction.

Dirt fought like a broken kora, strings all akimbo and out of tune.

Swoo suddenly slipped beneath Dirt's armpit, sliding around to take control of her from behind.

"You ready, Sis Dirt?" Swoo bellowed in triumph. "Eh? You ready?!"

A quick buck of Swoo's hips and Dirt felt her feet leave the earth, hauled up by the strength of another girl for the first time in years. In that moment, the shame of being so viciously Bowed by a NoBe didn't even occur to her. All she worried about was being dropped on her head, sand exploding all around her and raining into her eyes and mouth and nostrils. Her teeth would slam together, maybe even onto her tongue.

"Chaaaiii, what is this?!" a voice called.

Instead of flying backward, feet over head, Dirt was dropped back down to the earth. Instead of climbing off the ground with a head full of sand, she was standing, whole and unBowed. Swoo's arms fell away.

Only one person could make Swoo stop so suddenly. Only one person commanded such respect.

"Na fight, eh?" the voice said, and Dirt turned.

Sis Webba, the First of the Mud, the champion and leader of the Mud Fam, stood beside the ring, deep-black skin shining in the morning sun. Her round face was split with a grin, her thick nose flared in joy. She was the biggest of them, in every sense of the word. She was as wide as she was tall, with a good layer of fat over her muscles and a belly that thumped like a tree trunk when she smacked it. She clapped her thick, meaty hands. Hands that were feared all over the South for what they could do to a girl. Beside her, Little Snore immediately imitated Webba's clapping. Nana was a few strides away, stuck between wanting to clap along and wanting to cry.

"Young NoBe fighting na old, saggy branch, eh?" Webba said, laughing. "Bibi Snore, you see your sister?" She walked forward into the ring. "You see why she is 'Dirt,' eh? If I do not come, she will Bow na poor NoBe Swoo. Boom!" Webba made an explosion with her hands, eyebrows dancing in amusement.

Dirt was still breathing too heavily to talk, but she nodded to her Sis then bent forward, hands on knees, wheezing.

"Never!" Swoo shouted. "Sis Dirt cannot Bow me! Did you not see, Sis Webba?"

Webba went over and put an arm around Swoo. "Breathe easy, Swoo. Sometimes na saggy branch can be strongstrong, eh?" She let out a roar of laughter, one hand on her belly. "Strong Bow, my sisters, strong Bow," she said, strolling over to Dirt. She threw an arm over Dirt's shoulders as well. "You ripe, my Sis?" she whispered. "Swoo punish you, eh?"

Dirt enjoyed a small laugh, relieved that the fight had ended with her dignity intact. Even in her old age, she was just as nervous in a fight as she'd been when she was a Bibi.

Shameful.

She took a deep breath and straightened. "I am fine." She turned to Swoo and extended her hand. "Strong Bow, my sister."

She was met with a glare that could carve stone.

Swoo avoided Dirt's hand like it was a rotted fish, then looked to Webba, a plea in her eyes. "Sis Webba, before you come, I am winning. Do you not see?"

But Webba had already moved on to tossing Snore in the air,

spurred on by the Bibi's mad giggles. Swoo frowned and then left, tugging her handaxe out of its wooden block and wandering into the jungle.

"My Sis Dirt," Webba said, setting Snore down with an affectionate tug of the young Bibi's ear. "Come and speak with me in your boring voice." She headed back to the sleep hut.

Dirt nodded. "Slap na water," she said to the Bibi. "Five hundred Slaps before I come back." She ignored their groans. "Then I will teach you na Back Bow."

Nana and Snore lit up at that and immediately started practicing. Dirt followed the First of the Mud out of the ring.

The Mud sleep hut was only as big as it needed to be, rising scarcely above Webba's head and with just enough floor space for the five Mud sisters to sit in a circle around a meal. The girls spent most of their day outside: training, tending the garden, resting in the shade. They only used the hut for meals, sleep, and changing clothes.

The last of which Snore still hadn't figured out. She always left her discarded pants around, no matter how many times Dirt disciplined her for it.

"I am sorry, my Sis," Dirt said, collecting the latest pants from the center of the floor. It was an old pair handed down from Nana, light brown cotton with a border of little green jungle cats stitched around the leg holes. "Nana should not wake you like this. You need rest."

Unlike a Second, who had duties toward all the Fam's other sisters, a First only had one job: fight. Throughout the Bowing season, Bowers fought each other to determine how they ranked, from worst to best. Then those rankings were used to determine who moved on to compete in the annual God Bow tournament, a monthlong, high-stakes series of fights that determined the future of each competing Fam. While it was common for Seconds, Thirds, and even Fourths to qualify for the tournament, only a girl with the power, experience, and mental strength of a First had a chance to win it.

As such, the reputation and future of the Fam depended on the First's victories. With the final fight of the Bowing season less than a day away, Webba's rest was more important than ever, and it was Dirt's job to ensure she got it.

Webba shrugged. "Nana does not wake me. I am awake." She grabbed a mango from a fruit basket they kept in the corner and ate half of it in a single bite. At least she was eating properly. "I hear na old woman fight na NoBe, so I go and watch. Swoo almost Bow you, eh?" Her face lit with mirth while she chewed.

Dirt grunted. "Strong girl, Swoo," she admitted.

"Young girl, Swoo. 'Na fierce wind will spread na young seed but break na old tree.' And you . . ."

"Eh heh," Dirt said. When she and Webba were Bibi, the elder Mud Sis had been full of such wise sayings, but Dirt hadn't memorized them the way Webba had. "I am na old tree."

Webba's tone became uncharacteristically serious. "Almost na woman, eh? You have na plan?"

"For what?" Dirt asked, even though she knew what Webba meant.

"Na Bow is for girls," Webba said with exaggerated patience, as if explaining to a new Bibi. "Soon na Gods will Scar you and you must go. But where, Sis Dirt, Second of na Mud? Where then will my oldold sister go?"

"I have no plan, my Sis," Dirt sighed. The only way she didn't spend all day worrying about her life after Scarring was by worrying even more about Webba's fight. "I do not know what I will do. . . ."

The Gods had left the Isle long ago, but They still watched over it: Mama Eghodo the Lawbringer, Papa Oduma the Defender, Mama Ijiri the Trickster, and Papa Abidon the Liberator. When a girl reached her seventeenth year, They Scarred her face, marking her as a woman.

And Bowing was for girls. Girls only.

Dirt would be seventeen just after this season's God Bow tournament ended. Then her Scarring would come. When that happened, she would have to travel to Antie Yaya's compound, and she would never be seen again. As a young girl, Dirt had watched the elder Mud Sis say goodbye on the day of their Scarring, uncertainty in their eyes as they walked into the jungle. Soon Dirt would join them, begin her life as a woman.

Except Dirt had no idea what life as a woman was like. The only woman in all the South was Antie Yaya, but Antie Yaya was special. It was said that all the other men and women had been taken by the Gods, as a punishment for some ancient crime. Like every other girl in the South, Dirt's earliest memories were of being a recruit in the halls of Antie Yaya's compound, where she was taken care of by Antie Yaya and the Mosquito girls who worked for her. But at four years old, when the New Year came, she'd decided to become a Bower, and since then she'd lived with the Mud Fam, growing up among the secluded plot of jungle they called their camp. In her twelve years as a Bower, she'd never spoken with, seen, or even heard of another woman besides Antie Yaya.

"I . . . do not want to go," Dirt admitted. She felt like a coward. Scarring was tradition. Leaving the Fam was tradition. Traditions had to be followed above all else. "Na Mud is not ready," she said.

"Because we are few," Webba noted.

Dirt nodded, then gave Webba a desperate look. "Too few, my Sis."

Webba pursed her lips knowingly.

A Fam had to have five sisters. Anything less, and tradition demanded that the Fam be split apart, sending some of the sisters to one Fam, some to another. Some would likely leave Bowing altogether. If Dirt's Scarring came before the Mud could gain another sister, it would mean the end of the Fam.

That was why the God Bow tournament was so important. The day after the final match of the tournament was the first day of the new year. That was when the South's youngest girls would choose to become Bowers or, disgustingly, choose the life of a Mosquito girl. The God Bow tournament was a winner-take-all contest for that pool of aspiring Bowers. By tradition, all recruits had to join the Fam that had produced the greatest Bower of that season: the God Bow champion.

The only sure way for the Mud to survive was by winning the tournament and earning those recruits. And with Dirt on the precipice of adulthood, this season was the Mud's last chance.

Dirt wasn't going to leave her Fam without a future. She had always dreamed of being part of a large, mighty Fam. She was determined to see her dream made reality.

"Tomorrow," Dirt said, hesitantly, "you cannot fight as you always fight."

Webba raised an eyebrow. "Eh?"

"I have na plan."

Webba shook her head. "Na plan for my fight but no plan for your life. My Sis, you think too much."

Dirt had always been a worrier, true. But sometimes worry was the only thing that kept you safe. "Eh heh. I am your Second. I must think too much about you."

"Finefine," Webba sighed. "What is it?"

"You must lose."

Webba blinked.

Dirt sat and motioned for Webba to do the same. Then she explained her plan. All season, the Sis of the South were ranked based on their wins and losses. Despite being undefeated, Webba was ranked second, only behind the South's other undefeated Bower–Carra Carre, the First of the Vine and the reigning God Bow champion. And Webba's next opponent. If Webba won, she would take over the first rank. If she lost, she would remain second and be the second seed in the God Bow tournament. Both the one and the two seed had the privilege of not fighting in the first round, but the one seed would face a lower ranked opponent in the quarterfinals.

"So why lose?" Webba questioned. "If I win, I am one. One must fight four."

"Eh heh. And who is four?"

"Dream."

Sis Dream, the First of the Sand, was the only girl Dirt considered a true Slapper. Elusive, with near peerless footwork and hand speed, she would be a nightmare fight for Webba.

"Eh heh. And if you lose?" Dirt asked.

"I am two. Two must fight three."

"And who is three?"

Then Webba understood. She leaned back against the sleep hut wall, grinning. "Wing."

Sis Wing was the First of the Creek, one of the finest and most honorable Bowers in the South, and the greatest Rider in living memory. But Webba was one of the best Trappers in the South, and her specific style was an impossible matchup for Riders. She'd already fought and beaten Wing twice.

Webba pursed her lips in thought.

"So you see?" Dirt asked. "You lose to Carra Carre tomorrow, you fight Wing in na quarterfinal. Easy. And all that you learn from Carra Carre tomorrow you can use when you fight her in na final."

"Sis Wing is never easy, my Sis." Webba had always respected Wing, even though she trounced her every time they fought.

"Finefine, not so easy," Dirt conceded. "But we must win this season. We must."

Webba nodded. "This is true."

"With this plan, we will."

She knew the gravity of what she was asking. Webba would rather lose her legs than lose a Bowing match on purpose. But this season was their last chance. They had to do everything they could. Pride didn't matter. "I beg you."

For a moment, Webba seemed to really consider it.

But the moment passed.

"Breathe easy, my Sis," Webba said, waving a dismissive hand. "I am no foolish Bibi. I have na plan for tomorrow."

Dirt frowned. "What is it?"

Webba grinned, finished off her mango, placed the seed in the fruit basket, and grabbed another. She took a bite of it, eyes twinkling. "Na secret."

"Eh heh? From me?"

"Eh heh. Do not trouble your old mind."

"Webba, tell me! You . . . jumpy gekko!"

Webba laughed so hard she had to wipe away tears. "'Jumpy gekko,' eh? My Sis, you are truly oldold. Swoo must teach you to speak."

"I will learn," Dirt said dryly. "But what is na plan, eh? How can na Second be na Second if she does not know na First?"

"You know me," Webba said. She recovered from the laughter and leveled a warm look at Dirt. A look full of the love and trust they'd built over the years. "And I know you. You are my Sis. This Fam we have made . . . I will never let us fail. I swear by Mama Eghodo and Papa Oduma. I swear by Mama Ijiri and Papa Abidon." She extended a hand, palm up, fingers just slightly curled. "This is na season of na Mud. Our dream will come, my Sis, and na South will know we are great. They will know na Mud."

In all their years together, they had disagreed many times. But even when Webba refused to accept Dirt's battle plan, she would still tell Dirt what she intended. Now, in the biggest fight of their lives, Dirt would be blind.

She wanted to continue arguing, but she knew it would do no good. Webba wasn't asking for her counsel, she was asking for her trust. If trust were easy, it wouldn't be trust.

Dirt set her hand over Webba's, palm down. She curled her own fingers and wiggled them against Webba's palm. Webba did the same to her. A silly pact-sealing they'd thought up as Bibi.

"Show them," Dirt said. "Show them who we are."

Webba grinned, bits of yellow mango stuck between her teeth.

The Gods help them.

3

The Grand Temple

THE JOURNEY to the Grand Temple took hours. And Nana was already tired.

It was the dry season, so the trip was pleasant enough, with tropical flowers bursting all along the way in vibrant scarlets, plump cobalts, and searing golds. But like all the South, the path was choked by coils of jungle. It teemed with prowling cats and bulbs of bright fruit and lounging branches heavy with leaves. Mosquitos drifted predatorily, which meant the spiders were out in force, their webs splayed across the slim path to catch all they could, filling their bellies for the beginning of mating season.

The Mud sisters walked along the path in a column, Swoo leading the way with her handaxe, hacking through the vines and spiderwebs. Behind her was Webba, walking with head high and chest out, with the confidence every Bower needed to have on the day of a fight. Little Snore was in the center, wandering off the path to collect leaves, pick flowers, and harass gekko.

Nana was fourth in line, doing her best to keep Snore from getting lost to the forest while also staying quick enough to not earn a hurrying swat from Sis Dirt behind her. On top of that, she had to carry all the food and clothing the Fam would need for the day in a big basket atop her head. Balancing the basket wasn't much trouble, but balancing it while chasing after Little Snore and keeping pace ahead of Sis Dirt was hard.

Sometimes being the eldest Bibi wasn't very fun.

"Eyes up!" Swoo shouted from the front.

Ahead, Nana saw the thicket of damp emerald jungle give way to the hot cinnamon-colored sand of the Grand Temple grounds.

The Grand Temple was the biggest compound in all the South, bigger even than Antie Yaya's. It held six buildings, five of which were small tents, one for each Fam. The last building was an arena at the center of the complex, the Grand Temple itself. Taller than ten girls standing on each other's shoulders and wide enough to make a long footrace from one side to the other, it was a massive stadium of red bricks that seemed to be always crumbling, sprinkles of red sand weeping down the building's side and dispersing in the wind.

"Today na fighting daaaaay!" Webba suddenly sang to the sky, her voice pure and proud and joyous. She drummed a rhythm on her belly.

Today na fighting day-oh, today na fighting day!
Today na fighting day-oh, today na fighting day!

Swoo joined in first, bouncing and smiling, then Snore, lending her tuneless voice and skipping circles around Nana. Even Sis Dirt joined in.

Nana added her voice last, not because she didn't enjoy the singing, but because she had to make sure the supplies were stable on her head before trusting herself to sing and sway without dumping everything.

Together, the Mud sisters made their way across the sand, singing and dancing and having a fool of a time. They went into the tent designated for the Mud, where Nana could finally unload all their supplies.

But the work didn't end there.

Bowing was a ritual with three parts: eat, dance, fight. The fighting was the biggest spectacle, of course, but any Bower would admit that the eating was the most important part. Eat good, fight good.

After a long trek carrying the whole Fam's extra weight, Nana then had to prepare the meal. That meant sweeping the tent floor, laying out the cloth to sit and eat on, cleaning the dishes, and preparing the food. It was work she liked, and work she was used to doing, but it was still tiring. Snore helped, but she was just too little for some things, like carrying a pot of boiling water. And now that Swoo was almost a Sis, she preferred to tell Nana and Snore what to do rather than help do the work herself.

When the work was done, though, the meal was always amazing. There were generous cuts of fresh fruit—papaya, honey melon, pineapple—and several bunches of banana. Round discs of flatbread as big as a girl's head, vegetables soaked in a tomato stew, and several roasted fish that Swoo had caught, spines and eyes intact. And, of course, a wide dish of pounded yam—the only true food for Bowers—thick and sticky in the stomach like a stone at the bottom of a river. It was all arranged in clay bowls atop the blanket.

Once Webba sat and took a chunk of pineapple, the feast began.

They talked while they ate, but they didn't talk about Bowing at all. Nana loved that about Sis Webba. Most Bowers, like NoBe Swoo, only ever wanted to talk about fighting. But with Webba, they talked about food and dancing and gossip and everything except Bowing.

Soon the meal was over, which meant Nana could finally get to the part of Bowing day she enjoyed the most.

For the Fam, each visit to the Grand Temple meant an opportunity to trade for supplies. For Nana, it was a chance to talk to other girls, and even some of the boys, to learn what their lives were like and what they were interested in. None of that seemed important to the big sisters, but it was to Nana.

"We can go, Sis Dirt?" Nana asked once the dishes were cleared.

Before Dirt could respond, Snore darted out of the tent, cackling like a madwoman, her pigtails bobbing.

"Snore, we must ask!" Nana called. She gave an apologetic look to Sis Dirt, who just sighed and nodded.

"Go and catch that Snore," she said.

Normally, NoBe Swoo would join them. But when Nana looked to her, she was shooed along.

"I will stay," was all NoBe Swoo said.

With all the approval she needed, Nana fled the tent, ready to breathe in the fresh air.

Outside the Mud preparation tent, the breeze was warm, the sand glowed with soaked up sunlight, and all the world buzzed with the energy that only Bowing day could bring. Most of the South's boys and girls had turned up for the match. They were congregated along the outside walls of the Grand Temple arena, mingling and laughing and rushing from here to there.

Nana caught a glimpse of Snore's bobbing ponytails plunging into the crowd. She sighed, then stalked off after her sister.

Among the Isle's four groups, there was a clear hierarchy. At the top, of course, were Bowers. The Daughters of Oduma. No event was more important than Bowing, and no one commanded as much respect as a full Sis. Even a Bibi was higher status than any other boy or girl. Where Bowers moved, others made way.

Then there were the Flagga boys. The Sons of Ijiri. While Bowers were serious and solemn, Flagga boys treated life like every day was a celebration. Rather than living in large Fam, devoted to a discipline like Bowing, they lived in small groups and spent their days playing Flagga, a silly game where they stole flags from each other. There was no reason for it except to brag. No honor to earn, no recruits to win. There were plenty of Flagga out now, waiting with impatient exuberance for the fighting to begin. When they weren't playing Flagga, they could be found by their meager builds, colored headbands, and the devious light in their eyes.

"Bower girl!" a group of them shouted at Nana, waving. They were clad in brown pants and shirts–standard wear for supporters of the Mud. "Oos oos, Mud Fam!"

Nana gave them an appreciative nod back, but she continued walking. Flagga boys would talk until seeds grew stems.

Soon as she crossed from sunlight into the shadow of the Grand Temple's massive walls, she reached the Temple's market. Two rows of wooden stalls faced each other, hugging the building's long curve. Each stall displayed its wares: brightly dyed shirts and pants, face paints and mirrors, all manner of clay pots and utensils. Mosquito girls, the Daughters of Abidon, worked the stalls and sashayed down the avenue, chatting and giggling. Just about all of them wore some sort of jewelry—necklaces and bracelets and anklets, each glittering with colorful, carefully carved stones.

Nana couldn't take her eyes off their jewelry. Mosquito girls were third in the South's social order, and they were the only group that Bowers truly despised. Nana had never understood why. Yes, they were skinny and they walked around with high-heel shoes and they painted their faces to appeal to boys, but without Mosquito girls, the South couldn't function. They were Bonemenders, Weavers, Cookers, and more. They made almost everything Bowers needed, were always available to trade, and they always set a reasonable price.

And the jewelry.

One particular driftwood stall caught her eye. It held jewelry fit for Antie Yaya herself. Necklaces and bracelets and anklets glittering with rubies and emeralds and sapphires, extravagant cuts catching and reflecting the sunlight a thousand times. Each piece was more beautiful than the last, each stone the perfect sister to the other stones it shared twine with.

Bowers were strictly forbidden from wearing jewelry—tradition, of course. But Nana didn't even want to wear any of it, not really. She just wanted, desperately, to know how it was made. Bowing was all about destruction. Destroying distance between you and your opponent, destroying the opponent's grips and balance, destroying the other Fam's hopes of victory. Nana wanted to create. She could see herself sitting against a good tree, shaping stones into perfect ovals, braiding twine to thread the stones together, and taking all sorts of materials and combining them to create something beautiful. She loved her sisters, and she liked being strong, but she hated Bowing. And she hated even more the constant destruction that came with life as a Bower.

"Honored sister?" a voice said softly.

Nana nearly jumped out of her skin. Only a Mosquito girl would address her that way. But she'd gotten lucky. If a Bower had caught her looking at jewelry like that . . .

She turned quickly, responding far more casually than she felt. "Eh heh?"

A Mosquito girl was staring at her. She looked about Nana's age. She was nibbling on candied persimmons, four of them bunched on a stick, a smile on her thin face. Across the top of her dark hair, she wore a cherry-red cloth headband with an off-center bow, her short bangs curtaining her forehead. Multi-colored bracelets glinted on her wrists and a cute necklace with a red apple pendant dangled above her chest.

"You like na adorn, eh?" she asked.

"No," Nana blurted. "Adorn are for Mosquito. Not Bower."

"'Mosquito'?" The girl giggled, but had a scrunched confusion on her face. "We are not mosquito, we are Butterfly." She continued eating.

At first Nana had to stop herself from scoffing. Maybe they called themselves Butterflies, but that didn't make it so. They couldn't just choose to be called whatever they wanted.

But then Nana really looked at the girl. And the girl watched her back with a kind of muted interest, the way one may watch a team of ants carry a leaf up a tree. If Nana were eating such a sweet, she would have worn its stickiness all over her face and fingers, and Sis Dirt would have chided her to wash the stains from her clothes. But this Mosquito girl . . . her wrist was bent elegantly as she held the fruit in front of her mouth. Her teeth nibbled delicately. Her mouth wasn't even half full as she chewed. Nana had always wished she could treat food like that, like it was sacred. She wanted to take time and enjoy a meal, for once. Bowers treated food like it would disappear if you blinked. Sometimes while eating she looked around as her sisters crammed papaya and fish and pounded yam into their faces and she felt embarrassed.

This girl had an undeniable grace. Maybe they *were* closer to butterflies than mosquitos.

But Nana wasn't about to admit that. So she just stood quietly, awkwardly.

Thankfully, a group of boys came by to break up the staring contest.

"How now, Apple?" the first boy said. He was a big boy, much thinner than Webba, but a bit taller. He carried one side of a large wooden box, while another boy carried the other end. They took it behind the stall and carefully set it down on the sand. Two more boys came in carrying a box between them, each greeting the Mosquito girl in turn, calling her "Apple." All four boys bore colored bands tied high on their arms, and the first boy had a jet-black fox following silently in his footsteps.

These were Pusher boys, the Sons of Eghodo, and the Isle's fourth and lowliest group. Though Mama Eghodo was the highest of the Mamas and Papas, Pusher boys didn't enjoy such privilege. They were far bigger than Flagga boys, often taller than Bowers and sometimes as strong. But rather than fighting for glory in the Grand Temple, Pusher Boys spent their days transporting shipments all across the Isle, North to South, East to West. They were the only group that got to leave their homes and explore the Isle, and their only friends were each other and the animal companions, called Petti, that traveled with each group. They seemed like a humble, gentle bunch, and Nana had never understood why they were so lowly while the childish Flagga boys were so high.

Tradition, probably.

"Honored sister," the first Pusher boy said as he saw her, diverting his wide-eyed gaze to the ground. Once he said it, the other boys echoed him, each hastily smoothing out his clothes and standing like a Bibi about to be scolded.

"Breathe easy," Nana told them. "I am Nana." She hoped that would relax them.

"Na good day, Honored Nana," they all said in unison, not relaxed at all. They clearly hadn't spent much time around Bowers.

"Na Pusher boys," Apple said, her eyes still on Nana as she ate her snack, "bring more adorn for me. Do you want to see, Nana?"

This time, Nana hesitated. Of course she wanted to see them. But she wasn't supposed to.

"I am in na hurry," she finally said. "I must find my sister."

"It can be quickquick."

"No, I cannot."

"Why, eh?"

"I cannot," she repeated, her confidence wavering under the girl's questions. "I–"

"Bibi Naaanaaa!" Snore's voice pierced through the marketplace din.

Nana turned to see the youngest Mud sister plodding through the crowd, arms full of sweets. A trio of Mosquito-girl vendors chased behind her, demanding payment.

"Bibi Nana, come and pay!" Snore said, taking a bite of dried mango.

Nana nodded an apology at Apple. "I must go," she said, turning back to Snore before the Mosquito girl could question her again. She went to the vendors chasing Snore and haggled over the price of her little sister's sweets. As she was finalizing the deals, the first drums sounded from within the arena walls.

"Time for na Bow!" Snore shouted excitedly, spraying fruit all over a vendor's face.

Nana felt her gut clench. "Time for na Bow . . . ," she echoed.

She took Snore's hand and sped back to the preparation tent.

It was time to fight.

4

The Godskin

AS SECOND, it was Dirt's duty to help Webba warm up before a fight. A good warm-up was as important to success in a fight as a good meal. It increased fluidity, improved endurance, and, most importantly, prevented injury. Warm muscles bend, cold muscles snap.

Dirt stood across the hut from Webba, her ever-grinning Sis, and extended both hands outward to show her open palms. It was the traditional Bowing salute, the way a girl showed that she came to the fight unarmed and of her own free will, willing to accept any result: win or loss, safety or injury. She slapped her hands together, sealing the unspoken contract. Webba returned the salute, but ended it by walking forward with her arms out and wrapping Dirt in a hug.

Dirt rolled her eyes. It was a total breach of etiquette and a bad example to set for Swoo. But she returned it.

Then they backed away and the Bow began.

As big and strong as Webba was, it took a serious workout to warm her muscles, so Dirt had to push hard. They went through every position, the same patterns they'd done together for years. They knew each other's movements better than they knew their own. With Webba, it was always the same lazy Slaps, the same deceptive Rides, and the same wind-sucking Traps for which she was named—she left opponents feeling like they were tangled in a spider's web.

Strangely, Webba tossed in all sorts of new techniques this time. Silly, impractical things that would never work in a real fight. Dirt countered them with confusion.

"Focus, my Sis," she chided.

But Webba just laughed, then responded by Trapping and Bowing Dirt with terrifying ease.

By the time Webba finally had a sheen of sweat across her forehead, Dirt was drenched in her own and sore in a dozen places. She fell onto her back, panting.

"My oldold Sis." Webba laughed, bouncing lightly from one foot to the other. "You still Slap like Mama Ijiri."

Dirt tried to respond, but she was too focused on breathing.

Swoo watched in silent curiosity from the other end of the tent, no doubt absorbing the subtleties of Dirt and Webba's techniques, studying their shifts in weight and the placement of their feet. It was good that Swoo had stayed to watch rather than run off to play with the Bibi as NoBe usually did. As brash and emotional as she could be, she was maturing in her own way.

Just as the warm-up ended, the drums sounded from the arena.

It was time.

Dirt looked at Webba, hoping to see her sister's face turn serious.

Some hint that she understood the importance of the upcoming fight.

But Webba just grinned at her and put Swoo in a headlock, rubbing her knuckles into the NoBe's hair as Swoo flailed and protested.

Soon the Bibi returned with arms full of sweets and smiles on their faces. But they immediately set the candy down and donned serious expressions, even Snore.

"Bibi Nana, Bibi Snore," Dirt said.

They nodded, ready.

"Prepare na Godskin."

There's a difference between Bowing and God Bowing.

Bowing was a sport. A craft. A way of life. Being a Bower meant long runs before sunrise, hundreds of hours practicing technique until the muscles throbbed, years of being thrashed by bigger and more experienced girls. The days were exhausting and humiliating, the nights just brief moments of food and sleep before it all started over again. Eventually, all those hours and years and early mornings and sore nights turned a bumbling girl into a hardened fighter.

Dirt was a Bower. She'd been Bowing her whole life. She loved the sport, the camaraderie. Swoo was a Bower as well, and Snore. Even Nana was a Bower, no matter how reluctant.

But among the Mud sisters, only Webba was a God Bower.

Bowing was a fight between girls, but God Bowing was different. It was a clash between Gods, with girls as their vessels. A God Bower wasn't just a fighter, she was a house of the divine.

A Godskin.

In the story of the first God Bow, the Gods hadn't known how fragile humans were. They'd put so much of Themselves into the two God Bowers' bodies that the girls had nearly become gods themselves. Their fight had reshaped the once infinite jungle, creating the mountains, rivers, and valleys of the Isle. Afterward, the girls had died, entirely consumed by the power of the Gods.

That was how things were in the old days, long before even Antie Yaya was born. But the Gods had left the Isle long ago. Many believed there would someday be a Bower–a "True" Godskin–who would be able to withstand the Gods' powers, but until that day came, a God Bow was just a fight between two girls, each with her Fam there as support.

Still, traditions had to be maintained. So a God Bower still prepared herself to house a God. That meant eating constantly, to be as large as possible. It meant sleeping most of the day, to be well rested. It meant training almost every waking moment, to be strong.

It also meant dressing well. If you wanted to house a God, you had to look the part.

Swoo, Nana, and Snore flurried around Webba, stripping her of her baggy pants and halfshirt. Once she was naked, they built her new outfit piece by piece. They clothed her in a skirt made of palm fronds, with a belt of clay beads in a hundred colors. Clay bracelets–some thick, some thin–ringed each of her wrists and biceps. Atop her head, they placed a short, clay tower crown. It was perforated all around, with wildflowers sticking out of every hole as if the crown itself were in bloom.

The final touch was the Offer.

In the jungles of the South, there were five Fam–Sand, Rock, Creek, Vine, and Mud. Each Fam was named for their unique resource, the precious good that could only be found in their territory. The Sand Offer was the fine white sand of their beaches. The Creek Offer was jugs of cool, fresh water.

The Mud Offer was mud. Near thick as honey and pale brown in color, the mud surrounding the Mud camp was, like all Offers, believed to be blessed by the Mamas and Papas. It could heal bites, ease soreness, clear a stuffed head. It had a distinct scent, like brewed orange skins, and made muscles tingle cool when rubbed on the skin. Nana and Snore spent part of each day out in the brush surrounding the camp, gathering the mud and plucking it clean of grass and seeds and jungle debris. They mixed oils and crushed herbs into it, prayed over each batch, and kept it in the sun to slowly bake, churning it with a mixing stick each time the top layer coalesced into a solid film, bringing the cool mud on the bottom to warm at the surface.

Gathering and preparing the Mud Offer was a detailed and tiresome process, but it was the most important part of the God Bow, even more than the training. Training sharpened the body, and often the mind, but the spirit was another matter entirely. Only the Offer, blessed by the Gods, could ensure a girl's safety.

The Bibi dragged a bucket of the Mud Offer across the tent. Swoo climbed onto a low stone, raised the bucket over Webba, and poured out the contents. It covered her head, then shoulders, ran over the curves of her bare chest, down to her toes. The Bibi used their hands to even out the mud and wipe it away from Webba's eyes, nostrils, and mouth. As they worked, Dirt closed her eyes, hovered her outstretched hands near Webba, and prayed aloud.

Mama Ijiri na Trickster, give our Sis na courage
to Slap.

Papa Abidon na Liberator, give our Sis na grace
to Ride.
Papa Oduma na Defender, give our Sis na
strength to Trap.
Mama Eghodo na Lawbringer, give our Sis na
humility to Bow.
It is.

"It is," Swoo and the Bibi murmured.

Dirt broke a kola nut, gave half to Webba, and divided the other half among her sisters. They all placed their pieces into their mouths and chewed in unison. It was bitter and earthy and tasted like ancestors, if such a thing were possible. The taste of all the people and places and wisdom that were long gone, buried beneath the soil of time. Snore's whole face screwed upward in disgust as she chewed. Nana shuddered as she swallowed it down. But kola nut wasn't eaten for the taste. It was eaten for the blessing, for the bond between sisters, past and present. Sisters remembered and sisters forgotten.

By the end of the ceremony, clad in her Godskin, Webba seemed to disappear. In her place was some wild and powerful nature spirit with skin of soft, rippling rock, waiting to be inhabited by a God.

Then she grinned and she was Webba again. "You ripe?" she asked.

Dirt just grunted.

Webba laughed, patting Dirt's shoulder. "You are not. You are never ripe." She moved over to the tent flap, and the other Mud sisters came together behind her.

Two paths lay before the Mud. The first was the path of defeat.

It was a calm and easy stroll to oblivion. No recruits, the end of the Fam.

The other path was far better, but far more difficult. It was a jungle path blocked by vines and branches and tangled roots, all of them thick with sharp thorns. But it led to victory. Recruits. Survival. Their dream.

And this match could determine which path they walked.

"Mud sisters!" Webba called without looking back.

"Na Mud!" they all responded.

"We move!"

5

The Mud and the Vine

ONCE THE ARENA was cleared of other combatants and the audience fell into an anticipatory hush, Dirt and the younger sisters followed Webba forward, passing beneath the arch and into the Temple.

A surge of cheers filled the air. All around the arena, one by one, the fans rose to their feet to get a better view of the entering party. Most of the South's boys and girls had turned up for the match: Mosquito girls in their stilts and face paints; burly Pusher boys with colored bands wrapped around their arms, some with their Petti on their shoulders; Flagga boys with their endless energy and their whistling and whooping. Each was clad in colors corresponding to their preferred Fam—Creek fans in blue, Sand in yellow, Rock in gray, Vine in green, and Mud in brown.

As more of them saw that the Mud was entering, the cheers increased. As did the jeers. The Vine fans had finally seen the

Mud sisters and were letting their voices be heard, but they were soon drowned out by the Creek, Rock, and Sand fans. Those Fam didn't have their own Sis competing, but the charismatic underdog Webba was easy to love, while the fearsome champion Carra Carre was easy to hate.

Webba, ever the showwoman, stretched her arms out wide and basked in the crowd's adulation. She beat her chest and roared back at the audience like a newly freed beast, sending a visible tremor of excitement through the arena. This was why Webba was the First of the Mud. Dirt knew how to Bow. She knew how to teach it, and she knew how to be patient with young Bibi learning the craft. But the First was supposed to be the greatest Bower in the Fam. Greatness didn't mean having a master's knowledge, or even skill. Greatness meant inspiring others.

Dirt had always been inspired by Webba. She was proud to call her sister.

From the boxed seating section near the middle edge of the arena floor, a skinny Flagga boy raised his cane high, then brought it down on the talking drum slung across his shoulder. It echoed roundly, like a tree crashing into a pond. Another boy answered on his hand drum. Then another boy on a third drum, wide and deep. They played, one after the other, their beats weaving together into a pounding round of percussion that brought the few audience members who'd still been sitting to their feet. More instruments joined in, the harmonic chimes of mbiras and the trumpeting wail of algaitas. It all came together sonorously, filling the arena.

They had eaten. Now it was time to dance.

Webba raised one foot and slammed it down into the sand. Then she did the other foot, letting out a shrill ululation that was echoed by the fans. Their cheers rose further, shouts of encouragement and adoration spurring Webba on as she began her dance, feet pounding and arms gliding and hips cracking from side to side like a whip. All to the round, throaty beat of the drums.

Since Dirt's singing was notoriously croaky, Swoo had always been the one to lead the Fam when Webba fought. She raised her smooth, smoky voice while Dirt and the Bibi echoed her, booming the Mud anthem across the arena.

We are na Mud sisters! (We are na Mud sisters!)
We fight, oh yes, ooooooh!
We are na Mud sisters! (We are na Mud sisters!)
We never quit, noooooo!

As Webba danced, the crowd began clapping and singing along, drowning out the malicious whoops of the Vine fans. Dirt and the other Mud sisters joined in with their practiced steps, dancing low and fluid, firm and powerful—like mud itself.

Together, the Mud sisters danced across the Grand Temple floor. Once they reached the far side, they received a final round of cheers and applause as the drumming fell to a quiet heartbeat and their dance ended.

Minutes passed, and the Vine was nowhere to be seen.

"Where are they?" Little Snore asked, fighting with the breeze to keep her hair out of her mouth.

"They come late," Dirt said.

"Why?"

"Nana," Dirt said, "explain to your sister."

"Carra Carre is number one," Nana said. "In na God Bow, na fight starts when na high-rank girl comes. So it is polite to let na low-rank Fam enter first, or na low-rank girl will look like na coward."

Snore still looked confused.

"It is tradition," Nana sighed.

"Oh," Snore said. "But this is so loooong."

Snore was right. Being a little late was polite since it gave the lower-ranked Fam time to get prepared. But being too late was disrespect, a sign that the lower Fam's time meant nothing. It was a fine line, and as the Mud waited, the Vine crossed far past politeness and into clear disrespect. The crowd soon came to understand the insult being displayed. The Mud supporters began to grumble and shift uneasily, while the Vine fans sneered, heckling the Mud supporters near them.

Nana was counting to herself and taking long, calming breaths. Swoo's gaze was locked on the Temple entrance, as alert and focused as Dirt had ever seen her. Little Snore was asleep, her snores rumbling with such volume and texture that some nearby Flagga boys stared at her in disbelief and admiration.

Webba paced a lazy circle. Her chest and shoulders rose slow and fell with each breath. She rolled her neck, stretched and cracked her fingers, shook out one ankle, then the other. Dirt had never understood how she kept such control of her emotions before a fight. Especially now, given what they were up against. A fight with Carra Carre wasn't just a threat to one's winning record, it was a threat to one's physical health. The girl's skill was only surpassed by her sheer physical power.

After a long while, with the whole arena waiting in silence, the music began again, but with another tune. Whereas the Mud entrance music had been light and hopeful, this song was as heavy and foreboding as a storm cloud. Dirt looked over to the Grand Temple entrance.

The Vine poured in like a summer flood, a surging wave of green. Each girl had her head wrapped round and round in vines, leaving only two small holes for her eyes. Some said that the Vine girls concealed their faces because they were monsters, that the constant wetness of their hidden jungle camp had deformed their faces the way fingertips wrinkle after too much time in water. Others said the wrapping of vines wasn't concealment at all—it was their actual heads.

Whichever was true, the faceless horde marched into the Temple and began spreading into a formation of several blocks, each one a half-dozen girls across and as many deep. There must have been near two hundred of them, the larger ones in the front and the smaller ones lined up behind. Most seemed to be about Swoo's size, but there were at least twenty girls who were larger than Dirt and carried themselves with the confidence of full Sis.

A full third of the Vine girls were scarcely larger than Little Snore: last season's recruits, Dirt realized. After sickness had forced Webba to exit the previous God Bow tournament, Carra Carre had won every match with ease, defeating the First of each Fam without giving up a single point. She'd earned enough recruits to keep her Fam full for generations.

Dirt's heart sank.

All season, the Vine had brought impressive numbers—fifty, sixty—but they'd never brought the new recruits. Recruits were better off sitting in the stands, watching and learning and asking questions of the spectating Sis. But the Vine had brought theirs onto the sand in a show of force. They knew that the next class of recruits was watching. They knew the other Fam were watching. They knew what it would look like, their near-two hundred girls against the Mud's five. They weren't just showing up to Bow, they were sending a message that no matter what happened in this match, they were now the most powerful Fam in all the South, doubling even the Creek's numbers.

"Breezy bucks," Swoo cursed. "Every one."

"Why na Vine bring so many?" Nana asked.

"Because they are breezy," Swoo said, clenching and releasing her fist. "These foul, swinging sisters of goats."

"No. To speak to us," Dirt answered.

"Speak what?" Nana asked.

One path led to the end of the Fam. The other to their dream.

"They tell us to wake up," Dirt muttered.

The Vine settled into their formation, each girl still as a pillar. From among their ranks, a single girl stepped forward.

No, not a girl.

A God.

Her head was also wrapped in vines, but that was the only similarity she shared with her sisters. She was massive, a head taller than Webba and a belly heavier. Her muscles bulged against layers of thick fat, and her torso—which was most of her—was wide as a Bibi and thick as a palm trunk. Where Webba was covered in mud, this girl was dusted in green, as if leaves had been ground up and rubbed all over her. Palm fronds fanned out across her shoulders, sharpened like knives, and two small wooden rods were driven through her long nipples, supporting the lattice of thin vines that dangled across her chest and stomach.

She swept her gaze slowly around the arena, and everywhere

her eyes touched fell silent, whether they'd been cheering for or against her. When her eyes passed the Mud Fam, Dirt felt a chill tremble down her spine.

Webba must fight this girl?

Fear sealed her throat. In her heart, Dirt knew that no good could come of this fight. Or *any* fight with that girl, that behemoth, standing across from them.

Without warning, the Vine's champion released a guttural roar, a boom of sound that seemed to shred the arena air. The crowd was hushed but for the Vine fans. They began a low whoop, quick and clipped and threatening, a growing crescendo that the Vine sisters themselves added to.

And the girl stood, watching, basking in the terrifying praise.

Carra Carre had arrived.

As she raised a heavy fist, there was a collective intake of breath as thousands of stomachs clenched. Fists went up from all the sisters of the Vine. Then Carra Carre brought hers down. Not back to her side, but slammed down into her chest, over her heart. Her sisters did the same, a rippling sound of fists thumping against flesh.

"Na Vine!" They shouted in unison, marching in place, their fists rising and falling again on beat.

Fight!
Crush!
Na enemy!

Every stamp of their feet shuddered the arena grounds, every fist-raised shout was a shock to the senses. Where the Mud Fam had sung powerfully, like mud sloughing across a plain, there was a wild violence in the Vine anthem, like a band of wild monkeys surging through the jungle with fangs bared, swinging branch to branch as they bore down on a fresh victim.

The drums ended, but the Vine continued their chant, bellowing the last few words into the silence of the arena.

Crush!
Na enemy!

Swoo snarled. "Let them try. Oos oos, Webba."

Carra Carre strode forward with a calm sway, her bulk shifting with each step. Without hesitation, Webba went forward to meet her. The two approached the ring at the center of the arena grounds, its boundaries marked by sandbags. Both girls stopped at the ring's edge, facing each other across the span.

Suddenly, a joyful murmur arose in the crowd, breaking the Vine Fam's spell of fear. There were smiles and laughter, hands rubbing in anticipation, Flagga boys punching each other enthusiastically in the arm. This was the fight the boys and girls of the South had been waiting years for. Four times this fight should have happened over the years, and four times it had been foiled. Injury on one side, sickness on the other, one fight canceled when Webba withdrew to avoid fighting the previous Mud First, one fight canceled due to monsoon.

But now it was here. Both girls unbeaten. The question of who was the superior Bower would be answered. Not for all the recruits. Not yet. Rather for pride and glory, like in the old days.

Webba performed the salute, extending her arms out wide, palms open and facing her opponent, then slapping her hands together. Carra Carre responded in kind, her wingspan terrifying, her hands massive. Dirt was convinced she felt the wind from Carra Carre's palms smacking together, even across the arena.

Before Webba stepped into the ring, she looked back at her sisters. She did it every fight, tracing over each of them with pride and admiration in her eyes. Most Bowers never looked away from their opponents, but Webba wasn't most Bowers. She did things her own way.

When Webba's and Dirt's eyes connected, there was a pause.

"Na Mud," Dirt mouthed, nodding, sending Webba all the love and strength and confidence she could.

Webba winked, then turned back to face her opponent as she crossed over the sandbags.

The drumming began again, but it was a different beat. What had been a rhythmic dance beat was now an urgent war cry. It thrummed with foreboding rumble, but also a hopeful peal. A song to honor past bravery and inspire more. Music fit for the Gods.

They had eaten.

They had danced.

It was time to fight.

6

Sis Webba vs. Sis Carra Carre

THE MOSQUITO-GIRL timekeeper unstoppered a person-sized hourglass beside the ring, and as the sand began pouring, the two combatants took up their Bowing stances.

"Bow begin!" the timekeeper shouted.

Like most Bows, they started with light Slapping, pawing the air as they turned a slow circle around each other. Webba feinted a Ride, tightening her whole body as if to surge forward. Carra Carre jerked back in reaction. Then Carra Carre feinted a Ride of her own.

Webba didn't move. The crowd cooed.

Swoo cackled, then cupped her hands around her mouth and shouted, "Breeeeeezyyy!"

"Oos oos, Webba!" Nana and Little Snore shouted together.

Dirt watched, silent. To fans and Bibi, the exchange showed that Webba was more confident. But to the trained eye, it meant nothing. They were just gauging each other's reactions. As the slower girl,

Carra Carre was smart to be careful. It was part of what made her the champion–as big and as strong and as skilled as she was, she was also a thoughtful, cautious fighter.

Carra Carre suddenly took a long step forward, and Webba froze. She must have recognized the problem: If she backed up, that would put her back to the edge of the ring and Carra Carre would look to push her out–an instant victory. If she stepped forward, Carra Carre would grab her and lock in a Trap. As great a Trapper as Webba was, such a fight wouldn't favor her while those big muscles of Carra Carre's were still fresh.

Webba didn't back up. But she didn't step forward, either. Instead, she dived low, right between the thick legs of the Vine Sis, and rolled straight back up to her feet. She stretched her arms out wide, strutting around the ring with a grin that brought the audience roaring to its feet and set Swoo and the Bibi screeching like wild dogs.

Instantly, Carra Carre turned and charged into Webba's unguarded back. Right before impact, Webba tucked in her arms and spun away. Carra Carre skidded to the edge of the ring, catching herself just before she tripped over the sandbag barrier. Webba, light on her toes, Rode in to catch her opponent off-balance and from behind, but Carra Carre was too athletic: she turned and took up a defensive posture. Webba settled for a Trap around the bigger girl's waist.

Then the real battle began.

"Snore," Dirt said, never removing her eyes from Webba and Carra Carre as the two girls struggled for control of each other. "Na three types of Bow. What are they?" She asked such questions sometimes, to make sure the Bibi were watching for the right things, beginning to think like competitors.

"Front Bow, Back Bow, Counter Bow," Snore sang, reciting the song that Bibi were taught to help them remember.

"Good," Dirt said. "Nana, how many points for each?"

"Front and Back Bow are three points, Sis Dirt. Counter is one point."

The Front Bow was a forward push, often with a trip of the legs to send the opponent falling backward. The Back Bow was the most impressive, bending backward to flip the opponent over one's head. The third and most common Bow was the Counter Bow, and it involved turning an opponent's Front or Back Bow against her by Bowing her to the side. Each required strength to execute, but they required technique most of all. If a girl didn't have the right grip on her opponent or didn't shift her hips with enough snap or didn't off-balance her opponent properly before the attempt, no amount of strength could be enough to move a seasoned fighter.

After securing her grip and positioning, Webba pushed forward into a light Front Bow. When Carra Carre defended, Webba shifted all her weight in the opposite direction, veins straining against her skin as she launched her head back and hips up into a full Back Bow.

Dirt, along with the rest of the Grand Temple, held her breath. No girl had ever lifted Carra Carre like that. Ever.

For a moment, Carra Carre's legs swam in the air, unfamiliar with the feeling of being off the ground. But then she dropped her weight low, pulling Webba upright and negating the throw. Then she countered by turning her hips and falling sideways, driving Webba's back into the dirt.

"Counter!" the timekeeper called, raising a finger in the air.

One point for Carra Carre.

The crowd groaned.

"Swinging buck!" Swoo swore, slapping her hands in anger.

Webba slid out from under Carra Carre and jumped to her feet, shaking her head and giving the crowd a finger wag to let them know it wouldn't happen again.

That got a healthy round of laughter.

"Sis Dirt?" Nana said.

"Eh?" Dirt kept her eyes on the ring as Webba and Carra Carre resettled into their stances.

"Why does Sis Webba Bow like this today, eh? Does she not want to win?"

In truth, Dirt wondered the same thing. Webba had expressly refused to lose the match, even when Dirt laid out the strategic value. If she had changed her mind and was trying to lose, she didn't have to put herself at such risk with an opponent so dangerous. Dirt felt uneasy not knowing what was in her sister's mind.

But it wasn't a Bibi's place to question the First of the Fam.

"Nana, you are na Bibi or na Sis?"

"Na Bibi, Sis Dirt."

"So what do you know?"

Nana was quiet for a moment, then said in a morose voice, "Nothing, Sis Dirt."

"Eh heh."

The two combatants Slapped back and forth, Rode in and dodged, Trapped and broke Traps. Webba fought like she was possessed by Mama Ijiri Herself. Her movements were wild, acrobatic, playful. She mixed regular attacks with all manner of improbable techniques: Side Slaps and Cartwheel Rides and Ankle Traps. Dirt recognized them as the same techniques she'd used earlier, in sparring. It was one thing to use them in practice, but another thing entirely to use them in a real fight against the most terrifying God Bower in the South. But Webba was fearless. She'd turned the ring into a stage, and she was the only one with the script.

Even with her face hidden behind her vine mask, Carra Carre's growing frustration was clear. When she tried to push Webba to the edge of the ring, Webba found the center. When she tried a Trap, Webba danced out of reach. No matter how bold the Vine champion's techniques, Webba always seemed a step ahead.

As the time fell below half sand, Carra Carre remained a point ahead. But Dirt felt a change in the Grand Temple, both from the audience and from the shuffling uncertainty of the Vine Fam across the arena.

Carra Carre was struggling.

The invincible champion was dusted in the Temple's red sand, smudged in sweat. The lattice of vines dangling between her breasts bore half a dozen small cuts and breaks. With each exchange of Rides and Traps, Carra Carre seemed to take just a hair longer to get back into position. Her aura of dominance and fear suddenly seemed silly. Carra Carre was vulnerable. Mortal.

She was like any other girl, only bigger.

Whatever message the Vine had hoped to send was failing before everyone's eyes. Even when Carra Carre scored another Counter Bow and went up by two points, nothing changed. Webba kept to her plan of bouncing around like a madwoman, and the crowd was celebrating as if she were on her way to victory.

As Carra Carre tired, Webba began playing to the crowd even more. She Slapped inches from Carra Carre's face, goading her. She walked forward with her hands down, jiggling her belly, the height of competitive disrespect. Carra Carre could do nothing but back away.

Webba faked a Ride, then dove in with a Double Leg Trap. She slid in low, wrapping her two legs around one of Carra Carre's. It was a preposterous move, one so slow and ungainly that it rarely even worked on Bibi.

But Carra Carre was drained, and it was the last thing she expected.

By the time the First of the Vine reached down to untangle her leg from Webba's, she was already falling backward, with no hands to catch herself.

When she hit the dirt, the Grand Temple exploded.

"Bow!" the timekeeper called, punching three fingers to the sky.

With less than a quarter sand left, Webba had taken the lead.

Thousands of Flagga boys, Pusher boys, and Mosquito girls, arms over each other's shoulders, jumped in their seats, shaking the arena. Together, they sang another round of the Mud anthem.

We are na Mud sisters! (We are na Mud sisters!)
We fight, oh yes, ooooooh!
We are na Mud sisters! (We are na Mud sisters!)
We never quit, noooooo!

Nana and Little Snore danced and sang, hugging each other. Swoo sang along as well, making obscene gestures across the Temple at the Vine sisters.

Finally, Dirt understood Webba's genius.

By using an unusual style, Webba had shown Carra Carre nothing about how she really fought. If they met again in the God Bow tournament, it would be, for Carra Carre, as if they were fighting for the first time. Webba had learned Carra Carre's movements without revealing her own.

But she'd done even more than that.

She'd given the crowd an unforgettable spectacle. She'd demoralized the Vine and raised the status of the Mud in front of the season's biggest audience. She'd shown herself to be the greatest Bower in the South. She was on her way to beating the unbeatable.

When the two combatants returned to their feet, Carra Carre's desperation was clear. But so was her exhaustion. She advanced on Webba slowly, and Webba kept her distance, staying just inside the edge of the ring.

As the time trickled away, Dirt allowed herself a long exhale and a few proud notes of song beneath her breath: "We are na Mud sisters."

In a final, desperate attack, Carra Carre Rode in so clumsily and with such little force that the crowd laughed as Webba stepped to the side and Carra Carre fell face-first into the sand.

The First of the Vine climbed slowly to one knee, exhausted and defeated. The mossy green paint that had covered her skin was now largely smeared away, staining patches of the ring's sand. The lattice of vines between her breasts was torn and hung from one side. For her own part, Webba didn't look much better. She stood over Carra Carre with chunks of mud missing from her Godskin, all her bracelets broken and strewn across the sand, the crown on her head crushed into an unrecognizable clay mess, its flowers blown to the wind.

Carra Carre looked up at Webba and Webba looked down at her, and for a moment it seemed that the First of the Vine was truly broken.

"How can a Bow end?" Dirt asked the Bibi.

"Points," Nana said, "and Push."

Have more points when time ran out, or push the opponent out of the ring. But there was one more way.

"And?"

"Oh!" Nana said, brightening. "Bow Down!"

Carra Carre still hadn't risen to her feet.

Dirt nodded. "Points, Push, and Bow Down."

Bow Down was the third and rarest way a match could end. It occurred if one girl stayed on the sand for ten seconds, refusing to fight, accepting defeat. Often, her opponent would force her to speak her loss: "I Bow Down." But the count was enough. It happened occasionally among NoBe. Among Sis, it was unheard of. Better to have every bone broken than to concede.

As the last of the sand trickled down the hourglass, Dirt couldn't believe that she was going to see Carra Carre Bow Down. The shame would be unimaginable. Even if Carra Carre won the God Bow tournament, would the recruits be willing to train with a Sis who had experienced the humiliation of Bowing Down? They had no choice–it was tradition. But it would be an unprecedented situation.

Webba wasn't just beating Carra Carre and the Vine. She was, in a single brilliant performance, overturning the entire hierarchy of the South. The Mud was the new top Fam.

Every eye in the arena was focused on Carra Carre, waiting for her to give up.

But she didn't.

Instead, she tried one last Ride.

Suddenly, her muscles weren't exhausted. They weren't clumsy or slow. She moved so quick that it seemed less like she was expending the last of her energy and more like she had been saving all her strength for this very moment. She lunged at Webba so quickly that the crowd was still celebrating when she got her arms around Webba's waist, clasped her palms together in a bone-crushing Trap, and hauled Webba into the air.

In all their years together, Dirt could never remember seeing Webba lifted like that. She was too good. Too heavy.

But Carra Carre hoisted Webba onto her shoulder like she was a basket of dirty clothes. She drove up and forward with such force that she launched inches off the ground. In midair, she turned her shoulder down, switched her grip so that she was holding Webba by the knees. It was an illegal move. Any Bower of Carra Carre's experience would know not to grip below the waist.

And Carra Carre knew. She knew exactly what she was doing.

Webba, as frantic as she was, kept calm. She pushed away with proper technique, trying to turn her hips in the right direction. But she was unable to escape Carra Carre's destructive arms.

Dirt watched in disbelief as the two girls landed, first Webba in a burst of sand, then Carra Carre immediately after, all her weight drilling into the ground, her shoulder pressing into Webba's knee until there was a sick and hollow snap.

A moment of stillness followed, in which all the blood in Dirt's head drained away, pooling in her limbs.

Then pandemonium.

Before Dirt could react, Swoo was already halfway to the ring, sprinting across the sand with a finger pointed at Carra Carre, roaring curses. The Vine sisters were yowling a collective and victorious rage. Outrage, sorrow, elation, and confusion burned through the audience like a windblown wildfire.

Dirt's first move was to gather Nana and Little Snore into her arms and pull them back, as far as possible from whatever was about to happen.

"Stay!" she ordered.

Snore was looking around, confused.

Nana's eyes were round as coconuts. Tears streamed down both cheeks. She was taking breaths in rapid gulps.

"Nana!" Dirt said, taking the girl's face in her hands. "Nana, see me, eh? See!"

Nana was looking past Dirt, over at the madness in the ring, but Dirt brought her face closer until their eyes locked. She saw fear in her young sister. Concern, too, for Webba. But mainly fear.

"Breathe, my Bibi," Dirt said. "Breathe."

For years, she'd been teaching Nana breathing exercises for when she got anxious. They helped now. Nana slowed her breaths, the fear in her eyes gradually replaced with focus.

"Take Snore and be safe," Dirt ordered. "I will come and find you after, eh?" She tried to sound soothing, but could feel her own voice shaking. "Go!"

To Dirt's relief, Nana took Snore by the hand and ran toward the back of the arena.

Dirt turned and ran for the ring just as Swoo slammed a fist into the back of Carra Carre's head. All around the arena there were clashes of green and brown. Pusher boys jumped from the stands onto the sand, rushing for the ring to restore order. Vine sisters swarmed Swoo, and she disappeared beneath a violent mass of masked faces.

Among it all, Webba was writhing in the sand, clutching her destroyed knee. It was bent backward, like a bird's, a deeply unnatural thing that Dirt couldn't look away from even as it made her sick. She watched Webba try in disbelief to bend her leg the right direction, but the pain of it seemed to stun her into stillness.

Dirt wanted to help Swoo, but she had to trust the Pusher boys to break that up. Webba needed her more. She rushed into the ring and dived over Webba, shielding her sister from further injury as bodies tripped over them. She was almost relieved to see that it was just the one knee that was destroyed and not both.

"Shh . . . ," she said, stroking Webba's hair. "Shh, Sis. I am here, eh? I am here."

That was all she could say. She repeated it as the fighting roiled about them like a cloud of violence, a storm of fists and feet and flying blood.

All Dirt cared about was keeping Webba safe.

"I am here," she whispered, pressing herself into her Sis as bodies continued falling over them, crushing them into the sand. "I am here."

7

The Second of the Mud

DIRT SAT on the floor of the hut, watching in the dim torchlight as Webba fell into a grimaced sleep. The griff root was finally taking effect.

After Pusher boys broke up the brawl, Dirt and Swoo had carried Webba through the jungle and back to the Mud camp. The trip had taken the entire afternoon due to Webba's weight. By the time they reached the Mud camp, the sun was long gone.

The whole way back, Webba had moaned in pain, unable to speak more than a few words at a time. Once they laid her down in the sleep hut, Swoo went back out to find Nana and Little Snore, who had stayed hidden through the melee. Dirt remained at camp, straightening Webba's leg into place, heating water and pouring it over the swollen knee, and preparing the griff root tea to help her sleep.

Webba had done something special in that fight. Her brilliant strategy to not just defeat Carra Carre, but confuse and humiliate her, must have taken months to put together. And that wasn't even counting the fearlessness needed to actually stick to such a plan when that behemoth of a girl was breathing down on her in the ring.

Webba had taken the entire Mud Fam onto the path of victory, and for a moment, Dirt had enjoyed a glimpse of a clear future. One where the Mud was as plentiful as the Vine, with enough girls to last long after Dirt herself had moved on to the life of a woman.

Then Carra Carre happened.

Now the Mud Fam was back at a fork in the road, unsure which path they would go down. If Webba didn't recover in time for the first round of the God Bow tournament, there would only be the one path—the one that led to the end of the Mud.

The sleep hut door swung open. Dirt turned, relieved that Swoo and the Bibi were home and safe.

But instead of her sisters, it was a girl she'd never seen before. She wore skintight denim pants, with a patterned white blouse that was close around her chest but loose beneath, like a skirt for the belly. Her hair was long, bound in a ponytail that dipped below her shoulders, and her small, pointed face was mainly eyes.

She was skinny. No fat. Not even muscle. Not a Bower.

A Mosquito girl.

Dirt stood.

"Honored Mud Sis, I am Pebble." The girl spoke quickly and didn't make eye contact. If actual mosquitos could speak, that was how they'd do it. "Antie Yaya send me." She nodded her head at Webba. "To help." The white canvas bag of a Bonemender was slung over one shoulder, bulging unevenly.

As a rule, Dirt didn't trust Mosquito girls. They didn't have Fam like Bowers. They lived lonely lives, flitting from here to there, earning their meals by competing in the most senseless of ways. They competed to craft and trade baubles and dresses, competed to win the favor of Antie Yaya, competed for the affection of Flagga boys. Pusher boys were the lowest in the hierarchy of the Isle, but there was no one lower in Dirt's eyes than a Mosquito girl.

Still, if Antie Yaya had sent this Pebble girl, then Dirt would let the girl do what she'd been sent to do.

Dirt backed away, but kept her eyes on the skinny girl.

Pebble knelt beside Webba, peering at the damaged knee. She ran her hands around the area, then pressed on the black swell. Webba, still sleeping, let out a low groan.

"Skinny," Dirt said, "you enjoy your hands, eh?"

Pebble looked back, eyes wide, and nodded.

"Then you will not hurt my sister," Dirt said.

After a very gentle initial examination, Pebble began pulling medicine from her bag. First she rubbed various creams and oils into the injured area. Then she produced two short bamboo rods, set them on either side of the knee, wrapped them in broad leaves, and tied it all down with thin strings of palm twine. Lastly she prayed.

Pebble's prayer was different from how Bowers prayed. She didn't talk to the Gods or ask them for anything. She didn't dance. There were no drums or horns. She just sang their names, her voice high and fragile like a songbird's.

Dirt hadn't realized that Mosquito girls prayed at all. What did they have to pray about if they didn't Bow? It didn't take courage or strength to wear jewelry and strut around for boys.

Eventually, Pebble finished and began putting her medications back in her bag.

"That is all?" Dirt asked. She didn't know anything about Bone-mending, but that had seemed too quick to heal such a gruesome injury. Webba didn't look any better.

Pebble nodded and rose to her feet. She kept her gaze on the floor as she spoke. "Yes, Mud Sis."

"So when can she Bow, eh?"

Pebble glanced up, eyebrows bunched in confusion. "No . . . I . . ."

"Speak, skinnyskinny," Dirt said sharply. "Or you are sick?"

"I am sorry, Mud Sis. She cannot Bow for na long time."

"Eh heh, so how long? In na half moon, we will have na God Bow tournament."

Pebble shook her head. "No, Mud Sis."

"How long?"

"Many–" She stopped at Dirt's stare. But then something seemed to solidify in her. For the first time, she looked Dirt clearly in the eyes. "Many moons, Mud Sis. Your sister cannot fight in na tournament."

Dirt stared hard at the stupid girl. Even her name was stupid. *What girl wants to be na pebble, eh? Small and weak. She weighs nothing. Na wind can steal her.* "You come here why, eh?"

"I come . . . to help. To heal."

"You help nothing," Dirt said, nodding toward Webba's still-broken limb. "You heal nothing."

Pebble didn't respond, and Dirt didn't say any more. What more was there to say? It was clear that Webba was badly injured. Dirt didn't need the opinion of a foolish Mosquito girl to know that.

"Mud Sis . . ." Pebble's voice was back to its annoying wobble. "Na tournament . . ."

Dirt stared at her. "What?"

"Antie Yaya say you can send another sister."

Dirt shook her head. The stupid girl didn't understand. There was no one else.

Swoo was their best option. She had studied the Bowing of every elite Sis in the South, knew their strengths and weaknesses, the strategies they favored. And it was unlikely that any of them had studied Swoo. If she got favorable seeding, against an opponent who severely underestimated her, maybe she could pull an upset in the first round. Maybe if Swoo had the best performance of her life and if some of the other competitors got injured or sick and if the Gods Themselves came down and decreed the Mud to be Their favored Fam. Maybe if all that happened, some tradition-bucking recruit would go to the Mud instead of the winner of the tournament.

But Swoo wasn't a Sis. Not yet.

Only Sis could fight in a God Bow. And in the event of an injury, it was the duty of the next Sis in line to carry the Fam's honor into battle. Webba was the First, which meant the Second had to fight in her place. And Swoo wasn't the Second of the Mud.

Dirt was.

The door kicked open and Swoo appeared, sporting the results of the post-Bow brawl on her body. Her right eye was puffed and red, and there was dried blood smeared across a cut beneath her chin. A chunk of tightly curled black hair near the center of her forehead had been torn out. She had an arm around Nana, who had both arms around Little Snore. All three of them looked at Dirt, then at Pebble.

Little Snore stood on her toes to whisper loudly into Nana's ear. "Why is na Moskiki girl here?"

Nana covered the Bibi's mouth, her face apologetic.

Swoo was less tactful. "Go," she said in a flat voice.

Pebble scurried out of the hut, sliding past Swoo, who refused to make room for her to exit. Once the door closed behind the Mosquito girl, Nana and Snore rushed over to Dirt and wrapped their arms around her waist, burying their faces in her rolls of skin.

"You Bibi disappear, eh?" Dirt asked.

Nana said, "We hide like you tell us."

"I find them in na bush," Swoo added. She was walking curiously around the hut, gathering items. First she picked up a small canvas bag, then a bunch of bananas, then a hunting flute and several darts, and lastly her handaxe. "Nana have na stick like she will fight na Vine with it," she said, shaking her head. She picked up a shirt and inspected it before tossing it away.

"What are you doing?" Dirt asked.

Swoo slung the pack over her shoulder. "Nana, Snore, watch over Sis Webba, eh? We must go."

"Swoo, what are you doing?" Dirt repeated.

Swoo stopped by the door. "We will go and kill na Vine."

"Not we."

Swoo shrugged. "Then me."

"Not you."

"And who will stop me?"

Dirt sighed. She wasn't going to fight with Swoo. But she also wasn't going to let the girl go start a war. Given the size of the South and how hidden each camp was, it was nearly impossible to find another camp. But even if Swoo somehow managed to find the Vine, there were fifty of them for every one combat-ready Mud sister. Any conflict would only end with the Mud being destroyed.

"They mash up Sis Webba," Swoo said. "Who will punish them, if not us? You know Antie Yaya will not."

Penalties in Bowing were left to the Fam to enforce. Typically, a bad foul would lead to a brawl between Fam that wouldn't end until the offending girl had been beaten. But with the Vine so much larger than any other Fam, they must have known they were beyond consequence.

"In time, Swoo," Dirt said.

Swoo's eyes narrowed. "You breezy cluck. You will allow them to live?"

"When you are weak, you cannot fight power," Dirt replied. "'Na mouse will not bite na lion's tail.'" It was a quote she'd heard Webba say once.

Swoo sucked her teeth. "Then you will stay skinny and weak. How can you have power if you do not fight power?"

"We will, my sister. But not tonight."

"And so when?!" Swoo's voice suddenly leapt like a stoked flame. "When they mash me up, eh? When they mash up Nana and Snore and come and mash up na Mud camp? If not tonight, then when, *Sis*?" She spat the title.

"When Webba is healthy," Dirt said calmly. "When Webba is healthy, na Vine will suffer. But this night, our sister has pain."

"By Carra Carre's hand!" Swoo was shaking, her emotions seizing control of her. If Dirt couldn't find a way to calm her down, it was going to be a long, bloody night. "I swear by Papa 'Duma's chest, that swinging cow will bleed tonight!" She tightened her grip on her bag and turned to leave.

"Na Vine will bleed," Dirt protested, "but–"

Webba's voice cut through the commotion. It was dry and thin and a half whisper, but still hers. "You yowling kittens will not allow Webba sleep, eh?"

Dirt was the first to rush to Webba's side, but the others arrived immediately after. They each crouched beside the First of the Mud.

"Webba Bow all day," she continued, "she break leg, she does not eat, and still she cannot sleep. Chaaaiii."

The other Mud sisters all began speaking at once, issuing apologies and consolations and how-are-you-feelings and what-do-you-needs. Webba tried to respond, but her throat seemed to catch.

"Water," Dirt said, and Little Snore scurried outside to the water pump. After Webba drank several cups, she spoke.

"NoBe Swoo, how many Vine can you punish, eh?"

Swoo puffed up, but before she could respond, Webba shook her head. "Not enough, my sister. Be patient. 'When na sun rises, na Gods must always be there to greet her,'" she prayed.

"It is," they all responded.

And just like that, Swoo was calmed. Nana and Snore were reassured. Dirt was relieved.

Webba had a wisdom beyond her years, and a presence that felt like she had everything under control, even when she was broken and drowsy, lying helpless on the sleep hut floor. She was their leader for a reason.

After that, the Mud sisters went about their nightly routines. Nana and Little Snore brewed a pot of black tea with honey. Swoo grabbed tomatoes and green beans and black potatoes from the garden and chopped them into a pot using the same axe she'd intended to bury in Carra Carre's head just moments earlier.

Once food was ready, they all sat down to eat. They dipped long spoons into the soup, scooped up chunks of boiled vegetable, and washed it all down with cup after cup of sweet tea. During the meal, Swoo told them about the brawl at the Grand Temple. It was mainly half-true boasts about how she'd felt Carra Carre's skull crack like an old coconut when she punched it, and how she had knocked four—no, six!—Vine girls unconscious, including the one who'd busted her eye. And how they'd only brought her down because she slipped while kicking one of them in the face.

Nana and Snore nodded, enraptured by the stories. Webba, still dreary, wore half a grin. Dirt rolled her eyes, but found herself smiling.

After the meal, Nana and Snore cleared the floor and cleaned the dishes, then insisted that the older Mud sisters relax and watch a "show" they'd put together. Dirt settled down between Swoo and Webba while the Bibi began clapping and bouncing their hips from side to side until the other Mud sisters joined in. The show was mainly a song, with some short acted scenes about a Bower who went to save her Fam from an evil monster, but fell in love with the monster. Together, the Bower and the monster ate all the mosquitos in the South.

Their shows never made much sense. But they performed with such enthusiasm and confidence. It was the only time Nana ever looked confident, really. So the older Mud sisters allowed themselves to be swept up in the nonsensical story, to cower when the Bower confronted the monster, to coo when the two characters fell in love, to cheer when the two waged war on the mosquitos.

As it ended and Nana and Snore basked in the applause, Dirt realized with a knot of fear in her gut that there was only one stage left in the night: sleep.

Which meant that she had to tell them. Webba must have

already known how bad her injury was, but Swoo and the Bibi didn't. In their eyes, Webba was indestructible. Like Dirt, they would assume that Webba would be ready to fight by the God Bow tournament.

It was Dirt's duty as Second to tell them the truth.

"My sisters," she said as the applause died. "Sit, Bibi Nana. Bibi Snore."

Nana seemed to sense that something was wrong. She sat immediately, stroking her ponytail. Snore was still alight with energy from the performance. She began curtsying like the Mosquito girls did before dancing with boys, then she was so amused with herself that she fell into a fit of giggling. Nana had to wrap the girl in a hug and drag her down into her lap to keep her still.

After a short while, Dirt realized they were waiting for her to speak. But her heart was in her throat—she didn't want to open her mouth and have it spill out.

"My Sis," Webba mumbled. Her eyes were still shining with pain, but the meal and performance had returned some of the life to her face. "You have na seed in your chest. Add water."

Dirt nodded. She looked from kind Webba to skeptical Swoo to giggly Snore and uncertain Nana, whose skinny arms had never been meant for Bowing anyway. If Webba didn't recover before the tournament, it would be the end of the Mud. Dirt would become a woman without ever seeing her dream become reality.

"Antie Yaya send na Mosquito girl," she said. "She say Webba cannot . . . Webba is very hurt."

"How much hurt?" Swoo asked.

"Antie Yaya say . . . Webba cannot fight in na God Bow tournament."

Their reactions were what she expected. Webba gave a resigned sigh and closed her eyes. Nana's breathing shallowed. Snore stopped giggling, but otherwise didn't seem to understand. She looked from Nana to Webba, confused.

Swoo, though, was biting her lip uncertainly. Her forehead creased in a frown. "Sis Dirt," she said. "I am ready."

The girl had no delusions about the God Bow tournament. She knew she would be humiliated, maybe even injured, in a fight against the South's elite Bowers. Despite her quick volunteering, she wasn't confident. In fact, she was terrified.

Most girls ran when they were afraid, even Bowers. But not Swoo. At the end of the day, when worse came to worst, she was the bravest of them.

Dirt wanted to hug her.

"You cannot," Webba mumbled. "Dirt is Second."

Dirt had expected that answer. Webba would never embarrass her by letting Swoo, a NoBe, represent the Fam at the God Bow tournament. No matter how old she was and how ready Swoo was.

But she'd hoped Webba would say something different.

"Sis Webba, I am ready," Swoo repeated. She shifted, sitting up with her back straight, hands in her lap. "Every day I train, you know this. Train like it is my last day. I can eat. I can dance. I can fight. I know na Rock sisters and na Creek. I am not so fat, true, but I will never quit. Please." She had been speaking to the floor, but now she turned her eyes up at Webba. "I know you pick Sis Dirt. I understand. But I will show you. Please, allow me to show you I can fight for na Mud. I can God Bow. I am ready."

Swoo was a girl of unstable emotions. She laughed plenty, screamed in anger just as often, was as quick to sorrow as she was to celebration. But whatever she felt was always plain on her face, and in that moment, her desperation was clear. The tightness of her jaw, the shimmering wetness of her eyes. She had worked her whole life for an opportunity like this. Maybe not this soon, but that didn't matter. While Dirt was afraid of what would happen if she had to fight, Swoo was afraid of what would happen if she didn't.

As Second, Dirt should have challenged her. She should have asserted her place and demanded to fight on behalf of the Fam.

But she didn't. She couldn't. Swoo fighting in her place was exactly what she wanted.

After a long silence, Webba responded. "NoBe Swoo," she said, voice soft and careful. "You know na story of jungle cat and baby fish, eh?" Swoo nodded somberly, but Nana and Snore moved closer, curious. They always loved Webba's stories, especially new ones. "One day, jungle cat eats mama fish, but baby fish survives. Na jungle cat has pity, so she says, 'Because I eat mama fish, I will care for this baby fish.' She tries to bring baby fish on na land, but, as you know, baby fish cannot go. So baby fish stays in water and grows very small and skinny until, one day, jungle cat kills meat, waits until na bugs come to pick na bones, and then takes na bones into na water so baby fish can eat na bugs. Now, baby fish grows more bigbig and fatfat than all other fish. Then, after many moons, jungle cat makes baby jungle cat. One day, baby jungle cat falls in na water and, *shwoom*, na water takes baby jungle cat away. Jungle cat cannot swim, so she cries. But baby fish says, 'Do not cry, mama jungle cat. Na land is your place. Na water is mine.' Then she goes and saves baby jungle cat."

It was a simple, happy story, but Swoo's cheeks were streaked with tears by the end of it. She didn't look sad, though. Just determined.

"NoBe Swoo," Webba said. "You are fat. You are brave. You are na blessing to na Mud Fam. But na God Bow tournament is not your place."

Swoo flinched at the pronouncement, but otherwise kept her upright posture.

"Dirt will train for na tournament. But"–Webba slid her gaze to Dirt–"if Sis Dirt does not want to fight . . ." Webba rubbed the back of one hand against the palm of the other, then switched hands and did it again, shrugging. "'How can na grass know na sun better than na sky?' I am only na mashed up Sis who cannot fight. I will not stand in your way, NoBe Swoo."

Swoo's gaze was that of a starving dog looking at an unguarded meal–desperate, but suspicious. Waiting for something to come and swipe her good fortune.

Dirt felt heat rising up her neck. No matter what she decided, she would disappoint one of her sisters. If she chose to fight, it would ruin Swoo's hopes. But if she chose to let Swoo fight, it would break Webba's heart.

It wasn't a hard choice. It hurt, but it was clear what she had to do.

"I will fight for na Mud," Dirt said, and Webba's grin made her feel like she'd already won the whole tournament. Nana and Snore were smiling too. The way her three sisters glowed, all of them gifting her their trust in the most beautiful of ways, assuring her that they believed in her, was a promise of love and support. "I will fight in na God Bow tournament. I will show na South who we are. I will crush Carra Carre, and bring na recruits to na Mud."

Swoo didn't react at all. The desperation was still on her face. The determination too.

"I will fight," Dirt repeated, unable to calm the fearful rattle in her chest, "and I will win."

8

God Bow Training

2 Weeks until the Prayer

THERE WERE two weeks between the end of the Bowing season and the Prayer–the ceremony marking the beginning of the God Bow tournament. During this time, the entire Fam revolved around the life of the God Bowers. All the other sisters woke when the God Bowers woke. They prepared meals while the God Bowers trained. They kept the God Bowers' water cups filled. They served as coaches and sparring partners, as motivators, as masseuses, going to bed beside the God Bowers and waking up ready to fulfill all their duties again the next morning. It was a time of heightened focus for the entire Fam, a bond forged from the shared stress of preparation.

But this God Bow tournament was different. Webba was bedridden. The Bibi were busy fulfilling their duties and ensuring that Dirt didn't ever have to worry about food, water, or any other basic needs.

So it was just Dirt and Swoo.

Swoo trained alongside Dirt, but otherwise ignored her. On their morning runs, Swoo kept pace right beside Dirt, never going too far ahead despite her superior stamina. When Dirt returned to camp, sweat-soaked and panting, Swoo went back out into the jungle for another, harder run. During the afternoon weight lifting, Swoo seemed to be in an unspoken contest to lift as much as Dirt, despite her smaller size. She would work her way up slowly, lifting heavier and heavier rocks until she was trembling. When Dirt looked over at her, Swoo kept her gaze focused on the tree line, neck straining from the weight. When it was time to spar, Swoo instead trained alone, going through the Bowing sequence.

It didn't feel like they were sisters. It felt like they were competitors training against each other.

The rest of Dirt's days were spent at Webba's side, doing everything she could to help her sister heal. She made sure Webba was getting plenty of fish and pounded yam to keep her fat and strong. She massaged Webba's leg above and below the injury, rubbing it slowly and firmly with Mud Offer. She prayed, seeking Papa Oduma's favor. In the stories, He was said to value strength above all else. Why would He want to see Webba, His strongest Bower, set aside and broken, unable to do Him homage?

Most importantly, Dirt tried to keep Webba in good spirits—happiness was as powerful as any medicine.

"Remember Sis Bumi?" Dirt asked near the end of that first week. Webba always enjoyed reminiscing about the old days.

"Chaaaiii, Sis Bumi na Biter," Webba said, laughing. "You make that poor girl madmad."

"Me?" Dirt asked.

"You don't remember when she bite na first time?"

Dirt shook her head. As far as she could remember, Bumi had always been a biter. It had become such a problem that she'd been formally punished by the First, forced to do Bibi work for a whole month.

"Our last NoBe season," Webba said, "you Push her out three times, *gbe gbe gbe*. Then na fourth time, she grab your hand and bite."

That part was clear in Dirt's memory. "That is no true bite, my sister," Dirt said, doubtful. "Sis Bumi make play."

Webba stared for so long that Dirt thought she'd fallen asleep with her eyes open.

"My sister, at times you speak like you have na chicken brain."

"Eh heh?!"

"You are na NoBe. She is na Third of na Fam. And you Push her out. Chaaaiii!"

"Bite because of na friendly Bow?" Dirt waved a dismissive hand. "Not Sis Bumi."

"Bite because you make her look like she have no belly. After you, Sis Bumi becomes madmad for na half moon. Only then does she bite other Sis."

Dirt had always assumed Bumi was going easy on her in sparring. Why would a full Sis need to try her best against a NoBe? She'd never considered that Bumi had been truly upset over losing. She looked down at the scar on the back of her hand, a barely noticeable dent of white against the brown.

"You miss it, eh?" Webba asked softly.

Dirt looked up. Webba was regarding her the way Dirt might watch the Bibi fall asleep while holding hands.

"I miss Sis Bumi, yes. And na other sisters. But I like this Mud Fam. Even Swoo, that monkey neck."

"Not Sis Bumi," Webba said. "You miss na fight. *Na Bow.*"

Dirt shrugged. "What girl can miss her worst days?"

"You make many wins."

"As na NoBe. Every NoBe makes wins."

Webba was quiet for a while before speaking again. "You do not know yourself, my Sis. To be great, you must know yourself. To be na greatest, even more."

That was what Webba didn't understand. She thought everyone wanted to be great, like her. That everyone *could* be great. But some people were just average.

Dirt couldn't say that, though. Not after she'd promised to win the God Bow tournament.

She stood. It was time to get back to training. "You are right, my Sis. I will learn myself."

Webba sucked her teeth. "You sound way tired," she said skeptically. "Train well, Sis. Perhaps you will become na True Godskin."

Dirt snorted. "Perhaps. Or perhaps it will be Bibi Snore."

"Na Snore of na Gods."

When Dirt thought about how powerful and terrible Snore's nighttime rumblings were, the idea didn't seem so ridiculous.

"My Sis, come." Webba motioned her over, took a deep breath, and forced herself up on her arms.

Dirt, alarmed, threw herself under Webba's armpit. She did her best to act as a crutch as strained veins of agony sprung into Webba's face. But pain was part of the Bower's life, and Webba had her ways of dealing with it. She paused for a moment, took another deep breath, and tried to step forward. Even with most of her weight leaned on Dirt, it was too much. The moment her toes touched the earth, a spasm shot up her injured leg and she fell entirely on Dirt, breathing heavy through her nose and releasing the pain in slow, careful grunts.

Swoo came in then, face bright, her clothes soaked through with sweat.

"Sis Webba, I practice na Half Under Trap and—"

She froze, surveying the scene with a blend of shock and confusion.

Webba immediately wiped herself of any stress, standing upright on her one good leg. She flashed a smile. "Go on, my sister. Tell me."

"Are you okay, Sis Webba?" Swoo asked.

"Finefine. Tell me about na Half Under Trap."

But Swoo just stared. "You are trying to stand?"

"'Only na tree does not change place,'" Webba quoted, giving her belly a heavy smack. "I am too bigbig to be na tree. I must move."

"You do not need my help?"

Dirt managed not to roll her eyes. Webba had suffered one of the most grievous injuries of any Bower in memory. For the first time, she was feeling healthy enough to attempt to stand. It took courage to face so much pain.

Only Swoo could somehow make that about herself.

Webba's smile melted into a look so warm and loving that it was Dirt's turn to be confused.

"You are smart, NoBe Swoo," Webba said. "How can I call oldold Sis Dirt to help me when I have na strongstrong sister such as you?"

But Swoo didn't seem relieved. Her eyes flicked between Webba and Dirt. They brimmed with tears.

"Dirt, my sister," Webba said, motioning for Dirt to set her back on her mat. Once she was down, she continued, "You do not look tired."

"I am going to train now," Dirt said, puzzled. Nothing about the conversation was making any sense.

"A God Bower must be tired during training," Webba replied. "Always. NoBe Swoo?"

Swoo was looking up at the sleep hut ceiling. She took one deep sniff before looking back down at Webba. "Yes?"

"Until I am more strong, you must coach Sis Dirt, eh?"

Dirt was too stunned to say anything. The past week, Dirt had been training herself and Webba had seemed fine with it. She hadn't mentioned anything about Swoo taking over her coaching.

"Make her strong," Webba continued, closing her eyes and interlocking her fingers over her belly, the image of rest. "Show her how you work."

9

Coach Swoo

5 Days until the Prayer

SWOO WAS a fighter, through and through. Her favorite scent was sweat. Her favorite flavor was sand with a hint of blood, sweeter than any meat. She craved exhaustion, welcomed it like shade in the summer. Over the years, she'd forged her mind for the chaos of battle. Reshaped it to take all the stresses of expectation, all the audience's praise and wrath, all the hopes of her sisters, and turn them into rungs on her ladder to glory. She was built to stand across from a worthy opponent and argue with her body the only question in life that mattered: Who is stronger?

She was born to fight.

Not coach.

"If you want to cry, then cry and let us train," Swoo said.

She looked down in disgust at Sis Dirt. The girl—woman, almost—was on her knees in the ring, sweating and panting like a brand-new Bibi.

For years, Sis Dirt had lived the comfortable life of retirement. Training at her leisure, eating how she wished, practicing techniques only when she felt like it. She spent her energy senselessly, as if it had no value, yelling at the Bibi and telling Swoo how to Bow as if Swoo would not break her in a real fight.

A true fighter didn't know leisure. All she knew was the Bower's life: eat, dance, fight. A true fighter spent her energy wisely, stored it greedily, used it only when needed.

Dirt was no true fighter. Now Swoo had to spend a week trying to turn this lazy, overgrown Bibi into the God Bow tournament champion. All when Swoo should have been the one training and competing in the first place.

A worse fate, she could not imagine.

"Rest," Dirt panted from her knees. "My sister, allow me rest, eh?"

Pathetic.

"Ten . . . ," Swoo counted. "Nine . . ."

Swoo had set up a simple routine for their week. The first day, she had woken before the sun, nudged Dirt into consciousness. They started with a run through the jungle at an average pace, one any NoBe could have matched. But for a clumsy chicken like Sis Dirt, it was too much. She seemed to trip on every root, smack her head on every branch. Halfway into the run, she stopped to catch wind, wasting precious training time.

Back at camp, Swoo led a stretching routine that Sis Dirt groaned the whole way through. Then they did weighted technique training, Slapping and Riding and Trapping with a cloth sack full of rocks wrapped around their waists.

When the sun was fully up, they settled down to firstmeal. It was a small meal—fresh bananas, papaya, star apple, three hands of cashews and almonds, a half-dozen raw eggs—but Sis Dirt was holding her belly at the end like it would burst.

"Six . . . ," Swoo continued, unable to stop the growing smirk on her face. "Five . . ."

The afternoon was divided into two parts. The first half was light exercise, to tire the heart rather than the muscles. At least it was supposed to be light. But Sis Dirt's weak body couldn't handle it, never mind her heart. She didn't make it through a single drill without collapsing at least twice, shaking like the smallest branch of the oldest tree.

The second half was sparring. That was where Sis Dirt really fell apart.

"Two . . . one . . ."

In sparring, Swoo showed no pity. She was ruthless, overpowering, all the things a real fighter was supposed to be. If Sis Dirt couldn't fight Swoo, how would she fight a girl like Sis Hollo, the First of the Rock, whose Traps were so high and so tight they could choke the life from a girl? Or Sis Wing, the First of the Creek, with Rides so fast they made Swoo's look like those of a dying sloth?

So Swoo tossed Sis Dirt about like a bag of infested rice, equal parts ease and disgust. Her Rides met no resistance, even lifting Sis Dirt off her feet. Her Traps broke Sis Dirt down so easily, Swoo felt as if she'd become a True Godskin.

Only their Slaps were even. As much as Swoo hated to admit it, Dirt was likely among the best Slappers in all the South. Even while exhausted and broken and scared, Sis Dirt was full of Slapping tricks and feints that made her a frustrating girl to fight. Swoo could only imagine what she would have been like if she hadn't squandered whatever Bowing talent she possessed by letting herself waste away.

But she had, and Swoo punished her for it. She made Sis Dirt Bow more times than she could count, driving her hard into the ground, forcing her to eat so much sand she could skip her next meal. And each day, Sis Dirt quit. The first day, it was after a few brief sparring exchanges. The second day, she'd lasted longer, but not by much.

On this third day, she had lasted longer than the two previous days combined, but Swoo had still broken her.

"Zero . . . ," Swoo said. Sis Dirt fell back to the sand, unable to continue.

It wasn't a true fight, but Swoo still took satisfaction from the result: She'd made Sis Dirt Bow Down. Again.

Sis Dirt extended an arm up to Swoo, and Swoo looked at the thing in disbelief. She wanted to be helped up? After showing herself to be weaker than weak? After Bowing Down, and to a NoBe?

Even worse, this was the girl who Sis Webba loved so much. Not Swoo, who bore the same fighter's spirit as Webba. Who worked tirelessly to build the Mud Fam into greatness. Who dominated in the ring, proving herself to be the obvious heir to Webba's legacy of excellence.

No, it wasn't Swoo. It would never be Swoo. Sis Webba and Sis Dirt had a bond that she wasn't welcome to share, and she had to accept it.

But she didn't have to accept it happily.

Swoo ignored Sis Dirt's extended hand, leveled a cold stare at her weak and broken Sis, then turned away.

4 Days until the Prayer

Swoo started the day with an unusual run.

Normally, they took jungle paths, winding through the trees, jogging up and down dirt hills laden with thick roots and underbrush. But this time, Swoo led Sis Dirt toward the coast. It was a route she often took when she got a chance to run alone, without the Bibi to slow her down or Sis Webba to tell her to not stray too far from camp.

"Where is this we are going?" Sis Dirt asked between panting breaths as the stocky, broadleaf trees of the jungle began to give way to the lean, swooping palms of the Isle's coastline.

Swoo picked up the pace. If Sis Dirt had breath to talk, they weren't running fast enough.

Soon the soil dried into sand, and they could hear the lapping waves of the sea. The day was hot even in the early morning, and as the tree line dissolved and the endless blue horizon appeared, Swoo could think of nothing more refreshing than diving headfirst into the water.

But she couldn't. Not here. They were well beyond the Mud territory, in between the lands of the Sand and the Rock. Swoo had a good relationship with the Rock, but while the Sand girls weren't hostile toward the Mud, they wouldn't be happy with a surprise visit.

She continued running a while longer and soon reached their destination. Ahead, the pale gold sand gave way abruptly to gray stone that grew from tiny, smooth pebbles to jagged chunks as big as a Sis. The stones sloped up from the beach, making a high cliff along the water's edge.

"Ready?" Swoo asked, staring up at the cliff.

"Eh?" Dirt asked, hands on her knees, drowning in sweat.

Swoo took off at a sprint, careful not to cut herself as she sped up and over the sharp rocks. By the time she reached the top and looked back, Sis Dirt was still struggling up the bottom of the stony hill, moving with all the speed and coordination of a tortoise drunk on palm wine.

"Run!" Swoo shouted. "Move yourself! You misplaced fish."

Eventually, Sis Dirt reached the top of the cliff. Her legs were covered in shallow cuts, her palms raw from catching herself to avoid falling on her face.

Swoo looked out over the water. Other than the Mud camp and the Grand Temple, this was the part of the South she knew best. She breathed in the familiar salt scent of the sea, enjoying the unique pressure of the coastal winds against her skin.

"NoBe Swoo," Sis Dirt panted, sprawled on the rocks. "We must go."

"We are finefine," Swoo responded. They were just inside Rock territory, and she had no doubt the Fam's scouts were already watching them. Swoo had been there often enough to know that if their presence was a problem, the Rock sisters would inform them.

"We are in na Rock–" Dirt began, but Swoo cut her off.

"Sis Dirt, I must speak true."

It was just the two of them. No Bibi. No Sis Webba. There was no need for the pretense of peace that sisterhood sometimes demanded.

For a few seconds, the only sound from either girl was Sis Dirt's heavy breathing. "Eh heh," she finally said. "Speak true."

Swoo sat, dangling her legs over the cliff's edge. Far below, the water crashed in white sprays against the rocky beach. A group of Pusher boys were down there, inspecting stones before either tossing them back into the shallow water or lobbing them into a large wooden box. Their Petti, a small bear with black fur, ambled beside them, swiping at flashes of fish in the water. Swoo admired the Pusher boys for their strength and good sense, but she couldn't respect the work they did. Moving heavy things from one place to another took no skill, no focus or ferocity, no passion.

What a dull life.

"You are weak," Swoo said. "Body and mind. You are not na fighter. *I* am na fighter. It should be *I* who fights, not you. You must see this."

Sis Dirt didn't respond, which was all Swoo needed.

"Sis Webba will never love me as she loves you," she continued, avoiding Sis Dirt's gaze. "I know this. But I know too who I am. I will show Sis Webba what you and I see. This is not to dishonor you. All I want is to honor na Mud. On the day I do not love this Fam more than I love my own life, I will leave. But that day will never come, so I must give all I have to honor us."

She looked over at Sis Dirt then, and was not surprised to find her sitting calmly a safe distance from the cliff's edge, listening. Sis Dirt, for all her cowardice, always managed to keep calm everywhere except the ring.

"I understand" was all Sis Dirt said. She looked back out over the water, and together they watched for a while as the waves crashed below them.

When they returned to camp, they found Sis Webba seated up against the outside of the sleep hut. Nana and Snore were on one side of her. On her other side were two crude wooden crutches carved from the thick wood found deeper in the jungle. Sis Webba wore her usual grin, enjoying the cool early morning breeze.

Suddenly, all the anger and loneliness and pain Swoo had felt watching Sis Dirt help Sis Webba walk seemed senseless. Shameful, even. Sis Webba's health was more important than any petty squabbles.

"Sis Webba!" Swoo yelped despite herself, running from the tree line to crash into her sister.

"Look at this bigbig girl Swoo!" Webba said, laughing. "You run like jungle cat, eh?"

Swoo pressed her face into Sis Webba's shoulder, enjoying the familiar feeling, like stone coated in meat.

"Why are you out?" Swoo asked. "You need rest."

"Na time for rest is finished," Sis Webba replied. She grabbed her crutches, motioned Swoo away, and climbed unsteadily onto her one good leg. "You train Sis Dirt well, NoBe Swoo. But . . ." She tucked the crutches under her armpits and made her way to the edge of the ring, nodding for Sis Dirt to join her. Swoo moved over beside the ring with the Bibi.

"I am First," Webba said, cracking her neck one way, then the other. "I will teach my Second."

10

The Mud Pit

3 Days until the Prayer

DIRT WAS CONFUSED.

Swoo's training had been a nightmare. The runs had been lung-sucking, the exercises backbreaking, the spars humiliating. But she was training for the God Bow tournament itself. Being a God Bower wasn't supposed to be easy.

Then Webba had taken over, and the easiest day of Dirt's life began.

Instead of afternoon sparring, Webba just put her through light drills where she would often pause to adjust Dirt's technique and explain some concept. By the end, Dirt wasn't even sweating.

It was strange. Webba trained harder than anyone, so much so that when she was a NoBe, some of the Sis didn't like training with her because they were worried Webba would injure them before a fight. Dirt had seen glee in Swoo's eyes when Webba announced that she would take over. No doubt, Swoo had expected Webba to make Dirt's life even more miserable.

But, it was the opposite.

That morning, Swoo had still led the daily run, but it was clear Webba had given her the pace and route–it was less than half the distance and speed. The afternoon exercises were stretches, belly bends, and press-ups. Not very many, and all at a leisurely pace. No weights.

Dirt dared to hope that maybe Webba had changed her mind. Maybe she realized Dirt wasn't right for the tournament.

After secondmeal, it was time for sparring.

"This day," Webba said as Swoo and Dirt stood across from each other in the ring, "you will spar at five. Half power."

Swoo's face tightened, but she didn't say anything. Dirt couldn't make sense of Webba, but she took some comfort in the idea that Swoo wasn't enjoying any of this.

Sparring at half strength, Dirt did better than she would have expected. With Swoo's youth and speed constrained, Dirt's technique and experience made all the difference. For the first few minutes, she kept Swoo away with Slaps. Swoo tried to keep her composure, but Slap after Slap jolted her shoulders, halted her Rides, and bullied her around the ring until frustration got the best of her. She Rode in fast. Not full speed, but certainly more than a five.

Rather than being overwhelmed by Swoo's sudden change of pace, Dirt felt completely at ease. It was the sequence she knew best, the sort of fight she'd built her entire Bowing strategy around. Fight smart, use minimal effort, Slap and Slap until the other girl makes a mistake.

Then punish her.

As Swoo Rode in, Dirt didn't even need to Trap. She just lowered her hips and bent back, using her arms to guide Swoo's momentum over her head for a clean and easy Back Bow.

"Bow!" Webba howled, cackling. "Chaaaiii, Swoo! You allow Dirt to Bow you like that, eh? You and your whole head mash sand!"

The Bibi took Webba's cue, laughing wildly.

Dirt had forgotten how it felt. To see an attack and know its destination before the attacker did. To impose one's will on an opponent. There were no words that could capture the truth of it, no palm wine so intoxicating.

Suddenly Webba's training made sense. She wasn't doubting whether Dirt was right for the God Bow tournament. She was trying to remove *Dirt's* doubt. It was the sort of thing commonly done for a new NoBe, to help build her confidence before her first fight. Dirt was as far from a new NoBe as a girl could get, but it had worked just the same. For the first time in years, she felt good about her abilities.

As she rolled back to her feet, she extended a hand to help Swoo up. But Swoo bolted up on her own. She shook out each limb, bounced lightly from foot to foot. Her gaze was trained on Dirt, her face masked in a quiet and unnerving calm.

"Eh heh," Webba said, watching Swoo with a glint in her eyes. "Remember, only five. Half power."

They began again, and Swoo's prior frustration was gone, replaced by the same competitive mind that had spent the last season making fools of the South's best NoBe. Each time Dirt landed a firm Slap, Swoo moved with the blow, letting it skip off her. Each time Dirt tried to angle Swoo against the edge of the ring, the younger girl slipped away.

Soon Dirt's arms began to tire, and Swoo shifted to the attack.

"Sis, na time, eh?" Dirt called to Webba between heavy breaths.

When Webba didn't respond, Dirt glanced over at her sister only to suddenly feel arms around her waist, her legs leave the ground, her back drive hard into the sand.

"Bow!"

Dirt rolled onto her stomach and saw Swoo spring back up to her feet.

"Webba, na time," she repeated.

"I will tell you when na time is finished," Webba said, an uncharacteristically small smile on her face.

After two more Bows, Dirt was entirely sapped of strength, and Swoo discarded all caution. She attacked like a mad beast, darting in and out, Trapping Dirt from all angles, slamming and slamming and slamming her into the earth.

On the tenth Bow, with her lower back so damaged it was already swelling, Dirt stayed on the ring floor.

"I cannot," she said, trying to wipe sand from her forehead, but only replacing it with the sand from her hands. "My Sis, I cannot."

"Breathe easy, my Sis," Webba said. "No need to be quick."

So Dirt didn't rise for nearly a minute. Webba didn't count. There would be no Bowing Down. When Dirt finally got to her feet, she heard Webba call out.

"NoBe Swoo. Go ahead."

Then Swoo's arms were around her waist again. Raise. Dump. A stab of pain. Dirt was back on the ground.

"Webba, why–"

"No need to be quick, my Sis," Webba said again. "Breathe easy."

It continued that way deep into the afternoon.

Then into the evening.

Webba forced Swoo and Dirt to continue while she ate third-meal with Nana and Snore.

Finally, when the sky was black and Dirt had been driven into the sand once again, it was over.

"Eh heh. Time to make sleep, eh?" Webba called out of the darkness.

Swoo just grunted in response.

Dirt lay in the ring as the shuffling sound of Swoo's tired feet joined Webba's foot-and-crutches rhythm, the two sounds disappearing into the sleep hut. Her body felt like it had been thrashed by hot stones, a simultaneous beating and burning. The bones in her face rang like struck bells.

She was too battered to feel angry. Too tired for sorrow. All she felt, as she closed her eyes and let blessed sleep take her, was complete confusion.

If Webba was trying to build her confidence, she had failed.

2 Days until the Prayer

Dirt woke at Swoo's kick, blinking into the blue fog of the pre-sun morning. Sand was everywhere, embedded in her skin, tangled in her hair.

"We run," Swoo said. Even scarcely awake, Dirt could hear the sneer in her voice.

Swollen and sore, Dirt staggered to her feet. She was almost grateful for the dozens of bites she'd gained from sleeping outside. They distracted from the pain in the rest of her body.

It was all the same as the day before. Light run, firstmeal, easy afternoon exercise, secondmeal.

"Time to spar, eh?" Webba said.

Dirt nodded, nervous. She looked across the ring at Swoo, who wore a smile like that of a jungle cat that had cornered its prey.

"How much?" Swoo asked.

"This day is one," Webba said.

Dirt and Swoo both turned to Webba, eyebrows high in surprise. "Eh?"

"One is finefine," she repeated. "Breathe easy."

Dirt breathed a long, relieved sigh.

They sparred slowly, and Dirt got the better of most exchanges, all her years of technique and experience outweighing Swoo's greater athleticism. A few times, Swoo's frustration flared up, but a sharp word from Webba kept it from escalating.

The beating of the previous night had confirmed all of Dirt's fears about competing in the God Bow tournament. If a NoBe like Swoo could leave her a broken mess in the middle of the ring, what would the South's elite Bowers do to her? What would Carra Carre do?

The slower sparring gave her hope. She had weaknesses, yes, but also so many strengths. She didn't have to be the strongest girl, or the fastest. She just had to play to her strengths and avoid her faults.

Fight smart. As long as she did that, there was a chance.

"Finished," Webba said, raising a hand in the air.

Swoo looked disgusted. She wasn't sweating at all.

"Time for thirdmeal, eh?" Dirt asked.

Webba shook her head. "Not yet, my sister. We still must train."

"Train what?"

"Na mud pit."

Dirt looked at Swoo for an explanation, but Swoo only shrugged.

"Bibi Nana!" Webba shouted, turning to crutch herself back toward the sleep hut.

Nana and Snore came giggling out of the hut, hands clasped together, thumbs jostling for position in some game they'd invented.

"Yes?" Nana asked, not taking her eyes from the game.

"Where is na mud pit?"

Nana, distracted, pointed off toward the tree line.

"Bibi Nana!" Webba barked, cutting through their childish enjoyment. Both girls slapped hands to their sides and stared with big eyes at the First of the Mud. "Take us, eh?" Webba said more softly.

Only then did Dirt realize how little she'd seen the Bibi over the last two days. She'd been too tired to think about what they'd been doing all that time.

Nana and Snore led them a short distance into the trees, to a small clearing with soft ground. In the center was a square patch of mud as long and wide as Dirt was tall.

"Na mud pit," Webba said with pride. She dropped her crutches and sat with her back against a mossy tree trunk. "Go and step in it."

Swoo looked uncertain, but she trusted Webba. She walked over, placed a foot down on the mud surface, then lowered her leg until she was covered up to her knee in brown. She took her leg out, stared at the mud for a moment, then jumped in. Her whole body plunged beneath the surface before her head popped back up.

"It is cold!" Swoo yelped, hiding her shiver with a laugh as she wiped mud from her face.

Webba grinned. "It will not be cold long. Sis Dirt." She nodded to the pit.

Dirt's muscles were so sore, the mud pit was a blessing. She slid in gleefully, smiling for what must have been the first time all week.

The mud was cool on the skin, and came up to her shoulders. It didn't have the lovely scent of the Mud Offer, but it was far thicker, like being hugged by the ground. Dirt could barely move, but with the pain in her body and the heat of the day, she wasn't concerned with moving anywhere anyway.

"Why do we not do this before?" Dirt asked. All this mud around the camp and no Mud Sis had ever thought to do this.

"It is na oldold tradition," Webba replied. "Sis Prom tell me when I become na Sis. I believe now is na good time for tradition. It is finefine, eh?"

Swoo shrugged, seemingly confused.

Dirt closed her eyes, focusing on the pleasure of relaxing her muscles. "Very finefine."

"Good," Webba said. "Now." She clapped her hands. "Time for spar."

Dirt's eyes sprang open. "Eh?" she asked.

Webba's grin widened. She nodded.

Dirt sighed a long and sorrowful sigh, then began to climb out of the pit.

"No, my Sis," Webba said. "You will spar in na mud pit."

"My Sis, I cannot move," Dirt explained.

"Eh heh," Webba said. "So it will be quickquick. One Bow to make winner."

The light of violence returned to Swoo's eyes. "How strong, Sis Webba?" she asked.

Webba pondered that for a moment. "Ten," she said. "Fight strong, my sisters."

Dirt didn't even have a chance to Slap before Swoo Rode in. Startled, Dirt tried to back away, but the wall of the pit stood firm behind her. Swoo Trapped and tried to Bow, though both girls were too weighed down by the mud. Dirt then tried to assert her own Traps, but she was too slow, and Swoo was quick to stop every Trap she tried.

For the rest of the evening, Dirt struggled to break Swoo's crushing grips. It was exactly the kind of Trap-heavy fight Webba loved, the kind Dirt would never want. On the few occasions she managed to break Swoo's Trap and push away, Swoo Rode back in immediately, cutting through the mud like a crocodile.

Dirt felt Swoo tiring, but she felt herself tiring faster. Fear bubbled up within her. She realized that this night would be like the one before. Webba would let it continue as long as necessary. Whether on sand or in mud, she couldn't beat Swoo. She was too skinny, too slow. She was a coach, not a fighter.

"No!" Webba shouted.

With Swoo pressed against her, arms fighting for Traps, Dirt looked over to her sister. Webba was on her crutches, her eyebrows turned down—in anger or focus, Dirt couldn't tell.

"Fight, my Sis!" she said. "Dirt, you must fight!"

Dirt heard what Webba was saying, but she didn't understand. Her heart was pounding in her ears. Her muscles were screaming. She could feel her legs wobbling, unable to support her any longer. What more fighting could she do?

"Do not listen to na Whispers," Webba said as Swoo Trapped Dirt low around her waist, squeezing the air from her. "You are not breezy. You are not skinny. You are brave. You are fat. You are Dirt. Dirt can never quit! Tell yourself! You are brave! You are fat! You are Dirt!"

"Oos oos, Sis Dirt!" Nana shouted.

"Oos oos, Sis Dirt!" Snore muttered as she whipped a stick back and forth on the ground, swatting every insect in her path.

Dirt didn't know what Webba meant by the "Whispers," but she wanted to impress Webba. She wanted to make Nana proud. She wanted to inspire Little Snore. She wanted to put young Swoo in her place.

But she couldn't. She wasn't strong enough.

With a final effort, Swoo pulled Dirt away from the wall of the pit. Screaming into the sky, she hauled Dirt off the pit floor and swept her legs from under her, driving her into the mud.

Dirt held her breath just before her head slipped beneath the surface. She stayed under, too exhausted to push back up.

And too ashamed.

She'd failed Webba. She'd failed the Fam. Under the mud, she was buried, forgotten. No one was looking at her. No one was expecting anything of her. She was just another forgotten girl who couldn't disappoint anyone.

Then Swoo's arm dragged her up out of the mud and hot air flowed down into her burning lungs. She was unburied again, and everyone was looking at her, expecting something. She leaned back against the pit wall, breathing. Just breathing.

When she looked at Webba, the disappointment on her sister's face was as thick as the mud clinging to Dirt's body. She wanted to say something, to explain. But there were no words. Webba turned on her crutches to head back to the sleep hut, the Bibi in tow.

"Time for thirdmeal," Webba said. She didn't look back.

11

Forgotten Memories, Unspoken Words

1 Day until the Prayer

WHEN SHE WOKE on the final day of training, Dirt lay on the floor for a while, staring at the flat wooden slats of the hut ceiling. The sunlight filtered through the trees above, which shuddered in a breeze, setting the shadows of leaves playing and whispering like a troop of Bibi.

She had to tell Webba that she couldn't do it.

Not another morning run. Not another press-up. Not another sparring session. Webba was living in the past, blinded by sisterly love. She was placing her hopes in a girl who no longer existed, wagering the fate of the Fam on a memory.

The plain truth was that Dirt wasn't strong enough. Physically or mentally. She couldn't compete in the God Bow tournament. It had to be Swoo.

Now she just had to find a way to tell Webba.

Dirt suddenly realized that she'd woken up on her own. Webba hadn't called her. Swoo hadn't kicked her. For once, her morning was as peaceful as it had been before her tournament training.

She rolled to her side, but her sisters were all gone. Then she heard them just outside: the muffled patter of running feet, Snore's mad giggles, Nana's whiny protests, Swoo and Webba in murmured conversation.

When Dirt stepped out of the hut, eyes squinted against the sun, they all stared at her, waiting. Webba, balanced on her crutches, wore a grin that made Dirt pause in the doorway.

"Na good day, my Sis," Webba said.

The sweet scent of grilled plantain tugged at Dirt's nose. She looked around to find Swoo half obscured by rising steam, poking at the food over a ringside cookfire.

"Na good day," Dirt mumbled back. Snore bounced with energy. Nana looked at Dirt like she knew a secret that Dirt didn't. "What is it?"

"Training is finished," Webba said, crutching over to Dirt. "Today, we eat. Tomorrow, na Prayer. Next tomorrow, na tournament. Breathe easy, my Sis."

Dirt frowned, skeptical. But as Swoo and the Bibi returned to preparing food and Webba took a seat along the edge of the ring, she realized there was nothing to do but take Webba's advice.

All morning, the Mud sisters lounged in the shade, playing games in the sand and eating mounds and mounds of delicious food, even the sweet berries and grilled bananas that were normally off-limits to competing Bowers. Dirt let the Bibi style her usual mess of hair into neat, short curls. They taught her that thumb-wrestling game they'd learned and cackled with amusement as she lost to Webba again and again.

In the afternoon, after secondmeal, Webba retired to the sleep hut to take a brief nap. Dirt accompanied her sister, helping her down onto her mat.

This was Dirt's chance. Webba was in a good mood, relaxed and with a full belly. There wouldn't be a better time.

"My Sis," Dirt said, "we must speak."

"Sit," Webba responded, exhaling as she settled onto her back. "Make talk with me, eh? Let me hear your sleepysleepy voice."

Dirt snorted, then sat with her back against the rough driftwood wall of the hut.

"Yesterday," Webba said, "Swoo make you Bow."

Dirt swallowed. "Eh heh. I am tired and she is strong."

"She is NoBe. And she, too, is tired."

Dirt wasn't sure what to say.

"My Sis, you know na Bow as well as I," Webba continued. "Na body tire easy. But na mind . . . " She tapped a finger against her temple. "'Na jungle cat does not kill with only teeth.' You understand, eh?"

She did. A Bower's mind was as important as her body.

"My Sis," Dirt replied, "I do not have na mind like you. Like Swoo."

"No, you do not."

Dirt blinked. Maybe this would be easier than she'd expected.

"When you fight, I can see," Webba continued, eyes so intent that Dirt found it hard not to squirm. "When you begin, you are fine. Tongue to toe, you are strong. But Useyi Whispers to you His many lies. This I see. When He says you are breezy, you believe. When He says you are skinny, you believe."

Useyi. The God of Forgotten Memories, enemy of the Mamas

and Papas. He held in His hands all the lost souls whose names had been forgotten, a fate worse than death. However strange their ways, the Mamas and Papas wanted to see their human children succeed. Useyi wanted only failure. Because failures were forgotten, and the forgotten were His to play with for eternity.

But Dirt had never heard Useyi's voice. She wasn't even sure she would know it if she did. What did evil sound like?

"Why do you believe Him, my Sis?" There was a plea in Webba's voice. "You believe Useyi knows you, eh? My Sis, do *you* not know you?"

Dirt looked away. "I know, my Sis," she said. That was the problem. Dirt knew who she was. She was an old, retired Bowing coach who had no business fighting. It was Webba who didn't know who Dirt was. "This is why–"

"You are na Mud champion, Dirt. You are na God Bower. You will fight in na tournament. When Useyi Whispers to you, you must not listen to Him," she said. "You must speak against Him. You are brave. You are fat. You are Dirt. You hear?"

"My Sis, I cannot–"

"Speak it."

"Webba, I–"

"Speak. It." Despite the stone in her voice, Webba's face was strangely desperate. Dirt couldn't take seeing her sister like that. The mighty Webba, the First of the Mud, begging.

"I . . . am . . . brave," Dirt muttered. "I am . . . fat. I am, eh . . . I am Dirt."

"Eh heh, again."

"I . . . I am brave. I am fat. I am Dirt."

"Again. Loud."

"I am brave. I am fat. I am Dirt."

"Good, my Sis." Webba closed her eyes and took a deep, relieved breath. "Do not forget."

Dirt sat in silence with her sister for a long while before Webba suddenly spoke again.

"But what is it?" she asked.

Dirt frowned, confused. "What is what?"

"You say we must speak. Speak about what?"

Dirt stared, swallowed, opened her mouth, and closed it. This was her chance.

"Nothing, my Sis," she said. "Sleep easy, eh?"

Webba, eyes closed, flashed a grin, then exhaled into rest.

Dirt couldn't do it. She didn't have the courage to tell Webba that she wouldn't compete in the God Bow tournament.

But she knew who did.

Morning of the Prayer

Swoo was kneeling beside the ring, splitting wood with her trusty handaxe. Most of the wood in the South was too wet or soft to use for cookfires and torches, so Swoo had to collect branches from the right trees, sometimes trekking for miles to find what she needed. A small pyramid of chopped wood was stacked alongside the sleep hut, always stocked for the Fam's needs.

"You ripe?" Dirt asked.

Swoo grunted as she brought the axe down, splitting a long branch in half. *Thoonk.* She wiped her forearm across her sweat-slicked forehead. "Riperipe."

"Where are na Bibi?"

Swoo chopped one half of the branch down to usable size, then grabbed the other. "Playing." She brought the axe down. *Thoonk.*

Dirt sat on the ground, watching Swoo work. *Thoonk. Thoonk.* "Strong chop," she said.

Swoo blinked, then continued chopping. "Years ago, when Sis Webba tells me I must chop na firewood, I am not happy. I call it 'Bibi work.' Not for na fighter. But now . . ."

She brought the axe down on a particularly thick branch, cleaved it in a single stroke. Dirt wasn't sure she herself could have managed that.

"Now?" Dirt asked.

"Now I understand. I do not chop firewood for me, I chop for na Fam. Not *Sis Webba*," she emphasized. "Na Mud."

"Eh heh," Dirt mumbled. She knew what Swoo was really saying. Just because Webba chose Dirt didn't mean that was the best choice for the Fam.

And she was right.

Dirt didn't say anything for a while, just watched Swoo's axe chew through branch after branch until they were all about forearm length. Dirt rose to help Swoo carry the armload of wood.

"Let me help, eh?" Dirt asked, but Swoo shook her head.

"You cannot," Swoo said, her voice thick with sarcasm. "Na champion does not carry wood." She straightened her back and said with a suddenly stone face, "This is Bibi work."

As the Second of the Fam, it was Dirt's duty to fight when the First could not. But as the Second of the Fam, it was also Dirt's duty to do what was best for the Fam. Swoo stood before her, young, strong, ready for the role of Mud champion. Dirt knew that Swoo was testing her. Those chopped branches were a responsibility, one that Swoo would gladly hand over in exchange for the greater responsibility of being the Mud champion. Would Dirt be willing to make that trade?

"I will not stand," Dirt heard herself say. She wasn't sure whether she'd really said it aloud until she saw Swoo's eyes widen. "At na Prayer, when Antie Yaya calls. I will not stand."

Dirt extended her arms, ready to take over Swoo's "Bibi work." Sticks were a much lesser burden to carry than the future of the Fam. "You are na Mud champ–"

"Today na Prayer daaaaaay," Webba sang, emerging from the sleep hut.

Dirt jumped away from Swoo as if the girl were holding a basket of snakes. She wiped her sweaty palms along her pants.

"Today na Prayer dayoooooo." Webba crutched over to them, grinning at Dirt. "My Sis, you ripe?"

"She is ripe," Swoo said in a quiet, defeated voice. She brushed past Dirt to go add the bundle of freshly cut wood to the existing stack. "Our sister is ready."

12

The Prayer

THE PATH to Antie Yaya's was long and tight. Below, the earth was webbed and bulged with roots. Overhead, peeking out from behind the broad leaves and bunched pod fruit of the catappa trees, the sky oranged, then purpled, then blacked. The creatures of the night awoke, chirping and scuttling and cooing and shrieking in the dark like musicians all on a different tune.

Dirt led her sisters through the jungle, torch aloft. It had been a year since the last Prayer, but she remembered it well. She remembered watching Webba rise at Antie Yaya's call, how her sister had seemed so brave and powerful. A true Bower and a perfect Mud champion.

Now Webba expected Dirt to be the same.

They heard Antie Yaya's compound before they saw it. Muffled drumming cut through the trees, an invitation out of the damp and dangerous jungle. A voice skimmed over it, magnified by horn.

The voice called out, and hundreds of others responded from every direction. Dirt already knew what was being said, but as the Mud Fam continued forward, she was better able to make out the words.

"Mama Ijiri!" the lone voice boomed.

"Na Courage to Slap!" the others responded.

"Mama Eghodo!"

"Na Grace to Ride!"

"Papa Oduma!"

"Na Strength to Trap!"

"Papa Abidon!"

"Na Humility to Bow!"

When Dirt and the Mud finally emerged from the tree line, the drumming and chanting washed over them in a flood of sound. They raised their own voices, adding to the chorus.

Ahead of them, in the center of a deep basin in the earth, Antie Yaya's compound sat on a low plateau, lit by torch and moonlight. It was a palace of gray-brown limestone, with smooth ripples in the rock that looked carved by wind. Its long main hall stretched across the plateau, divided by dozens of ornate columns. At the center, a trio of plumed crests rose from the roof like stone pineapples. All around the compound was a field of shortgrass, green and vast and soft enough to seat thousands. The smell of roasted meats, vegetables, and plantains drifted on the cool evening breeze.

Webba paused in her chanting. "We are here," she said, peace in her voice. Antie Yaya's compound always felt like returning to a home they'd forgotten, a place where the very soil knew them. "You ripe?"

Dirt didn't trust herself to speak. She nodded.

"Na Prayer, na Prayer!" Snore sang, flapping her arms.

Swoo continued the chant, eyes ahead, face tight. She was still hoping, Dirt knew. Hoping that when Antie Yaya called for Webba's replacement, Dirt would stay seated and she would be the one to rise instead.

Dirt was hoping for the same.

They continued forward, onto the stone bridge that curved over the gap of sunken earth between the edge of the jungle and the plateau of Antie Yaya's compound. Girls from all around the South crowded onto it like fish swimming together upstream. Antie Yaya's was a sacred place, where the usual divisions and hierarchies weren't tolerated. So Bowers and Mosquitos, girls from each Fam, moved side by side. All around Dirt, they ran to excitedly embrace old friends, flip each other's hair, slap each other's bellies, cackle at jokes only they knew.

Among the rush, much smaller girls weaved about, often moving against the traffic of the bridge. Some of them pushed small carts laden with food—corn here, sticky rice packed into bamboo there—and rushed over to any older girl who made eye contact, ready to trade. Some were supervised by Mosquitos and others were like wild animals, chasing and smacking each other and creating a general madness that earned the occasional thwack from a Bower. They were all younger than Snore, and they all looked unfinished, in a way—with neither the firmness and growing belly of a Bower, nor the spindly, costumed frame of a Mosquito. These were the children of the forgotten. These were the descendants of those girls who had gone to Antie Yaya upon their Scarring and were never seen again.

These were the recruits.

At other Prayers, Dirt had scarcely noticed them. But now she couldn't take her eyes off them. These chaotic little hawkers were the key to the Mud's survival. At the end of the day, more so than any praise or glory, they were the only prize that mattered. They were the future.

Dirt would be a woman soon. Was this what awaited her? Creating one of these children and sending her to Antie Yaya? How did that even happen? Some girls said the Mamas and Papas gave children to women. Some said women got children from men, which didn't make much sense. Dirt herself couldn't remember the woman who created her. Now, for the first time, she wondered whether that woman could remember *her*.

The Mud sisters moved through the throng of girls, forming as best they could a protective circle around Webba. As uncomfortable as it must have been for her to cross the bridge on crutches, she didn't seem to mind. She flashed grins and waved a hand at the girls who called out to her over the chanting. Even injured, Webba was a star.

When they reached the other end of the bridge, Dirt sighed in pleasure at the feel of grass beneath her feet. Grass was rare in the jungle, where the tall thicket of trees soaked up most of the sunlight. At Antie Yaya's, the grass was crisp and prickly between her toes, almost tickling. As they walked together toward the building, Snore and Nana took exaggerated, giggling steps, toes splayed.

Dirt pointed out a spot beneath an old, bent tree with a few young Mosquito girls sitting in its higher branches. "Let us go there, eh? We can sit under na tree."

"Too far," Webba shouted over the chanting, giving Dirt a curious look. "Na Mud champion must sit in front."

Dirt gave a tight-lipped smile and nodded.

There were always open spots near the foot of the building. The Mosquito girls preferred to leave plenty of space for the Bowers rather than suffer the indignity of being bullied out of their seats. The Mud sisters took one of the openings, leaving room for Webba to stretch her leg and lay her crutches beside her.

To their left and right were all Bowers, mainly Creek and Sand sisters that Dirt greeted with eye contact and firm nods. There was a question in their eyes as they nodded back. They were wondering which Mud sister would fill Webba's footprints.

Dirt couldn't help looking past them, over to the mass of vine-wrapped heads to their far left. One head poked up above the rest, the largest girl in all the South. Seeing Carra Carre made Dirt feel a soup of emotions—sadness, fear, anger.

And confusion.

Before Carra Carre became a Sis, the Vine had been a modest Fam. Powerful, but reclusive. Even last season, when Carra Carre had dominated the God Bow tournament like no girl ever had in memory, she'd done so honorably. This year, something had changed. To deliberately maim another Bower was beyond imagination. Was it just the humiliation of losing to Webba that made her lash out?

Or was it something more?

Finally, the voice leading the chants fell quiet, and the congregation ceased chanting as well. The silence was all-consuming, a sacred hush no girl dared to break. The few girls still standing eased themselves quietly onto the grass, crossing their legs, waiting.

Ahead of Dirt and her sisters, two dozen gray steps led up to the altar in front of the building, where Antie Yaya sat upon a giant clay throne, her long arms draped on the armrests. She wore a green-and-black flower-pattern top and skirt with a matching head wrap.

A coral bead necklace with gold dividers gleamed above the swoop of her neckline. She must have been as old as forty, the oldest person Dirt had ever seen. But she was beautiful for a slim woman. She was poised. Powerful.

And unsettling.

Antie Yaya's blinks were long and slow. Her eyes, splayed wide, occasionally rolled in her head before she refocused them. The torchlight darkened her neck, making it look like there was an emptiness between her body and head. Her cheeks were high and full and lovely, yet her jaw was unnaturally tight, as if she were clamping back a scream. Snore crawled into Dirt's lap, seeking comfort from the sight.

Was this what a woman was? No belly, no sisters, nothing to fight for; just a pretty thing in a too-big chair, telling young girls what to do while trying not to scream? Antie Yaya had always looked severe, but now Dirt found her unsettling for another reason.

Her mouth came unstuck slowly, strings of spit between her lips. Then she spoke in an airy voice that carried across the compound.

"Tonight marks the beginning of a new world," she said, vacant gaze sweeping her audience. "And the Gods sit among us."

The unfamiliar words she used. The way she drew long on some sounds. Antie Yaya had a strange way of speaking.

Over the years, Dirt and Webba had traded theories about why. Maybe Antie Yaya was from the North, East, or West, and people spoke differently there. Maybe it was how all women spoke.

Maybe Antie Yaya was just weird.

But the answer that felt the most true, and that most girls accepted, was that Antie Yaya wasn't from the Isle at all. She was sent by the Mamas and Papas to guide and protect the children of the Isle. Her speech was the language of the Gods, translated into something their ears could understand.

Or maybe she was just weird.

"There was a world before this one," the old woman said as a light drizzle began, "where the Gods lived and loved and cried and celebrated. And fought. How they would fight." She smiled sadly, as if reliving a fond memory. "Oduma the Defender against Ijiri the Trickster. Abidon the Liberator against Eghodo the Lawbringer, Queen of the Gods. How the earth would shake beneath the nations. The blood." Her smile disappeared. She blinked slowly. "The bloodshed, the lives forgotten. What is left when the Gods wage war?"

Her eyes settled firmly on the assembled girls. She looked from face to face, seeming to take in every single girl in just a few moments. Dirt shivered when their eyes briefly locked. She held Snore tighter.

"So they chose others. Two to fight in their stead. Two chosen, two sacrificed. Two then." Her face went slack and she closed her eyes for a long moment. When she opened them, she seemed calmed, almost warm. "And two now. Through you, the children of the new world, the Gods return. Two will fight, but only one will prevail. The True Godskin."

Her words were punctuated by a punch of thunder from the western woods, one so loud Dirt felt it in her chest. Strangely, there was no flash of lightning. Drizzle turned to rain, falling in light drops.

"Daughters of Oduma, rise!" Antie Yaya proclaimed. "The Sand!"

Dirt looked to her right and saw three girls stand from among the cheering Sand Fam. Dream was the First of the Sand, her arms long and thin like skipping ropes, her face always looking like she was making an important decision. Beside her were Hari and Zuna, the Sand's Second and Third. Zuna was in her first season as a Sis, a young prodigy who had finally found her stride after being only an average NoBe.

"The Rock!"

Hollo, Nat, and Ask stood, arms over each other's shoulders, swaying their hips to the singing of their sisters, flashing smiles. Typical Rock girls.

Snore shifted in Dirt's lap, leaning her head back so her mouth was by Dirt's ear.

"Sis Dirr," she whispered loudly, "who is she?" Snore jutted her chin up at Antie Yaya.

Dirt smoothed the girl's hair, confused.

"She is Antie Yaya. Now, quiet."

"No," Snore insisted. *"She!"*

A girl stood in the wings of the altar, out of the rain. She was nearly hidden in the shadow of a pillar, but Dirt recognized her. Ebe. She was one of the last Bowers of the now-gone Bush Fam. She'd been among the best NoBe of Dirt's era, using tricky Rides and unpredictable Bows to offer a headache to any opponent. Everyone had expected her to be among the South's elites when she graduated to being a full Sis.

But that expectation was never fulfilled. In her last match as a NoBe, Ebe had suffered a humiliating loss to Wing of the Creek. She never competed again, and soon the Bush Fam had no girls left and was dissolved.

"She is Ebe," Dirt said.

Dirt had heard the rumors of Ebe becoming Antie Yaya's assistant, but she hadn't believed them.

"The Creek!" Antie Yaya wailed.

Wing, the First of the Creek and the biggest threat to Carra Carre now that Webba was out, stood and waved to the crowd. Splash and Sevi, her Second and Third, joined her. All three girls had thick legs and heavy bellies, which they drummed on as their sisters whooped.

Dirt looked from Wing back to Ebe, uncomfortable with the contrast. Wing was nearly as large as Webba, a Bower in her prime, full of life. Ebe's skin was loose, her posture bent. She was a girl diminishing into nothing. Their lives had taken such different paths since their fight.

"Who is Ebe?" Snore asked.

Dirt didn't know how to answer.

Ebe was no longer a Bower. She was no longer a sister of the Bush. She had no sisters to enjoy, no Fam to remember her or tell her story. The great Bowers were remembered forever, even when their Fam was no more. But Ebe had never become great. She'd given up too soon.

"She is . . . ," Dirt said, watching the girl with pity. "She is no one."

"The Mud!" Antie Yaya called.

And all eyes turned to Dirt.

13

Champion of the Mud

A WARM TERROR lanced through Dirt's chest. Snore stared up into her face from within her lap. "Sis Dirr!"

Time seemed to slow as she looked from one sister to the next. Nana looked as nervous as Dirt felt, eyebrows raised in anticipation. Webba wore a glowing smile and gave a small nod. "Oos oos, Dirt."

Then she looked at Swoo. She expected to see rage, maybe jealousy. But Swoo's face was pleading, eyebrows bent in desperation, legs braced to stand. Dirt stared at her for so long that an unrest grew in the crowd.

Finally, she looked back to the dais. To Ebe. To the girl who had been defeated by fear and ruled by shame. The girl who had lost both her Fam and her chance at greatness, all because of one bad match. A girl whose Fam had been all but forgotten and who herself was fading from memory.

And Dirt stood.

A murmur rolled through the crowd. None bothered to hide their surprise. They all knew Dirt. They knew she was no fighter.

Dirt looked out over the thousands of assembled girls. The Creek Fam with dozens of girls in their ranks, fat and strong and intimidating. The Sand and Rock Fam, who were smaller but always moved with confidence and cheered with pride, as if they were as large as the Vine.

Then there was the Mud. Just five girls, one on crutches, one a child. Girls with mismatched clothes and meek demeanors, whose feeble cheers couldn't make enough sound to wake a baby.

That had to change. That's what Dirt's standing meant. She had to change it.

"Oos oos, Dirt!" Webba howled, and her sisters picked up the call.

"Oos oos, Sis Dirt!!"

"Oos oos, Sis Dirt!!"

Dirt turned back to Antie Yaya, trying her best to portray a pride and confidence she didn't feel. Antie Yaya's wandering gaze came to a stop on her face, and there was a long, disquieting pause. The old woman's firm jaw enjoyed a brief looseness, as if she were going to say something.

Then the rain picked up into a steady shower. She glanced up at it, and when she looked back down, her jaw was tight again and the moment was over.

"The Vine!"

Carra Carre rose like a mountain out of the sea, leaving her Second, Verdi, standing shadowed behind her. As Carra Carre raised a meaty fist, a murmur of admiration spread across the gathering. She beat her chest three times, her sisters punctuating each beat with a sound that was half grunt, half howl.

With all the competitors on their feet, Ebe emerged from her haunt behind Antie Yaya, dragging out a wooden board as tall as she was and twice the width. It was divided into four columns, each one holding long, cut-out rectangles, arranged in pairs. The first two columns held four pairs each, the third held two, and the final column held just one. The tournament bracket. The leftmost column was for the first round. It held the numbers five through twelve, set so that the higher numbers were paired with the lower–five against twelve, six against eleven, and so on. They'd have to compete to advance to the second round–the quarterfinals–where the top four seeds were already entered.

Dirt eyed the empty two-seed slot, where Webba would have been if she were healthy. Now that slot would be filled by Dirt.

Ebe picked up a gray stone slate that had a "1" etched into it and a smear of green paint across its face, representing the First of the Vine. When she put the one slot in the second round, Carra Carre let out a roar that spurred a wave of cheers from the Vine.

Dirt watched with her heart in her throat. She knew there would be an uproar when she received the second seed. Those seeded below her had spent a whole season proving themselves, while Dirt had been little more than a sparring partner. But it was her only chance. The higher seeds faced the lower ones, which meant she'd get easier competition as the second seed. If she had any chance at sneaking out a victory or two, that was going to be the way.

But when Ebe placed the second slate, it wasn't for Dirt. It had a "1" with blue paint, for Wing, the First of the Creek.

"No!" Webba shouted, but she was drowned out by the crush of cheers from the Creek sisters.

Dirt's name wasn't on the three-seed slate either. That was Dream of the Sand. Then Hollo of the Rock. The Firsts of all the other Fam were placed ahead of her. Disappointing, but Dirt couldn't say it was unfair.

The rain poured on, fat drops drenching through clothes. Girls around the plaza began to exclaim in alarm, bunching together and holding their arms over each other's heads in a failing attempt to keep dry. This sort of sudden, powerful storm was common during the wet season, but Dirt had never seen a storm like this during the dry season.

Ebe, shielded from the rain by the building's overhang, continued placing the rest of the slates. Nat, then Splash, Seconds of the Rock and the Creek. Then Carra Carre's Second, Verdi. Sevi of the Creek came in at eighth seed, making her the highest ranked Third, followed by the Sand's Second, Hari.

Only then did Dirt's name appear. Tenth seed. Ranked among the Thirds. It was the lowest possible seed she could've been given without it being an outright insult to the Mud.

As the second seed, she would have immediately advanced to the quarterfinals, waiting to face the winner of the match between the seventh and tenth seed. Instead, Dirt was in that very match, waiting to face the seventh-seeded Verdi. Verdi, the right hand of the defending God Bow champion, the strategic mind behind the South's most powerful Fam, and a terrifying Bower in her own right.

Dirt couldn't shake the sense that Webba's match had been prophetic; the First of the Vine had defeated and maimed the First of the Mud. Maybe the fight between Seconds would end the same.

The rain picked up further, and Antie Yaya's compound became obscured by droplets, whipped on by a cruel wind. Speeding water sliced across the skin, roared dull in the ears, filled the world with the scent of damp.

Soon, Dirt couldn't see anything more than a stride away. Webba and Swoo were taking in the storm with wonder and confusion, but Nana was shrunken in fear. Snore was asleep. Dirt could feel the presence of the thousands of other girls around her, but she couldn't see them behind the deluge. She was almost grateful; she was finally saved from the stares and mutterings.

Suddenly, like a boom of thunder, Antie Yaya's voice cut through the howling rains.

"Oduma the Defender," she prayed, "He of the Untempered Heart, whose chest turns spear and arrow alike, whose Shield defends the Isle against Useyi and the Forgotten, who stood alone against the legion in the Ingue Pass." Antie Yaya's voice became increasingly fevered, a wild wail. The rain came down harder, until Dirt could no longer even see her sisters beside her. She was alone, trapped by the storm as Antie Yaya's voice descended on her from every angle, a colorless shroud of prayer and rain. "Look upon Your daughters, Brave Oduma. See into their hearts. Pour unto them Your spirit. Choose, oh Oduma, Your Godskin!"

Dirt felt a swell in her chest, as if she'd taken three deep breaths at once. A throbbing rush in her head. A sudden crush of her limbs. Something pulled her spine until she could no longer feel the grass beneath her feet. Instead, she was floating, her skin tingling so hot it crackled. She felt like it was only a matter of time before she would burst like an overripe melon.

Not far off, Dirt saw what looked like a point of blue light, and she immediately knew that it was her own reflection. She had become a grounded star, cold and burning at the same time.

Then it was over, and Dirt collapsed to her knees like a puppet whose strings had been severed. The storm receded, suddenly thin enough that she could see the concerned expressions of her sisters and hear the whispering of the girls around the green.

Dirt climbed back to her feet, to stand with the other champions. Not far away stood Carra Carre, who watched Dirt with an unfeeling flatness in her eyes. Dirt held her gaze, tried her best to show no fear, then turned to look up at Antie Yaya. The old woman looked even older, worn out by the ceremony. She waved a hand and Ebe hurried over to help her to her feet. Soon after, the two of them disappeared into a door farther back in the building.

The Prayer was over.

Dirt was fighting in the God Bow tournament.

And the fate of the Mud depended on her winning.

14

The God Bow Tournament Begins!

OUTSIDE THE TENT were the sounds of Bowing. Drums and horns wove music. Flagga boys, their voices high and eager, laughed and joked and traded insults with each other. Mosquito girls shouted across the sand, trading for eggs, coconut, palm oil, and more.

But inside the tent was silent. Dirt stood in its center, too nervous to do anything but breathe. She wished she could be like Webba before a fight, full of life and humor. She wasn't Webba, though, and she wasn't full of anything but cold fear and warm bile.

As Webba prayed and broke the kola nut, the Bibi lathered Dirt in Offer with slow, deliberate motions, like they were painting a wall. Dirt had long ago forgotten the feeling of having the sacred Mud on her skin. Forgotten how heavy it was, how much it symbolized the weight of the Fam. She'd also forgotten that it was applied as much as a massage as a costume. The Bibi's little hands were soothing against her skin, almost rubbing away her anxieties.

Almost. She still felt like throwing up, and the bitter taste of kola nut didn't help.

Webba's Godskin was elaborate, with clay rings and bracers, twig anklets, and a flowery crown, all arranged like the armor of a jungle queen. Dirt's was much simpler. No clay beads, no flowers. Just eight pieces of clay jewelry: one bracer around each elbow, wrist, knee, and ankle. They were plain and functional rather than etched with patterns like Webba's. Her Mud Offer was applied in several thick layers rather than Webba's thinner coat, and instead of a tall crown laden with flowers, her crown was a ring of snapped twigs and jungle mulch.

She looked like a mudslide.

Nana and Snore stepped back and looked her up and down, unable to hide their disappointment with the result.

"Sis Dirr," Snore said as Nana tried and failed to shush her. "Sis Dirr look . . . bad."

"Fat!" Nana shouted over her sister. "Sis Dirt look fatfat."

"Whatever na Gods speak," Dirt said to herself as much as to the Bibi. If her Godskin was plain, then it was meant to be plain. She couldn't control that. Godskins were determined by the Mamas and Papas, carried out through the Bibi.

Fighting fashion was the last thing on Dirt's mind anyway. She looked around at her sisters, Webba on her crutches, the Bibi and their hopeful faces, Swoo standing by the tent flap, arms folded, lost in thought. They were all depending on her.

"NoBe Swoo," Webba said, looking at Dirt with an unusual somberness.

"Eh?"

"Take na Bibi. Na Sis must speak."

Swoo looked from one Mud Sis to the other, then gathered up Nana and Snore and left the tent.

"My Sis," Webba said. "'Na girl with stone legs cannot swim.'"

"My legs are not stone."

"And na Grand Temple is not na river. But same and same, you must breathe easy. Be free."

Dirt swallowed and nodded. "Thank you, my sister. I understand."

"Eh heh. So let us go." She crutched over to the tent flap and held it open.

Dirt took a step forward, but just that one step melted through her resolve. The bile in her stomach rushed up her throat and she turned to a tent corner, splattering the day's meal onto the sand.

Some Godskin she was. What God would want a girl who was huddled in the corner of a preparation tent, legs quivering, lording over a splash of her own insides?

After a moment, she turned shamefully back to Webba.

"I am sorry," she mumbled, eyes downcast.

"Eh? Why?"

"I . . ." Dirt didn't want to admit it, but she didn't know what else to say. "I am afraid." It was the truth. The humiliating truth. It should have been Swoo.

"Eh heh!" Webba said, all too cheerfully. When Dirt looked up, she saw that Webba was smiling, leaning casually on her crutches as if she weren't at all worried that the fate of her Fam was in Dirt's shaking hands. "Na Bow is life, my Sis. If you are alive, how can you not be afraid? Do you think Verdi is not afraid?"

Dirt frowned. "I have seen you in many Bows. You are not afraid."

"No." Webba shrugged. "But I am mad, my Sis. I am na madmad woman. I love to fight."

Dirt blinked.

"But you are not me," Webba said softly. "I know you. You are afraid. Finefine. But you are powerful. Who can Slap like Dirt? Who can make na girl Bow like Dirt? Who has na courage to spar with Swoo? Who has na grace to teach Nana and Snore, those helpless and honey-minded Bibi? Who has na strength to break my Trap? Eh? Who has na humility to be na Second when she is greater than na First?"

Dirt couldn't tell if Webba was joking. It didn't take any courage to spar with a NoBe. Nana and Snore were both attentive students. Webba's Traps nearly bent her in half–she only broke them when Webba went easy on her. And there was no ambiguity about who the greatest of the Mud was.

"I know you," Webba said. "But *you* do not know you. I know you can win. I know you can make Verdi Bow. I know you can make Carra Carre Bow. You are brave. You are fat. You are Dirt. Speak it."

"I am brave. I am fat. I am Dirt," she mumbled.

"Eh heh! Loud, my Sis!"

"I am brave. I am fat. I am Dirt."

"AGAIN," Webba shouted, intensity in her eyes. "Loudloud!"

A warm energy filled Dirt's face, calmed her stomach.

"I AM BRAVE. I AM FAT. I AM DIRT."

"Good, my Sis," Webba said, nodding, and Dirt was surprised to find herself breathing heavy, muscles tight, her fear dissolved. "Do not forget."

Webba had always said that Dirt would be a top-ranked Bower if she ever decided to compete. Webba had never doubted her, and wasn't doubting her now. And who knew Bowing better than Webba?

Dirt opened her mouth to apologize for her self-doubt, but Webba raised a hand and shook her head.

"Not here," Webba said. "Whatever you will say, say in na ring."

She extended her palm facing up, fingers slightly curled. Dirt smiled, then set her hand over Webba's, palm down. They wiggled their fingers against each other's palms, like they'd been doing since they were Bibi.

"You ripe?" Dirt asked.

Webba responded how she always did. She grinned.

Dirt's match was the last of the day, but they went to the Grand Temple early to watch the other matches. A side tunnel exclusively for Bowers made it easy to watch without having to deal with the crowds.

The first Bow was between Nat, the Second of the Rock, and Zuna, the Third of the Sand. It was a quick one. Zuna was a newer Sis, too inexperienced to fend off a strong Trapper like Nat. After wading through a few Slaps from Zuna's long arms, Nat secured a Trap and bullied Zuna out of the ring for a Push.

In the second match, the Creek's Third, Sevi, Bowed the Sand's Second, Hari, all around the ring. At half sand, the score was 13–0. Sevi's sisters stopped coaching for the remainder of the match, instead just singing and dancing as Sevi made her beleaguered opponent eat sand over and over.

The third match saw a surprising performance from Ask of the Rock, who came within a point of defeating the highly regarded Splash of the Creek. It was a humbling moment for young Ask, who had been leading for most of the match only to have her inexperience lose it for her in the end. As the Creek Fam roared in victory and gathered for a celebratory dance, Ask knelt at the edge of the ring with a dry cloth over her head and her shoulders bouncing from sobs. Her sisters surrounded her for a supportive group embrace, then helped her out of the arena.

Between matches, the Mud Fam kept Dirt ready. Nana and Snore reapplied Mud Offer as it hardened or slid off her. Webba had her do jumps, squats, and short sprints to keep her muscles warm. She also talked her through strategy.

"Na plan," she said.

"Slap, Slap, Slap," Dirt replied. "And Bow." Verdi was a strong Trapper, so Dirt would have to keep her at a distance with Slaps and be ready to execute counters when, hopefully, Verdi lunged forward in desperation.

"Sis Dirr will win?" Snore asked.

"Of course!" Nana cheered.

Swoo had been quiet all morning, doing her duties but otherwise being neither encouraging nor combative. Now she eyed Dirt curiously.

"If na Gods speak it," Dirt said.

"Only if you stay awake," Webba added, flicking Snore's nose, "you noisy piglet."

When the ring cleared from the third match, it was time.

They left the side tunnel and made their way to the main entrance, where they lined up. Dirt stood in the front, her heart racing, her breathing quickening.

But she was ready.

"Who are you?" Webba's voice was sturdy, confident.

"I am Dirt," she responded. *I am brave. I am fat. I am Dirt.*

As the drums pounded, Dirt strode out from the shadow of the entrance arch into the sun beating down from a clear sky. As much as she felt the heat of the day, she felt the eyes of the crowd more. Flagga boys and Mosquito girls, Pusher boys and all the Bowers who were done competing for the day. Fans from every Fam in waves of green and blue, brown and yellow and gray garb, like a sea of multihued grass. All the boys and girls of the South watching her every step.

The Godskin suddenly felt much heavier.

But she was ready.

She swept her gaze back and forth, watching the audience sway to the music. Watching them watch her.

"We are na Mud sisters!" She heard Swoo's voice peal high and clear from behind her.

"We are na Mud sisters!" the other sisters echoed.

"We fight, oh yes, ooooooh!" Dirt croaked, realizing she was late to join in.

"We are na Mud sisters!"

"We are na Mud sisters!" the Mud Fam responded, louder this time. Dirt felt their voices rumble in her chest.

"We never quit, noooooo!"

She danced her best across the arena, emboldened by the presence and voices of her sisters. She was surprised by how good it felt. How powerful it was to lead her sisters in a dance before the world. Even as basic and clunky as her moves were, even with Webba being nearly immobile on her crutches, even with Swoo's smooth dancing skills making Dirt's own look silly, Dirt felt nothing but free. This was why Swoo and Webba had put her through such torturous training. There was no way fighting Verdi would be more difficult than what she'd already been through. The hard part was over. She just had to do what she'd trained for.

She was ready.

When she got to the far side of the arena and the dance was finished, she took a few deep, slow breaths, the same way she'd taught Nana.

I am brave. I am fat. I am Dirt.

The music dropped to a subdued heartbeat as they waited.

And waited.

And waited.

The Mud sisters waited as the sun sailed past its peak, as the crowd tapered down to boredom and then ramped up to restlessness, some leaving the arena altogether. A few skirmishes broke out among groups of impatient Flagga boys. Eventually, Mosquito girls came out and traded sweets to keep the masses occupied.

Swoo gritted her teeth, nostrils flaring. "They disrespect us like this, eh?"

Nana was laid out on the sand, holding a broad leaf over her head to shield herself from the sun. Snore was asleep on her belly, snoring.

"It will not help them," Webba said. She was still all smiles, despite the sweaty marsh of her armpits and the pain that must have been flaring in her one good leg from being upright for hours. "'Too much rain will drown na seed, but will only make na tree stronger.' Respect or no respect, Dirt will make Verdi Bow."

The sun was past midway, the hottest part of the day, by the time the Vine arrived.

They rolled into the Grand Temple entrance in full force, just as they had for Carra Carre's match with Webba. Heads wrapped in vines, knees high as they marched, fists pounding against chests. Many of the spectators who had left earlier followed them in, making it look like the Vine had brought half the South to support them.

Na Vine!
Fight!
Crush!
Na enemy!

A cold stone of intimidation settled in Dirt's gut.

It was one thing to watch the Vine from behind Webba. It was another matter entirely to have those hundreds of vine-wrapped heads staring blankly at you, those massive bodies marching like a single entity, the earth reverberating with their weight, the air shuddering from their chant. She wasn't just fighting Verdi. She was fighting the entire Vine Fam, their years of sweat and toil, their hundreds of training partners, all their collective experience and strength.

She wasn't ready. She wasn't ready at all.

The drumming quieted. The Vine let out a final chant and stilled. Verdi emerged from their ranks.

She strolled past her sisters, touching a few of the Bibi and NoBe on the shoulder, nodding to one Sis, clasping hands with another, all with her eyes locked firmly on Dirt. At the front of their ranks, she stopped. She was nearly Webba's size, with less weight in the legs and more in the chest. Green-brown vines coiled down the length of her arms, like snakes around two thick branches. From within her mask of vines, her eyes shined violet like two glinting jewels. Dirt realized this was the closest she'd ever been to Verdi. She had never noticed the strange color of her eyes before.

The music changed from the dance to the fight. The drums picked up speed and the algaitas blared. Dirt spared a final glance back at her sisters. Snore had woken up and was praying for Dirt in a loud whisper. Nana watched Verdi, lines of stress creasing her forehead. Swoo was clenching and unclenching her hands, wearing a scowl that could melt sand into glass.

Webba was just smiling. She gave Dirt a small wave.

Dirt stepped up to the ring. Distantly, she could hear the cries of support from Mud fans, but the rest of her world was the fear-enhanced sounds of her own body: fogged breathing, a throbbing heart, her thighs rubbing against each other with every step. Verdi strode toward her and crouched, extended her arms out wide, showed empty palms in salute. Dirt did the same, and Verdi's eyes narrowed in what Dirt could only interpret as a smirk.

Then the girls crossed the sandbags into the ring, the time-keeper overturned the hourglass, and the Mud and Vine fought again.

15

Sis Dirt vs. Sis Verdi

THERE WAS a brief moment of circling and pawing Slaps in which Dirt thought that all her weeks of anxiety—all her years of refusing to fight—seemed like overreaction.

It is na spar, she thought. *Same and same.*

Then the moment ended.

Verdi's Ride was faster than Swoo's. Her Trap was stronger than Webba's. Her Back Bow launched Dirt into the air, the world tumbling over itself, and the tail of her back drove into the earth, all her weight bearing down on a single bone.

"Bow!" the timekeeper called, raising three fingers.

Pain screamed up Dirt's spine and her legs tingled strangely.

The crowd howled. "Verdi! Verdi! Verdi!"

It is not na spar, Dirt realized as she climbed back to her feet, exhaling pain with short, rapid breaths. Sparring was practice. It was about learning and improving and safety. No matter how hard

Swoo or Webba went, they weren't trying to hurt her.

This fight was about dominance. About winning at all costs. Verdi wasn't just willing to hurt her, she *wanted* to. Dirt had worried so much about how her mind would handle a fight that she'd forgotten the physical experience, the speed and brutality of it.

As soon as Dirt was upright, Verdi was on her again, Riding in like a sudden storm. Dirt shuffled backward, trying to avoid the Trap. But to no avail. Moments later, she was picking herself off the earth again, spitting sand out of her mouth.

"Bow!"

She was down six points and it wasn't even a quarter sand.

Behind her, Swoo's desperate shouts buzzed on the edge of Dirt's awareness. To her left and right, the crowd rumbled on the brink of disinterest as they realized she had no chance. Before her, Verdi stood impetuously, her eyes alert, her Godskin fully intact while Dirt's was cracked and broken and half strewn about the sand.

"You throw up, eh?" Verdi's sudden speech made Dirt freeze.

She stared, unsure of what to say.

"I can smell you." She spoke so casually, as if they were two friends sitting around camp. "Many girls throw up before na fight. You are afraid, eh?"

Dirt didn't trust herself to speak. She shook her head.

"No?" Verdi's mouth was hidden, but Dirt could hear her smile. "Na lie."

Then Verdi was on her again.

Their fight became a pattern. Dirt wasn't able to stay upright for more than a few seconds before she was forced to Bow again. Bow after Bow after Bow. After each fall, she began to fear what Verdi would do to her once she stood, fear the gleeful roar from the crowd as her back hit the ground, fear that moment of inhaled sand, the spluttering and spitting and the sticky heat in her chest that made breathing nearly impossible.

At just past half sand, the score was 25–0. It was an unheard of score gap, especially at the high level of a God Bow tournament. But it was what Dirt should have expected. All the training and meals and strategizing couldn't change the truth that she wasn't good enough. She'd never been good enough. In the very pit of their hearts, Webba and Swoo were fighters. In the very pit of her heart, Dirt was a coward.

After another hard Bow, Dirt climbed back to her feet and glanced at her sisters. Snore's face was confused, looking from Webba to Swoo to Nana, searching for answers. Dirt could only imagine how it felt for her to see her big, strong older Sis be thrashed by a stranger. Nana had her eyes half covered behind her palms. Swoo's jaw was tight with anger.

Webba was shouting. Dirt hadn't noticed before due to the wall of sound from the audience, but now she focused on Webba's lips, straining to hear.

"Na Whispers!" she was saying. "You are brave! You are fat! You are Dirt!"

Dirt hadn't even realized the Useyi's Whispers had wormed into her mind again. They had sounded like her own thoughts, her own long-held fears. But thanks to Webba, she could hear them for what they were. Words of doubt and fear braiding into her self-belief.

Verdi Rode in, slipped behind her, hauled her into the air, and Back Bowed her onto the back of her neck hard enough to make the world blink white and ripple like a struck pond.

"Bow!"

"Speak it!" Dirt heard Webba scream.

She tried to think the words, but she couldn't hear them over the Whispers. She wasn't brave. She wasn't fat. She was weak, and now everyone in the South was seeing it. It was hard to believe anything good about herself when she was in the middle of such failure.

Dirt struggled back to her feet, wiping sand from the back of her head, unsurprised to feel that her crown had been crushed. A few twigs remained stuck in her hair, but more of them were scattered around the ring, along with her broken bracers. She watched the last tenth of sand trickle toward the bottom of the hourglass, accepting defeat and humiliation and the end of the Mud Fam. She was grateful she hadn't been injured. But guilty, too. Webba had sacrificed her body fighting for the survival of the Fam. Dirt just had scrapes and bruises, some swelling on the back of her head. She would be fully healed within a week. Webba would carry her injuries for months.

Verdi Rode in again, intent on Bowing Dirt a final time for no reason other than cruelty. The Vine fans cheered, pounding their feet, bloodthirsty. The Mud fans, and even the other Mud sisters, all wore a uniform look of loss.

All except Webba. Webba was still willing to fight. Her crutches were forgotten on the ground. She was balanced on one leg, both hands cupped around her mouth. She sucked in all the air she could manage and bellowed at the top of her lungs.

"You are Dirt! You are Dirt! SPEAK IT!"

The match was already over. If she couldn't sacrifice her body the way Webba had, the least she could do was repeat Webba's words.

"I am brave," she said aloud. "I am fat. I am Dirt."

Her head rippled again. Not from the impact of a Bow, but from the sound of the words.

Of course she was brave. There were no cowards in the God Bow tournament. If she were such a coward, she would have let Swoo fight, no matter how hard Webba pushed.

Of course she was fat. She trained with some of the best Bowers in all the South. If she were so skinny, Verdi wouldn't now be gleaming with sweat, chest rising and falling with deep breaths.

And of course she was Dirt. The Second of the Mud, sister to Webba and Swoo and Nana and Snore, former prodigy of the Mud Fam. If she weren't Dirt, she wouldn't still be standing after being Bowed over a dozen times, down 40–0 in what could be her last-ever God Bow.

I am brave. I am fat. I am Dirt.

This new truth clashed with her doubts and fears like a flood against a jungle fire, filling her with a clean, purifying steam. She felt its scouring heat boil beneath her skin, through her head and chest to each toe and finger.

Then she felt nothing.

No fear. No doubt. No bruised back or sore arms. No swollen legs, no weak joints. Her mind was completely silent. Blessed silence. Peace.

Verdi seemed so small. So insignificant. She barreled forward, crouching for another Ride, but Dirt just stepped to the side and Verdi charged through empty air, almost flinging herself out of the ring. It was as simple as that.

All around the arena, the energy shifted. The thousands of resigned spectators sat up in their seats.

Verdi quenched her momentary confusion with action, Riding at Dirt again. This time, Dirt simply stretched out a palm, connecting with Verdi's shoulder. The Second of the Vine came to a jarring halt, all her momentum destroyed in an instant, sending a gust of sand kicking up and past Dirt.

The Vine sister's eyes widened. Then Dirt Pushed. A shove to the shoulder, enough to keep a girl away, but nothing more.

Verdi blasted backward, flipping over herself, ripping a trench in the sand as she tumbled. The sandbags at the edge of the ring did nothing to slow her. She split through them, sending spectators scrambling as she sped across the Grand Temple and smacked into the arena wall with such force that cracks webbed out from the impact point. Chunks of dense red sand broke free and plummeted all around her. She slid to the floor, head slumped on chest. Her eyes were open, but she stared unfocused out at nothing, groaning.

In an arena filled with thousands, no one made a sound. Dirt looked at her hand, expecting to find it had turned to stone or was steaming with heat. But it was just her hand. The same hand she'd always had.

"OOS OOS, DIRT!!"

Webba was speeding across the Grand Temple, at first swinging herself along her crutches, then tossing them aside to hop on her one good leg. She plowed into Dirt, nearly sending them both to the ground before Dirt caught her.

"She is Dirt!" Webba screamed into the sky, laughing. "She is Dirt!"

Webba shouted and celebrated and hop-danced about the ring. Like nothing unexpected had happened. Meanwhile, the arena sat in stunned silence. Across the grounds, a few Vine NoBe rushed to Verdi's aid. Other than a low groan and a slow, uncoordinated blinking, the girl showed no signs of awareness. Blood leaked from the back of her head, staining the sides of her vine mask.

Dirt had imagined a thousand ways the fight with Verdi would go. She lost most of them, often in brutal, humiliating fashion. A quick Push out of the ring. Bowed onto her head and knocked unconscious. Forced to Bow Down after having her bones broken and flesh rubbed away by rough sand. In a few of her imaginings, she achieved the upset of a lifetime, winning on points or tricking Verdi out of the ring somehow.

She had never imagined this.

Dirt turned in a slow circle, looking out at the audience. A stiffness formed wherever her eyes fell, a collective ceasing of breath.

"We are na Mud sisters!" Webba sang, her voice thick as poured honey.

It took a moment for the other sisters to respond, but Swoo picked up the call.

We are na Mud sisters!
We fight, oh yes, ooooooh!

"We are na Mud sisters!" Webba sang again, pumping her arms for the crowd.

We are na Mud sisters!
We never quit, noooooo!

They sang it again, but this time the Mud fans in the stands joined in. Not in their usual raucous energy, but with a hushed reverence that made Dirt's spine tingle.

As everyone sang in her honor, Dirt watched the Vine carry Verdi away and retreat from the arena. The last of the Vine to leave was Carra Carre. She stopped at the arena entrance and looked back at the Mud, her eyes catching Dirt's. Like the rest of the Grand Temple, Carra Carre stared at Dirt in disbelief.

Dirt was sure her own face looked as disbelieving as Carra Carre's. Because even though she had imagined a million endings to her match with Verdi, she never could have imagined that she–Sis Dirt, the Second of the Mud–would be a Godskin.

A True Godskin.

16

The True Godskin

NANA HAD NEVER seen a drunk person before. But as she watched Swoo finish a third cup of palm wine, she was fairly sure Swoo was drunk.

"Sis Diiiiiiiirt!" Swoo howled into the sky, raising her clay cup high. "Sis Dirt will be na God Bow Chaaaaampion!"

Around the ring of the camp, their Flagga-boy guests cheered and started playing music again, all pounding drums and twangy kora. Webba invited them to the camp sometimes, after big victories. The boys always accepted, of course—it was an honor for them just to spend time with Bowers. Nana found the boys smelly and noisy, and she didn't like that the younger ones teased her, but they were good drummers and one of them played pretty songs on the algaita, so she didn't mind their visits.

Like Bowers, and unlike Mosquitos and Pushers, Flagga boys also lived in Fam. These seven boys lived in the same muddy area of the South as the Mud Fam, though they weren't allowed to harvest Mud Offer like Bowers were. In private, they probably called themselves the Mud Fam, but around Bowers, they were just the Mud boys.

NoBe Swoo led the Mud boys in a dance, bouncing around the ring with a few of them lined up behind her, palm wine sloshing over her hand. Sis Webba stayed a safe distance away, unwilling to risk being jostled in the dance circle. But she swayed on her crutches, grinning and dancing with Snore to the music. Sis Dirt sat outside the ring at the high table set for the victorious fighter. Fresh fruit, smoked corn, and walnuts—a rare treat—were laid out on the table before her, an offering brought by the Mud boys. She looked her usual self. Not angry, but not *not* angry.

Of the big sisters, Nana liked Sis Dirt the most. She was more gentle than NoBe Swoo and more nervous than Sis Webba. Nana herself was always nervous, so Sis Dirt made her feel less lonely. But Sis Dirt was always so serious. Even at a party in her honor, she looked like she'd rather be training or coaching or cleaning, anything other than just celebrating.

Nana sat on the edge of the Mud camp with her back against a tree, sliding stones onto a thin string of twine. It was her first time making a bracelet. All week, once she'd finished her duties, she'd been going out and secretly collecting stones. She'd had to pick the perfect moments to sneak away, often when the big sisters were busy with training. The party was the perfect distraction for her to work on it.

She held her creation up to the torchlight. All the stones were deep blue, in a dozen different shades. She smiled at it, then made a silly face.

"I am Nana," she said, giggling. She knew the bracelet couldn't see or hear her, but she had to introduce herself to it somehow.

"What is that?"

Nana startled, stuffing the bracelet into the back waistband of her pants. She looked up to find Snore standing in front of her, half a corncob in her mouth, pigtails tied with colorful, celebratory twine.

"Nothing!" Nana said.

"Candy?"

"No, it is nothing."

Snore blinked, then took a nibble of corn. "Bibi Nana, les us play," she said, spraying bits of yellow.

"I cannot now, Snore."

"Why? Les us plaaayyy."

"Because I am tired."

She wasn't tired at all, but she didn't want to play. All she wanted to do was finish her bracelet, and she couldn't do that with Snore around. Snore herself wouldn't care, but if she mentioned it to any of the big sisters . . . Nana could hear Sis Dirt's scolding at just the thought of it. "Na Bower cannot wear na adorn." And Nana would never see the bracelet again.

Because tradition.

"Why are you tired?"

"Because I am tired, so let me rest." She hoped she didn't sound irritated. It wasn't Snore's fault. "We will play soon, eh?"

Snore shrugged and left, unbothered as ever. Her brain only lived one moment at a time. Once the prospect of playing with Nana was gone, she was on to the next thing–in this case, plucking individual kernels off the cob and using them to make a circle around Webba that must have been intended as some sort of trap.

Webba pretended to be stuck once the circle was finished. Snore cackled.

Nana sighed and pulled the bracelet back out.

"Bower Nana."

Nana sighed and stuffed it away again.

This time, one of the Mud boys stood before her, bent at the waist with an overly charming smile. Nana couldn't remember his name. It would probably be Beakfoot or Dizzy Eyes or something. The Flagga boys had the strangest names. "Come and dance, eh?"

She almost gagged on the stench of unwash that wafted off him. Smelly. Now she remembered. His name was Smelly. "I cannot, I am t–"

But he'd already taken her by the hands and pulled her to her feet.

Or he tried to, at least. He was older than her, she thought, but not any larger. And she was a Bower. Not only was she stronger than him, but she was also trained in the arts of moving the body, maintaining balance, making herself feel heavy. He tugged once, blinked down at his hands in confusion, then pulled again, harder. Nana slid forward a little, but otherwise didn't budge.

Smelly looked at her in awe. "Chaaaiii, strongstrong girl."

Nana didn't know what to do with the compliment. She pulled her hands from his grip, twisted her fingers around each other, and scrunched her shoulder uncomfortably. "I must see my sisters."

She fled, scurrying away from him to the other side of camp and ending all hope of finishing her bracelet that night. Smelly's friends broke into laughter, teasing him. She didn't like that they'd all been watching her.

But she didn't *not* like it either.

She would have liked to dance, maybe. Not with Smelly, but one of the other boys. Maybe. Or maybe if they were Pusher boys instead. They were low status, but they were big and strong and peaceful. And they had their cute little Petti.

But Nana had never spoken to one before. Pusher boys spent their time with Mosquito girls.

Nana often wondered what her life would be like if she were a Mosquito girl. Butterfly girl. That girl, Apple, had taught her that they were really called Butterfly girls. Maybe if Nana were a Butterfly girl like Apple, she wouldn't have just one incomplete bracelet. Maybe she would have racks of bracelets. And necklaces, too. And anklets. All in half a hundred different designs, each unique and crafted with care. Not just for herself, but to share with other girls as well.

It was an impossible desire, of course. Bowers didn't paint their faces or talk to Pusher boys or hide their feet in shoes. Bowers didn't make jewelry.

With her attempts to work on her bracelet foiled, Nana strolled to the high table. She grabbed a rambutan, peeling off the red skin with green hairs.

"Sis Dirt?" she asked, holding out the white fruit.

Sis Dirt turned her attention to Nana slowly, as if waking from a dream. Several knots swelled out of her forehead, and the left side of her chest was bruised black. Verdi had left her mark.

"Nana," she said, letting out a long breath and taking the fruit. "You are enjoying, eh?"

"I like na music," Nana said. "But it is loudloud."

"Indeed."

"You are enjoying, Sis Dirt?"

For a while, Sis Dirt didn't say anything. The music filled the silence. The drums slid into a new beat that earned howls of joy from the Flagga boys. Two of them launched into a dance Nana hadn't seen before, swaying in unison, then jerking to a halt, then swaying again, keeping to the rhythm. NoBe Swoo watched attentively, no doubt remembering every detail and adding it to her own repertoire.

"My body," Sis Dirt said. "All over, I hurt. All my muscle and bone. But I win."

"Everyone says you are na True Godskin. Na Gods choose you, Sis Dirt."

"Eh heh."

"Do you feel different?"

Sis Dirt looked at Nana in surprise.

"I . . . In na ring, I feel powerful. Way fatfat. And I feel . . ."

Nana stayed quiet, let Sis Dirt find her words.

"I feel I can do anything. And when I look at Carra Carre, I see in her eyes she is afraid. She knows I will come for her. She knows that she can no longer punish na Mud."

Nana watched a rare smile bloom on Sis Dirt's face, small and shy. It made Nana happy, seeing Sis Dirt happy. During the training for the God Bow tournament, none of them had been happy. Not really. Even Snore had been less than herself. No matter how confident Sis Webba was, they'd all been afraid for Sis Dirt. Or afraid that NoBe Swoo would lose her temper and do something regretful before the tournament began.

But Sis Dirt being a True Godskin, her victory over the Vine—it seemed to mark a new beginning for the Mud. Who could stand before Sis Dirt the Godskin in a Bow? Once she won the tournament, the Mud would win the season's recruits, and everything would be easy again. There'd be more Bibi to help maintain the camp and expand the garden. More training partners for Snore and Nana instead of just each other.

"But . . . ," Sis Dirt said, her smile vanishing. She raised a hand to her face, rotating it in the moonlight and studying it as if it were a stranger's.

"Eh?" Nana asked.

Swoo's voice roared from the ring, cutting through the conversation.

"We are na Muuuud Sisters!" Swoo howled, cup in the air, glistening with sweat from her dancing.

The Mud boys laughed and joined her song. "They are na Mud sisters!"

"We fight, oh yes, ooooooh! We are na Muuuuuuuuuuuud!"

"They are na Mud sisters!"

"We never never never never never never . . ."

Swoo hopped about the ring, once for each "never," until she stumbled over the sandbags at its edges, catching herself against the high table. Somehow, she didn't spill any of her palm wine.

"Ohh, my sister!" NoBe Swoo shouted from an arm's reach away. "My sister, my sister, my sister." She set her elbows on the table and leaned forward. "You will tell us, eh? How now? How you zoomzoom Verdi like she is na new Bibi? Verdi just *konk* her head. Shoooooo"–she made a motion with her hand like it was a spear sailing through the air–"ooooooo *KONK*! You see na Vine sisters, eh? Chaaaiii!" She cackled. "All eyes. Like spiders. Sis Dirt is clever. Cleeeever! Tell us how, clever sister."

Sis Dirt shook her head. "I do not know, my sister. Na Gods favor me."

NoBe Swoo climbed onto the table. It took her nearly half a

minute, complete with wobbling, cursing to herself under her breath, and knocking several platters of food to the floor. The Mud boys finally spied the free entertainment and quieted the music, laughing and poking each other as they watched NoBe Swoo.

She moved her face inches from Sis Dirt's. Nana could imagine the stink of palm wine on NoBe Swoo's breath. She winced on Sis Dirt's behalf.

"Na Gods?" NoBe Swoo whispered loudly.

Dirt pursed her lips. "Climb down, NoBe Swoo."

"Na Gods favor *you*?" Swoo slurred, eyebrows shooting up. "Favor . . ." She fell back onto her butt, right into a bowl of roasted corn. The Mud boys erupted in laughter.

"Swoo," Sis Webba said, crutching over from beside the sleep hut, "you are tired. Go and sleep, eh?" She shot a glance at the Mud boys, which evaporated their mirth.

Swoo waved a dismissive hand. "I train. I pray. These two things, every day. And na Gods . . . na Gods deny me. Na Gods make Carra Carre fat and strong."

"NoBe Swoo," Webba said, more edge in her voice. NoBe Swoo looked over, confused. Almost scared.

"Na Gods mash you up, Sis Webba," she explained in a pleading voice. "First of na Mud. Our champion. Na Vine mash you up. Break you. Na Gods allow this." She looked at Nana, who froze, scared that NoBe Swoo would have words for her. But her older sister just looked off into the jungle and hurled her cup across the night, clouded liquid sloshing out in droplets as the cup sailed past its intended tree target and landed noiselessly in the dark.

NoBe Swoo collapsed back onto the table, prompting stifled laughter from the boys.

"Trip," Sis Webba called out, "you and your Flagga must go home, eh? We must sleep."

The boys immediately began packing their instruments and palm wine, then trickled out of camp.

"Am I not fat?" NoBe Swoo called out to the sky, eyes closed. Nana saw a tear trickle down her cheek. "Am I not brave? Eh? Why her?"

Sis Dirt rose from the high chair. "It is late" was all she said as she walked off toward the sleep hut.

But Nana saw how uneasy Sis Dirt looked, and how briskly she walked. She wasn't just going to bed. She was escaping.

"Why her?!" Swoo screamed.

The celebration was ruined. But Nana didn't blame NoBe Swoo. This was the life of the Bower. They all liked to dance and sing about the Fam, but sometimes a Fam wasn't fun at all. Sometimes they competed *against* each other as much as they competed *with* each other. Sometimes they got jealous of each other and said mean things. Sometimes they even hurt each other, physically or worse. The big meals and fun dancing didn't change any of that.

"Snore! Nana!" Sis Webba called, but she had her eyes on NoBe Swoo, pity on her face. "Come and sleep, young Bibi. Come morning, Swoo will be finefine."

Nana went over to Sis Webba, where they were joined by Snore. Together, they retired to the sleep hut. But Nana could hear NoBe Swoo's muttering clearly, the words Sis Dirt had moved so quickly to avoid.

"Why Dirt?"

17

A Test of Fear

TEN STRIDES above the earth, the air was cleaner. Pure. No scent of droppings or lingering ash from cook-fires. No training-grounds sweat. The breeze was powerful and cool against the skin.

Carra Carre knelt on the edge of the rough wooden platform overlooking the Vine camp. Below, her sisters were waking. Each Sis had a squat home that sat on its own wooden platform. Each platform jutted from one of the jungle's lombi trees, rising thick and mossy into the sky. The many-trunked behemoths were like bundles of leafy sticks gathered by the Mamas and Papas and driven into the earth.

Below the Sis were several layers of NoBe homes, where they lived as many as three per hut. The Bibi lived even farther below, crowding into houses six or seven at once. Long vines stretched from the upper homes to the lower ones, to make for a quick descent through the camp. Several NoBe were taking the lines down to lead the Bibi on their morning runs, sliding with gleeful faces as they held on to both ends of an oil-slick cloth. Each tree was outfitted with wooden ladder rungs for the trip back up.

Beneath all the airborne wooden platforms and crisscrossing vines, the mighty River cut through the land, deep as memory and swift as time. Not only did its lapping waves mask the sound of the near two hundred girls who lived above it, but it made the Vine the most inaccessible camp in all the South. Unless a girl had some way to traverse the water, and a desire to risk the wrath of the hippos and crocodiles that skimmed its surface, the only way to get to the camp was a long, narrow plank bridge that extended out to the nearest bank. And that was nearly impossible to see from land, obscured by strategically placed brambles and leaves.

The Vine camp was an invisible fortress.

Some of the younger sisters waved up at Carra Carre as they left for the morning run. Some gave silly salutes or sillier smiles. Children. She didn't acknowledge them. It was good that they were happy, but children could always find joy. It was their way. She, however, was nearly a woman. The First of her Fam. She had responsibilities, and she could not laugh, smile, or wave until her Second was healthy again.

Or avenged.

"Cee Cee!" Nuna called in her lazy lilt. Carra Carre looked two trees over and a stride below, to where the Third of the Vine leaned casually against her hut. "Again you don't sleep, eh?"

"No."

"My Sis, I am sorry," Nuna said, somber.

It was an old tradition to keep watch over an injured Sis. Carra Carre had never seen it in her lifetime, but Antie Yaya had mentioned it a few times in her stories. Typically, all the Fam's Sis would rotate watch duties, but Carra Carre had elected to keep watch herself. She'd spent the last three days and nights willing her eyes awake as she prayed for Verdi's quick recovery.

"It is fine," she croaked back, her voice stale from disuse.

"What do we do?" Nuna asked.

"Wait for Verdi."

"I mean na Mud. What do we do now, eh? Na Gods choose that skinnyskinny, Dirt. Our sisters are afraid. How can–"

"We wait for Verdi."

Nuna nodded, held Carra Carre's eyes for a moment, then turned away.

"Vine Sis!" she called out over the camp. With Verdi injured, Nuna was acting Second. It was her job to lead the Sis in training for the day. "Wake up, you snoring goats! Chaaaiii, how you don't wake each other, only na Gods know."

Carra Carre had tried to sound confident in Verdi's return, but in truth she wasn't sure what the Gods desired for her sister. No girl left a Bow unscathed, true. But in all her years of Bowing, she had never seen a girl hurt the way Dirt had hurt Verdi. Even hours after the match, Verdi had seemed confused, had spoken in a slow mumble. Physically, she would heal, of course. Mentally, though? Spiritually? Carra Carre wasn't sure.

And what of Webba?

The thought had haunted her since their fight, the refrain of a song she couldn't stop singing to herself. Verdi had insisted it was what the Gods desired. The Gods visited her in her dreams, and they'd tell her things, show her visions. Carra Carre hadn't believed it in their younger years, but time had proven Verdi true. The Vine was the most powerful Fam in memory, and Carra Carre herself was the greatest Bower in the South, just as Verdi had predicted so many years ago.

So when Verdi had told Carra Carre to break Webba, she listened. She ignored her doubts, suppressed any admiration she had for Webba as a competitor and a fellow First, and did what had to be done. For the Fam. The end of Webba meant the end of the Mud. The end of the Mud meant more recruits for the Vine. There was a war coming, Verdi said, and the Vine would need all the recruits they could if they were going to win.

But Carra Carre couldn't forget the sinewy snap of Webba's leg against her shoulder, the way that Webba, who was normally so brave and smiley, had screamed like Useyi's own fingers were reaching for her throat. Why would the Gods want that?

Then Dirt had fought Verdi. Dirt. The retired Second of a failing Fam. A girl whose Ride was slower than those of half the Vine's NoBe. Who was meek and skinny and breezy even in her prime. Somehow, that girl was a True Godskin. It made no sense, and it made Carra Carre wary. What other reason could the Gods have for choosing her if not to punish the Vine? For the first time, Verdi had been wrong. Or she'd misunderstood.

Dirt the Godskin was the consequence of that misunderstanding.

"My sister . . ."

Carra Carre heard a voice so faint she wondered if the lack of sleep was playing with her ears.

"Little Cee Cee," the voice said.

There was only one person who called her that.

Carra Carre spun to her feet, turning away from her camp overlook to the hut behind her. Verdi was braced against the doorway of her squat home, hands wrapped knuckle-tight around each branch of the entry's wooden frame. In just a few days, the injury had taken so much from her. Her skin was light, barely brown at all. Her arms, normally her strongest and most defining feature, had slimmed. Her belly was as large as ever, but sat a little lower, as if some of the muscle behind it had been lost.

She didn't smile as Carra Carre rushed over to wrap her in a hug, but then again Verdi seldom smiled. That, at least, remained the same.

"My Sis, how do you feel?" Carra Carre asked.

"Better."

"And your head, eh?"

She nodded slowly, as if to prove it was still firmly attached.

"You sleep?" Verdi asked.

"You know I cannot sleep. Let us sit, you need rest."

Carra Carre grabbed a woven mat for them to sit on, then called down to some strolling NoBe to bring up tea.

They sat together, legs crossed and facing each other as they had since they were young Bibi. They'd been best friends since the beginning, back when Verdi had been the bigger of the two. Now, even though Carra Carre was the First and the younger sisters all looked up to her, Verdi was still the true mind of the Vine. As much as Carra Carre had just kept watch all night because she wanted to protect her sister, she also hadn't known what else to do but stay by Verdi's side.

"You remember na fight, eh?" she asked.

Verdi pursed her lips. "I remember na beginning. She has na strong Slap. Strongstrong. But she moves too slow, too loose. Like na NoBe fight before na first Bow."

Carra Carre nodded. It was said that before their first Bow, NoBe were only a little ahead of Bibi. After, they were only a little behind Sis. The speed and violence of real combat sharpened a girl's technique.

"I think," Verdi continued, "how Papa Oduma must favor na Vine to give me such simple fight. And then . . ." She blinked and sighed. "I wake up outside na ring and my head is like na empty coconut."

A senior NoBe, Murua, climbed up the rungs on the lombi tree with a reed across her shoulders and a lidded clay cup dangling on each end. She scampered over and set the cups down, nodding in respect to Verdi and then Carra Carre before taking a vine line back down to the lower platforms.

"So what can we do?" Carra Carre asked. She didn't expect an answer, and was surprised at how quickly Verdi responded.

"We will punish na Mud."

"How, my Sis? If na Gods choose Dirt . . ."

"Who says na Gods choose Dirt?"

"Your coconut head," Carra Carre joked.

Verdi didn't smile.

"My Sis," Carra Carre continued, "I am strong. But . . . I cannot defeat Papa Oduma Himself."

"You think she has Papa Oduma's favor, eh? You think she is na True Godskin?"

Carra Carre frowned. Verdi was the only girl who had felt Dirt's power firsthand. If she didn't believe it . . . "What else can it be?"

Verdi's eyes suddenly gleamed. "A test," she hissed. "Did I not tell you na Gods will return?"

She had, Carra Carre realized. Days ago, before the Prayer, Verdi had told her that change was coming. She'd had a dream, one that hadn't meant anything at all to Carra Carre, but that had been clear as sky to Verdi. She said she'd seen thousands of Bowers, more than all the Fam in the South combined, kneeling in an open field and looking up at the clouds as if they might fall. Verdi said it meant the Gods were coming back, and that Bowers had to be ready to receive them.

"Did I not tell you na Gods will change na Isle?" Verdi continued. "No more Creek and Sand, Rock and Mud. No more Mosquito girl and Pusher boy. One Isle, united under na Gods."

Verdi stuck a finger in her tea and swirled it. When she pulled her finger out, she stared with wide, fevered eyes at the spiraling gray liquid. "Why will na Gods come back to na Isle for this Dirt girl? Who is she, eh? Second of five. From na skinnyskinny Fam. How can Papa Oduma choose her? Does she have power? Eh? Does she have faith?"

Verdi left space for an answer, but Carra Carre knew she wasn't supposed to fill it. She looked into her sister's eyes and saw the same unwavering confidence she'd always seen. Everyone called Bowers the Daughters of Oduma, but only Verdi truly believed it. Only Verdi truly thought that the Isle was promised to them.

Verdi stood suddenly, and Carra Carre rushed to help her. She led her back to the ledge of the platform, overlooking the camp.

A group of NoBe was at the center of camp, standing around and watching little Jaldi, a small but prodigious NoBe, try to complete the Climb. The Climb was a vine that dangled from one of the camp's tallest trees, down to just above a cut-away circle in a wooden platform, exposing the waterline. It was common knowledge among the Vine that the Climb was impossible to finish. Most girls weren't strong enough to make it even halfway. The few that made it farther eventually had to make a decision: (1) give up and go back down before they got too tired, or (2) risk reaching the top but be so exhausted that they fell into the predator-filled water below.

Verdi had been the first girl to ever complete it.

"It is not na test of strength," she'd told Carra Carre in her first year as a Sis, just before she started her ascent. "It is na test of fear." She'd climbed all the way to the top and a quarter of the way down before she lost her grip and plunged into the River. Only by luck had none of the creatures eaten her. Yet she'd emerged from the waters a hero.

Jaldi was only a quarter of the way up and already she had the look of fear in her eyes that most girls had when attempting the feat.

"Papa Oduma will not choose this Dirt, my Sis," Verdi said. "*You* are Papa Oduma's champion. But you must first earn His favor. And how will you do this?"

"I do not know, my Sis," Carra Carre sighed.

"Fear," Verdi hissed. "Why do you never lose? Eh? I see your fight with Webba. She is better than you–"

Carra Carre shifted uncomfortably. It was true. Webba was the most skilled Bower Carra Carre had ever seen.

"–but she does not have your fear. When she almost makes you Bow Down, I see it in you. Na fear of defeat. Na fear of shame. Na fear of disrespect. Na fear that your Vine sisters will no longer love you. All that fear you use to defeat Webba. To destroy Webba. You see how strong that fear makes you, eh?"

Far below them, young Jaldi was frozen less than halfway up the Climb, too scared to go either up or down. The other NoBe rushed over to rescue her before her grip failed.

"Papa Oduma does not choose breezy Bowers, my Sis," Verdi said in a voice that was so distant it reminded Carra Carre of Antie Yaya. "You must learn to control this fear to become na True Godskin. Not only when you are near defeat. Always. Do you not see? It is na test."

Carra Carre didn't have Verdi's faith. She'd always found sweat, discipline, and training to be more reliable than the Gods. She trusted long morning runs and hours-long workouts under the sun, heavy stones cradled in her arms. She prayed by working high among the camp's dangling vines, gripping so tight her fingers couldn't unfurl the next day. She worshipped the fight. The clash of one's will against another's. The certainty–the undisputed truth–of victory.

She didn't have much faith in Papa Oduma or any of the Gods.

But she had faith in Verdi.

"Na test . . . ," Carra Carre said, watching the other NoBe console Jaldi as she walked away from her failed attempt at the Climb. "Na test of strength? Or na test of fear?"

Verdi looked at her for a moment without saying a word.

Then she smiled.

18

Finding Quiet

6 Days until the Wing Fight

DIRT HAD ALWAYS imagined what it would feel like to be a true Godskin.

In Antie Yaya's stories, the Godskins were founts of unlimited power. Their stomps were earthquakes, their leaps threatened the clouds, their claps could split the wind. Dirt imagined the Godskins of old were big and fat, with bellies like no other. Their every meal was a feast, their every story an epic tale, their every laugh echoed through the jungle. They were always confident, full of joy.

She'd never imagined how scared they must have felt.

Power earned can be a wonderful thing, but power given is a curse. Dirt didn't feel any more confident or joyous. She didn't feel any fatter or bigger of belly. She just felt like she'd been given something she didn't deserve. The Gods, even Papa Oduma, were notoriously fickle. Sis all across the South prayed more than she did, worshipped with more passion, and danced as if every step was for the Gods. Yet it was Dirt who was given this gift. The peace. The quiet. She'd never known how loud her mind was until that moment of divine silence. The hot, yearning tug of muscle on bone as she commanded her body into the slightest of actions. The concussive force she'd released. How weightless Verdi had felt, like a pebble in her hand that she knew she could throw farther than her eyes could see.

No girl deserved that power. Especially not Dirt. What would happen when the Gods realized they'd chosen the wrong girl? If they could give it so easily, they could take it away just as easily.

What if they already had?

When she aired these worries to Webba, her Sis provided a simple answer.

"We will see."

There was a week between each round of the tournament. The first day was usually for resting, but Webba woke Dirt early and they spent the entire morning re-creating the Verdi fight, even using some of the Offer to rebuild Dirt's Godskin. Swoo was supposed to play the role of Verdi, but she was sulky, hungover, and too ashamed of herself to leave the hut, so Nana took her place. Together, the Mud sisters went through the movements of a Bow: eat, dance, fight. Dirt Bowed Nana all over the ring, slinging her about effortlessly as Snore cheered and giggled like a madwoman. Not once did Dirt feel the power of a Godskin.

She wasn't surprised. She tried to move on to other training, but Webba wouldn't allow it.

"Again," she'd say, and Dirt would square off with Nana while Snore watched on. Each time, Dirt failed to feel anything.

"What is it?" Webba asked after the tenth or so try. By then, the sun was at its peak and the day was so hot that Snore had to move the eggs into the shade so they wouldn't cook in their shells.

"I cannot," Dirt said, sweating, panting, hands on her knees. "Na Gods are not here, my Sis."

Webba narrowed her eyes. "What do you hear?" she asked.

"Eh?"

"You hear something," she said. "Close your eyes. What is it?"

Dirt listened, first with her eyes open, then closed. She heard those familiar voices, telling her what she lacked, reminding her of all her failures and shortcomings, insisting that their words were truth.

"Na Whispers," she said.

Webba nodded. She didn't have to say anything else.

I am brave, Dirt thought. *I am fat. I am Dirt.*

The affirming words were fire against the chill tendrils of Useyi's Whispers, dissolving into that comforting, cleansing steam of the mind.

When she opened her eyes, everything seemed so clear. The crisp sheet of blue sky; the warm, round glow of the sun; the tree canopy like a thousand soft, green hands, fingers splayed and interlocking; each grain of sand between her toes, rocking gently with the wind. Webba had lost weight since the injury, muscle turning to fat turning to nothing. Each strand of Snore's pigtails could be counted from afar.

Dirt distantly heard Webba shout for Nana to advance. She watched Nana move forward cautiously, Slapping slowly. So slowly. Between her Slaps, there was a whole island of time to exploit. Dirt didn't bother Slapping back. She Rode in, closing the gap between them like snapping her fingers.

She plowed into Nana and, before she could stop herself, launched them both out of the ring. They flew across the open air, speeding toward the jungle. She pulled Nana against her chest as they left the ring and punched into the tree line. She rotated her body, smacking back-first into a towering palm. The tree released a massive clap as its stocky trunk split.

Dirt slid to the ground, Nana still in her arms. The top half of the tree fell right after, whistling to the earth and crashing just beside them.

The Mud sisters sat in silence, even Snore.

Until Swoo came staggering out of the sleep hut, hastily hopping into her pants, panic on her face.

"My sisters! What is it?!"

She froze when she saw the downed tree, Nana's pale face, Dirt's disbelieving one.

Webba was the first one to laugh, of course, but the rest of them weren't far behind. The Mud sisters laughed until their faces ached and their hands were wet with wiped tears.

Then Dirt did it again.

19

Birds, Palms, and Anthills

5 Days until the Wing Fight

IT WAS the easiest week of Dirt's life.

The first thing she did each morning, with Webba to guide her, was silence the Whispers.

"Make quiet," Webba would command. "You are brave. You are fat. You are Dirt."

Then, after Dirt had proven what she could do with her Godskin power, Webba would have her release it. Quiet and release, quiet and release, a dozen times.

After that, Webba had her do a series of strange new exercises that she said were supposed to help her use her powers better.

"Count them," Webba said, nodding at the birds sitting among the trees.

"Eh?" Swoo asked, confused. "Count na birds? For Sis Dirt or Bibi Snore?"

"Na Godskin must improve, always," Webba said.

"Improve counting?!" Swoo asked, incredulous. Swoo, for once, was right. Dirt raised a questioning eyebrow.

Webba nodded, an answer.

There must have been a dozen or two. It wouldn't take very long to count, but it still seemed like a waste of time.

"One," Dirt began, eyes hopping from bird to bird, "two, three, four . . ."

Suddenly a spray of sand flew into the treetops, causing the birds to take flight in a cacophony of wild caws. Dirt turned to see Webba smiling, rubbing her palms together to rid themselves of the remaining sand. "Eh heh," Webba said, "now count, quickquick!"

It was considerably harder to count the birds as they flew.

After bird counting, Webba had her climb to the very top of a palm tree. Dirt found it nauseating. As a Bibi, she'd climbed trees often, to collect banana and coconut. But that had been many years ago, and many pounds lighter. A fall that a Bibi may laugh her way out of could do real harm to a Sis.

"Sit, my Sis," Webba told her.

Dirt sat at the center of the palm, where the base of the branches formed a suitable, if prickly, seat. She took a deep breath and closed her eyes.

"No, my Sis," Webba called up. "Eyes open. Look and see. Breathe easy, eh?"

Dirt reluctantly pried her eyes open. Looking down at the camp from so high up made her feel dizzy, and suddenly it seemed impossible to breathe properly. She was there for nearly an hour before Webba called her down.

After the birds had been counted and the treetops had been sat upon, Webba had Dirt stand on an anthill. Just stand, unmoving. This time, Webba encouraged her to close her eyes.

"You must feel na ants," she explained.

Dirt did her best to ignore the dozen tiny tickles as the ants scampered over her skin, but once a pinch of her skin flared in pain from a bite, she yelped and hopped away, much to the delight of Snore.

When all of Webba's unusual exercises were done, Dirt didn't feel like she'd accomplished anything. But Webba wore a smile of deep satisfaction.

That was when the real training started.

In the afternoon, Webba would have her make quiet again. With the power of the Gods surging through her, the regular daily workout became the simplest thing in the world. She could launch herself as high as the trees with a press-up, did more belly bends and squats than ten girls combined, hauled boulders twice her size and tossed them into the air as easily as she'd toss an orange. For once, it was Swoo who was drenched in sweat, breathing heavy, pleading for a break. Before the day was over, it was clear there was no physical feat Dirt couldn't accomplish.

But Webba had a new plan by the next day.

"Today you will Slap" was all Webba said after Dirt returned from her run with Swoo.

"Why, eh?" Dirt asked, wiping a smattering of sweat from her brow while Swoo collapsed in the ring, exhausted. "I can run to na sun and back. You think I cannot Slap?"

Even with the little exercise Dirt was doing as a Godskin, the softness of her body had already begun to melt. Her arms were tightening, her belly growing in size and firmness, her neck and face rounding out with fat and muscle. And as her body had re-formed, so had her confidence.

"Eh heh, you see?" Webba said, grinning. "Bibi, look at your big-big sister. This proud cow. Before today, she cry." Webba contorted her face into a mask of anguish. "'My Sis, I cannot,'" she whined. "'My Sis, I am tired.'"

Nana and Snore cackled with delight.

"That is not me," Dirt said, bouncing her eyebrows at the Bibi. "That is Sis Dirt. This," she said, pointing to herself, "is Sis Dirt na Godskin."

"Chaaaiii!" Nana and Snore cheered.

Swoo, still flat on her back, called out from the ring. "True, Sis Webba. Sis Dirt throw away Sis Verdi like na old durian. Why must she Slap?"

"Because she is na Godskin," Webba said. "Na Godskin must improve, always."

Webba had been saying that all week, and Dirt didn't understand it then any more than she had before. With the powers of the Godskin, Dirt wasn't sure a hundred girls could stand up to her, much less one. Yet Webba had insisted that she keep up her training, as if any of what they were doing would make a difference. At times, as much as she had tried to suppress the feeling, Dirt found it irritating. For whatever reason, the Gods had chosen her. She was the True Godskin, the first in memory, even a memory as old as Antie Yaya's. Webba knew everything there was to know about Bowing, but this was something different.

What could Webba possibly know about being a Godskin?

Still, Webba was her First. Dirt set her feet, rolled her shoulders, extended her arms, palms slapping down on the air in front of her.

Slapping had always felt natural to her. A girl didn't have to be agile to be a Slapper, unlike being a Rider. She didn't have to be strong, like a Trapper. She just had to be cautious, careful, tactic–

"No," Webba interrupted. "I say *Slap*."

Webba dropped her crutches, hopping on one leg until she found her balance. Then she started Slapping. Not in the churning, fluid way Dirt Slapped, but with force, like her arms were switches cut from a tree and she was whipping the backside of an unruly Bibi. That was why the technique was named as it was–the Whip Slap. It was a powerful technique, designed to spear a girl in her chest and shoulders, damaging her muscles over time. But the technique was useless in competition. With anything except perfect placement, it could easily end in broken fingers.

Dirt stared, stunned. She'd never seen Webba Slap like that before, with such power and precision. She hadn't even realized Webba still knew the Whip Slap.

Trust Webba to perfect new techniques while on crutches.

When Webba finished, she took a long, deep breath, then flashed a grin. "*Slap*," she repeated before retrieving her crutches.

Dirt nodded, took up her fighting stance, and began Slapping again. It was difficult to do what Webba asked. She hadn't practiced the Whip Slap in years, and her body couldn't quite recall its rhythm and timing.

By sundown, Dirt still hadn't figured it out.

"Breathe easy," Webba said. "It will take time."

. She practiced the Whip Slap for several more hours, but only made slight improvements. Her frustration grew. She was wasting time practicing a technique she would never use even if she weren't the Godskin.

When she went back to the sleep hut for a late dinner, she told Webba how she was feeling. But Webba disagreed.

"Na Godskin must improve, always," she said.

It was a foolish waste of time, and Dirt was growing impatient with Webba. She loved her sister. She loved Webba more than she loved herself. But Dirt had accomplished something that was beyond Webba's guidance. All her life, she'd heeded her sister's wisdom. But maybe that didn't make as much sense anymore.

Maybe it was time for Dirt to listen to herself.

20

Reclaiming Pride

3 Days until the Wing Fight

DIRT LED the morning run, pounding through the jungle. She didn't stumble over any roots. She didn't slip on any slick leaves. She didn't run into any trees. Filled with her Godskin power, her reactions were too fast for nature to catch her off guard.

Behind her, Swoo wasn't having such a good time.

"Sis Dirt, slow!" she shouted. "Slow, you rushing rooster!"

It was Dirt's turn to ignore Swoo's pleas.

She continued through the jungle until the thicket gave way to sparse palms and the jungle floor gave way to coastal sand. Soon they reached the foot of a stony cliff, the same one they'd visited just days before. Last time, Swoo had run ahead, speeding up the incline. This time, Dirt leapt from the sea-level stones to the top of the cliff in a single bound.

She sat on the edge of the cliff, overlooking the water while waiting for Swoo to catch up. Last time they'd been here, her mind had swirled with thoughts of falling, of her body being smashed by waves, smeared against the cliff. Now those thoughts seemed absurd. The original Godskins had created the oceans. How could the ocean be any danger to her?

"Sis Dirt," Swoo said as she dragged herself over the final rocks and collapsed beside Dirt. "na Gods punish you." She turned her face to the sky and closed her eyes, chest heaving up and down.

Dirt smiled. Humility looked lovely on Swoo.

"You know why I bring you here, my sister?" Dirt asked.

Swoo was too tired to speak. She just shook her head.

"I must apologize," Dirt said. "Before, I am too afraid to tell Webba I will not fight. I see that hurts you."

"Eh heh," Swoo said, then she fell silent. Dirt watched the auburn sun climb the horizon, the water lap calmly against the cliff. "I disrespect you before. In na training," Swoo added after a long pause. "This is . . . not fine."

An apology? From Swoo? Dirt looked at her sister with a raised eyebrow, impressed. Swoo scrunched her face up in embarrassment and looked away.

Dirt laughed. "You and I are same and same," she said. "Too proud."

"*I* am proud," Swoo responded in an uncharacteristically soft voice. "*You* are not proud enough. You are na Godskin. Every Bower in na South will push their First from this cliff to be you. If Oduma says I must throw Nana into na water to be na Godskin, you will all see Nana fly."

"NoBe Swoo!" Dirt scolded.

Swoo waved a hand dismissively. "Nana is skinny, she will be finefine. And if I am na Godskin, I can make na Mud more powerful than any Fam in memory.

"But I am not," Swoo said without a touch of bitterness. She looked directly into Dirt's eyes. "My big sister Dirt is. So I will give everything to her, now and forever."

Dirt extended a hand, and once Swoo took it, she pulled her sister into an embrace. Sisterhood was complicated. Sometimes she truly believed that Swoo was the worst thing in her life. Other times she felt Swoo's love so fiercely that she couldn't imagine living without it.

They embraced briefly before separating.

"Swoo, you are right," Dirt said. "I am not proud enough."

She thought of the Whip Slap, and how Webba, who was broken, had mastered it. How could Dirt let a Trapper learn such a skill better than her? Where was her pride as a Slapper?

Just saying it ignited a fire in her. For the first time in years, she felt the desire for competition, for dominance.

Suddenly she stood. The ocean winds tugged and pushed at her.

"Watch, Swoo," she said, swallowing. "See your sister, na Godskin."

Normally, a jump from that cliff would be death. Even if a girl managed to jump far enough away to avoid being shattered against the rocks at the cliff's base, the impact with the water itself would break her.

But Dirt was no ordinary girl.

She took a calming breath. *I am brave. I am fat. I am Dirt.* Once in her Godskin, she leapt out over the water.

"Sis Dirt!" Swoo screamed in horror.

But Dirt didn't feel any fear. Only peace. Only freedom.

As she dived headfirst, the glistening water rose up to meet her. She punched into the surface and was immediately surrounded by colors as a rainbow of fish dispersed around her. Bright trees of orange-gold coral branched beneath her on the sea floor, beside tall seaweed forests waving in the currents.

After a moment, Dirt kicked back above the water. High on the cliff, Swoo looked down at her with a mix of disbelief and admiration.

"Sis Dirt, you are madmad!" she shouted before breaking into laughter.

2 Days until the Wing Fight

Dirt woke early on the next day of training, determined to master the Whip Slap before her sisters woke. She Slapped the entire morning, carefully altering the roll of her shoulders, the incline of her arms, the lean of her weight.

Until it finally happened. Somehow, brain and body reached an agreement, and her arm rolled just right, her hand coming down on her imaginary opponent with concentrated force, drilling through the air.

She felt a surge of pride as she stood with one arm outstretched, breathing heavily as the morning dew steamed in the blushing sunlight. She'd done it. Webba had put a challenge before her and she'd met it, like a true competitor.

The sound of applause caught her by surprise. Webba was leaning against the wall of the sleep hut, grin on her face, clapping her large, meaty hands together.

"Chaaaiii! Look at my strongstrong Sis."

Dirt restrained her smile and shrugged. "It takes me two days. For na simple Slap."

Webba shook her head. "Two days, she says." She raised her

voice, calling into the sleep hut. "My sisters, wake and wake. Come and see what your big sister Dirt can do."

As proud as Dirt was, it was embarrassing to have the young ones woken up over a Slap technique they had all seen before. The Bibi rubbed weary eyes as they trailed out of the sleep hut, hands shielding against the sun. Swoo was more alert, but not by much. She looked around with brows bunched in confusion, as if certain there was nothing Dirt could do that was worth starting her day with.

"Again, my Sis," Webba said.

Dirt felt ridiculous. Now that she could execute the technique, she didn't understand how it had given her so much trouble in the first place. It was simple enough. She did it a few times in a row, each one sharper than the last.

"Chaaaiii . . . ?!" Nana exclaimed, ever eager to please, yet unsure what she was supposed to be impressed about. "Way strongstrong, Sis Dirt."

Snore yawned and blinked a long, slow blink.

"This is na waste of my eyes," Swoo said, walking back to the sleep hut.

Dirt couldn't fault their boredom. She didn't like that Webba had put her in such an uncomfortable position.

"Not like this," Webba said, shaking her head. She stretched out a hand, catching Swoo before she could leave. "Again, my Sis. But make na Whispers quiet."

"It is fine, my Sis, I–" Dirt began.

"*Make quiet*," Webba repeated.

Dirt sighed, mentally reciting her mantra until she felt the familiar power of the Gods coursing hot through her. Then she set her feet and let loose two Slaps.

Her arms rolled without resistance, lighter than the air they cut through. Energy surged from her shoulders to her hands to her fingers and then exploded outward. Like spears driving through clouds, two visible bolts of wind ripped across the camp. They smashed into a palm at the edge of the tree line with enough force to blow chunks from its trunk.

Swoo stared in frozen silence. Nana's eyes were bowls. Snore was on her feet in an instant, running across the ring to inspect the tree. She rubbed a palm over the exposed tan interior. Then she looked at her hand, sniffed it, and licked it. She patted the tree's opening and grinned back at her sisters.

"Sis Dirr, you break na tree!"

Dirt herself couldn't quite believe it. But when she looked at Webba, there was a knowing smile on her sister's face.

"Two days it takes you, eh?" Webba said, grabbing her crutches and stuffing them under her armpits. She moved off toward the water spigot to make her afternoon tea. "Chaaaiii, very slow, my Sis."

21

Trading Dreams

1 Day until the Wing Fight

FOR YEARS, Dirt had dreamed of building the Mud into the biggest Fam in the South. Hundreds of sisters strong, all of them supporting each other, enjoying life together, pushing each other to be great. In her mind, Webba had been the one to lead them toward that dream. Dirt was meant to be a supporting character, there as a witness to Webba's rise.

But the story had changed. Now she was the one to lead them down that path, to bring greatness to the Mud.

Because Dirt was a True Godskin. Powerful. Chosen.

The rest of the day was a blur of joy. She practiced her new Whip Slap—"na Spear," Swoo started calling it—ate heavy meals, danced and sang and laughed with her sisters. Webba's injury felt like it had happened a year ago. The chaos and despair they'd all felt was a fading memory.

On the last day of training, the day before the fight, the Fam traveled to a nearby slope. It was in the heart of the jungle, but few trees dotted its length, and it was covered in the creamy brown-red mud they used to make the Offer. In their Bibi days, Dirt and Webba had spent a lot of time evading chores by slipping and sliding down the hill, laughing with their sisters, wasting the day away until an angry NoBe came calling.

"Na Mud Slide!" Dirt said when she saw it. She couldn't help but smile. It had been so long.

"Today na sliding daaaaay," Webba sang, sitting down at the lip of the hill and scooting forward. "Today na sliding day-oh!"

Before Dirt or any of the other sisters could stop her, Webba pushed off down the slope. She gained speed as she skimmed along the slick mud, weaving around one tree then another with her braced leg stiff in the air. When she slowed to a halt on the level ground at the bottom of the hill, the other Mud sisters let out a collective breath, exchanging nervous laughter.

Webba raised two triumphant arms in the air. "Na Mud!!"

They spent the better part of the day taking turns down the slope. The Bibi were just happy to slide around in the mud, but Swoo turned it into a competition with herself to see if she could stay on her feet for the entire slide down. By the end of the day, she was sliding down the hill upright, at full speed, with spins, jumps, and other tricks thrown in.

Dirt started the day alongside the younger sisters, sliding down the slope with ease. With the power of a Godskin, balancing was nothing for her. She even easily performed a backflip that Swoo had been repeatedly failing. After that, she spent the rest of the morning just watching. That giggle in Snore's mouth, that smile on Nana's face, that joyful glint in Swoo's eyes. They were all made possible because of Dirt's strength. She was finally the big sister they deserved.

In the afternoon, the Bibi gathered fruit from the surrounding trees and Swoo came back with fish from a nearby pond. The Mud sisters enjoyed secondmeal atop the hill, under the soft sunlight that shined through the tree leaves. When the meal was over, the younger sisters all fell asleep, Snore sprawled on top of both Swoo and Nana. Dirt and Webba sat beside each other, keeping watch.

"Thank you, my Sis," Dirt said. "For today. I enjoy it."

"Today is not for you. Today is for me. Snore wants to cook today and she is so happy I cannot tell her that she will poison all of us."

"So you bring na whole Fam out to play and eat fruit and fish?"

"How can I know we will have fruit and fish?" Webba asked, shrugging. "I think it better to eat na mud."

Dirt laughed.

Webba's eyebrows shot up. "What is this sound my very serious sister makes, eh?"

Dirt sucked her teeth but couldn't force away her smile. "Go to sleep, you silly duck."

"How can I sleep?" She suddenly looked at Dirt with eyes full of admiration. "Look at you. My Sis, na True Godskin."

"I am." It felt good to say.

"And now you have na Spear."

"I do." That felt less good to say. She was still irritated at Webba's training. Even though Webba had turned out to be right about the Whip Slap, Dirt didn't like how much Webba presumed. She had never been a Godskin. "But how do you know?"

"Know what?"

"Na Spear. Na Whip Slap. How do you know what na True Godskin can do?" she asked.

She expected Webba to be surprised. To admit that she didn't really know anything. Instead, Webba pursed her lips, then lay back, arms behind her head as she stared up at the tree cover.

"You know our dream, eh?"

"Na big Fam. Most big in na South."

"Eh heh. When I am na girl and we dream it, I know I must be strong to make this dream. And I always think . . ."

After a few seconds of silence, Dirt looked over at Webba to find a strange smile on her face and a bashful flare to her nostrils. "What is it?"

Webba shook her head and grinned. "I always think I will be na True Godskin. I think if I am na Godskin, I can fight for na Mud, win for na Mud. So I spend manymany days thinking about na Godskin. How na Godskin Ride, Trap, Bow. And Slap."

She kept her eyes firmly on the leaves above.

Dirt stared at her sister, a world of realization collapsing onto her.

I take Webba's dream, she realized.

She'd assumed that Swoo would have always dreamt of being a True Godskin, but it had never occurred to her that Webba had felt that way. Webba had always seemed as powerful as any girl needed to be. But why wouldn't she? What Bower wouldn't want to be chosen by the Gods themselves?

When Swoo had found out Dirt was the Godskin, she'd gotten drunk and cried in front of Flagga boys.

But Webba had been nothing but loving. She'd tried to pass on all she knew and imagined about Godskins to Dirt. Even as Dirt enjoyed everything that Webba herself had hoped and yearned and worked for, Webba didn't feel anything but happiness for her sister.

Dirt lay back to rest her head on her sister's shoulder.

"My Sis," she said, as Swoo and the Bibi all held hands in sleep, Snore's rumbling echoing among the trees.

"Eh?"

"Thank you."

22

Sis Dirt vs. Sis Wing

THE CROWD was the largest Dirt had ever seen.

It looked like every Flagga, Mosquito, and Pusher in the South was crammed into the Grand Temple. There may have even been some Pusher boys from the other parts of the Isle, judging by the number of Petti that Dirt didn't recognize–fierce, long-legged dogs, tiny lizards that fit in a boy's hand, great golden birds with white, translucent wings.

Her name was whispered on every lip. Was Sis Dirt truly the Godskin? The Second of the Mud? That retired girl?

When Dirt moved forward, out from under the shadowed arch of the arena, the murmurs of excitement became a powerful quiet. A moment of reverence yawned on as she crossed the sand.

Then the music kicked up and the cheers came with it.

Raucous and rabid, the crowd rose to its feet and released a crush of sound that rumbled the arena floor. An entire wing of the arena was brown-clad Mud fans. The Flagga boys in the audience led a dance, with Pusher boys and Mosquito girls joining in, all of them swaying as one. The Sand fans were nearly as fevered in their cheers, with many of the yellows joining the sea of browns, and even the boys and girls of the Rock cheered Dirt's entrance, despite their friendly relationship with the Creek.

The Creek fans were silent, but it was a focused quiet, the proper respect for a formidable foe.

The Vine booed and hissed as if Dirt was fighting one of their own.

It was strange to have fans. Dirt knew she should have been flashing smiles, smacking her belly, and adding fuel to their fire. But she had never been comfortable with attention in the way that Webba was. These people were a distraction she didn't need. A nice one that gave her tickles in her stomach, made her cheeks hot with pride and embarrassment, lightened her steps. But still a distraction. She did her best to block out their sound.

I am brave. I am fat. I am Dirt.

Webba, voice as full and powerful as ever, started the singing. Dirt danced her best, but it was still Swoo whose dancing got the crowd going the most.

They had barely reached the far side of the arena when the cheering came to an abrupt halt, replaced a moment later by a new, quieter wave of cheers.

Unlike the Vine, Wing and the Creek didn't make the Mud sisters wait. They strolled through the Temple entrance nearly a hundred girls strong, singing in that distinct Creek way that was less about the words and more about how long and beautiful a note could sound.

Creeeeek Boooooweeerrr!
Creeeeek Poooooweeerrr!

The Creek Bibi and NoBe carried baskets of paradise leaf, a rare beauty of a flower that only grew along the edges of their territory. The girls did a shuffling dance as they spun the paradise stalks in their hands, dispersing the flower's golden, heart-shaped seeds into the air. The seeds drifted up to the audience, showering the arena in tiny flecks of gold, like sunlight made solid.

Dirt had forgotten how much she loved the Creek's entrances. Normally, she would clap along, even when they were fighting Webba—Webba didn't mind since she herself would often sing and dance with the opposing Fam. But it was different now. Dirt was prepared to end the Creek's best chance at winning the tournament. And even injure Wing, if necessary. It didn't feel right for her to celebrate a Fam right before fighting them.

Snore had no such reservations. She cheered and laughed and ran around, trying to catch the paradise-leaf seeds as they glittered down.

As Creek sisters advanced in skill, they were allowed to train in increasingly deep parts of their creek, where a girl's strength was the only thing keeping her from being swept away in the current. As a result, each girl sported a length of pale skin that revealed her rank. The Bibi were only pale at their feet, a sign of little skill. The NoBe were pale up to midcalf, and many of the full Sis had pale skin up to their waists.

Wing, as she strode out ahead of her sisters, singing with full throat, was pale up to her neck.

She was possibly the greatest Bower to ever come out of the

Creek. A girl that any Fam would have been proud to have. She wasn't as big and strong as Carra Carre nor as clever as Webba, but she could move in ways that no other girl could, with a speed and grace that frequently left crowds stunned. During the previous God Bow tournament, she had been the only Bower to even get close to scoring on Carra Carre. She wore a simple Godskin with the customary knee-wrap, waistcloth, and tattered half shirt of the Creek. But she accented it with a blue band wrapped around her forehead and blue tassels running through her short braids. Her Godskin would have looked meager on any lesser Bower. On Wing, it was just a reminder that she didn't need much to impress the Gods. Her skills were enough.

Wing joined the Creek's dance, to a roar of approval from the crowd. She glided from one end of the arena to the other; she jumped and touched her toes in midair; she fell into a full split.

She turned the Grand Temple into a stage.

Her sisters backed her up, flowing in unison like a river. By the end, the entire arena was on its feet, clapping along to the Creek anthem.

After the dance, when the music shifted to the song of the Gods, Dirt and Wing met at the ring. Wing's face, so expressive during the dance, became entirely empty of emotion, her muscles loose, eyes so calm that she almost looked disinterested.

Dirt knew her own training. She knew of all the superhuman feats she'd performed. Just minutes before, she'd known that she was the most powerful girl on the Isle. Yet she still felt an uncomfortable stirring in her gut as she stared into Wing's eyes. It was easy to imagine success from a safe distance, but it was a different matter in the ring, facing down a girl who was intent on breaking her. There was no fear in Wing's face. She didn't seem at all worried about what Dirt had done to Verdi.

The two competitors exchanged open-palm salutes and stepped into the ring. Then the timekeeper unstoppered the hourglass.

"Bow begin!" she cried.

I am brave, Dirt thought. *I am—*

"Sis Dirt," Wing said.

"Eh?"

Wing faked a Ride, forcing Dirt to stagger back. Then she began moving in a strange way, sliding slowly forward, then wrenching quickly to the side, then dropping to her knees only to bounce back up. It was impossible to tell what she was going to do or where she was going to go next, and Dirt found herself focusing entirely on tracking Wing's movements.

When Wing suddenly Rode in, the act was so quick and forceful that it threw Dirt to the sand and nearly out of the ring, no Trap or Bow required.

"Bow!" the timekeeper called.

An easy three points that silenced the crowd.

But the Bow gave Dirt exactly what she needed—a break. A moment with her back against the warm sand. An intermission where only the sky remained in her vision, blue and clear and free.

I am brave. I am fat. I am Dirt.

When she got back to her feet, her mind was quiet, filled with clarity and the power of the Gods.

Her Whip Slap, na Spear, rended the air at her fingertips, sending a barrel of wind across the ring. It crashed into Wing's chest and sent her staggering backward.

The crowd erupted. This was the power they'd come to see.

Wing's icy calm melted, and her eyes widened. She braced herself against the sandbags along the ring's edge, arms across her chest, leaning into Spear after Spear. Then Dirt Rode in, so fast that the First of the Creek was still squinted and braced against the next Spear. Dirt extended a finger forward onto Wing's shoulder and pushed just the slightest bit, enough to tip her out of the ring.

"Push!" the timekeeper cried. "Na winner is Sis Dirt of na Mud!"

It took a moment for the crowd to react. Some rubbed their eyes, as if their vision were playing tricks on them. But eventually they came to understand what they'd just witnessed, and they began a modest, disbelieving applause.

Wing stood from the sand and patted herself off. Then she took Dirt's arm and raised it into the air. The audience cheered louder, with more fervor. Other than the Vine fans, the whole audience hollered, launching into the victor's song—the Mud anthem.

"Dirt!" Wing shouted over the singing crowd. She held Dirt by the shoulders, a grin on her face to rival Webba's. "Na Daughter of Oduma. Strong Bow, Sis."

"Strong Bow," Dirt said. She was surprised when Wing wrapped her in a hug.

"Your Sis Webba," Wing said. "She is na good girl. Fat. Clever." She pulled back, looked Dirt in the eye. "Go and punish Carra Carre."

Before Dirt could answer, she was tackled to the ground by Swoo and the Bibi, buried under their cheering and giggles. They sang with the crowd, the Mud anthem filling Dirt's ears. With Webba's smiling face and helping hand, Dirt climbed back to her feet and left the Grand Temple with her sisters. She did her best to acknowledge the fans on her way out.

They crossed the sand back to the tent. Nana and Snore were chasing each other, giggling so hard that drool sprayed from their mouths. They tumbled into the sand in a fit of laughter, only to rise and repeat the cycle. Swoo was reenacting the fight, Slapping against an imaginary Wing, then hopping over and being that same Wing, dramatically reeling from the Slaps. Webba watched Swoo with an amused grin.

Dirt breathed in the morning air. Victory was a sweet, sweet feeling.

A sudden pain bloomed in Dirt's face, running up from her chin to her cheek. It started as a dull throb, but with each second it grew worse, deepening and sharpening until it felt like some unseen knife was being driven into her skull and carving its way up to her eyes.

Something was wrong.

Dirt wanted to scream, but she handled the pain the way a Bower would—gritting her teeth and accepting it.

When she raised her hand to touch where the pain was, she was stunned by the sudden scorch of her fingers, as if she'd touched a log straight out of the fire. She snatched her hand back and looked at her fingers to find Offer from her Godskin. And blood. Black blood so dry that it looked days old.

What is this? What is happening to me?

Dirt slowed as her sisters walked ahead. She touched her face again. Same heat. Same black blood, mixed into the Offer. She turned in a circle, searching until she found the only thing that could help her make sense of what was happening. Nearby, a Mosquito girl's wooden trading stall had what she needed.

Dirt started toward it.

"My Sis," Webba asked, "where are you going?"

Dirt didn't slow down. "I am coming," she mumbled, hand cupped over her cheek. "Go inside."

The pain didn't matter anymore. She could barely feel it. All she could feel was terror.

"Mirror," she said as she reached the Mosquito girl's stall, turning her face away from the stall's other patrons.

"Eh heh?" the girl responded, taking a jug of water from one customer in exchange for three red bracelets. "Trade mirror for what? You know this mirror is very finefine and–" She froze once she finally turned to Dirt. "Na Godskin?" she asked, then shrieked it again before Dirt could respond. "Na Godskin!!"

As a crowd of fans began to form, Dirt snatched a small hand mirror from a display shelf and bolted, running until she reached the tree line and could hide among its shadows.

Then she raised the mirror to her face.

She'd never used a mirror before, but she'd seen Mosquito girls use them to look at themselves as they applied face paints. When her face was centered, she took her hand off her cheek and at first saw nothing out of sorts. Her face was fine.

Until she saw a small dot of black, just beneath the Offer. It was a disquieting, shifting black, like a river at night. Dirt wiped the Offer away until she could see the spot more clearly.

A line of that strange black ran up from her chin to her cheek, where it bent into a semicircle that followed the curve of her eye. She could see clearly that the black was moving, and it glowed with a soft light, like black flames were burning from a canyon within her face.

She reached up to touch it again, and found it had cooled a

bit, no longer scorching. But it was there. And it would stay there forever, she knew.

She was Scarred.

It wasn't supposed to happen until her seventeenth year, still weeks away. Antie Yaya's Mosquitos must have messed up the birth records. Or maybe the Mamas and Papas had just decided to make her a woman early. People had to stick to tradition; maybe the Gods didn't.

Dirt wanted to run. She wanted to bury herself in the jungle and disappear. She wanted to jump into the sea and sink to the bottom. She wanted to be anywhere else. Anyone else.

But she was just Dirt. Dirt, whose Scarring had come.

Dirt, the woman.

23

An Offer for Offer

"SIS DIRT go, '*bom bom bom*,' and you see Wing? Her face go, 'Chaaaiii, this Dirt will kill me.' How can na girl like Wing fight our Sis Dirt, eh? No girl is so fat! No girl is so brave! We are na Muuuuuud sisterrrrrs!"

Nana watched NoBe Swoo strut around the preparation tent, singing, dancing, as happy as if she herself had won the fight. Sis Webba, seated on the tent floor, sang along lightly. Snore joined in, too, following behind NoBe Swoo and mimicking her dance.

Sis Dirt stayed seated. She didn't sing. She hadn't even rubbed the Offer from her face. None of that was too surprising from Sis Dirt, but Nana didn't expect to see such a miserable look on her face, not after a victory like that. She had worked so hard the last week, improving her abilities and mastering na Spear. She'd beaten Wing, one of the greatest Bowers in all the South, and she didn't have a single injury. Could nothing make her happy?

Nana crossed the tent to sit beside Sis Dirt. She tried to lean her head on her sister's shoulder, but the Second of the Mud startled, pulling away and looking at Nana as if she were a snake.

"Sis Dirt?" Nana asked, confused.

Sis Webba leaned over with a grin. "Your big sister is tired, my Bibi. Let her rest, eh?" She looked at Snore and NoBe Swoo. "Swoo, take na Bibi. Go and make play before you give your oldold Sis Dirt na aching head."

With a last concerned glance at Sis Dirt, Nana followed NoBe Swoo, who carried a giggling Snore on her back, as they all left the tent.

Sis Dirt's match had been the first of the day, so the sun was still climbing the sky, warm but not blazing. Not a long distance away, near the arena entrance, hundreds of people streamed out through the open entryway, jumping and shouting and cheering, making a parade lap around the arena while they waited for the next match.

NoBe Swoo's eyes brightened as she saw the crowd. "Eh heh, look at these party cats! Let us join them, eh?"

Before Nana could protest (a crowd that big meant a lot of pushing and sweat and bad odors), NoBe Swoo was speeding across the sand, Snore bouncing and cheering on her back. Nana didn't follow. Instead, she headed for the Grand Temple market outside the arena's walls.

She strolled the market, stopping in front of various food stalls. But she wasn't looking at the food. She was looking out of the corner of her eyes at nearby jewelry stalls, admiring the craftsmanship and memorizing patterns that she could try later.

She was walking from one food stall to another, eyes on a

stunning green anklet sitting on the counter of a jewelry stall, when she bumped into someone.

"I am sorry!" she said as she turned to see the person she'd bumped into.

It was the Mosqu–Butterfly girl. The one with the cherry cloth headband and short bangs. The one whose name matched the pendant glistening at her neck.

"Apple . . . ," Nana said.

"Nana," the girl responded, smiling. She had a small clay cup in her hand full of cut-up fruit chunks. "How now, Bower girl?"

Nana smiled back. She'd spent the last couple of weeks trying to learn to make jewelry, and here was the girl who had started her on that journey. It was good to see her.

"I am finefine," Nana said.

"What are you doing?" Apple asked.

Nana shrugged. "Sis Webba says I can play."

"This is play?"

"Well . . ." Nana was almost afraid to say it. She lowered her voice to a whisper. "I am looking at na adorn." She nodded her head over to the nearby jewelry stall and its magnificent green anklet.

Apple eyed the stall for a moment. "It is fine," she said judiciously. "I can show you some adorn more finefine."

Nana couldn't imagine anything much more beautiful than what she was already looking at, but who was she to argue with a Butterfly girl about jewelry?

"Show me!"

Apple took her hand (somehow Apple's hands weren't sticky from the fruit–amazing!) and led her down the dusty market avenue, skipping by stand after stand. They got many stares as they passed. Friendship between Bowers and Butterflies was rare, which made Nana all the more grateful for Apple's.

After a short jaunt, Apple stopped at a wooden stand no different from any of the others, though this one had a group of Butterfly girls sitting around it. Before they approached, Apple pointed them out.

There was Pom, whose earrings and socks were carefully mismatched–her typical style. There was Mimi, the youngest. She was just five, but with her heeled shoes and thickly dyed lips, she was intent on acting like an older girl. Lily and Rose were two bananas in a bunch, both clad in simple jeans, dark blue blouses, and lightly dabbed cheek rouge, but Lily was the talkative one while Rose mainly just repeated what Lily said.

Then there was the oldest girl, Pretty. Nana didn't need Apple to explain anything about Pretty. Everything about her was obvious.

She was a perfect model of what a girl should be. When every other girl had sand in her hair after a long day at the Grand Temple, Pretty's hair was clean. When every other girl's lips were dry and dehydrated, Pretty's thick lips glistened wetly. Few girls had hips like Pretty's, already widening beyond her waist, and fewer still had the beauty gap between their front teeth–Mama Eghodo's teeth.

Sis Webba was beautiful, but she was beautiful like a Bower: dark skin, an easy smile, big arms, and a bigger belly. Pretty was even darker than Sis Webba and was the ideal Butterfly. She was tall, mysterious, curved like a wave atop water. Nana didn't know whether Pretty had been given her name by others or she'd seen her reflection and chosen it herself, and she didn't ask. Either way it was accurate.

Nana hated admitting it to herself, but she would trade almost anything to look like Pretty.

As Nana and Apple approached the stand, none of the other girls paid them notice. They were all focused on Pretty, listening to her tell a story about one of the many Pusher boys who competed for her attention.

"So this boy says, 'Oh, Pretty, let me make you na mama so we can go and live with na Gods.'"

"Chaaaiii!" the other girls cooed.

"You know what I say?"

They leaned forward, waiting.

"I say, 'You see me, eh?'" She raised an arrogant eyebrow. "And he says, 'Eh heh, na most sweet girl I have seen.' So I say, 'That is enough of na Gods for you!'"

The girls erupted in rapid, high-pitched giggles, a strange blend of noise that sounded to Nana like a tree full of birds. Bowers didn't laugh like that.

"That is what I say to him!" Pretty continued. "And then his face is . . . eh . . ."

"Heartbroken?" Pom offered.

"Heartbroken," Pretty said immediately, as if she hadn't heard Pom at all. "That sillysilly boy. That neck of na snake."

That earned more giggles from the other girls.

"Eh heh, Apple, how now?" Pretty said, suddenly turning her attention to Nana. "Who is this one?"

Nana felt fire rush into her cheeks as Pretty's gaze fell on her. She felt like she was being weighed, judged. The laughter died down as the other girls turned to look as well.

"This is Nana. She is my friend."

"Na Bower friend?"

"She likes adorn," Apple explained.

Pretty scoffed, then rose from her side of the wooden stall and walked over to them. She seemed even taller up close, and her skin was smoother. And her hips were wider. And her face more skillfully contoured by paints. The closer she got, the more impressive she was.

Apple spoke again, nonplussed. "I say I will show her adorn."

"Eh heh," Pretty mumbled to herself, looking Nana up and down. "Why you like adorn, Bower girl?"

Nana thought of a million and one things to say, and they all tried to come out of her mouth at once, resulting in a clog of words around her throat and no sound coming out at all.

"Is Na Bower girl . . . ?" Pretty began. "Are you, eh . . . ?"

"Deaf?" Pom offered.

"Deaf?"

"Speak, Nana," Apple said, chewing casually on her fruit.

"I like adorn," Nana finally blurted, digging into her waistband and pulling out the new bracelet she'd been working on. It wasn't done yet, but she liked the red-yellow-black pattern of the stones, like snakeskin.

Pretty barely spared it a glance before rolling her eyes. She threw her head back and laughed loudly, which spurred the other girls to laugh as well. Nana looked at Apple, unsure how to respond. Apple just shrugged. Suddenly Pretty raised her fist in front of Nana's eyes.

Dangling from her grip was the most beautiful bracelet Nana had ever seen. Instead of the tiny stone chips Nana worked with, this one had a dozen large stones, all thick, rare, and precious. They were each different colors, different shapes, all glowing in the morning sun. A fire red stone with flecks of green brushed up against a black stone with tiny holes all along its surface, and beside them both was a plain gray stone with a vein of gold down its center. Nana could only imagine how long it had taken to gather those various stones, polish them, set and bind them just right. And how much fun it had been.

"You like, eh?" Pretty asked.

Nana nodded, transfixed.

"Oh well," Pretty said, turning abruptly and hiding the bracelet from view. "Na Bower cannot wear it." She sat on a high stool, crossing her legs. "Na Bower are way fatfat."

All the girls laughed, but Nana didn't understand what was so funny. It was the first nice thing Pretty had said to her.

"Thank you, Mosq–Butterfly Pretty," she said. She wasn't sure how Butterfly girls used titles, or if they used them at all, but she hoped it was accurate.

Pretty only sneered. "You want be na Butterfly, eh? So you can wear adorn?"

No, Nana thought immediately. She was a Bower. She had a Fam. She never wanted to be a Butterfly girl, no matter how nice their jewelry was.

"If you want be na Butterfly, bring me Mud Offer," Pretty said. "One bowl."

Nana looked again to Apple, but she wasn't sure what she was looking for. Maybe some sign that Pretty was joking. Or some reassurance that the idea was ridiculous. Nana was a Bower. Why would she want to lower herself to become a Butterfly?

But Apple just stared at her. She didn't say anything.

So Nana didn't say anything either.

"Nana!" NoBe Swoo's voice rang out from the far side of the market. Nana watched NoBe Swoo looking around for her, calling out. Snore sat on NoBe Swoo's shoulders, twisting the elder sister's hair.

"One bowl?" Nana asked, more to herself than Pretty. But Apple smiled at that.

"One bowl," Pretty repeated.

"Nana!" Swoo called again

Nana watched Pretty, uncertain of how she felt and what she wanted. Finally, not knowing what else to do, she turned away from the Butterf–the Mosquito girls and ran.

24

A Hidden Scar

THE PREVIOUS First of the Mud was a girl named Sis Prom. She had never been more than an average Bower. Even as a young NoBe Webba would regularly thrash her in practice. But she was a great mentor to the younger sisters, and she fulfilled her duties as best she could. Sis Prom often talked to them about the future, about what to expect when her womanhood came.

"I will go to Antie Yaya," Sis Prom said one afternoon. They were sitting beside the ring as Webba, still a brand-new Sis, showed the new NoBe, Swoo, a variation of the Pull Trap.

"And then what, eh?" Dirt had asked.

Sis Prom had a cautious way of speaking, as if any wrong word could bring the sky down. "I believe she will make me go East."

"Why East?"

"No girl can know. It is said Useyi is in na East. Na Mamas and Papas need strongstrong Bowers to fight Him."

"Then why send you?" Dirt had been more flippant in her younger years.

Sis Prom chuckled. "Goodgood question, my young Sis. I do not know what na Gods want for me. But when my time arrives . . . Webba, be kind!" Webba had Trapped Swoo with one arm and was poking a wet finger into Swoo's ear. She looked over her shoulder at Sis Prom and grinned.

Less than a week later, Dirt woke to find Sis Prom tearfully stuffing clothes and fruit into a bag. Even in the dark, Dirt could see two black lines across her cheek. By the time she realized that the day of Sis Prom's Scarring had come, her sister had already fled into the night. It was a shock to see Sis Prom leave like that, suddenly and shamefully before the other sisters could even wake to say goodbye.

Now, as she sat across from Webba on the tent floor, Dirt kept expecting tears to come. Yet her eyes were dry. She just felt scared, her insides tied into a knot. This long after a fight, she should have changed out of her Godskin. But she was terrified to move at all. If she brushed her face wrong, her Scarring would be revealed.

I am brave. I am fat. I am Dirt.

The last week of training had planted the words so firmly in her head that they'd become her natural response to fear. Except they felt useless now. Hollow. Webba's coaching, Swoo's long hours of sparring, the Bibi constantly gathering food, preparing her meals, keeping the ring clean and the mud pit filled and the Offer prepared. All that work from her sisters. They'd done everything they could to make her the greatest Bower in the South, and she'd failed them. Not in the ring, against Carra Carre or any other girl, but in her own body.

She was a woman now. Greatness was for girls.

"My Sis . . . ," Webba said.

Dirt would have to do the same as Sis Prom. Leave her sisters, go to Antie Yaya, and be sent to the East. Maybe that meant a fight with Useyi Himself. Maybe that meant something else. In doing so, she would forfeit the God Bow tournament, the Mud would get no recruits, and the Mud Fam would end. Swoo, Nana, and Snore would have to find their own ways, likely being scattered to different Fam, who would treat them as outsiders until they proved themselves.

It was how things had to be.

"My Sis . . . ?" Webba pressed.

But what if it wasn't?

She was already hiding her Scarring, and nothing had happened. Antie Yaya hadn't ordered her capture. The Gods hadn't whisked her up and flung her Eastward. Aside from the dulling pain in her face, she didn't feel any different. She didn't look any different either, as long as the Scarring stayed covered. So no one else knew. She could hide it. And if she hid it, she could continue to Bow. She could win the tournament.

Then when the season was over, she could fulfill her duty and go to Antie Yaya. It wouldn't matter if everyone found out then. The Fam would survive and the Gods would understand. Why did being a woman have to mean abandoning the life she loved to fulfill some tradition?

"Dirt."

At her name, Dirt realized she'd been staring at nothing, and hadn't heard any of what Webba had been saying.

"Eh?"

"I say you are special, my sister," Webba said, reverence in her voice. "Sis Dirt na Godskin."

"Eh heh . . . ," Dirt said absently. "Thank you, my Sis." She managed a small smile.

"You are tired," Webba said with a sympathetic laugh. "Breathe easy, na day is almost finished."

"Almost?"

"We must go and watch your opponents."

Dirt had forgotten there were still more fights. Dream versus Splash, Hollo versus Sevi. Nat versus Carra Carre.

"Change your clothes, eh?" Webba said. She grabbed a halfshirt and pair of pants and tossed them to Dirt.

Dirt caught them and stared. A mental image of herself tumbled in her mind, changing into the halfshirt a dozen different ways, each of them ending with her smudging the Offer from her face and revealing her scar to Webba.

"I will change," Dirt said. She stalled by brushing some of the remaining Offer from the rest of her body, picking at tiny bits of mud on her elbows, patting some off her thighs. Finally, when everywhere but her face was clean of Offer, she swallowed and stood.

Swoo, blessed Swoo, burst through the tent flap with Snore on her shoulders and Nana in tow.

"Sis Webba! Sis Dirt!"

As Webba turned to them, Dirt brought the shirt over her head more smoothly than she knew she could, and calmly moved Offer from her forehead to cover up whatever parts of the Scarring the shirt may have exposed. Her heart pounded. With no mirror available, she could only pray that she hadn't revealed her Scarring to the world.

"Na Bow will start soon," Swoo said.

"Sis Dirr," Snore began, "me and NoBe Swoo go to na parade for you."

"Parade, eh?" Webba responded. She motioned for NoBe Swoo to help her onto her crutches. "All for your bigbig sister here?"

Snore nodded and smiled at Dirt.

"Did you go to na parade, Nana?" Webba asked.

Nana shook her head, a strangely pensive look on her face. "I go and see . . . friends," she said.

"Eh heh . . ." Webba gave her a curious stare before turning to Dirt. "My Sis, you have Offer on your face." She extended a thumb to wipe it off.

Dirt jerked her head away, hand cupping over her Scarred cheek. "I have na cut. From Wing."

For the slimmest of seconds, Webba seemed to weigh in her mind the possibility of what Dirt had said. But the time passed in an instant, and Webba nodded, grinning. "You ripe, my Sis?" she asked.

Dirt's heart was beating like a talking drum. Everything in her stomach wanted to come up. It took all her willpower to not constantly touch her face to make sure she hadn't made a mistake that would end her life as she knew it.

She was not all right. She would never be all right again.

But Webba was smiling at her. Snore was smiling at her. Even Swoo was smiling, a strange look of admiration on her face. They were all looking at her with such warmth, such love. Her sisters. She couldn't let them down. No matter what, she would compete in the God Bow tournament.

This Fam had to survive.

"I am ripe," Dirt lied, smiling as well. "Riperipe."

25

Another Skin

THE MUD SISTERS entered the arena through the Bower-only side entrance, hidden from much of the audience. But the crowd still rose to their feet with cheers when they saw Dirt. She waved, smiled, nodded at some of the young girls who called out to her. Not because she'd grown comfortable with the cheers—quite the opposite. She felt like if she didn't play the role of Godskin perfectly, they would suspect something was wrong. They would figure out her secret.

The Fam made its way to the reserved Bower seating, where their peers received them with as much passion as the fans. The Rock girls jumped from their seats, cheering and hollering and being as rowdy as ever. Several of them stood and moved out of the Mud Fam's way, falling into exaggerated curtsies while some of their sisters cackled. Sis Ask, who had been eliminated in the first round of the tournament, greeted them with particular warmth, hugging each of the girls and thanking Dirt for beating the Creek for her.

It all almost made Dirt smile, despite her Scarring. Almost.

The Creek girls were less excited to see Dirt and the Mud. A few of the NoBe smiled at Swoo, but the Sis only granted Dirt a curt nod. Wing was nowhere to be seen. Given how fresh Wing's defeat was for them, Dirt appreciated that they were at least civil.

Unlike the Vine.

There were only a few Vine girls in the stands, one Sis babysitting a group of young Bibi. The Bibi hissed at the Mud like a den of snakes, but at a sneer from Swoo they stayed in their seats. Dirt didn't recognize the Vine Sis, but her eyes narrowed behind her vine mask as if she'd known and hated Dirt her entire life.

As the Mud settled into seats beside the Rock sisters, the second match of the day began. Dream, the First of the Sand, versus Splash, the Second of the Creek. The match that would determine Dirt's next opponent. It ended quickly. After being Bowed early, Dream dominated the fight with all manner of Slaps before scoring a Push before half sand. Dream would be Dirt's next opponent.

The Sand sisters in the Bower section roared in victory, and the Creek girls deflated. With Wing and Splash out, they only had one girl left in the tournament.

That girl was Sevi, who, just a short while later, fought and lost against Hollo, the First of the Rock. At the defeat, the Creek sisters left the stands, escorting an emotional and apologetic Sevi from the arena. The celebration of the Rock went on for a steady five minutes, which was modest for them.

Before the final match of the day, Dream and her victorious Sand sisters returned to the arena to a smattering of cheers. They made their way to the Bower section, and Dream marched straight up to Dirt as if they had scheduled a meeting.

"Second of na Mud," Dream said, standing over Dirt. Dream was surprisingly thin for a Sis. She was of a height with Carra Carre, but scarcely half the weight, with long limbs and a face of weird proportions—droopy ears and a small mouth, thick lips but a thin nose.

Dirt understood the challenge in Dream's voice, but she responded respectfully. "Sis Dream. Strongstrong Bow."

Dream scrunched her nose in disgust. "You are not na True Godskin," she said. Her sisters nodded in support behind her. "You are na fake. And I will show na people"—she pointed a finger out to the crowd, who cheered as they realized what was happening, energized by the confrontation—"who you are. It is!"

"It is!" the Sand echoed.

Dirt knew she should have done something, if not to defend her own honor and that of her Fam, then at least to give the crowd the show they were hoping for. But she couldn't muster the outrage. Dream hadn't said anything false. Dirt was a woman among girls. A fake.

As the silence continued, Dirt's shame only grew.

"Dream, did Wing not punish you last season?" Swoo was on her feet, cracking her neck one direction, then the other. "Did my bigbig Sis Webba," she continued, climbing over a seated Nana and Snore to stand face-to-face with the much taller Dream, "not Bow you on your cantaloupe head, you sleepy goat? Eh? Sis Dirt will mash you, you sticky-minded snake!"

Dream's eyes enlarged at the insults, and her throat rolled with something that surely would have led to violence had Webba not intervened.

"Sit, NoBe Swoo," Webba said, laughing. "Sis Dream is First of na Sand. She does not have time to make chatchat with you, you young jungle cat."

Swoo didn't move, but there was a visible decline in her aggression, and everyone seemed to exhale a bit. Some of the Rock fans in the audience sucked their teeth in disappointment at the decreasing tension.

"Go and enjoy na win, Dream," Webba said. "'Na dog must eat quick before na cat arrives.'" Even seated with a destroyed leg, the authority and threat in Webba's voice sent the Sand away, muttering to each other about what they would have done to Swoo if it weren't for Webba.

Once they were gone, Webba looked at Dirt with a slight scrunch of confusion on her face. Dirt turned away.

The music flared to life again for the last match of the day: Nat of the Rock versus Carra Carre.

The Rock entered the Grand Temple first. With just twenty or so girls, the Rock would have been the South's smallest Fam if it weren't for the Mud. But what they lacked in numbers, and perhaps in intelligence, they made up for in swagger. Each one sported stylish hair, with gray chalk markings swirling across her skin and that perfect, charismatic blend of joy and confidence. Nat, the Second of the Rock, led the way through the arched entrance, flanked by Hollo and Ask, her First and Third. Hollo led the singing, her smooth, rich voice skating on the crowd's cheers.

Na Rock Fam!
Most strong Fam in na land!
And when we Bow
Make you say 'wow'!

Luckily, they were better dancers than they were songwriters.

They all shuffled together in a left-left-right-right type of dance that had become popular across the South. No doubt Swoo would know its name; Dirt didn't. The Rock added their own flavor to the move by flapping their arms to the side, in and out and in, whooping and shouting encouragement to each other as the arena rose to its feet to dance and clap along with them.

Nat, usually so fluid, looked stiff. Even as she danced, her brows were tight, and Dirt could see her taking long, measured breaths. She was nervous. The poor girl had to fight Carra Carre in her second-ever God Bow tournament. More than likely, she would lose quickly and painfully.

When the Rock finished, Nat took her position on the far side of the Grand Temple, watching for the Vine's entrance.

To Dirt's surprise, that didn't take long. Carra Carre led the way, and no matter how many times Dirt saw her, the girl looked too big to be real. Clad in their masks, marching in unison, the Vine entered with their usual chants and salutes.

But something felt different about them.

It was in the way they held their heads, the confidence of their steps. Whereas their previous entrances had always seemed like a performance, this one felt like they'd actually become the army they'd been pretending to be. Triumph and violence radiated from them like heat from summer sand. Dirt didn't know what had caused the change, but it made her uneasy.

"Breezy clucks," Swoo said. She must have felt it too. "They have na plan."

The music shifted from entrance to battle, and the two girls took to the ring, Carra Carre dwarfing Nat.

Dirt felt a sudden simmer of anger. The Vine had the most Bowers. The biggest Bowers. They had Carra Carre. They had everything a Fam could want, but it wasn't enough for them. They wanted to intimidate. They wanted to humiliate and destroy, as they'd done to Webba.

This was why Dirt had to hide her Scarring, just a little bit longer. For the first time, someone could do something about the Vine's brutality. Of all the girls who had ever lived on the Isle, the Gods had given *her* the power—no one else. Girl or woman, she had a responsibility to give Carra Carre and the Vine the divine punishment that they deserved.

Even if that meant lying to her sisters. Someday her sisters would understand. All the South would understand.

Down on the Grand Temple floor, the timekeeper turned over the hourglass to start the match.

Nat charged across the ring, trying the same aggressive Trapping she'd used in her first-round fight. Carra Carre didn't even take up her fighting stance. As Nat sped toward her, Carra Carre grabbed the Rock girl's wrist.

Dirt didn't see the grab. No one did. One second, Carra Carre was standing still and the next she had her hands around Nat's thick wrist like an eagle's talons wrapped around a branch. Nat tried to pull her wrist back, but it didn't budge. She tugged with her whole body, first with technique and then with reckless desperation. A confused mutter swept the arena.

Ice formed in Dirt's belly. "No," she breathed.

Carra Carre flung her arm back, as if she were throwing a stick out into the jungle. But it wasn't a stick she was holding. It was Nat. She screamed through the air, flying ten strides above the ground into a hastily clearing section of the audience. One brave Pusher boy caught her, and he may well have saved her life by slowing her impact. But Nat was moving too fast for him to truly save, and the sound of their bone-snapping collision filled the arena.

Before anyone could scream for help, Carra Carre jumped, arcing high into the air above the highest seats in the Grand Temple. All eyes looked up, but lost her in the glaring sun until she came whistling back down into the box of Bower seats. She crashed back to her feet just two rows in front of Dirt and the Mud.

The Rock sisters between Dirt and Carra Carre scrambled away in a panic, toppling over their seats and each other in order to escape. Carra Carre didn't move. She stood among the chaos she'd created, her chest heaving, veins bulging against her skin, eyes alight with the lust of combat, burning from within her mask of vines. She stared straight ahead.

At Dirt.

Dirt thought to stand up. Bowers were strictly forbidden from fighting outside the ring, but if Carra Carre wanted a war, she was ready.

She thought to make quiet. To challenge Carra Carre right then and there, destroy her in front of all the South.

She thought to do to the girl worse than what she'd done to Verdi, to dismantle her so badly that the Vine would never recover.

She thought to finally avenge Webba.

She thought all these things.

But when she tried to stand, her legs wouldn't work. She felt like she was back in her first God Bow again, the one from all those years ago. Her first and last. The one in which she'd been paralyzed by a mental sandstorm of fear and doubt.

I am brave. . . . I am . . . I am fa . . . I . . . I . . .

The sandstorm was too loud, drowning out the words in her mind. All she could do was stare back at Carra Carre, unable to think, unable to breathe, unable to do anything but sit and hope that the First of the Vine wouldn't break her the way she'd broken Webba and Nat.

But Carra Carre didn't attack her. Instead, after a long and terrifying moment, she turned away and hopped back down to the ring. She was greeted by her sisters, none of whom seemed surprised to find that their First could leap through the sky or throw a girl like discarding a banana peel. Together, the Vine all began marching, pounding their chests, screaming their chant into the stunned silence of the Grand Temple.

Na Vine!
Fight!
Crush!
Na enemy!

As the haunting echoes of the Vine anthem sailed in from outside the arena, Dirt again became aware of her surroundings. Up in the stands, Nat's sisters rushed to her aid, as did some of Antie Yaya's Bonemenders. The Rock fans were wiping tears from their eyes, shaking their heads, hugging each other. Some of the other fans were doing the same.

As the audience began trickling down to the arena floor and out its arched entrance, their mutterings caught the wind and sailed back to where Dirt sat. They were saying what every boy and girl in attendance had come to believe. What Swoo said with the subtle tightness of her lips. What Nana said with the pity in her tired gaze. What Webba said in her vacant, disbelieving stare.

What Dirt was saying in her own heart.

The Gods had chosen another skin.

26

Preparing the Chicken

"SLAP NA WATER!"

More than two hundred arms swam through the air, slapping down on an imaginary water line.

"Ride na wind!"

The army of girls surged forward, low and agile.

"Trap na fire!"

So many hands smacked together that it sounded like a tree had split.

"And Bow to na earth!"

They all bent, in as many ways as there were girls. The Bibi and younger NoBe performed just slight bends. They had never bitten into the sweet fruit of battle; they didn't yet know how much power it took to throw a girl. The older NoBe and new Sis, on the other hand, bent so hard they nearly slammed into each other, eager to show their strength and youth. The older Sis, those still in their physical prime but with the wisdom of the years, bent just right, keeping their technique strong and tight but not wasting any more energy than they needed.

Carra Carre paced back and forth atop her high platform, among the thick tree trunks of the Vine camp, admiring her Fam. It was a rare day. As First, she didn't get many occasions to actually train her sisters. All her time was spent focused on her own development.

But since defeating Nat, she'd become something more than a First. The usual admiration her sisters had for her had become reverence. Every step she took was studied by a dozen onlookers, as if the secret to receiving the Gods' favor were in the weight of her footfalls. NoBe ran to give her water even when she didn't ask, even when she'd just drank a cup, just to be around her.

It was all a bit overwhelming.

But it felt good.

For once, she felt like the First she was supposed to be. Not just a big brute. Not just the body to Verdi's brains. But like an actual leader, one who inspired her sisters.

Before the Nat fight, Dirt's abilities had sent ripples of fear through the Vine camp. Now her sisters were filled with a defiant strength. As she watched them train down below and saw the confidence in their bodies and the conviction in their eyes, she realized how close they had come to despair. She vowed they would never go back to that feeling. Not while she was the First of the Vine.

"Again!" she shouted.

"Na Vine!" her sisters responded, arms churning as they began the sequence again.

"Little Cee Cee."

Carra Carre turned to see Verdi struggling to climb up the last few rungs of the ladder to the platform. Her mind had recovered so much from the fight with Dirt, but her body had yet to regain its strength.

"My Sis, are you not tired?" Carra Carre asked, running over to help her sister. "Go and sleep."

Verdi shrugged off Carra Carre's helping hands and finished her ascent before responding. "I am na Vine sister. Does na vine sleep?"

Carra Carre sucked her teeth. "Does na vine speak? So quiet yourself."

She'd hoped it would make Verdi smile, but Verdi just blinked a slow, strange blink that made Carra Carre feel uneasy.

And guilty.

At home, she was Little Cee Cee. But in the ring, she was Carra Carre, the most feared Bower in the South. She'd done the right thing in defeating Nat, and defeating her in a way that sent fear through the other Bowers. But when she saw the effects of what Dirt had done to Verdi, she couldn't help but think about how much suffering her actions caused Nat and the Rock.

She would do it again if she had the chance. A thousand times if that was what her Fam needed. Because victory was the only way to ensure the future. Winning was everything.

But it didn't always feel good.

"I see words in your mind," Verdi said, hobbling over to sit on the edge of the platform, dangling her feet half a hundred strides above the camp below. "Speak to me, Cee Cee. 'Words are made for na mouth.'"

Carra Carre sat beside her, looking out at the Vine sisters training below.

"Why do na Gods give me power, eh?" Carra Carre asked. "To mash up other girls? Can I not win and make no pain?"

Verdi was quiet for a while, long enough that Carra Carre almost repeated herself in case her sister hadn't heard.

Finally, she spoke. "My Sis, is it wrong to kill na chicken?"

Carra Carre frowned. "These are not chicken, Verdi. These–"

"Please, answer."

Carra Carre sighed. "You must kill na chicken to eat it." It seemed like the answer her sister wanted. Sometimes bad things had to be done for good results.

"And if you do not eat it?"

"What else can be done with na dead chicken?"

"Throw it in na river. Is it now wrong to kill?"

"Is . . ." She couldn't fathom why anyone would throw away a perfectly good chicken. Why were they still talking about chicken? "Is . . . Sis Nat na chicken?"

"Kill or do not kill," Verdi said in a dispassionate voice. "Only na why is important. Eat na chicken is finefine. Toss na chicken is bad-bad. But this way and that way, na chicken is dead. Na *why*, my Sis."

Just then NoBe Murua climbed onto the platform. Carra Carre looked over at her, but Verdi kept her eyes forward.

"What news?" Verdi asked.

"Sis Verdi, we find tracks," Murua said.

Carra Carre raised an eyebrow. "Tracks?" she asked. Why were they looking for tracks?

Verdi ignored her, continuing to speak to Murua. "Eh heh. You follow them?"

"Yes, Sis Verdi," Murua reported. "But they disappear over leaves. We do not see mud."

Carra Carre didn't understand. "My Sis," she said, low enough for only Verdi to hear. "Why do we look for mud?"

Verdi was quiet for a moment, then said, "Thank you, Murua. You may go."

Once Murua was gone, Carra Carre stared hard at her sister. "My Sis, what is this, eh?" She didn't like secrets. She was still the First of the Vine, and decisions still had to go through her. "Tell me."

"I tell Murua and her NoBe to look for na Mud."

"Na Mud . . . ?" Carra Carre frowned. "Why?"

The South was large. Carra Carre couldn't imagine how a girl from another Fam could ever find the Vine camp, and she assumed the other camps were equally hidden. Even if a girl knew exactly where to look, she would be tracked and turned away the moment she entered Vine territory, long before she reached the camp itself. Why would the Mud even waste the effort?

Verdi kept her gaze out over the camp, where a mass of NoBe and Bibi had gathered to watch little Jaldi attempt the Climb again. The "test of fear" that so few girls even attempted. She was persistent, that one. She would make a great Sis someday.

"My Sis," Verdi said, "if I can show you what na Gods show me . . ." She shook her head, and for a moment her face bore an uncommon expression. Not doubt–Verdi didn't have a single seed of doubt anywhere in her considerable mind or body. But perhaps hesitation. Caution. "When na Mamas and Papas come, we must have na army ready for them. All na Bower united as one Fam. One Second. One First."

Verdi turned to stare at her with such intensity in her eyes that Carra Carre had to keep herself from leaning away.

"I understand," Carra Carre replied. "So I must defeat Dirt."

"And so you will. But we cannot let na silly Bow decide na future. This fight will not take place in na Grand Temple."

She will attack na Mud camp, Carra Carre realized with horror. Murua and the NoBe weren't out looking for the Mud sisters. They were looking for the Mud camp.

An attack on another Fam's camp would be a breach of tradition so severe that Carra Carre didn't even know what the consequences could be. She could barely stomach the depths they'd already gone to for victory. There was no way she could allow full war against another Fam. There was no honor in that. Problems between Bowers were meant to be settled in the ring.

"My Sis . . . ," Carra Carre began. "We cannot."

"We can," Verdi said. "We must."

"Do you not believe I will defeat her in na ring?"

"You will win. You never lose."

"So why–"

Verdi stood so abruptly that Carra Carre sucked in a breath, fearful that her sister would plummet off the platform. But Verdi stood balanced on its edge, fearless.

And in that one second, it was immediately clear the difference between them. Everything Carra Carre did was because of fear. Everything Verdi did was because of fearlessness.

It didn't matter who was the First. The leader of the Vine was clear.

Down in the camp below, Jaldi, not even a quarter of the way up, fell from the Climb.

"Breathe easy, Little Cee Cee," Verdi said, stretching her arms out wide, buffeted by the wind. "And remember na *why.* We will eat na chicken. We will not toss it."

Carra Carre took a long, slow breath. Verdi's fearlessness had built the Vine. Was now, with so much at stake, the time to oppose it? She had to trust her sister. She had to ignore the sinking feeling in her stomach, the morbid certainty that the path ahead would end in disaster.

"But first," Verdi said. "We must kill it."

27

Snore Makes a Friend

"BIBI NANA," Snore said, "why–"

"Shhh!" Nana put a finger over her lips, her head cocked toward the sleep hut.

"Bibi Naaaanaaaaaaaa, I wanna–"

"Shh, Snore! I cannot hear!"

They were crouched in the garden, just behind the sleep hut. The big sisters were inside, talking in quiet voices. Snore didn't know what they were talking about, but she didn't see why it mattered anyway. They never talked about anything fun. Sis Webba used to, when she wasn't broken, and NoBe Swoo did sometimes, after someone won a fight. But big sisters were just boring people. A simple truth.

Now even Nana was boring. Instead of playing (it was a perfect day for playing–no fights, no Offer to gather, nothing), she was trying to listen to a bunch of old ladies talk. What about running through the jungle? What about climbing trees? What about making Bower dolls from brush and palm twine?

When Snore demanded that Nana play with her (she stomped in a circle around her, chanting, "Bibi Nana, les us play!"), Nana became upset and started talking about something Snore didn't care about.

"Carra Carre is na True Godskin," Bibi Nana said. "Before, Sis Dirt can defeat Carra Carre easyeasy, but now maybe she will lose. And if she lose, na Mud Fam will vanish because Sis Dirt will soon go be na woman and na Mud will only have four. A Fam must have five sisters."

Snore stared. It all sounded very boring, except one part. "Vanish?" she asked, intrigued. She imagined a gekko vanishing into the leaves. That seemed fun.

"Not like na gekko," Bibi Nana said absently. Then she frowned, like she wasn't sure if she was saying something good or bad. "If Carra Carre is na True Godskin . . . maybe na Gods do not want na Mud Fam to be. Maybe na Gods want us to go . . ." She was quiet for a bit, then looked at Snore again. "You understand, eh?"

"I must make poopoo," Snore said.

She stood and headed for the trees, leaving Bibi Nana to her listening. She didn't have to poop, but if Bibi Nana didn't want to play, then she would play on her own.

So she went on an adventure. A special mission for the Gods. Right away, she found Papa Oduma Himself waiting for her not far into the jungle. "Bibi Snore," He said, His face swirling into existence in the trunk of a tree, "na big Sis are very boring. Even Nana."

Snore nodded. Finally, someone understood her.

"My strongstrong Bibi Snore," He continued, "I need you to figh my enemy."

"Papa 'DooDoo," Snore said, kneeling in respect. "I will figh for you. Who is na enemy?"

"Na moskiki," He said. "Chaaaiii, they are here!"

A swarm of mosquitos appeared around Snore, each one as big as Sis Dirt, each standing on two legs like a human. Snore immediately began fighting, Slapping the insect monsters so hard they exploded, Trapping them until they split in half in an explosion of monster goo, Bowing them onto their heads and feeling them crush flat beneath her.

They were no match for her, and after a short time she stood panting, covered in mosquito bits but filled with power. Then she heard a buzzing, one that grew louder and louder until it felt like it was in her head. Beside her, several trees toppled over, and from behind them came the Queen of the Mosquitos.

"Na Moskiki Quueeen!" Snore howled, jumping into battle.

But she froze as she heard a delicate whine.

That wasn't part of the adventure.

Her imaginary world melted away–the trees unfelled, the mosquito queen popped out of existence, Papa Oduma's face turned back into the tree trunk. She heard the soft whine again, followed by a sharp hiss. The jungle was Snore's favorite place, and she knew all its sounds.

Especially animal sounds.

She ran toward them, stopping to take cover behind a thick tree. Ahead of her was the sight she'd expected: a jungle cat cub, back reared, fur raised, ready to fight. Across from it was a baby poke-poke, with its snout narrow and back full of long quills.

The poke-poke was trying to keep its back to the cat, but the cat darted around to the animal's face, hissing and swiping a furry, harmless paw. It was the poke-poke that was whining. It kept calling for help as it tried to escape, but the cat continued blocking its prey.

Well, that wasn't very nice.

"You!" Snore shouted, and both animals turned to her.

Snore strode forward, stepping between the two and facing down the cub, her back to the poke-poke. She squatted, extended her hands to show she was unarmed. The Bowing salute. Though she was a young Bibi, she was still a Bower and a sister of the Mud Fam. She had to represent her Fam with honor.

The cub blinked as Snore took up her Bowing stance.

"Come and figh me!" she barked.

The cub lunged. Snore startled and closed her eyes, trying to Slap its nose but missing. It barreled into her, both of them toppling to the jungle floor in a tumble of skin and fur. All her Bowing training scattered from her mind as she latched her hands onto the animal's face and tried to tear its cheeks off. In return, the cub latched its blunt-toothed bite around one of Snore's pigtails, thrashing its head back and forth.

After nearly a minute of cheek tugging and hair gnawing, both parties were tired. Snore let go first, then the cat followed soon after. They sat and stared at each other until Snore reached out and placed her hand on the cub's head.

"Nubbi," she said. It was a good name.

It let out a feeble yelp, closed its eyes, and brushed its head against Snore's hand.

Snore knew Sis Dirt wouldn't let her keep the cub, but Nubbi was her friend now and friends were the third most important thing in life: (1) sleep, (2) play, (3) friends.

So she made a silent vow.

Every morning, while the other sisters were sleeping, she would come back and play with Nubbi. By the time the other sisters realized what she was up to, she would be at least as big as Sis Webba, and then she wouldn't need their permission.

It was a perfect plan.

"Good plan, eh?" Snore asked.

Nubbi purred her agreement.

28

Sisters and their Secrets

6 Days until the Dream Fight

SWOO WAS the first one up.

She liked the feeling of a new day, when it was just her and the world. Even the sun was still asleep, rubbing its eyes and yawning awake.

In the center of the ring, she stood in her Bowing stance, Slapping slowly and carefully. She focused on the clench and release of each muscle, the air drawing in and out of her body. People were always impressed by her speed, but few knew that her secret was slow training. The body can't do fast what it can't do slow. As a Bibi, she'd wake up before the rest of the Fam and spend each morning moving as slowly as she could through the four movements of Bowing. With all the added responsibilities of being a NoBe, she appreciated the rare morning she could get back to the training that had made her.

And think. The best part of a new day was that she could think in peace.

Carra Carre loomed in her mind. Large and heaving, filled with the power of the Gods, challenging Sis Dirt from a leg's length away. Yet Sis Dirt had done nothing. No, less than nothing. She'd stayed in her seat, cowed by a superior girl.

Pathetic.

After the Mud Fam had returned to the tent, Sis Dirt claimed that something was wrong with her powers. She claimed that she'd tried to find the silence and challenge Carra Carre, but it hadn't worked.

Swoo didn't care. It didn't take divine power to stand up when challenged. When Carra Carre broke Sis Webba, Swoo charged into battle without hesitation, not caring that she was only a NoBe challenging the reigning God Bow champion. It didn't take the favor of the Gods to be brave.

But Sis Dirt, of course, was a coward.

Swoo sank down into a Ride as slowly as she could, muscles tight and shaking. She let out a long, stabilizing exhale.

It should've been Swoo. Win or lose, she would have fought fearlessly. Even if Sis Dirt won the next-round fight against Dream, she would inevitably face Carra Carre, and her cowardice would bring the end of the Mud Fam.

Then what?

Swoo had to start thinking about the future.

She would never join the Vine, even if they invited her. But she had three other options. The Creek would take her. Wing would love to mentor another skilled Rider, and Swoo could only imagine the tricks Wing could show her. The Sand had few NoBe, and could use another.

But the Rock would be the best fit. They were good girls with big bellies, who danced and laughed as well as they fought. More importantly, they were similar to the Mud. They were a small Fam, and they were in need of a Rider like Swoo, which meant she would stand out. Good. She didn't want to just be another NoBe at another Fam. She wanted to be great. The greatest Bower in the South, for as many seasons as the Mamas and Papas would allow. Every moment she spent with this dying Mud Fam put her further from the greatness she deserved.

She had to leave.

Swoo continued moving through her training, slowly but powerfully, like a river over rocks. As she finished the sequence, she bent as far into a Back Bow as she could. Then her weight took over, and the top of her head settled into the soft sand.

That was when, upside down, she saw Nana walking out of the trees toward the sleep hut, a clay bowl in her hand. She froze, wide-eyed, under Swoo's gaze.

"Nana," Swoo said.

Nana stared back. She looked scared, even for her. "Na good day, NoBe Swoo."

"Na good day." Swoo swung her legs up over her head into a headstand, wincing from the strain of weight on her neck, until her feet came back over to the ground. She stood upright and took in the sight of her sister. Why was there mud all over her hands? "Where you go, eh?"

Nana first shook her head, then shrugged. "I go make peepee."

"In na bowl?"

Just then a head poked out of the sleep hut door. Sis Dirt peered out, face half hidden by the door. She surveyed the area for a moment before spying Swoo and Nana. Then she disappeared into the sleep hut and came out a few seconds later wearing a thin strip of white cloth bound to her right cheek. An apparent injury from the Wing fight.

"Na good day, my sisters," she said.

"Na good day, Sis Dirt," Nana and Swoo said together.

"I must make peepee," Sis Dirt said before anyone asked. Why was she carrying a canvas bag with her to go pee? "Where is Snore?" she asked suddenly.

Swoo shrugged. Snore had still been sleeping when Swoo left the hut.

"I don't see her sleeping this morning," Nana said. So Snore must have snuck out after Swoo but before Nana. That girl was a master of doing what she wasn't supposed to do.

Just then, there was a rustling in the nearby trees, and all three sisters spun toward it, falling into their Bowing stances.

Snore came tumbling out of the thicket, giggling madly as she and a jungle cat cub climbed over each other. They rolled across the ground, pushing and pawing, carrying on all the way to the ring. They only stopped when they bumped into Swoo's leg.

Snore immediately scrambled to her feet, eyes wide as she looked at her sisters. The cub, still in play, hopped onto Snore's shoulder, teeth tugging the youngest Mud sister's ear. Slowly, it realized playtime was over.

"Na good day, sissers," Little Snore said with as much formality as she had ever shown.

"Na good day, Snore," Nana and Sis Dirt said in unison.

"Does this Fam not sleep?" Swoo asked, exasperated.

"Little Snore," Sis Dirt said, "Where do you go, eh?"

"I go . . . make peepee."

"Eh heh. And what is this jungle cat you have?"

Snore stared for a moment, and Swoo could see the thoughts running through the little girl's diabolical mind. Should she lie? Should she cry and apologize and hope Sis Dirt would take pity on her? Should she throw a preemptive tantrum and demand to keep it? Should she just go to the hut and go back to sleep?

None of those. She tilted her chin up and took a long, smug blink.

"She is Nubbi," she said with a haughty "hmph," then skipped clumsily over to the sleep hut, Nubbi bouncing alongside her in confusion.

Nana hurried after Snore, back to the sleep hut. Sis Dirt went out into the jungle to relieve herself–or do whatever she intended to do with that canvas bag. Soon, Swoo was alone again, and she felt a heaviness in her stomach.

For all their tiring strangeness, she loved her sisters. She'd give anything for her sisters, for the Mud. She never wanted to leave them.

But she had to. And she had to leave soon.

29

Face Paint

5 Days until the Dream Fight

WEBBA SAID there was no problem.

She said it was no surprise that Carra Carre had been chosen. She said the Mamas and Papas often rewarded those who didn't seem to deserve it. She said that it was okay Dirt had been caught off guard by her challenge. She said that Dirt had still been chosen for a reason. That she was still a True Godskin.

Webba said a lot of things.

But Dirt knew better.

The Gods had chosen another skin. And Dirt knew why.

She just couldn't tell her sisters.

The previous day, Dirt had woken early to conceal her Scarring. She rose just before the sun and rushed out into the jungle to the edge of the nearby stream. There, she stared at her reflection in the water, at the deep black groove cut into her face, its endlessly shifting dark, its cold flames. The pain was gone. At least the physical pain. But looking at her face, the face of a woman, hurt her heart in a way she'd never imagined. That Scar was a reminder that whether she told her sisters or not, she was no longer one of them. She was no longer a sister of the Mud Fam. At least Ebe was Antie Yaya's helper. Dirt was nothing, no one.

After that first day, Dirt knew the bandage she'd planned to use would no longer work. What sort of cut could Wing have caused that would bleed for days? She could sense that the other sisters were already getting suspicious. Little Snore kept trying to pull it off, convinced Dirt was hiding something fun under it, and Swoo seemed to be waking up even earlier than usual, trying to catch whatever secret it was she thought Dirt was hiding.

At least it felt that way. She couldn't be sure if her sisters were actually starting to watch her more closely or if she was just losing her wits to paranoia.

Either way, she was driven to a method she never in her life thought she'd consider: face paint. She had a small canvas bag that she kept hidden in her spare clothes, filled with all her face painting tools. At the stream, she mixed pale brown Mud Offer with scorched tree ash until it formed a dark brown paste that matched the color of her face. Then she'd use a flower stem to apply it and a brush formed from short grass to smooth it into her skin.

It was humiliating work. As she did it, she almost wished her sisters would discover her, so that they could banish her to Antie Yaya's. Even that would've been more dignifying than painting her face like a Mosquito girl.

But her sisters never came. And so after painting over her Scarring and checking her reflection in the stream, she would return to camp with her breath held, terrified that each of her sisters could see right through the paint.

And there her sisters would be to greet her with warm smiles and quick embraces.

Dirt considered just telling them. What did it matter now that she wasn't going to win the tournament? At least if she told them, they could prepare for the coming end of the Fam.

She considered telling them, but when she saw the hope in Webba's eyes, she couldn't. She just couldn't bring herself to steal that hope from her sisters. All she'd ever wanted was to make the Fam bigger, happier, more stable. Telling them would do the opposite of that.

So in the days leading up to the Dream fight, Dirt trained as hard as ever.

"Na Whip Slap," Webba instructed. "One hundred times."

Dirt stood in the center of the ring and performed the Whip Slap. No problem.

"What is this?" Webba asked. "Na *Spear*."

She knew Webba wanted her to make quiet. Webba wanted her to draw on her power as a Godskin. But she wasn't a Godskin. She was a woman.

I am brave. I am fat. I . . . I am . . . She tried, but each word flickered in her mind with the image of Carra Carre standing over her, eyes radiating heat, overflowing with the power of the Gods. And with the image came fear. And with the fear came all of Useyi's Whispers.

If she were so brave, why did she cower when Carra Carre challenged her? If she were so fat, why had she faltered against Wing, and even given up a Bow? What did it matter if she was

Dirt? Dirt was a woman now, not a Bower at all, much less a God-skin.

Even though she could recognize the thoughts as Useyi's, she couldn't do anything to dissolve them.

She tried the Whip Slap again, and it was just a Whip Slap.

Swoo let out a short bark of laughter, as if a bitter truth had been confirmed. But Webba looked at Dirt in utter bewilderment, like she'd grown an eye in the center of her neck. Then her face softened.

"Your head is loudloud, eh? Take your time, my sister."

Time wouldn't help, but Dirt pretended it would. With each passing day, she failed to make her mind quiet, but each day she told Webba she was feeling better and better. To help her make quiet, Webba had her do more of those strange drills: counting birds, sitting on trees, standing on anthills.

"Sis Dirt."

Nana held a cup of water in her face. Afternoon training had just ended, and she'd only received two ant bites. She sat in the ring, trying not to scratch the two angry swells of skin.

"Thank you, my sister." Dirt took the cup and paid Nana with a brief rub of the head. Swoo was gone, off on another run. Snore's loud slumber issued from the sleep hut. Webba was off behind the tree line, relieving herself.

It was just Dirt and Nana, yet Dirt was still a little surprised when Nana sat down beside her.

Not long ago, Dirt's main role had been Nana's teacher. The girl was thin but strong, with a natural sense of balance that was better than even Swoo's. She and Nana used to talk all the time about the Fam and Bowing and life. But since Webba's injury and the tournament, Dirt's role had changed. She no longer knew what was going through the Bibi's head.

"Sis Dirt," Nana said, an uncommon focus on her face, "what will you do when you cannot be na Bower?"

Dirt felt a rush of heat to her face before she realized the question was harmless. Nana couldn't know about her Scarring, and if she did, she wouldn't be so bold as to ask. Something else was on the girl's mind.

"Nana . . . you call me old, eh?" Dirt joked.

Nana didn't smile. She still stared off at nothing. "Can na Bow be all of life, Sis Dirt? No other thing?"

"What other thing?"

"Maybe . . ." She glanced at Dirt, then averted her eyes. "Can you be na But–Mosquito girl?"

Dirt blinked. She hadn't expected that, and it took her a moment to understand what was really being asked. The poor girl was scared, and it was Dirt's fault. The younger sisters were depending on her to win the tournament, but between Carra Carre's powers and Dirt's inability to summon her own, they must have been starting to fear for their future.

"My Bibi," Dirt said, "you can be na Bower as long as you like. Understand? Soon, you will become na NoBe, and some day you will be na Sis. More fat than your Sis Dirt. More fat than your Sis Webba."

Dirt put her arm around the girl's narrow shoulders, brought her close. Swoo was returning from her run. Webba was just coming back from the jungle, moving carefully on her crutches. Snore was stumbling blearily out of the sleep hut, rubbing her eyes awake with one hand and dragging Nubbi along the ground with the other.

Their private moment was over. Dirt climbed to her feet, ready to return to training.

"Breathe easy, my sister. I will punish Carra Carre," she said, hoping Nana would believe what she herself didn't.

30

The Gekko and the Guava

1 Day until the Dream Fight

EACH DAY of the week seemed to crawl, full of suspicion and paranoia and shame. But the week as a whole seemed to disappear in a blink, and suddenly Dirt found herself a day away from another tournament fight.

The final day of training went well, even with Webba pushing her hard and Swoo being Swoo. When the training was done, the Mud retreated to the sleep hut to prepare thirdmeal. Dirt sat exhausted but relaxed in the sleep hut as the Bibi prepared the meal and spread it out before her. While she was making her way through the platters of fish and vegetables and pounded yam, the Bibi were putting on a show.

"Give me na meat!" Snore shouted.

"Never!" Nana responded, giggling.

They wrestled around the cramped sleep hut. Not like Bowers, but like two Flagga boys who didn't know push from pull, tumbling all over each other. On one occasion, they even fell against Swoo, who shoved them away with a mixture of irritation and amusement.

Dirt couldn't make sense of the story, but she enjoyed watching it. Nana was happy again. Webba was smiling. Swoo and Snore were in a playful mood. Dirt's week of reassuring lies had finally worked. They had come to believe she could win, with or without the favor of the Gods. That was why they could dance and eat and laugh so freely. The gift of the strong was to let others take peace in their strength. For so long, Webba had been the one to give them that gift, and now it was Dirt's turn.

Maybe it didn't matter that her strength was a lie.

Snore and Nana reached a point in the show where the characters were forgotten. The Bibi faced each other and began playing an old clapping game called the Gekko and the Guava, singing the game's song, swaying their hips in time, and clapping a complex series of claps.

Papa 'Duma, my sister sleep
She sleep until her belly shrink
And when she wake, she go and eat
Na Gekko and na Guava!

After the first verse, Webba scrambled to her feet, forgoing her crutches in favor of just hopping up on one leg and joining the Bibi. She looked comically large next to the tiny Bibi, and had to hunch her shoulders to keep her head from pressing up against the sleep hut roof. Snore and Nana laughed madly at Webba's grinning participation, and they transitioned smoothly into a three-person clapping pattern, singing and swaying together.

Papa Abi, my sister cry
She cry until her eye go dry
And when we ask, she no know why
Na Gekko and na Guava!

"Look at these legless chickens dance!" Swoo said, sucking her teeth but unable to hide her smile as she got to her feet. There was a roar of glee as she joined, and as they all clapped the next verse, they stole moments to look at Dirt. They goaded her with glances and grins until, finally, she stood and joined on the final verse, clapping and singing and swaying like she was a Bibi again.

Mama Eghi, my sister win
She win and make na dance begin
And when we dance, we shake and spin
Na Gekko and na Guava!

They all dissolved into puddles of laughter, collapsing to the soft wood of the sleep hut floor, limbs all entwined. Soon the chorus of her sisters' easy breaths—and Snore's rough, rumbly ones—filled Dirt's ears as they all drifted off to sleep. She remained awake for a bit longer, unable to remove the smile from her face.

Carra Carre was waiting, yes. But Dirt couldn't think about that yet. First she had to fight Dream. And she would win, because she had to.

Because the Mud was worth it.

31

Sis Dirt vs. Sis Dream

DIRT STOOD with her sisters in the main entrance of the Grand Temple, heavy in her Godskin. She'd spent the morning reviewing her strategy with Webba. Her fight against Dream would be Slapper against Slapper, and Slapping was a game of finesse, a game of cleverness. It wouldn't matter as much that Dirt wasn't as young or as strong as her opponent.

I'm ready, she told herself.

But before her own fight, there was the other seminal match: Carra Carre versus Hollo, the First of the Rock. Hollo and her sisters entered the arena to more fanfare than usual. Even though they left a hole in their formation where Nat would have been, they danced as cheerfully as ever, doing their best to put on a show for the crowd.

"How is Sis Nat, eh?" Webba asked.

"Badbad," Swoo said. "Carra Carre break her back. Na Rock take her to Antie Yaya to heal."

Webba exhaled in a way that made Dirt look over at her. Her jaw was tight, tilted up at an angle that Dirt hadn't seen since they were children. Anger. A bubbling, violent rage. She wanted revenge, Dirt knew. Both for what Carra Carre had done to her leg, and the revenge of a competitor, to have a second chance at a foe who had bested her, no matter how cravenly.

Dirt put a hand on the back of Webba's neck, gave her a supportive pat and rub. Webba didn't look at her, but she exhaled again and there was an easing of tension around her jaw and shoulders.

Webba's burdens were Dirt's now. She had to do what her sister no longer could.

Carra Carre and the Vine marched into the arena with a confidence they didn't deserve, pounding their chests like a gang of foolish Bibi. They weren't Bowers, they were bullies, building their empire on the pain of other girls.

"I hate them," Swoo said.

"It is," Webba added bitterly.

Carra Carre strode into the ring to meet Hollo, and the two exchanged salutes before settling into their Bowing stances. The timekeeper turned over the sand, and the fight was on.

When Carra Carre was finished crushing Hollo into unconsciousness, the Rock Fam rushed their First out of the arena, calling out for any Bonemenders. As they passed by the Mud, Dirt's heart seized at the sight of Hollo, the terrifying dangle of her legs, the impossible bend in her spine.

Dirt realized that she was shaking. Not out of fear, but out of anger. With each win, the Vine only got more arrogant, more ruthless and destructive. It had to end.

"You will show them, my sister," Webba said. "Breathe easy. You will show them who you are."

Dirt took a long, calming breath. She'd never been more ready for a fight.

From within the arena came a low rumbling of drums and an anticipatory murmur from the crowd. It was time.

"Who are you?" Webba asked as the younger sisters fell in line behind Dirt.

"I am Dirt."

"Ripe?"

"Riperipe."

As they entered, some fans rose to their feet, cheering wildly and singing along to the Mud anthem as Dirt and her sisters danced across the hot arena sand. Some stayed in their seats, a look of skepticism or even outright disgust on their faces. Most of the crowd, though, leaned forward, excited but cautious, unsure of what to expect but ready to enjoy it.

Soon questions would be answered, and rumors would be quelled. Was Carra Carre truly the new Godskin? Had the Mamas and Papas chosen a new champion? Or had Sis Dirt been a fraud the whole time?

Just as the Mud reached the far side of the Grand Temple, the Sand entered. They rushed in together like a sudden storm, fifty girls spreading out into a circle and singing to the sky, their voices mixing as freely as the grains of sand along their beachside home. Dream led the song, her sisters responding in tune.

When I call my Sand sisters, all my sisters answer me!

(Answer me, eeeey eeeey eey!)
And with all my Sand sisters, we will fight na
enemy!
(Enemy, eeeey, eeeey, eey!)

As they sang, one girl twirled a quick circle, then another, then another. In no discernible pattern, the girls spun like the many winking eyes of some friendly beast. The randomness made it all the more beautiful, a visual delight that drew cheers when a few of the girls happened to twirl at the same time.

They ended with a flourish, each girl grabbing two hands of sand and tossing them into the air, then bowing their heads as the grains rained upon them.

"Chaaaiii, look at Sis Dream dance, eh?" Swoo exclaimed, admiration on her face. And then, after a long pause, added in an unconvincing voice, "But Sis Dirt will win, maybe."

It was as much of a compliment as Dirt could hope for.

With the song done and the dancing finished, Dirt stepped into the ring across from Dream. The First of the Sand was short and compact, with legs as thick as storm clouds. She wore her hair in a single braid down her back like a great brown snake. Her Godskin was simple, clean; multicolored cloth braided around each thigh, woven cloth covers on each of her fingers and toes, and a glistening blend of oil and white sand–the Sand Offer–spread over her skin, twinkling like stars against a brown sky.

Most Bowers considered Dream the best Slapper in the South. But, as a fellow Slapper, Dirt wasn't as impressed. Her Slapping was flawed; there just weren't any other elite Slappers to take advantage of it. Other than Dirt.

As the two girls faced off in the ring, Dream's eyes were sharp, unwavering. Dirt felt a rush of uncertainty that made her want to look away, but she forced herself to stare directly into Dream's eyes. She saw a wildness there. A desperation.

Then they backed away from each other and performed the Bower salute. Dirt took up her stance and the hourglass was unstoppered.

"Bow begin!"

Dirt tried to make quiet. Useyi's Whispers surged in her mind, but she spoke firmly against them.

I am brave. I am fat. I am Dirt.

As she looked at Dream, she felt the Whispers fading for the first time in a week, and she dared to hope that maybe she'd been wrong. Maybe the Gods hadn't abandoned her.

But over Dream's shoulder, far off and hazy in the sandy arena, Dirt saw a girl wearing a vine mask. She couldn't tell who the girl was or even whether she was a Bower or just a costumed fan, but the sight of her made Dirt think of Carra Carre again. Carra Carre the Godskin.

Useyi's Whispers burst anew across her every thought.

Dream prowled forward, cautious and cunning. Her eyes were wide and attentive, her muscles clenched, veins bulging along the surface of her skin. She was treating Dirt like a snake, like one mistake could be the end.

Her slow approach gave Dirt time to refocus. She didn't need the Gods to defeat Dream. She hadn't expected their power anyway.

She began lightly Slapping the air, and Dream immediately dived to the side, rolled dramatically, and sprung back to her feet. Confused laughter rippled through the crowd, but Dream didn't seem to have done it for their amusement. Her eyes were heavy on Dirt.

Dirt, confused, took a step forward. Dream bounced away. Dirt raised her hands for another Slap and Dream dived to the side again, rolling, then jumping back up to her feet. Dirt watched it all with disbelief, and almost joined the crowd's laughter as she realized what was happening.

Dream was terrified.

It was obvious now. She was skittish, clearly expecting every Slap to be a Spear and every Ride to be too fast for her eyes to track. She must have spent the last week training to fight the divine. Dirt almost felt bad for her.

But the ring wasn't the place for feelings.

Dirt charged forward with a feinted Ride, backing Dream to the edge of the ring. Once Dream's feet touched the sandbags, however, the Sand champion panicked and instinct took over. She sprang forward, catching Dirt by surprise with a firm Trap and an immediate Bow.

But Dirt had spent the last few weeks getting Bowed endlessly, so she didn't even have to think as she shifted her weight, throwing Dream to the side and landing on her.

"Counter!" The timekeeper raised a finger.

It was only one point, and a clumsy point at that. But it was a point that Dirt herself had scored. Against one of the South's elite Bowers, the First of her Fam. And Dirt had done it not with the power of the Gods, but with her own power. She took the moment on the ground to overcome her disbelief, to accept that she could actually beat Dream. She was going to win.

The crowd saw things differently. A buzz swept through them as they began to realize that something was wrong with Dirt's powers—after all, Dream hadn't been sent flying out of the arena.

When the fight resumed, Dirt took the center of the ring, throwing out Slap after Slap in a broken rhythm to keep Dream guessing and on the retreat. On several occasions, she almost Pushed Dream out. But each time the Sand sister flung herself away from the ring's edge. The crowd loved the tension, inhaling in unison each time Dirt cornered her opponent, then cheering wildly each time Dream escaped.

By half sand, Dirt could see that Dream was getting tired. Not just from the fight, but from the fear. Being afraid is exhausting, and her arms were starting to lower, her feet starting to slide out of stance. Dirt continued to counter her Slaps and wear her down, careful not to get Trapped again.

Dream ducked under Dirt's attempted Push and crawled frantically away from the edge of the ring before scrambling back to her feet. Then she Slapped twice, quickly. To Dirt, they looked like regular Slaps, just a measure of distance to keep her away.

Too late she saw the sand fly from Dream's hands, and by the time she thought to move her head, searing pain blinded her, blackening the world. She screamed, one hand flying to rub her eyes, the other shooting out stiff as she spun wildly around, trying to defend herself against an opponent she couldn't see. She spun and spun, stumbling about the sand. She just needed to get a hand on Dream, to grab and hold the girl until her eyes cleared.

There was a wave of outraged noise from the crowd, then a voice that Dirt knew too well shouted curses from the depths of her chest.

"NA SWINGING BUCK!"

Then the sound of flesh smacking into flesh. Bodies thudding onto the ground. Dirt staggered around, still trying to clear her eyes as snarls and grunts and more curses filled the air.

Finally, she managed to open one eye, only to find Swoo sitting atop Dream, a fist raised in the air and a face full of fury. Just then, a wave of Sand sisters washed over the NoBe, grabbing her arms and feet, pulling her away.

"You CHEAT!" Swoo howled, kicking her feet, thrashing her head, biting the hands that held her. "You throw sand in my sister's eyes, you breezy cheat!"

The commotion continued until Pusher boys began jumping down to the Temple grounds to free Swoo and separate the two Fam. Swoo stalked back and forth in front of a row of peacekeeping Pusher boys, shouting profanities at the Sand. The Sand sisters were out of their minds with rage. The indignity of a NoBe attacking their First was too much to bear, and it took a few hundred Pusher boys to keep them from tearing Swoo apart.

The Mosquito-girl timekeeper trotted around the madness to get to Dirt, peering hard at her face. "Can you see?" she asked.

If Dirt said yes, the match would continue, but she didn't think she could fight well with one eye. If she said no, the match would end, and the winner would be determined by points: a coward's way to win.

She needed time. So she didn't answer.

The timekeeper held her hand in front of Dirt's left eye, three fingers up.

"How many?" she asked.

After some hesitation, Dirt said, "Three."

The timekeeper tucked her fingers down, then raised what looked like three fingers again.

"How many?"

Dirt blinked rapidly, then rubbed her damaged eye, only to wince from the grind of sand beneath her eyelid. "Three?!"

The timekeeper gave her a pitied look, then turned away to address the audience.

"No!" Dirt screamed.

Unfortunately, the girl didn't listen.

"Sis Dirt of na Mud cannot fight," she said. "Na Bow is ended!"

32

Growing Apart

JEERS AND HISSES rained down from the crowd. There was no more singing and dancing, no more smiles. Only outrage.

"Na lie! Skinnyskinny Dirt!"

"Breezy Dirt!"

"Na fake Godskin!"

Dirt realized that even fans in the closest seats may not have been able to see the sand fly into her eyes. They must have believed that Dirt was faking it. That she was ending the match because she was too scared to fight without the power of the Gods.

The timekeeper raised her arms for quiet, turning a slow circle so all could see that she had an announcement to make. The crowd hushed itself.

"Sis Dream of na Sand cheat," the timekeeper said, and the crowd exploded again with jeers and hisses, especially the Sand fans. Dream herself, standing among her sisters, just shrugged. She knew what she'd done. A Pusher boy had to retrieve a speaking cone for the timekeeper so that she could speak over the crowd. "So na Bow is finished. Na winner, one point against zero"—the timekeeper extended a hand out toward Dirt—"is Sis Dirt of na Mud!"

The arena rumbled, a mix of the Mud fans' cheering and the rest of the audience's displeasure. Swoo helped Dirt to her feet, and under the rage of the audience, the Mud left the Grand Temple.

There was no celebration when they returned to camp.

When she beat Verdi, Dirt got some small revenge for Webba and, more importantly, discovered her Godskin powers. In her fight with Wing, she'd grown in her power, gained better control of it, and sent a message that the defeat of Verdi wasn't a one-time thing.

But this victory was meaningless. The rules, not Dirt, had beaten Dream. She hadn't gotten any revenge, she hadn't grown in her power, she hadn't sent a message to the other Fam. And to top it off, a shameful fight had broken out between the Mud and Sand, souring the relationship between the Fam. The Bow would be recorded as a win, but on the path to defeating Carra Carre and ensuring the survival of the Fam, it was several steps backward.

And her sisters knew it.

Swoo had leftover rage from her one-woman battle against the Sand, and she let it spill over onto Dirt. That night, she stewed silently, helping the Bibi prepare thirdmeal but not speaking to anyone. The next day, Webba had everyone take the day off from training, for Dirt's eye to recover. But Swoo went out running anyway, disappearing in the morning and not returning until well into the afternoon. When they ate, Swoo was silent, but Dirt would occasionally feel the younger girl's eyes on her and look up to find Swoo glaring.

But it wasn't just Swoo.

Nana seemed uncharacteristically distant. That first night, when Snore asked her to put on one of their shows, she laughed nervously and looked away. It hadn't seemed so strange then, with all the post-fight tension, but she declined again the next day, and the next. Dirt spied her frequently staring into the woods, as if something from across the Isle were calling out to her and it took everything she had to not get up and go to it.

But it wasn't just Swoo and Nana.

The night of the fight, Webba had been her usual self. She was full of grins and congratulations, praising Dirt for her victory. "Every win is na blessing." But she woke the next morning somber, told everyone to take the day off, then spent most of it sleeping. Or at least appearing to. Dirt knew Webba well enough to know what her breathing sounded like when she was asleep. Though Webba's eyes were closed, her breathing was casual, as if she were still awake. But when Dirt called her name, she didn't respond.

Then the next day, Webba seemed a different person entirely. She was already up by the time Dirt returned from covering up her Scarring. She stood in the center of the ring, teeth gritted, straightening her broken leg so that her foot touched the ground. She tried to lean on it, but winced and shifted her weight away. Then she tried again, and again, each time flinching against the pain, but each time putting more weight on the injury.

"Strong move, my Sis," Dirt called out, and Webba seemed to startle. Dirt couldn't remember ever seeing Webba startle. Instead of flashing her usual grin or even wearing her pain plain on her face, Webba just stared back without expression.

"Today na training day," she said. "Wake Swoo and na Bibi."

That day was as challenging as any Dirt had experienced since the beginning of the tournament. Webba barked orders, one after another in a constant stream, demanding that Dirt adjust every ounce of her weight, ensuring that not a single toe was curled that should have been straight. Even when Dirt was confident she'd done a technique flawlessly, Webba found something to correct. If Dirt was unable to instantly fix her mistake, Webba found some physical punishment. Press-ups. Boulder lifts. Another round of sparring with Swoo.

At the day's end, as the sunlight yawned violet over the treetops, Dirt fell to a knee in the center of the ring. A hundred aches and shallow scratches crisscrossed her body. She was dripping sweat. Her head was ringing from the Bow, and she was so exhausted she wasn't even scared over whether all that hard sparring had rubbed the face paint off her Scarring, exposing her.

Webba didn't have words of criticism or encouragement. "Go and rest" was all she said.

They ate thirdmeal in near silence, Dirt too tired to speak and the other sisters seeming to sense Webba's mood. As Dirt lay down for bed, she wanted to say something. A joke. An apology. Even just "na good sleep, my sisters."

But she didn't say anything. Nor did her sisters.

She'd always dreamed of the Mud Fam being the biggest Fam in the South, with Webba as its champion and her at Webba's side. For years, they'd worked toward that dream, only to have it dashed in just a few weeks. Whatever faith the Mud sisters had placed in Dirt before the fight was gone. None of them said it, but not a single one of them believed she would beat Carra Carre. Not even Dirt.

Not even Webba.

Instead of Dirt's dream, her nightmare had come true. The end of the Fam she loved so much.

And they all knew it.

For the first time in their lives, the Mud Fam drifted off to sleep without a sound.

33

What Sleeps in the Jungle?

4 Days until the Carra Carre Fight

BIG SISTERS could be so weird.

Snore didn't always know what was going on with them, but she knew it was weird. Sometimes Bowing was fun, like when they got to hug each other and throw each other and fall in the sand. Sometimes it was boring, like when they had to run and pick up heavy rocks and talk. The big sisters spent all week doing the not-fun stuff more than the fun stuff.

Very weird.

The big sisters were so focused that they didn't notice Snore was gone all day. Or maybe they just thought she was with Bibi Nana, but Bibi Nana was becoming weird, too, even though she wasn't very big yet. Sometimes Bibi Nana would sneak out of the camp and not tell anyone where she was going.

So it was just Snore. Snore and Nubbi.

Together, they prowled the jungle, the two of them pouncing

on every bug, swiping at every mosquito, climbing every low branch, eating every sweetberry. They fell asleep a lot, too, dozing off against the base of a tree—or inside it, if there was space and no one else living in it.

It was on their third nap, late in the afternoon, that Snore woke because she thought she heard something. That was normal for her. Sometimes she woke herself up with her snoring. But this didn't sound like a snore. It sounded like movement.

Snore stood, Nubbi blinking awake beside her.

"Bibi Nubbi, do you hear?" she asked the cub.

Nubbi looked up at her but didn't stir.

Snore heard it again. A rustle above her in the impenetrable web of thick branches and feathered leaves. She took up her Bowing stance and turned a slow circle, eyes wide and ears open. Nubbi jumped to stand beside her, snarling this way and that.

This time, Snore didn't hear a thing.

But she saw something. Two dark eyes, not twenty strides away, peeking from amidst a fray of fern leaves and drooping vines.

Snore froze in her Slapping, hands out in the air. A breathless fear tightened her chest in a way she'd never felt from all the snakes and jungle cats she'd seen in her short life. This was different.

Bibi Nana would've screamed.

But Snore just turned, scooped up Nubbi, and ran as hard as she could back to camp.

34

Butterflies and Bowers

"NANA?"

The call came through the trees. Apple's voice.

"Here!" Nana called back, standing and dusting herself off.

This far into the jungle, it was hard to find specific places to meet. But Nana and Apple had managed to think of a clearing they both knew, about an hour east of Antie Yaya's.

As Apple emerged from the thicket, the first thing Nana noticed was the string of round, orange beads around her wrist.

"You are wearing it!" she squealed.

Apple raised her wrist. "How can I not?" She showed it off proudly.

Nana had worked hard to make that bracelet for Apple. She'd been sneaking away from the camp to gather and carve the stones where her sisters couldn't see. It felt so good to see someone wear and appreciate something she'd made with her own hands.

She hugged her friend, the first hug she'd given or received in a while. That felt good too.

"Are you ready?" Apple asked when they separated. "Did you bring na Offer?"

Nana nodded, patting the cloth bag slung over her shoulder. The clay bowl of Mud Offer gave a muffled clunk.

Apple's eyes lit up. "Good. So we go."

Their trip through the jungle was more play than trek. They talked about all kinds of silly things, giggled and chased each other around tree trunks, and stopped to pick flowers to put in each other's hair.

It was such a pleasant difference from the tense mood at the Mud camp. Things had often been difficult since the God Bow tournament started, but once Dream threw the sand into Sis Dirt's eyes, Nana had known it would get worse. Chaos. Screaming. Fighting. Blood.

And for what? Nana had always liked the Sand girls. They were friendly and they danced well and their Godskins were very pretty. Now they were her enemies.

Bowers liked to make fun of Butterfly girls, but Butterfly girls didn't fight each other like animals and walk around with broken arms and knotted heads. Butterfly girls learned more than just how to hurt people—they learned how to create. To serve others. To make the Isle a better place.

Butterfly girls had a better life.

By the time Nana and Apple emerged from the tree line, Nana had almost forgotten where they were going.

But then she saw Pretty.

They were far away from any of the Bowing territories, firmly in Butterfly land. The dark, sweaty jungle behind them gave way to a crisp blue sky, with a field of tall grass sloping down to a narrow brook. Pretty and her girls were over by the water, with a large basin of dirty clothes sitting among them. Two of the girls, the twin-like Lily and Rose, were washing blouses in the water, passing a brick of soap back and forth. Pom, with her mismatched colors, was adjusting a clothesline that extended down from a nearby tree, making room for more clothes to dry while young Mimi frolicked beside her.

Pretty wasn't working beside the others. She lounged in the grass, head against a soft log, telling stories.

"One Flagga boy say to me, 'Pretty, my brother say he love you. But I say I love you. So who do you love?' So you know what I tell him?"

"What do you tell him?" Lily and Rose asked in unison.

"I tell him—wait. Mimi!" She extended her hand, pointing at a bowl of mixed fruit just barely beyond her reach. At Pretty's command, little Mimi left her place beside Pom and ran over to the bowl. She handed it to Pretty, then was shooed away.

"I tell him"—Pretty paused for drama, looking side to side as if she were about to tell a secret. Then she struck a pose, framing her face between her arms—"'I love *me*!'"

Cackling laughter, first from Pretty, then from the other girls.

"How now, Butterfly?" Apple called, grinning as she walked down the slope toward the other girls.

"Apple! Now finefine!"

"Now fine!"

Nana followed at a distance, staying near the top of the slope. Pretty made her feel uneasy.

"You bring na Bower girl, eh?" Pretty said, waving. Even her wave was beautiful. "How now, Bower girl?"

"Her name is Nana," Apple said.

"I bring na Offer," Nana said. Could the other girls hear the shake in her voice?

Pretty extended her arms out, fingers wiggling. The twins left their laundry and ran to Pretty's call, each grabbing an arm and pulling her to her feet. She took a moment to smooth her dress—a beautiful flower-print top that left her shoulders bare, poofed at the arms, and flowed down past her knees—before walking up the slope to Nana.

Pretty walked a slow circle around Nana. Nana hated the girl's theatrics, but she stayed silent.

"You do not understand, Bower girl," Pretty said. "Offer is nothing. Just na . . . eh . . ."

"Symbol?" Pom offered.

"Symbol. To show you will trade Bower for Butterfly. Fam for Butterfly. Everything for Butterfly."

Nana knew that. She'd always known that. But hearing it out loud set her heart bumping with doubt.

She couldn't leave the Mud Fam. Leave her sisters, who had raised her and loved her all her life? Who had taught her everything she knew and lived by? Especially Sis Dirt, who had fought so hard to win the tournament for them? If she left, the Mud would only have four sisters. That wasn't enough. It would mean the end of the Fam, even if Sis Webba healed soon.

She couldn't do it.

But she still found herself reaching into the bag and pulling out the bowl. She removed the top to reveal the creamy beige Mud Offer within.

Pretty froze, eyes stuck on the Mud Offer. The Mud regularly traded with Butterfly girls, so she must have seen it plenty of times before. But the look in her eyes was still a hungry one. A possessive one. Nana didn't like it.

"Speak my words," Pretty said suddenly, eyes snapping up to Nana's. "I want to be na Butterfly."

Nana swallowed. She looked to Apple, who was beaming, then back to Pretty's dark, hungry gaze.

She wasn't meant to be a Bower. She never had been. Her sisters would understand, she told herself.

They would understand.

"'I want to be na Butterfly,'" she repeated.

And once she said it, she felt all the guilt leave her. She felt light. Buoyant.

"I do not want to be na Bower."

"'I do not want to be na Bower.'"

"Butterfly are skinny."

"'Butterfly are skinny.'"

"Butterfly are beautiful."

"'Butterfly are beautiful.'"

"Butterfly are, eh . . ."

"Poised," Pom offered.

"Poised."

"'Butterfly are poised.'"

"But Bower are fat," Pretty said with a strange sneer.

"'But Bower are fat,'" Nana repeated, proudly.

"And way ugly."

Nana blinked, frowned to herself. That wasn't true at all. "'And way ugly.'"

"And rubbish."

"Pretty . . . ," Apple said, frowning.

"Speak my words!" Pretty demanded.

"'And . . . rubbish.'"

"Fat, ugly, rubbish."

The feeling of lightness disappeared in an instant. Each word sank heavier into Nana's gut. "'Fat, ugly, rubbish.'"

Pretty's face was all triumph. "Na mud." She extended her hand. "Give me."

"You are bad, Pretty," Apple said, her voice flat and sad. "Way bad."

Nana didn't quite understand what was going on, but it seemed that the oath was over, at least. She extended the bowl forward.

Pretty's hand came up fast. Nana saw it coming—years of Bowing training made her hard to surprise. But it was fast enough that by the time Nana realized it was an attack, it was too late. Pretty smacked the bowl into Nana's face, a pale brown spray across her eyes, into her nostrils and hair.

Then there was laughter. Squealing, wheezing laughter. So gleeful and proud.

Even then, Nana didn't understand. She looked at Pretty through watery eyes, trying her hardest to keep her composure. She focused on her breathing to stay calm.

"Am . . . am I na Butterfly now?"

They only laughed harder. The twins were doubled over against each other, each keeping the other from laughing herself to the ground. Pom's laugh was loud and clipped, like a dog's bark. Mimi let out an unrestrained gale of laughter, checked to ensure the other girls were still laughing, then continued. Pretty had one hand across her belly and the other hand pointing a finger in Nana's face.

Then Nana understood.

She turned to Apple first, who was glaring at Pretty. But all she did was glare. She didn't say anything, didn't do anything.

Nana then looked at Pretty, whose pointed finger had a smear of Mud Offer on it. She pushed the finger away from her face.

Pretty kept laughing. She brought her finger up again, but Nana Slapped it away, then Slapped again, slamming her palm down on Pretty's shoulder.

The laughter stopped.

Pretty's face squeezed into something entirely unpretty. She raised her finger again, this time pushing it directly at Nana's nose.

"You fatfat Bowe–"

Nana dropped low and Rode forward, catching Pretty around the stomach and driving the breath out of her lungs. She secured a Trap, arms wrapped tight, then burst upward, hauling the Butterfly girl off her feet. Pretty put up a flailing resistance, but she was slow and skinny and untrained. Nana tossed her down the hill as easily as she would've thrown Snore, the other girls watching in wide-mouthed shock. Pretty slammed into the earth a half dozen strides down the slope, then tumbled over stones and dirt clods before splashing into the marshy soil by the brook's bank.

By then, Nana was already running back through the jungle, stumbling over roots as she navigated through weepy eyes. She ran almost the entire way home, ignoring the pain in her lungs as much as the pain in her heart.

She was unaware of the eyes watching her every step.

35

Sis Dirt vs. NoBe Swoo

DIRT SAT with her back against the rough wood of the sleep hut, staring into the jungle. Out in the dark, gekko chirped—*yrrrree yrrrree*—and the branches swayed in slow unison with the breeze. Swoo and the Bibi were preparing thirdmeal, the heat of their cookfire warming the air. Webba had fallen asleep in the hut, a respite from the flaring pain in her leg.

There was a cloud of exhaustion around the camp as each girl struggled to carry her own burden. Webba's smile had been rare all week. Swoo was being quiet rather than her usual argumentative self. Nana seemed on the verge of tears and flinched whenever she was called. Even Little Snore, normally so carefree, sometimes stared out into the jungle like she was afraid of something out there, fingers gripped in Nubbi's fur.

"Sis Dirr."

Little Snore skipped over, dragging poor Nubbi along the ground by a paw. She hadn't yet learned that you couldn't carry a cub the same way you carried a doll.

"Sis Dirr, thirdmeal ready."

Dirt took a deep breath. She imagined, out in the dark of the jungle, another version of herself that lived on another mud plot, in another part of the South. There was no God Bow tournament for that Dirt. No Carra Carre. No Gods coming in and out of her life. No impending end of her Fam. Just eating and dancing and laughing and Bowing with her sisters.

"Sis Dirr?" Snore asked, head tilted. Nubbi shook out of Snore's grip and climbed into Dirt's lap, nuzzling her belly.

"I will come," Dirt said, exhaling. She scooped up Nubbi, took Snore's hand, and walked into the sleep hut.

The blanket spread over the center of the room was piled with food: platters of jollof rice, tomato-and-pepper soup, shredded papaya with chili and peanuts, chunks of chicken, and grilled plantains. All of them fresh, their scents twirling into the nose with each inhale.

Dirt set Nubbi down and took a seat beside Webba, patting her sister gently awake. Webba yawned and looked around at everyone as she scooted up to a seated position.

"Let us eat" was all she said.

It was another silent meal. They passed dishes around, ate their fill, and stared at each other while avoiding stares in turn. When the food was finished, the Bibi cleared the dishes, then lay on the floor atop their sleep mats.

"No show, eh?" Dirt asked.

For a moment, Snore brightened. She raised her eyebrows and looked over at Nana. But when Nana didn't respond, Snore scrunched her nose in disappointment.

"Let us play," Dirt suggested, standing. She herself didn't much want to play, but she couldn't just let them all slide deeper and deeper into gloom. "Na Gekko and na Guava."

This time, even Snore didn't respond.

Dirt took Nana by the arm and dragged her to her feet. She set the girl's feet in position, raised her hands.

"Up, Snore," Dirt said.

Snore stood.

"Eh heh," Dirt said. She clapped, then extended a palm for Nana.

"Sis Dirt," Nana said, eyes downcast. "I . . . I do not want to play."

"Why, eh?"

Nana didn't speak for a moment, then shrugged.

"No why? Good. So you can play. Snore?"

Snore looked to Webba, who was staring off into nothing, then to Swoo, whose gaze was stonily on Dirt. With neither responding, she put her hands out, ready to play.

"Papa 'Duma, my sister–" Dirt began, but a tear streaming down Nana's cheek stopped her.

"Nana, what is it?"

Nana fell to the ground, brought her knees to her chest, and covered her face in her hands. Snore abandoned the game to sit down beside her.

"Bibi Nana, are you afraid?" Snore asked.

Dirt stood alone in the center of the room. "It is na game, Little Snore. She cannot be afraid of na game."

"She is not afraid of na game, you sandy swine," Swoo said.

Dirt rounded on the NoBe. "I do not ask you, NoBe–"

"You cannot make quiet." Swoo's voice was accusatory. "That is why Nana is afraid. You cannot become na Godskin, so you cannot defeat Carra Carre."

"I can try–"

"Sis Webba cannot fight. I cannot fight. Nana cannot fight. Little Snore cannot fight." She stabbed a finger at Dirt. "Only *you* can fight," she spat, face twisted with contempt. Then she looked away as if she wanted to throw up. "So we are afraid. Na Mud is finished."

The wall torch fluttered from a sudden gust. Out in the dark, gekko chirped. Dirt watched as Nana's tiny body shook, as Snore's blank face scrunched in concern, as Webba's shoulders fell.

Dirt could remember the Bush family. She remembered intimidating their Bibi, competing against their NoBe, talking with Webba about how their Sis would do against the Mud Sis at the time. Even though she'd watched their numbers dwindle over the years, it had seemed so sudden when the Bush Fam finally disappeared. From the outside, they had looked like their usual, confident selves. Was this what it had looked like from within? A quiet misery, hopeless and hostile? Sisters injured and angry, arguing with each other, unable to look each other in the eye?

Was this the end?

"Webba will heal," Dirt countered. "When she heals, na Mud–"

"Who do you lie to?" Swoo said. "Us? Or yourself?"

"I do not lie."

"Another lie."

"Mind your mouth, Swoo."

"And if I do not?" Swoo leapt to her feet, temper boiling, veins straining against her neck. "Bigbig Sis Dirt, eh? Cannot fight Carra Carre, but can fight NoBe Swoo."

"I will fight Carra Carre."

"And lose, you breezy goat," she said. "Because na Gods favor you, but you are too breezy to see it. You think we are blind, eh? You think we are all fools to believe na Gods abandon you? Why? If you are no more na Godskin, speak why!" She stopped pacing, awaiting Dirt's answer.

Dirt knew why the Gods had abandoned her. She'd hoped to wait until after the tournament to reveal it to her family. But what did it matter now?

She opened her mouth to tell them the truth. Then she froze. She remembered the fear in the eyes of Sis Prom, their previous First. She remembered her face as she fled the hut that day, never to be seen again. The shame. Sis Prom had known what would happen if she told her Mud sisters about her Scarring. She wouldn't be one of them anymore. They would have looked at her like they looked at Mosquito girls, shunned her until she left the camp, as they had to the Scarred Sis before her. Sis Prom had never been a great Bower, but she was wise. Better to disappear in the night as the First of the Fam, the Mud champion, than to stand in shame before the sisters she loved so much.

Dirt couldn't bear to see her sisters realize that she wasn't one of them anymore.

"No why, eh? Then let me speak it." Swoo leaned closer, speaking directly into Dirt's ear. "You are na coward."

"You are afraid for na Mud, eh?" Dirt fired back, turning to look the NoBe in the eyes. "That is why you attack Dream?"

Swoo pulled back, rage and confusion warring across her face.

Dirt was done being nice. She was done playing peacemaker.

Everything was always about Swoo. Calming her, appeasing her recklessness and emotions. Season after season, Dirt held her tongue, ignoring the bad influence Swoo had on the Bibi. Meanwhile, Swoo and her ego did nothing but ruin the reputation of the Fam that Dirt and Webba had built.

No more.

"You worry na Mud will be no more," she said, "so you go and fight Dream? Maybe na Rock will see you and think you fatfat, eh?"

For a quick moment, Swoo looked away in embarrassment, confirming Dirt's suspicion. But only for a moment.

"I . . . ," she retorted, heat flooding her face. "I attack Dream for na Mud!"

"Na Mud?! Chaaaiii!" Swoo had Mama Ijiri's own arrogance. "Who is na Mud? *You* attack Carra Carre. *You* attack Dream. And if na Vine fights back, eh? Na Sand? You will fight them all, eh? Fight all girls and trees and monkeys in na South. Bravebrave NoBe Swoo! Bigbig belly Swoo!" Dirt shook her head. "No. You attack Dream for yourself!"

Those who didn't know Swoo thought she was angry when she yelled, but it wasn't true. Yelling was normal for Swoo. It was when she was quiet that her true anger came out.

"Every Bower," she said in a low, calm voice that rattled from the shake in her chest, "every Flagga, every Pusher, every swinging Mosquito in na South will remember Swoo." She bit her lip, as if she were trying to keep her next words in. But she changed her mind. "But you are weak, you saggy branch. You give nothing to na Mud. You sacrifice *nothing* for na Mud. I will not remember you. None will remember you."

To be forgotten was to become Useyi's for all eternity. There was no graver insult.

All the rage seemed to rush out of Swoo, leaving only emptiness. She stared at Dirt like Dirt was nothing to her. Like she was looking at a Mosquito girl.

Then she left the hut, stepping over a still-weeping Nana and out into the dark.

"My Sis," Webba said.

You are weak. You are scared. You are Dirt.

Dirt collected herself, then turned, ready to enjoy Webba's calming warmth and the gaze of someone who still looked at her like she was a sister of the Mud.

Except Webba wasn't looking at her. She had her good knee up, an elbow propped on it, her hand on her forehead.

"Webba?"

"For many years, you believe in me. When everything is wrong, you believe. Always. And it is enough." She raised her face, and her eyes were cold. They didn't look like Webba's eyes at all. "But when I choose you and not NoBe Swoo, it is not enough. When I speak that you are great, it is not enough. Na Mud needs na Godskin. *You* are na Godskin. But you are too afraid to be great. I believe in you, my Sis. I will always believe." She shook her head. "But it is not enough."

Dirt blinked once. Twice. Then a third time as tears began to burn at her eyes. Then everything began to fail. Her breathing became shallow and runny, her lips quivered, her stomach turned over and over itself, and her heart ripped in two as easily and messily as overripe fruit. A single tear escaped her eye, trailing down her cheek, and she immediately wiped it away.

How could everything be so horrible?

Then Nana screamed, panic in her voice. "Sis Dirt, your face!"

Everything in Dirt's body seized up as she realized what she'd done. She looked down at her hand, at her fingers that had just wiped her tear away, and saw a brown smear of face paint.

36

Mama Ijiri and the Mountain

NANA LOOKED between Sis Dirt and Sis Webba, confusion and terror bubbling up within her.

Then Sis Dirt ran. She crashed through the sleep hut door, out into the night, leaving dust and silence behind her.

Nana had seen Sis Webba angry. She'd seen Sis Webba sad. She'd seen Sis Webba surprised and confused and, of course, happy.

But she'd never seen Sis Webba scared.

The First of the Mud was still staring at the sleep hut door even after Sis Dirt had left, her face slack, her eyes empty. Nana couldn't tell if she was breathing.

"What is na cut on Sis Dirt's face?" Nana asked, failing to keep her voice from shaking. She knew the answer to her question, but she wanted it to be anything else. A cut caused when doing chores. An injury from training with Swoo. Anything but what it was.

But she'd never seen an injury like it. That deep black gorge, shifting like leaves in a pitch-black night.

Sis Webba looked over at Nana and Snore, and their presence seemed to startle her, snapping her out of her daze. "Breathe easy, Nana."

"But . . . Sis Dirt has na Scarring. Why, Sis Webba?"

Sis Webba bit her lip, clearly uncertain. "Because she is na woman."

"Sis Dirr is na woman?" Snore asked.

"So she must go?" Nana added.

"Yes, but . . ." Sis Webba shook her head. "Breathe easy, young Bibi. Everything is finefine."

But Nana knew that was a lie. Everything was very much not finefine. Sis Dirt had to leave. NoBe Swoo was gone. Even if she came back when she calmed down, she had never left the Fam before. Not like that. Something had been broken that couldn't be fixed.

Even Little Snore seemed to understand something severe had happened. She took Nubbi into her lap, stroking her fur. "No more Mud Fam, Nubbi," she said. "Now we are na Little Snore Fam."

"We are still na Mud Fam," Sis Webba said with a gentle smile. "Today, we are."

Nana felt new tears sting her eyes. She hated crying in front of her sisters. She always did it, but she knew it just made her look weak. Then they consoled her and she only felt weaker.

Webba extended her arms out. "Come, my sweet Bibi. Come, come."

Despite her desire to appear strong, Nana rushed into Sis Webba's arms. Her big sister's warm body was always so comforting. Her rolls of thick fat were soft as a cloud, and her belly had a calming, empty sound when Nana put her ear to it, like the inside of a conch.

"You know na story of Mama Ijiri and na mountain?"

Nana loved Mama Ijiri stories. Unlike aggressive Papa Oduma stories or scary Useyi stories, Mama Ijiri stories were always funny and clever.

But she hadn't heard this one. She shook her head. Snore did the same.

"Eh heh." Sis Webba cleared her throat. "Long ago, Mama Ijiri wants to walk across na Isle. She walks for many moons, until one day a bigbig mountain is in Her path. It is so wide She cannot go around, so high She cannot see na top. So clever Mama Ijiri makes na fire to burn down na whole mountain. Na mountain burns but does not go away. Then She takes na bamboo stick and fills it with lightning from na sky. She throws na stick at na mountain and BOOM!" Sis Webba clapped her hands together, making Nana jump and Snore giggle with pleasure. "But na mountain is finefine. So Mama Ijiri then digs a deepdeep hole all around na mountain, so that it will fall and na earth will swallow it. But no matter how deep She digs, na mountain is deeper."

She paused and put her hands in her lap, as if the story were over.

"Go on! Go on!" Snore cried.

Sis Webba smiled. "You want to know?"

They nodded eagerly. Nana didn't care how the story ended. Just hearing Sis Webba's voice made her feel calm, made her feel like the fight between NoBe Swoo and Sis Dirt had only ever been in her imagination.

"So Mama Ijiri does nothing," Webba said. She pursed her lips, eyebrows bent sadly. "She sits down and says, 'I try my best, great mountain, but I cannot move you.' And then, with na bigbig shake, na mountain stands up and walks away."

Silence.

Nana blinked. "Sis Webba, is na story finished?"

"Finished. Do you understand?"

She shook her head.

Sis Webba let out a long, tired sigh. "Scar or no Scar, na Mamas and Papas choose Sis Dirt. She is na True Godskin. Na greatest Bower in na South. But she will only believe when she is ready. If Mama Ijiri cannot move na mountain"—her voice dropped to a soft murmur, as if she were speaking to herself—"how can I?"

Just then, footfalls sounded outside the hut. Nana looked up, hopeful that Sis Dirt or NoBe Swoo were returning.

But she felt Sis Webba's muscles tense. Nubbi squirmed out of Snore's arms and growled at the door, fur standing on end. As Nana listened, she heard more than one pair of feet. More than two. More than ten.

The footfalls came to a sudden stop and a voice called out to them, "Na Mud! Come out! And bring your sister Dirt!"

37

A Visit from the Vine

2 Days until the Carra Carre Fight

NANA OPENED the sleep hut door for Sis Webba but stayed behind it. Sis Webba didn't spare a glance back at her younger sisters, but she did mutter a message before crutching out into the night.

"Go and hide," she said.

As soon as the door closed, Nana took Snore, who had Nubbi under an armpit, and ran to the back corner of the sleep hut. There, she pushed out a small section of the wall. They squeezed through the opening, out into the cricketing dark, then rushed over to huddle in a bushy thicket on the edge of the jungle. Nana stayed hidden in the tree line, but crept around until she had a full view of the camp.

Sis Webba stood just in front of the sleep hut, leaned casually on her crutches. Across from her, in the ring, at least a dozen Vine sisters stood in a V formation, all their heads wrapped in vines. Verdi was in the center, unmistakable even without her Godskin, her violet eyes reflecting the moonlight.

"Nana–" Snore began, but Nana clamped a hand over the girl's mouth. They needed to stay quiet.

"A good night, Sis Verdi," Sis Webba said.

Verdi's eyes roved the camp. "Where is Dirt?"

"*Sis* Dirt," Webba replied, "is not here."

"So go and bring her."

Sis Webba smiled. "You find us, eh? How?"

"We watch," Verdi said. "We listen. We follow. You Mud are not careful."

"'Na mouse walks with fear where na cat runs with pride.'"

Verdi was silent for a moment, anger visible in the narrowing of her eyes. "Move yourself, Webba. We will search your camp."

"Na tournament is soon. If you want Sis Dirt, you will see her."

"There will be no tournament."

Nana frowned. What did Verdi mean by that?

Sis Webba raised an eyebrow. "Eh heh . . ."

"I know you can feel it." Verdi's voice was suddenly a sharp hiss. She spread her arms out wide and looked up at the night sky. "Na Gods. They are *here*. They come to make this world new. And They choose us, na Bower, to lead Their children. *All* Their children." She dropped her hands, leveled her gaze at Sis Webba. "Na Vine will unite na South. Na whole Isle. We will be one Fam, and Carra Carre will be First of na First, and na Gods will let us lead Their new world. Your Dirt cannot stop this."

"So you are afraid," Sis Webba said calmly. "You fear you cannot defeat Dirt in na ring, eh? You know all na South will see my Sis crush na Vine, so you must defeat her here, eh? With these very loyal dogs?" She gestured to all the Vine girls standing at attention. "Bravebrave, Verdi."

Verdi's eyes narrowed again behind her mask. She raised a hand and the group of Vine Sis with her fell into Bowing stances.

Snore pulled Nana's hand down from her mouth and whispered, more quietly than Nana had ever heard her.

"Nana, someone is behind me."

As soon as Snore said it, Nana could feel another presence. She turned her head slowly and saw the dark shape of a Vine sister huddled in the night a few strides behind them. Then she turned back, suppressing the bone-chilling scream she felt well up within her. Screaming wouldn't do anything but tell the rest of the Vine where they were. She wrapped her arms firmly and protectively around Snore. She had to be strong.

"It is fine," she whispered back, hiding her fear. "Sis Webba will come."

When Webba didn't react to the Vine Sis in their Bowing stances, Verdi raised her voice. "One more time will I say this—move yourself, Webba!"

Sis Webba crutched forward a step and all the Vine sisters stiffened. "As you can see, Verdi, I cannot move so well. You will have to move me."

Silence.

Then one of the Vine sisters, probably a young Sis trying to impress the older ones, stepped forward, confidently approaching Sis Webba.

Sis Webba's crutch whipped up into the girl's head, exploding against her skull in a burst of wood. The second crutch came up immediately after, bashing the next nearest Vine sister in the belly hard enough to double her over and snap the crutch in half.

Sis Webba dropped the remaining shards of wood in her hands

and took up a one-legged Bowing stance, balanced effortlessly.

The rest of the Vine sisters charged in. Sis Webba Trapped the first girl around the waist and swung her around to smash the next in the face. She Front Bowed the next girl into the earth, dropping all her weight onto the girl's jaw, then she rolled forward to her feet, ducked a Slap, Trapped another girl from behind, and Back Bowed her onto her neck. Even as the Vine surrounded her and landed blow after blow, she continued to flow from one attacker to the next. She seemed to be in five places at once, flashing here and there between slashes of moonlight, dispatching each girl with brutal efficiency.

Nana had spent years watching Sis Webba train, but she'd never seen her move so perfectly, with such power and speed and precision. When it came to Bowing in the ring, Sis Webba fought strategically, with a goal of winning. But this wasn't a Bow. This wasn't the Grand Temple, and there was no timekeeper. Here, Sis Webba's only goal was to destroy.

And she was good at it.

More than half of the Vine sisters were laid out in varying states of injury and unconsciousness by the time Verdi called a halt to the fight.

"Stop!" She looked at her fallen sisters, disgust in her voice. "Even broken, Webba, you are strong."

"Too strong, eh?" Webba said, grinning. She was glistening with sweat, breathing heavy, sporting bruises all over, and cradling two fingers that bent unnaturally at their joints. It was clear she couldn't keep up the fighting much longer.

Then Verdi raised a fist and another twenty Vine sisters emerged from the jungle to take the spots of the fallen.

"Eh heh. Too strong." Verdi's violet eyes flared. "We must break you more. Murua!"

Sis Webba's eyes widened and she sprung forward into action, plowing into another Vine sister as the others closed in on her.

Nana felt movement behind her, then strong, calloused hands clamped down on her shoulders.

"Breathe easy, little Bibi," a voice said.

Instinctively, she froze. That was always her reaction, to stay put and wait for the big sisters to save them.

But NoBe Swoo was gone. Sis Dirt was gone. And Sis Webba was tired on one leg, fighting the Vine by herself. No one was going to save them. Nana was the big sister now.

She raised her foot and stamped it down on the foot of their Vine captor, but all that earned was a chuckle. "If you do not fight, we–"

So Nana snapped her head back, relieved yet disgusted by the crunch of bone and pained grunt she earned for it. The hands fell away from her shoulders.

"I am sorry!" she shouted. "Snore, run!"

They sped away, running through the trees in no particular direction, concerned only with fleeing. Feet pounded after them, but it was dark, and they knew the jungle around camp better than anyone. When they managed to create enough distance from their pursuer, Nana led them to a tree with a knob near the bottom, one they'd climbed hundreds of times.

"Up, Snore! Up, up, up!"

With Nubbi in her hands, Snore struggled to climb. Nana had to push her up, climb after her, then push her up again to the higher branches until they were several strides above the ground, hidden among the foliage. The Vine sister who had been chasing them came into view shortly after, rustling slowly through the jungle, peering around in the dark. Nana let out a relieved breath as the girl continued on past their tree without thinking to look up.

From that high up, Nana had a clear view of Sis Webba. She was restrained between four Vine Sis, bloodied and battered, lips swollen, one eye blackened. Her head hung down on her chest, and it seemed to take all her energy just to stay upright.

"Nubbi!" Snore exclaimed.

Nana looked over to find Nubbi bounding down the tree branches, growling once she hit the ground and charging toward Webba. Snore slid down after the cat, too quickly for Nana to catch her.

"Snore!" Nana hissed, but her sister was already jumping down from the tree.

Nubbi dived at one of the Vine girls, sinking baby teeth into her knee and slashing short claws across her calf. The Vine sister gave her leg a strong shake that sent the cub flying across the sand, where Snore scooped her up, staring angrily at the Vine.

For a moment, Nana considered jumping down to get Snore. If she could get to her sister fast enough, they could make another run for the jungle and lose themselves among the trees.

But more Vine sisters appeared. One snatched Nubbi out of Snore's hands while another hauled Snore up by the arms, her two small wrists trapped in the Vine girl's single meaty palm. Several of the sisters eyed Snore's tiny footprints, their eyes following them until they were lost in the dark of the jungle. Nana pressed herself flat against a branch, trying to make herself invisible.

NoBe Swoo would fight them. Sis Webba already had. But Nana

couldn't do it. She couldn't even breathe. She'd already tried to save Snore once and she'd failed. She wasn't a fighter like the others. She didn't even like Bowing.

She just wanted to make bracelets.

At the sight of Snore in the Vine sister's hands, Sis Webba raged with renewed strength, flinging one of the restraining Vine sisters half across the camp before two more rushed to hold her in place.

"You and I, Verdi!" Sis Webba snarled. "Leave na Bibi out. If you win, na Mud will surrender. You and I. Sis and Sis!"

Verdi stared for a long, quiet moment.

"This is fair, Webba. Way fairfair." She waved her hand and the Vine sisters released Sis Webba, who stumbled, teetering on her one good leg before managing to take up a Bowing stance.

Verdi was one of the best Bowers in the South. Even if Sis Webba were at full health, it would be a close fight. As injured and beaten as she was, Sis Webba had no chance, and she knew it.

"Wait . . . ," Verdi said. "Sis and Sis, yes. But you are na First of na Mud. I am only na Second. This is not fair." She turned and walked away. "Cee Cee!"

Carra Carre sped out of the darkness like a bat swooping through the night, steaming with the power of the Gods. Sis Webba reacted, Slapping twice at Carra Carre's chest. But she was too slow, too weak. Carra Carre Rode in, Trapped Sis Webba around the waist, and hauled her effortlessly into the air. All of Webba's punches were mosquito bites, and Carra Carre's head was a mountain. The First of the Vine didn't seem to even know she has being struck as she rolled Sis Webba in her hands, turning her face to the sky.

Then she brought her down.

Nana would never forget the way Sis Webba's head snapped to

her chest from the sudden drop. The way Carra Carre brought her knee up, hard and fast. The grinding sound of knee against spine, and the stunned and terrible exhale from Sis Webba.

The terrifying dangle of Sis Webba's legs, her spine so destroyed that they were no longer in her control.

Sis Webba's eyes rolled back into her head. Her whole body went limp. Carra Carre tossed her across the camp, sending her crashing into the sleep hut in a clatter of wood.

Then there was only wind, a light breeze traveling indifferent across the clearing. None of the Vine sisters cheered or whooped. Even Snore and Nubbi were silent, staring wide-eyed at the shattered sleep hut and their shattered sister sprawled among its remains.

Nana kept a hand tight over her mouth, stifling her horrified sobs.

"Young Bibi," Verdi called out, turning a slow circle so that she could be heard from any angle. "You have seen what you have seen. Tell you sister Dirt. Tell her na Vine will wait for her surrender."

38

The Wisdom of Antie Yaya

HOURS HAD PASSED since Dirt fell asleep in the jungle. She decided that she'd rather be among the spiders and jungle cats and angry, territorial monkeys than let her sisters see her weep. In exchange, she'd earned the most painful sleep of her life, her whole body burning with bites and aches.

Yet that pain was nothing. Nothing at all compared to the pain in her heart.

Her sisters had seen her Scarring. Her life as a Bower was over. She would never see Webba again.

She felt sick.

Overhead, the sky was at its darkest, and Eghodo's Eye twinkled above, marking North. She couldn't go back to camp, and it didn't make sense to spend the rest of the night in the jungle. So she climbed to her feet, gathered her bearings, and began the journey to the only place left for her: Antie Yaya's.

With her sisters around her, the jungle had always been home. But alone, this deep into the night, the jungle was a nightmare, all dancing shadows and distant shrieks and errant, ghostly brushes across her arms. Even the trees became her enemies. Their branches danced in the breeze, seeming to grab for her when she wasn't looking and bludgeon her with their dangling fruit.

When she finally reached the edge of the tree line and looked out over Antie Yaya's compound, she exhaled a deep and shaky breath.

Dirt had never been to Antie Yaya's outside of Prayers. She was taken aback by the emptiness. This late, there weren't even many Mosquito girls out, just a few of them up chatting or sneaking a late-night snack. There were none of the young recruits out–they must have been sleeping. As Dirt made her way across the stone bridge, she received raised eyebrows and reproachful sucking of the teeth. Normally, Mosquito girls treaded fearfully around Bowers, especially a full Sis. But they could all see Dirt's Scarring. They knew she was no longer worthy of fear. Dirt would have enjoyed flinging Mosquitos from the bridge like rotten leaves, but they were right to disrespect her. She was no longer Dirt, the Second of the Mud. She was just a girl–a woman–and she had no right to walk among them.

She soon crossed the grass and arrived at the foot of Antie Yaya's palace, not far from the spot where she'd been sitting just weeks before, when she'd foolishly declared herself to be champion of the Mud.

Antie Yaya was slouched on her throne, eyes half-closed in sleep, a bowl of guava slices perched delicately on her armrest. Dirt wondered if the woman ever stood. Was that what a woman did? Sit in a chair all day, waiting for people to bring her food and wash her clothes and tell her what was happening in the world beyond her vision? Had she ever left her compound?

Dirt opened her mouth to speak, but a shush cut her off.

Ebe stood on the far side of the dais, back hunched, skin drooping in thick, puckered arcs. Her eyebrows were bent together in anger and she held a single upward finger to her lips.

"Don't bother, Ebe," Antie Yaya said. "I'm awake."

Antie Yaya was suddenly alert, staring down at Dirt, eyes glittering as she bit into a crispy slice of raw guava. She looked like a different woman since the last time Dirt had seen her. On the night of the Prayer, Antie Yaya had seemed split between two worlds, half in the heavens and half on the Isle. Now she seemed unified. The gaze she leveled at Dirt was endless and wise, the kind of look a tree would give a seed.

"Antie . . . ," Dirt said, mouth dry.

"Why are you here, Bower girl? Shouldn't you be out wrestling somewhere?"

Dirt swallowed. She couldn't speak in Antie Yaya's way, so she tried to be as clear as possible. "Antie, I come today because I am now na woman and–"

"Do you all talk like that?" Antie Yaya interrupted, taking a deep breath. "I thought it was just the skinny ones. Whatever you're going to say, make it quick."

"I . . ."

She didn't have it in her to say it again. It hurt too much.

Antie Yaya's eyebrows drew in tight for a moment, then raised lightly. "Oh, I see," she said. "Your face."

Dirt couldn't speak. It was shameful enough that her sisters had seen her Scarring, but now Antie Yaya herself was asking about it.

Antie Yaya rose suddenly. She turned and walked off into the dark rear of the dais, Ebe scrambling behind. "Bower girl, come with me."

This was it. Dirt looked back over her shoulder, back at the life she'd lived before, to her camp and her Fam and her sisters.

To Webba.

Then she turned and hurried up the stairs after Antie Yaya.

Dirt turned down narrow hallway after narrow hallway, doing her best to keep pace with Antie Yaya's quick steps. Dirt had never been in a stone structure before, and it made her feel uneasy, trapped. Along the walls, torches glowed every dozen strides, but between each one was a dark stretch that made Dirt want to hurry forward into the safe light of the next torch.

Not only did the light provide some small comfort in the strange building, but it revealed the wondrous art etched into every inch of the walls. Crowned people and tusked beasts and fiery mountains. Marriages and funerals and wars. An entire history was mapped out in the walls of Antie Yaya's palace, every story of the Mamas and the Papas and their creation of the Isle. Dirt recognized Papa Oduma by his tree trunk of a torso and the great, eye-shaped shield he carried. Papa Abidon always seemed to be laughing, drinking, surrounded by admirers, while Mama Ijiri was always solitary or moving among crowds with a mischievous smile.

Mama Eghi was the most impressive. She stood on mountain-tops, in crowded plazas, in sacred jungle clearings. She was always speaking. Her words changed the world around her, breathing life into those who listened. They turned desert into lush green, fruiting jungle into icy plains. She was always depicted with a crown as well, a resplendent cone that marked her divinity.

And every now and then, randomly appearing among the beautiful artwork was a pair of gnarled hands with sharp fingers. The disembodied hands hovered all throughout history, especially the battles and funerals, anywhere souls could be taken and hidden away from memory.

Useyi.

Dirt thought that if giving up her life as a Bower also meant she wouldn't have to feel Useyi's Whispers in her mind again, then maybe it wouldn't be so bad.

"How much of this do you know?"

Antie Yaya had stopped and was looking at the wall drawings. Dirt moved next to her.

"I know many stories. Sis Habbi tells us when we are Bibi. And Sis Prom when we are NoBe."

"Stories . . . ," Antie Yaya said, eyes glowing with torchlight. "He takes our memories, this one. Useyi. The God of Forgotten Memories. Do you know what that means?"

It seemed pretty straightforward to Dirt, but she suspected Antie Yaya wanted a more interesting answer. So she didn't respond.

"It's a paradox," Antie Yaya said. "If they are forgotten, they aren't memories." She reached out and traced a finger along a carving of Useyi's hands. "Your forgotten memories can only become someone else's stories. That's what all stories are. Memories others have forgotten."

A group of recruits suddenly spilled out of one of the various rooms that lined the hallways. They immediately looked up at Dirt, eyeing her with curiosity and fear.

She couldn't help but stare at them. They were so small. So unburdened. They were like Snore, but even more innocent and wide-eyed by the world. Some of them gave her a small smile. An especially brave one waved and muttered, "Na good day, Honored Sis," spurring a wave of giggles from the others.

"And look at this group," Antie Yaya said, turning from the wall drawings to corral the recruits back into their shared room. "If you all slept as much as you laughed, the world would be better for it."

Dirt realized that in just a few days those sweet girls would all be Vine sisters. She'd never understood before that the recruits needed the Mud as much as the Mud needed them. Now because of her failure, they would all soon be wearing vine masks and bullying the other girls of the South.

And she would just be a forgotten memory. Like Ebe.

A story for someone else to tell.

Dirt looked over at Ebe. The girl looked back without a hint of emotion in her face.

"Don't mind them," Antie Yaya said, returning to the hallway and striding toward their destination. "You have more important things to worry about."

"Sit," Antie Yaya said. "Ebe, draw a bath."

They were in a large room, empty but for a bed and a pair of cushioned chairs that were not unlike Antie Yaya's throne. A circle of torches hung from the ceiling, illuminating the room. The whole space smelled like flower petals.

Dirt fell into one of the chairs and went immediately rigid at the feel of the cushion against her. It was soft. Impossibly soft. She imagined someone plucking all the feathers off a bird and binding them in a bag. Only a madwoman would use feathers in such a way, but that was how the cushion felt.

"What is it?" Antie Yaya asked, sitting in the chair across from her.

"Na chair . . . how can it be so soft?" She squirmed in it a bit, raised herself up, and fell back down again.

"Feathers," she replied. "It's filled with feathers."

"Eh heh . . ." *Madmadwoman*, Dirt thought.

"Have you ever sat in a chair before?"

She'd sat in the stands of the Grand Temple before, but those were benches. And they didn't have feathers to cushion your bottom.

She realized that she must have been sitting wrong. Antie Yaya was leaned back, legs crossed. Dirt was hunched forward, knees wide, elbows on thighs. She refused to cross her legs like that–it was just impractical. But she slowly leaned back and did her best to mimic the older woman's ease.

Antie Yaya stared at her for a long moment before speaking.

"What's your name, Bower girl?"

"I am Dirt."

"I thought so." A corner of her mouth turned up in a crooked smile. "You're the Godskin."

"I . . . I am."

"You're all anyone talks about, even the skinny ones. 'Sis Dirt na Godskin! Sis Dirt na Godskin!' I hadn't expected you to be so small."

Dirt wasn't sure what to say about that. Now that she was sitting across from Antie Yaya, she realized the woman wasn't very big. A finger taller than Swoo maybe, and probably of similar weight. How big had she expected Dirt to be?

"So you've come to me about your womanhood?"

The change in conversation was jarring.

"Yes, Antie Yaya. I have my Scar." She gestured to her cheek. "I am na woman."

"And?"

"And . . . so I . . ."

"Antie Yaya," Ebe interjected, standing in the shadows along one side of the room, "na bath is ready."

"Thank you." She waved a hand and Ebe left the room, closing the door behind her. "It's for you," she said to Dirt. "Get undressed."

Dirt didn't much feel like a bath, but she wasn't going to argue with Antie Yaya. She stood and began to pull her pants down.

"Not here!" Antie Yaya said, extending a hand to block Dirt from view. "Come."

Antie Yaya took her over to a side room that Dirt hadn't noticed. In it sat an iron basin that was big enough for a girl to lie in. It was more than half-filled, with coils of heat steaming off the water.

"Go ahead," Antie Yaya said, stepping out of the room.

Na hot bath?

It didn't make much sense. Baths were something a girl did in cold streams, not hot iron bowls. Bowls were for soup.

But Dirt pulled her clothes off anyway and tested the water with her toes. It wasn't boiling, but she still felt like a human tea leaf when she climbed in.

That wasn't to say it didn't feel nice. The water came up to her shoulders, wrapping around her snug and warm. It had a strong aroma of ginger, and Dirt even saw with alarm that slices of ginger and lavender were floating along the surface.

Chaaaiii! This woman will cook me!

"How is it?" Antie Yaya said, reappearing in the doorway.

"It is finefine," Dirt said. "Thank you, Antie Yaya."

"Does it help?"

Dirt frowned. "With what?"

"Everything."

How could a hot bath fix everything?

It seemed that Antie Yaya just wanted to let her soak so that everything could be fixed, but Dirt had to ask the question that had been on her mind.

"Must I go East?" Dirt asked.

"To fight Useyi?"

Dirt nodded.

"Where did you hear that?"

"Na stories."

"You would leave your sisters?"

"If I must," Dirt said firmly.

"And who says you must?"

Stories. Common knowledge. Tradition. "I am na woman now. I must leave na Fam and go East." She shrugged. "It is."

"'It is,'" Antie Yaya repeated with a short, sharp laugh. "'It is!' 'Na stories!' Do you children truly not know anything else? What lies beyond the Isle?" she asked, suddenly changing topic.

Dirt shook her head.

"What lies at the center of the Isle?"

"I do not know."

"Why do Flagga boys play Flagga? Why do Pusher boys have Petti? Why do Butterfly girls wear face paints? Why do Bowers Bow?"

"Because . . ." Dirt felt like the answers to those questions were obvious, but when she tried to summon them, they were nowhere to be found.

"You don't know," Antie Yaya said.

Dirt nodded, frowning.

"Wrong. You don't *remember*. Useyi's hands have been busy, it seems."

Dirt knew Useyi claimed memories. She'd always known that. But she'd never realized how much he took, not just from her, but from everyone. She'd never realized how little she truly knew about the world.

"Can you tell me?" she asked, not sure if she was prepared.

"Of course not!" Antie Yaya said. "You think Gods take memories that I have the power to return? No, Bower Dirt, I only tell you this so that you'll trust well the words I'm about to say." She leaned forward. "All these things you don't know, I do. I know more about this world than you likely ever will, and I am telling you now, with as much conviction as I have ever said anything, that no one can tell you how to live your life. Girl or boy, young or old, Bower or Butterfly, Uncle or Antie. No one. All girls must choose lives of their own."

"But it is—"

"Don't say it," Antie Yaya warned, holding up a finger. "Tradition is important, I know. Tradition makes you strong, helps you understand where you come from so you can better understand where you're going. But not all traditions are true. Some are only made to keep you in a box that others were too afraid to break out of."

Dirt wasn't sure what to say to that. Tradition was bigger than any one girl. Even bigger than Antie Yaya. It came from the Gods themselves.

Didn't it?

"I tell you this because the Gods are returning, young one. These are not traditional times. These are dangerous times. Desperate times. And you are a Godskin. If any girl allows herself to be trapped within the box of tradition, we will all soon suffer. More so if that girl has a gift like yours."

Dirt chewed her lip, digesting Antie Yaya's words. Of everything she said, only one thing really mattered. "So . . . ," she finally said. "If I must choose . . . I can be na Bower? I can fight?"

Antie Yaya's face softened. "Of course," she said, her voice gentle.

Immediately, Dirt's eyes began to sting. She blinked to clear the oncoming tears away, then splashed her face with warm bath water. Her Scarring was supposed to have been the end of her life as a Bower, the end of her God Bow tournament, the end of the Mud. But now it was the beginning. An opportunity. Greatness didn't have to end at girlhood.

She was still a Bower. The God Bow tournament wasn't over. The Mud could still fight.

But that wasn't why she was nearly crying. She was near tears because she knew that none of it mattered. No matter what Antie Yaya said, Dirt still didn't have the powers of a Godskin.

And Carra Carre was still waiting.

Antie Yaya insisted that Dirt spend the night rather than risk a journey through the dark jungle, so Dirt slept in the strange, cushioned bed Antie Yaya provided for her. She didn't like it. It was like sleeping in pounded yam. Her spine felt loose and unsupported, and the blanket made no sense given how warm the night was. When she rolled it up and moved it to the side of the bed, she still had ample space to stretch her limbs. She preferred sleeping in the cramped sleep hut, with her limbs tucked tight and her sisters warm beside her.

She didn't sleep long. After a few hours, she was awake, gathering the clothes, tools, and seeds Antie Yaya had left for her. She'd hoped to be gone before anyone else was awake, but when she got out to the front dais of the building, the sky was beginning to lighten from evening black to early morning purple and Antie Yaya was already seated on her throne.

"Na good day, Antie Yaya," Dirt said, setting her bag of supplies over her shoulder.

"Good morning. You didn't sleep very long."

"I must go back to my sisters, Antie." Dirt looked out at the jungle stretching across the horizon, the trees' spindly shadows in the morning haze. The jungle looked infinite from where she stood. She felt extra small.

"So you will fight tomorrow?" Antie Yaya asked. "You and the other Godskin?"

Dirt swallowed, nodded. "And I must win. For na Fam."

"I'm sure your Bower sisters will still love you if you lose."

Antie Yaya didn't understand. Dirt wouldn't have any sisters if she lost.

"Maybe I will come and watch," Antie Yaya said with a small smile. "See for myself what all the uproar is about."

Dirt turned back to the old woman and fell to a knee, head down. "Thank you, Antie."

"Stand up, Dirt."

She stood.

"You have a long and difficult path ahead," Antie Yaya said. "May the Gods grant you bravery. May they grant you strength. May they grant you certainty in who you are."

I am Dirt.

She looked up to find Antie Yaya staring out into the distance, face tight. Behind her, standing in the shadow of a pillar, Ebe watched. Dirt gave her a curt nod, which she was surprised to see Ebe return.

She stood and turned to leave, but was struck by a final thought.

"What about Sis Prom, eh? And all other Sis who have na Scarring? All na oldold people like you. If they do not go East, where are they?"

Antie Yaya pursed her lips, as if she weren't going to speak. But then she said, "I don't know." There was a subtle, fearful shake in her voice that stunned Dirt. "No. I don't *remember.* That's why I need you, Godskin. That's why we all need you. To be ready to fight so that we don't all become forgotten memories."

Dirt didn't know what that meant, but it seemed like she was searching for answers that even Antie Yaya didn't have.

So she left, down the steps and back into the jungle. She was halfway back to camp when she felt something was off. The monkeys that were typically up at this time were nowhere to be found. Fruit had been picked that they normally left on the tree. There was a whiff of sweat on the breeze, too thick for the small Mud camp to produce.

Then she saw footprints just ahead. Dozens of pairs, all moving in the same direction away from the Mud camp.

And something else, spattered in small drops among the prints, nearly imperceptible in the dark—blood.

39

Broken Sisters

1 Day until the Carra Carre Fight

DIRT RAN.

She sped through the jungle, dipping beneath and dodging around branches, tearing through newly spun spiderwebs, nearly tripping over herself in her haste.

Soon the familiar chunky mud smell of camp caught her nose and she slowed to a stalking pace, stomach and chest clenched to keep her breathing silent. After a short while, the trees thinned and she was able to see the Mud camp.

It was destroyed.

The sandbags around the ring were torn and scattered, scraps of white canvas littering the grounds. All over, the sand was gouged up, splotched with dirt and leaves and bits of broken wood. Then she saw the sleep hut, caved in, nothing more than debris.

Dirt walked out of the trees and into the nightmare, staring around in disbelief.

"Sis Dirt."

Startled, she turned toward the sound with her hands up, ready to fight. But it was just Nana, seated with her back against the collapsed sleep hut, knees to her chest. She was so small, so still that Dirt hadn't noticed her.

She rushed over to crouch beside Nana and wrap the girl in a tight hug. Nana didn't hug her back. She didn't react at all, neither stiffening in resistance nor softening into Dirt's embrace.

"Nana," Dirt said. "What happened, eh? Tell me."

"Na Vine," she said, her voice surprisingly clear.

"'Na Vine' . . . ," Dirt repeated, confused. "I do not understand."

"Na Vine. They take Snore. And Nubbi."

Dirt's heart froze in her chest.

Sweet Snore. Innocent Snore. Her big sisters should have been there to protect her. Swoo and Dirt and Webba. But Swoo had abandoned them. And Dirt almost had too.

"Where is Webba?" Dirt asked sharply.

Nana's face drained of blood. She turned to look at the sleep hut.

Dirt looked from the rubble to Nana and back, trying to make sense of it. She went over to the mound of shattered wood and began picking through it, first slowly, then in a craze, tossing wood aside with her bare hands, ignoring the accumulating cuts and splinters. With each throw, her desperation grew, each piece of tossed wood counting off a second she was losing as Webba lay trapped.

Trapped, she hoped. Nothing else. Just trapped.

Finally, one piece of wood revealed Webba's perfect face, round and black, with thick cheeks and eyes closed to the world.

Dirt prayed. She wasn't Antie Yaya. She wasn't some Mosquito

Bonemender. She was only a Bower who had once been favored by the Gods and who hoped that maybe they still had enough affection for her to answer just one more prayer.

When she saw the shallow rise and fall of Webba's chest, Dirt sighed out all the breath she had, relieved.

"Webba?" she said, pulling away more pieces of wood. "My Sis, you can hear me, eh? Webba."

Webba's eyes rolled behind their lids, but didn't open. Something was very wrong. "Nana," Dirt said, waving her over.

Together they cleared the rest of the rubble and maneuvered Webba onto flat ground. But Dirt didn't know where to even begin treating Webba's injuries. There were too many to count, from her battered head to the swollen discoloration spreading all along her ribs and sides.

Then Webba started shaking.

Her jaw rattled in a wholly terrifying manner that sent Nana scrambling away. Spit bubbled out from between her teeth. Her entire body convulsed like it was being bathed in lightning.

"Webba!" Dirt screamed, holding Webba's face in her hands, doing her best to keep her teeth from smashing against each other. "My Sis, I am here!"

As Webba continued to shake, an unbearable helplessness settled into Dirt. She could feel Useyi's presence nearby, watching and waiting for Webba to pass into memory, where he could take her into his clutches. She kept her eyes on her sister, etching every detail into her mind, refusing to let Useyi have her. Not Webba. Never Webba.

"I am here, My Sis," Dirt said, over and over and over. "I am here. Please . . ."

Dirt was so intent on Webba that she ignored the taps on her shoulder. It took Nana's urgent voice to get through to her.

"Sis Dirt!"

Dirt looked up to find a thin girl standing beside her. She had a white canvas bag in her hands and was already setting it on the ground, pulling out supplies.

"Honored Mud Sis, it is okay," Pebble said. "I am here."

Pebble ordered Dirt and Nana to leave while she worked on Webba. Dirt ignored her at first, sitting by Webba's side and asking question after question to better understand what was going on. But eventually Pebble rounded on her with a fierceness Dirt had never seen out of a Mosquito girl.

"Go!" she shouted, eyes wide and the strain of the task before her already plain on her face. "Honored Sis."

Dirt took Nana and left.

They went into the jungle, tracking the footprints left behind by the Vine. Dirt didn't expect they'd lead all the way back to the Vine camp, but she hoped for something. Anything. Maybe Snore had escaped. Maybe they'd gotten tired of carrying her and dropped her off somewhere. Snore could be a handful.

Throughout their search, Nana recounted everything that had happened during the Vine's attack.

"And so they come for me, eh?" Dirt asked.

"They say you must not fight tomorrow."

"Why?"

Nana shook her head. "Sis Verdi is way confusing. She say na Gods are coming and na Vine must be na only Fam. Then Carra Carre can be 'First of na First.'"

It was probably confusing for Nana, but it made sense to Dirt. Antie Yaya had said as much. The Gods were coming back. The Isle was changing. Many traditions were disappearing—clearly Verdi thought the tradition of Bowers not fighting outside a Bow could disappear along with them.

By midday, they'd lost the trail to a shallow creek, but Dirt kept them going. They scoured the nearby jungle no matter how treacherous the path, climbing mounds of jagged stone, reaching into the hollow trunks of trees and down into wide-mouthed rabbit dens. Once, whether by the delusion of hope or the fog of fatigue, Dirt thought she found Snore. But it was only a nest of intertwined roots at the base of a tree, partially covered by a bit of discarded cloth.

As the sky darkened and the treetops drank most of the moonlight, it became impossible for Dirt to tell footprint from hoofprint. The jungle began waking up, creatures of all sorts leaving new prints that misled them. She was crawling on her knees, tracing her finger along the inside of what turned out to be a paw print, when Nana interrupted her.

"Sis Dirt, it is late."

Dirt sat back on her heels and let out a long, defeated breath. "I cannot find Snore," she said. She hadn't expected to. But it still hurt. She could only imagine how scared and lonely Little Snore felt.

"It is fine, Sis Dirt. I know you cannot."

Dirt looked at the young Bibi. Really looked at her. Something was different about her. Her face looked sharper, harder, like she'd aged five years in five hours.

"Let us go back," Dirt said. If she hadn't found the Vine with full light, she wasn't going to find them in the dark. Further searching only put her and Nana at risk of attack, by the Vine or anything else.

Dirt began the trek back to camp, and Nana walked close beside her, suspicion in her voice.

"Where do you go?" she asked. "After you fight with Swoo."

Dirt swallowed. "I go and see Antie Yaya."

"For na Scarring?"

Dirt nodded.

"You do not say goodbye?"

"I . . . do not," Dirt said. She failed to keep the shame out of her voice.

Thankfully, Nana didn't push further. "But you come back. Even though you are na woman."

"Antie Yaya says it is fine."

"Why?"

"It is not simple."

"And so?"

Dirt glanced at Nana and raised an eyebrow. It was uncharacteristically bold of her. Nana stared back, undaunted.

Dirt sighed. "I am na Godskin."

"Only na Godskin can choose her life?"

"No."

"So who else?"

Dirt stopped. The trees around them were familiar—they were almost back to camp. "All girls must choose. This is what Antie Yaya tells me. Tradition guides us, but it does not make us."

Nana stared at Dirt like she was looking upon Mama Eghi herself. Her eyes were intent, lips parted in awe.

"What is it, eh?" Dirt asked.

"All girls must choose?"

Dirt gave her a curious look. "Yes . . ."

Nana nodded, her mouth setting into a straight, resolute line. Before she turned to continue walking, her eyes lingered for a bit on Dirt's Scarring. Dirt had to keep herself from covering her face out of self-consciousness. She needed to get used to the staring—this wouldn't be the last time.

When they emerged back into camp, Pebble was seated on the ground beside Webba, her thin body slack with exhaustion, chin hanging on her chest.

Dirt feared the worst. "Pebble." She went over to her and crouched to meet the girl at eye level. "How is my sister?"

Pebble looked up. "Honored Sis, she is fine. But . . ." She grabbed a stick from the ground and climbed to her feet. "Look, please." She stood next to Webba and pressed the stick down on Webba's hand, into a finger. Webba groaned and her finger twitched.

Then she pressed the stick down onto Webba's thigh. Then her knee. Then her foot. One leg, then the other.

No response.

"I do not understand," Dirt said.

But she did.

"Her legs . . . ," Pebble said. "She will not walk again."

Webba. Brave Webba. Sweet Webba.

Swoo's words echoed in Dirt's mind. *You give nothing to na Mud. You sacrifice* nothing *for na Mud.*

Webba had sacrificed. Day after day, month after month, year after year, she'd spent her life building the Mud, preparing her sisters for the once-in-a-generation moment when they could finally win a God Bow tournament. She'd been willing to fight Carra Carre, a Godskin, to protect the Mud Fam. Dirt knew firsthand what the power of a Godskin could do to a girl. Webba had as much of a chance of beating Carra Carre as beating the sun.

Yet she'd fought anyway.

In her first fight with Carra Carre, Webba had sacrificed one season for the Fam. In this fight, she'd sacrificed all future seasons.

All for the Fam.

"We will remember you, Pebble," Dirt said, a hand on Webba's leg. She couldn't take her eyes off her broken sister.

"Thank you, Honored Sis."

"And Blessings to Antie Yaya for sending you."

"Antie Yaya does not send me," Pebble said. "Your sister sends me."

Dirt frowned. She looked to Nana, who shook her head.

"Not this one," Pebble said. "Na angry one."

Swoo.

"You see her?" Dirt asked.

"Eh heh . . . not long ago, she comes to me." Pebble looked between Dirt and Nana, confused.

"Where is she now?" Dirt asked.

Pebble shook her head. "I do not know, Honored Sis. After she leaves me, she goes north."

The Mud camp was west of Antie Yaya's. If Swoo was traveling north, then Dirt had no idea where she was headed. But it meant she wasn't coming back. Swoo was truly gone.

This wasn't just the end of Webba's journey as a Bower. Swoo was gone. Snore, kidnapped. From five, they'd become two.

It was the end of the Mud Fam.

And like the end of anything, the memories would only last so long. Then they would fall into Useyi's clutches and all would be forgotten. Swoo's rage and brilliance, Snore's endless energy,

Nana's delicate kindness. Webba's strength. Webba's bravery. Webba's smile. As impossible as it seemed, Dirt knew she would someday forget Webba's smile. What good was a heart when the mind forgot everything that heart held dear? She wanted to rip hers out of her chest and leave it buried in the soil, beneath the only home she'd ever loved. Let the worms make use of it; it only brought her pain.

Instead, she pulled Nana close and laid her own head on Webba's unfeeling legs and let her heart fill so much with love for her sisters that it broke.

40

How the Gods Choose

The Day of the Carra Carre Fight

DIRT DIDN'T REMEMBER falling asleep.

She woke with the back of her head resting against Webba's belly, Nana curled in her lap. The sun was barely up, and the dewy haze of the previous night still clung to the world. Birds sang, monkeys yelped, and a breeze sighed through heavy branches. All the South was waking up to a peaceful morning.

Except the Mud Fam, which was just three girls in a shattered hut.

Dirt remembered saying goodbye to Pebble, watching her trudge back through the jungle in the dead of night. She'd judged that girl unfairly. Pebble was skinny, yes. And she couldn't fight. But she had a different kind of strength. She'd chosen a path and she walked it with dignity and resolve.

Maybe Mosquito girls weren't all bad.

Dirt and Nana put together a breakfast from the remains of

their garden. It was a meager meal, not one worth setting out properly. Dirt ate on the sleep hut floor beside Webba. Nana didn't sit with her. Instead, she placed a wide, flat rock near where the ring used to be and sat there, staring into the jungle as she ate.

By half noon, it was time to leave. It was time to go face Carra Carre.

Despite her meal, Dirt had never felt so empty. Despite the bright and beautiful day, she'd never felt so afraid. Despite being in the tournament finals, a position most Bowers could only dream of, she'd never felt like such a failure.

She cleaned her bowl and stored it in what used to be a corner of the sleep hut. Now it was a stack of splintered wood, piled a stride high.

"No food for Webba, eh?"

Dirt whipped around. Webba was still laid out, both legs braced by wooden rods, her hands over her stomach. But her eyes were open. Her breathing had steadied.

Dirt rushed to her sister's side, reaching her just a step before Nana, who sprinted across the camp to gently lay herself across Webba's torso.

"Sis Webba," she murmured, a prayer.

Webba's arms still worked and her chest was still strong, so she wrapped Nana in the tightest hug Dirt had ever seen.

"When na Vine comes, I do not save you, my Bibi," she said, and the pain of her words was plain in her face. "I try my best, but . . . I am sorry."

"It is fine."

"You are bravebrave."

Nana sat back on her knees, wiping tears from her cheeks. "But . . . I do not save Snore."

"We will bring Snore home," Webba said, a sudden darkness falling over her face. But then she exhaled and smiled a bitter smile. "Look at me play toughtough. Na broken Sis."

Nana looked shocked. She'd likely never seen Webba–joyful Webba, gallant Webba–in such a miserable state. Dirt wasn't sure she had either.

"Sis Webba is not broken," Nana said. "Maybe your legs do not work, but–"

Webba shook her head in a short, frustrated manner, silencing Nana. Then she winced and rubbed her throat. Nana immediately rushed off to go prepare more tea.

"You are here, eh?" Webba asked, finally acknowledging Dirt. "What of na Scarring?"

Dirt shifted uncomfortably. She explained her visit to Antie Yaya's, and all the things Antie Yaya had told her. When she was finished, she kept silent, awaiting Webba's judgment. Just because Antie Yaya was fine with her remaining a Bower didn't mean Webba would be.

Webba let out a long breath. "So I keep my sister?" she asked, her voice shaking with emotion, her eyes brimming wet.

Dirt took one of Webba's hands in her own. "Always."

"And na Bow? Carra Carre? You can fight, eh?"

"I can," Dirt said. "But . . ."

"Eh?"

Nana returned with a full cup of griff root tea. Webba drank nearly half of it in a single gulp.

"I must not, my Sis," Dirt said. "Na Vine will punish Snore."

"Eh heh . . . ," Webba said. "And who can save Snore, if not na Godskin? When Snore is safe, you can Bow."

"And what of Swoo? I must find her."

"Swoo will return. Breathe easy."

Webba always saw the best in people. But Webba didn't always see the truth in people. Dirt understood Swoo for what she was–a winner. She liked being a winner more than anything else, and if she didn't think the Mud could help her win, she would go somewhere that could.

"Save Snore and punish Carra Carre," Webba said. Then she eyed Dirt curiously. "Or . . . you do not want to fight?" Webba asked.

"I do. I must. But . . ."

Webba closed her eyes and went quiet. She stayed that way for so long that Dirt feared she'd fallen asleep again.

"My Sis, I must go," Dirt whispered.

"You remember what I say before?" Webba said, opening her eyes. "Before you go to Antie Yaya?"

Dirt would never forget. Webba had never spoken to her that way before. "You believe. 'But it is not enough.'"

"I believe. Na Gods believe. Antie Yaya believe. When will it be enough? When will you know you are great?"

"My Sis, I cannot make quiet–"

"And why not, eh?"

"Because . . ."

Before, she thought she'd lost her power because of her Scarring. But was that true? If Antie Yaya didn't care about her Scarring, would the Gods?

"I do not know," she finished with a sigh. "I struggle, my Sis. I am not you."

"Yes!" Webba hissed. "You are not me! Do you not yet understand? My Sis, I am not na Godskin. All my life, I dream that I will be na Godskin. But I can never be. Because I am Webba. I am fatfat. I am strongstrong. When I fight, I am happy. I feel peace. You see this, eh?"

Of course she did. Webba enjoyed fighting. She enjoyed it more than anything else in life. And any fear she felt before a fight dissolved when she was in the ring. Swoo was the same way.

"But you . . . ," Webba continued. "When you fight, I see you have fear. You have no peace. To fight, you must overcome. This is why you are great. This is why na Gods choose you."

Dirt stared at her sister in disbelief. "My Sis, what do you speak, eh? If not for Carra Carre, you overcome every girl."

"Yes, and I have power, my Sis," Webba said. "But this is who I am. I do not choose to be me. For true power, you must be who you are and more. You must know fear and choose to be brave. You must not overcome na other–you must overcome yourself."

Nana stood, picking up a bag of food and Mud Offer. It was time to go. "Sis Dirt . . ."

"You see, my Sis?" Webba said. A tear rolled down her cheek. "You are not me. You will never be me. You are Dirt. And when you know who Dirt is, you will know you are enough."

Dirt squeezed Webba's hand, kissed the back of it, then climbed to her feet. She took a moment to commit her sister's face to memory. Her skin as smooth as a moonless night. The curves of her ample, always-smiling cheeks. The wide, sculpted caverns of her nose. Webba was a gift, greater than any gift the Gods had ever granted.

"I must go," Dirt said. With how quickly everything had collapsed over the last few days, she felt the need to say something profound, to speak her heart fully in case this turned out to be her last chance. "I . . . I will remember you, my Sis."

Webba closed her eyes again, a small smile spreading on her face. "Do not remember me, Sis Dirt of na Mud. Remember yourself."

41

The Newest Mosquito

DIRT ATE ALONE on the floor of the preparation tent.

She ate. Not to gain size or even enjoy the food, but to keep to the Bowing ritual: eat, dance, fight. She'd lived by it her whole life. Even now, when nothing made sense, she couldn't think of anything else to do. The familiarity brought her comfort.

She stretched. Not to warm her muscles, but to imagine that Webba was there with her, coaching her, advising her.

I am brave. I am fat. I am Dirt.

She prayed. Not to ask for courage, grace, strength, and humility, but for the safety of Snore and Swoo.

The tent flap opened and Nana returned, chewing on plantain chips. Her back was straight, her chin uplifted. Ever since the Vine attack, the girl moved with a certainty that Dirt had never seen in her. The attack had changed her, and Dirt hadn't yet figured out if it was for the better.

"You ripe, eh?" Dirt asked.

Nana stopped just inside the tent entrance, chewing. "Ripe-ripe."

"Outside is fine?"

Nana nodded. "When na Vine comes . . . we will save Snore?"

"I will fight," Dirt replied. "I will fight to bring Snore back."

She left unspoken what would happen if she failed.

I will Bow Down, she admitted to herself.

Nana's brows dipped, followed by a sudden timid shift in her posture. She looked scared, uncertain. This was the old Nana, from before her newfound confidence.

"You have na seed in your heart, Nana," Dirt said, recalling one of Webba's sayings. "Add water."

Nana sank delicately to her knees and sat back on her ankles. She was sweating, Dirt saw.

"Sis Dirt, I do not want you to be madmad with me."

Dirt frowned. "Nana, you are my sister. My only sister with me on this day. Speak free."

That only seemed to make Nana more concerned. She opened her mouth and closed it a few times, then took a few long, slow breaths the way Dirt had taught her so long ago.

"I do not want to be na Bower," Nana said, finally. "Tomorrow, I will be na Butterfly girl."

Dirt let loose a long, tired sigh.

In the end, it wasn't her Scarring that had ended the Fam. It wasn't the God Bow tournament or a lack of recruits. Her sisters each had their own lives to live. And the time had simply come for them to do so.

She wasn't unaware of the irony. She'd left Antie Yaya's so she wouldn't end up like Ebe, and yet now they were the same—the last of their Fam.

After a long silence, she finally croaked out, "Why?"

Tears sprang immediately to Nana's eyes. "Sis Dirt, I do not like na Bow. I like to make adorn."

"Adorn . . . ?" Dirt asked, confused. "You will leave na Mud for ado—"

"I want to be skinnyskinny," Nana added, frantic. "I like na finefine dress and I want to speak with na Pusher boys and dance with Flagga boys, maybe. I do not like to fight and na blood and . . . and . . ."

The poor girl. Dirt knew the pain of wanting a different life than the one expected of you. She knew the courage it took to choose to be yourself.

Dirt extended her arms and Nana fell into her embrace, overcome with tears.

"I am sorry, Sis Dirt," she said between sobs.

But Dirt understood. Nana had never been a Bower. Not truly. She was good at it, and she enjoyed parts of the Fam life, but she wasn't a fighter. Her life deserved to be filled with blouses and bracelets, not broken bones and black eyes.

All girls must choose, Dirt thought with sadness. Even if she didn't like their choices.

"So you will be na Mosquito girl, eh?" Dirt said. "You think because you are na Mosquito, I will not call you 'Bibi Nana'? You think we will not sing and dance together?"

Nana's smile unfurled like a spring flower, from a pursed bud to a toothy grin.

Dirt wiped tears from Nana's cheeks and buried her face in

Nana's hair. She did with Nana's girlish smell what she'd done with Webba's face—committed it to memory, its delicacy and softness and warmth.

Then the music flared up. The band was playing in the arena.

It was time.

"Tomorrow," Dirt said, "is tomorrow. But today is today. And today, you are na Mud sister."

Nana exhaled a sigh of relief and nodded. "Yes, Sis Dirt."

"Eh heh," Dirt said. "So come." She climbed to her feet and stood in the center of the tent. "Prepare na Godskin. We must dance."

42

Brave. Fat. Dirt.

IN THE STANDS of the Grand Temple, the boys and girls of the South were all on their feet. They were there to watch the God Bow tournament, a match between two Daughters of Oduma.

The champion Carra Carre. The First of the Vine. The greatest Trapper in the South. Favored by Papa Oduma Himself. She was fighting to establish the dominance of her Fam, to strengthen her legacy, to be remembered by all.

Her opponent was the unlikely contender Dirt. The Second of the Mud. Formerly retired Slapper. Maybe favored by Papa Oduma, but maybe not. She was fighting for the survival of her small Fam and the honor of her fallen Sis, Webba.

The fans had given up their time and energy to be there that day, having been promised a violent end to the story.

None of them realized that the story might not end as they'd hoped.

Dirt looked out at the crowd as she danced into the arena. If it could be called dancing. She walked forward, vaguely on rhythm. Nana shuffled beside her. All around, the normally cheering Flagga boys and Mosquito girls and Pusher boys booed their entrance. At first Dirt thought it was because of her pathetic dancing. But the hostile crowd's words began to float down to her.

"Na fake!"

"You will lose!"

"Na fake Godskin!"

In the Bower seating section, the other Fam watched in silence. The Creek beside the Sand, the Sand beside the Rock. They were curious rather than hostile, only interested in who would emerge victorious. And to scout for next season, to see if there was any way they could begin preparing to fight a Godskin.

Dirt led the singing of the Mud anthem, with Nana's wispy echo as her only support, a stark departure from the harmonized sound the Fam had managed at full strength. The wall of jeers from the audience washed out their singing entirely, but they sang all the same.

When she got to the far side of the arena, Dirt stopped and turned to take in her surroundings. For once, she wasn't nervous. Somehow, it hadn't yet hit her that this was the tournament finals. That Carra Carre would be walking through the entrance any moment. The last couple of days had been so vivid, so terrifying and emotional, that this experience seemed drab by comparison, like a dream with muted sound and color.

"You ripe, Sis Dirt?" Nana asked.

Dirt almost smiled at Nana's attempt to fill Webba's role.

"Riperipe," she said. "For whatever comes."

The Vine didn't make them wait. Moments after Dirt and Nana settled into their positions on the far side of the Grand Temple, the Vine's hundreds of pounding feet made the arena floor tremble. They filed in as they had each time before, spreading into their ranks, faces veiled by vines. They marched their angry march and sang their angry anthem.

Every inch of their vine-covered heads exuded victory. They could easily tell by the Mud's diminished numbers that their attack had done its job. They knew the Mud were in no shape to oppose them.

When their entrance was finished, Carra Carre stepped forward into the ring. She looked relaxed, as she had before all her other fights. Behind her, Verdi was the opposite, spilling over with energy. She paced in front of the Vine's ranks, bouncing with excitement, her violet eyes wide and visible even from across the arena.

Dirt walked into the ring and stared up at Carra Carre, the girl who had maimed Webba, not once, but twice. Not for a season, but for a lifetime. Ruined not just one Bower, but an entire Fam. She was even bigger up close than from afar. Truly a mountain of a girl. Yet, for such a brute, her eyes were brown and soft behind her mask. She looked down at Dirt not with anger or contempt, but an almost Bibi-like curiosity.

Carra Carre didn't salute. Neither did Dirt. Verdi grew more impatient as the moments passed. They were expecting Dirt's surrender.

"Where is Snore?" she said instead, loud enough for the crowd to hear.

Carra Carre's curiosity turned to suspicion. "Bow Down," she said in a low voice. "Verdi will bring your sister."

"I must see her," Dirt said.

Silence.

Then Verdi shouted. "Say what you must say, Dirt!"

Were they worried what the crowd would think of them kidnapping Snore? It was a treacherous act, true, but the Vine seemed past caring about such things.

No, it was more than that. Dirt looked past Carra Carre, past Verdi. She saw that the other Vine sisters were shifting as they stood, uncomfortable.

Something was wrong.

"Where is my sister?" Dirt asked, her heartbeat drumming in her ears, picking up speed. "Where is Snore?"

Papa Oduma, defend Little Snore. Do not let this Bibi suffer for na weakness of her big sisters.

"Say what you must say!" Verdi repeated. She was frantic, eyes darting all around. "Say it!"

Dirt swallowed. She knew Webba wanted her to fight, but she couldn't do it. Not as long as they had Snore. She wouldn't be able to live with herself if they did to Snore what they'd done to Webba. She put nothing past the Vine.

"I . . ." Dirt licked her lips, tried to quell the sickness in her stomach. "I will not fight na Vine." The Mud was already finished. A fight with Carra Carre wouldn't have changed that, no matter how it ended. "I Bow D—"

"BREEZY SWINGING BUCKS," a voice shouted, a primal shrill that split the air.

All heads turned to the Grand Temple entrance, where two girls stood just behind the ranks of Vine sisters. One girl was taller, with her cloud of tight curls shaved on the sides and puffed in the back.

One of her eyes was swollen black and shut, but the other was wide open, full of fire. Her right arm dangled as if it were no longer connected to the shoulder, and blood splotched her skin in the sort of strange yet specific places that told the story of a fight.

The other girl was tiny and undamaged, with hair in pigtails and a small jungle cat cub bundled in her arms.

Dirt's heart nearly leapt from her chest. She drowned in relief.

"You think you can punish na Mud, eh, you dog's tongues?" Swoo's voice was stretched out and dried, exhausted. "Come in na night. Break our sleep hut. Take our Bibi. You think we will not punish you back, you everlasting swine?! You undermating gekko!" She trudged forward, limping but keeping an arm around Snore.

And suddenly everything made sense. Dirt thought back to the night of the first fight between Webba and Carra Carre, how she'd had to talk Swoo out of waging a one-girl war against the Vine. This time, Dirt hadn't been around to stop her.

She hadn't betrayed the Mud at all.

She'd saved them.

Swoo showed no fear of the Vine girls to her right and left, which seemed to inspire hesitation among their ranks. None of them tried to stop her as she approached Verdi at the front of their formation. Verdi was a head taller than Swoo and more than double her weight, but when they stared into each other's eyes, it was Verdi who took a step back.

Swoo took her good arm off Snore's shoulders and raised it into the air for everyone to see. Her palm was black, covered in ash.

"Go and see your sisters, Verdi! Go and see your home. Go and see how NoBe Swoo of na Mud punishes na Vine." The evil curl of her smile told the whole story.

Verdi blasted Swoo with a punch that sent teeth spiraling across the arena. Swoo crashed to the sand.

A roar went up from the crowd, but Dirt didn't hear it. Nor did she hear Nana's scream. Rage erased her senses, blinding her, deafening her. A rage that burned so hot or so cold that she couldn't tell which it was. All she felt was the burning.

Snore fled the violence, running around the ring to Nana's waiting arms, the two of them scurrying away to safety.

Swoo, dazed, struggled slowly back up to a knee. She stared Verdi in the eye and spat blood out of the side of her mouth.

"You strike me, eh?" she slurred, grinning red. "Strike me again, Verdi, you violent goat." She stood and walked even closer to Verdi. "For each strike you deal to me, my sister will deal you. You see her?!" Swoo pointed over to the ring. To Dirt. "She is bravebrave. She is fatfat. She is—"

Verdi smashed her forehead down onto Swoo's nose, and this time there was no loss of teeth, just a quiet burst of blood and Swoo's body crumpling to the ground.

As Dirt charged across the arena, all she could think about was breaking every bone in Verdi's body. She'd broken her once before. Easily. She would do it again, in a way the girl would never recover from.

But then Carra Carre was in her way, a body far larger, far stronger, far harder to break. Dirt skidded to a halt. Carra Carre looked down into Dirt's eyes and Dirt looked back up, entirely unintimidated by what she saw.

This was even better. Carra Carre first, then Verdi.

Dirt hopped back to her side of the ring. She didn't bother with a salute.

"TIMEKEEPER!" she shouted.

"Bow . . . ," the timekeeper said, unstoppering the hourglass. The crowd of Flagga boys and Pushers and Mosquito girls and Bowers, all the boys and girls of the South, raised their voices in anticipation and swung their colored cloths in circles over their heads and pounded their feet until they sounded like thunder rolling around the arena. "Begin!"

43

Sis Dirt vs. Sis Carra Carre

DIRT RODE IN. She didn't care that she couldn't make quiet, and she didn't care if Carra Carre could. She didn't care about winning. All she cared about was destroying the Vine, dismantling their Fam the way they'd tried to dismantle the Mud. She wanted to make them watch their Fam fall apart piece by piece.

Carra Carre dodged aside, but Dirt Rode in again. She reached out for a Trap, but Carra Carre Slapped forward, pushing Dirt back, her long arms keeping Dirt from securing any hold.

Dirt stepped away to reset, and wasn't surprised when Carra Carre did the same. She was surprised, though, when Carra Carre closed her eyes, dropped her arms to her sides, and took a deep breath.

"No!" Dirt screamed. Carra Carre was trying to make quiet, trying to access the power of the Gods that Dirt had lost. She couldn't allow it.

Dirt leapt across the ring, secured a Trap around Carra Carre's waist, and pushed for a Front Bow. But the bigger girl countered, quicker and smoother than a girl her size should have been able to manage. Dirt went weightless for a moment, then slammed on her side into the sand.

"Counter!"

Dirt jumped to her feet, charged in, and was countered again.

"Counter!"

She charged in again, hard Slaps to a quick Ride, Trap, Bow sequence. Carra Carre twisted, sent her flying.

"Counter!"

Three points down and her muscles starting to tire, Dirt's rage began to diminish. Only then did she realize how foolish she'd been.

She was never going to overpower a girl like Carra Carre. Her only hope had been to stay light and evasive to tire Carra Carre out, similar to what Webba had done. Instead, she'd only exhausted herself.

Dirt looked back at her sisters. Swoo had found her way over to the Mud side of the arena and was seated beside Nana and Snore. She watched intently as she held a red-soaked shirt to her nose. Nana looked stiff with fear, while Snore, disturbingly, wore a blank, faraway stare.

They were depending on her. She had to be smarter.

She backed away, put her arms down. Carra Carre did the same. The crowd sensed the change and fell into an anticipatory hush. The only breaths taken were by the two competitors.

Dirt wasn't going to beat the Vine champion without being able to make quiet. She'd known that going into the match. She could either lose quickly with doubt in her head or win with a clear mind.

I am brave, she thought. *I am fat. I am Dirt. I am brave. I am fat. I am Dirt. I am brave. I am fat. I am Dirt.*

Breathing deeply, slowly, she recited the words Webba had taught her what seemed like ages ago. She didn't just recite them, she tried to believe them. She was brave, not a coward. She was fat, not weak. She was Dirt. She was enough.

She tried to believe it.

She tried.

But the Whispers.

If she were so fat, why had Carra Carre just countered her with so little effort? Where was her bravery when Webba had told her the truth and she'd run weeping from the camp? When had being Dirt ever helped anyone?

Dirt tried the chant again, over and over, speaking against the Whispers as strongly as she could. But nothing happened. She couldn't do it.

Carra Carre, however, could.

A tremor ripped across the Grand Temple grounds, fans wobbling on their feet and looking around in sudden fear and discomfort. Then another tremor, then more, one after another. Soon it was clear they were emanating from the same point: Carra Carre. Energy steamed off the First of the Vine like a mirage under a hot sun. Beneath the vine mask, her eyes flew open. Dirt saw power in them. Power and confidence and . . .

Carra Carre roared into the air, arms out and veined, straining from the power. Then she became a blur, moving quicker than the eye could make sense of. But Dirt had already seen what she needed to, seen the deep-rooted truth that no amount of speed could obscure.

Relief.

Carra Carre had been relieved when she found her power. As if she hadn't been sure it would come at all. As if she didn't know what she would have done if it didn't.

As Carra Carre streaked toward her, Dirt felt like she was finally seeing her for the first time. She wasn't just big and strong. She wasn't just the First of the Vine, the biggest and most powerful Fam in all the South. She wasn't just a champion Bower.

She was a girl.

A girl fighting in the biggest tournament in the South. Fighting to defend her title. Fighting for the ambitions of her Second. A girl who didn't believe she was worthy of the power of the Gods any more than Dirt did.

It was just as Webba said. Carra Carre hadn't been chosen because she was the best Bower. The true power of the Godskin came from that very fear, and the ability to defeat it. Carra Carre had been chosen because she was scared. Because she didn't believe she was worthy. Because she had to overcome the Whispers in her mind to make quiet.

Just like Dirt.

Suddenly Dirt felt like she was in a mudslide, Webba's words crashing into and over her, refusing to be ignored. Everyone believed in her. Not just Webba. Snore, with her endless hope. Nana, who didn't even want to be a Bower. Swoo, who had risked her life to ensure Dirt could fight. Verdi, who had so feared facing Dirt in the Grand Temple that she'd broken tradition to sabotage her.

And Carra Carre, whose relief said everything.

They all believed in her.

The only person who didn't believe in Dirt was Dirt.

"Oos oos, Dirt!" Swoo's cracking, beaten voice.

"Oos oos, Dirt!" sang the Bibi.

"Oos oos, Dirt!" shouted voices from the crowd, people she'd never met and would never meet. Boys and girls who had never Bowed a day in their lives and who didn't understand the enormity of the task they were asking when they cheered for her to beat Carra Carre.

Before, she'd been trying to make quiet by speaking over the voices with her own. By trying to drown them out. But when she lost faith in herself, her own voice wasn't enough.

Now, she realized that she didn't have to speak over the Whispers at all.

She just had to listen to different ones.

So Dirt listened to all the South. All the boys and girls who believed in her. Friends who loved her and enemies who feared her. Antie Yaya and Ebe out at their compound. Her sisters—them most of all.

She should've listened to them all along.

The power flooded into her just as Carra Carre's hands shot forward in a quick shove. Dirt met her halfway, smashing palms against palms, fingers interlaced with her foe's. Their colliding energies shockwaved out in an explosion of light, blinding hot and burning bright, sending the ring's sandbags spinning in every direction. Hot sand pellets skipped off Dirt's legs before embedding themselves in the Grand Temple walls.

Dirt pushed forward and Carra Carre slid back. Slowly at first, then with increasing speed. Carra Carre suddenly twisted, with enough force that Dirt felt her fingers nearly snap. She pulled her hands free and Rode in low, Trapping Carra Carre around her massive waist, driving her across the arena. She slammed her against the sand-brick wall, which caved in at the impact, crumbling down on both their heads.

Enraged, Carra Carre countered with a Trap of her own. Dirt felt like a tree had fallen across her chest, stealing her breath, watering her vision. Carra Carre jumped both feet onto the arena wall behind her and exploded forward, driving Dirt all the way back toward the center of the arena.

Dirt hadn't expected any less. She turned Carra Carre's anger and momentum against her, bending back at the hips and launching the First of the Vine over her head to crash at high speed into the sand.

"Back Bow!" The timekeeper raised three fingers.

Tie game.

The crowd's cheering deafened and shook the arena. The ring had been destroyed, and the arena itself was damaged, with hot sand flying everywhere. Yet the crowd was more enthralled than ever. Dirt looked over at the timekeeper, that skinny Mosquito girl, and gave her a nod of admiration–she was committed to her duty.

The girl nodded back.

Then Carra Carre slammed shoulder-first into Dirt's gut and the fight resumed.

Dirt countered again with a Back Bow, but Carra Carre was a quick study. The Vine behemoth flipped through the air, spinning end over end like a thrown stick before landing on her feet. She charged back into battle as Dirt Slapped the air, sending a parade of concussive Spears ripping across the arena. Carra Carre blocked the first three blows with her forearms. But she slipped the fourth, tilting her head just enough.

Dirt clenched her teeth in frustration as her Spear crashed into the audience, sending spectators flying. As Dirt unleashed Spear after Spear at her foe, Carra Carre sped in one direction, then another, darting around the arena grounds.

As quickly as Carra Carre was moving, Dirt's eyes were ready. It wasn't so different from the counting birds training she'd done with Webba. She tracked Carra Carre from point to point, keeping the girl from getting even a moment's rest.

Still, Carra Carre was too quick to hit, and each errant Spear smashed holes in the red walls of the Grand Temple, pulverizing the sand into clouds of dust. Soon the entire arena floor was a ring of fog, with Dirt in its center. Only the fans in the highest seats could see Dirt turning like a girl surrounded by jungle cats, eyes peering into the dust. The rest of the fans murmured in confusion, complaining to their friends.

Dirt couldn't see anything beyond her arm. She listened intently for Carra Carre's footfalls, but between the audience and the band's music, her ears were useless.

Just before the dust settled, Carra Carre emerged from hiding, Riding in and Trapping Dirt, arms veiny and tight around Dirt's waist. Rather than driving into a Front Bow or bending for a Back, Carra Carre leapt straight up, rocketing them into the air with such force that she drew a trailing funnel of sand with them.

Dirt's heartbeat tripled in rhythm as the earth below shrank. As the top row of fans descended toward her, then passed below her. Bowing used momentum, converted it, redirected it. But Carra Carre had taken them straight up. There was nothing to redirect. Stuck in Carra Carre's thick arms, there was nothing Dirt could do. Even as she thrashed and struggled, Carra Carre didn't budge.

At the top of the jump, in that breath of time freed from weight and the tightness of one's own body, Dirt remembered Webba's training again: the tree climbing. She'd been that high before, sitting atop the jungle canopy.

There was no need to panic.

Then they fell in a spiral, heads toward the ground. Dirt didn't fight it. She slowed her breathing, relaxed her muscles. She was going to hit the ground. She couldn't change that. But she could roll with it, minimize the damage.

The fans blurred into view like distorted drawings. Their arms were dangling rather than raised to the sky, mouths yawning up rather than jaws slack, expressions of horror and awe.

That was all she saw before the world went black.

44

The True Godskin

DIRT WOKE to tiny, wet drumbeats against her skull.

When she opened her eyes, the world was still hazy, incomprehensible. She couldn't hear anything but a high-pitched peal. She sat up, but everything swam sideways. Vomit erupted from her belly and poured out of her mouth, thick as honey.

Her sight returned before her hearing did. She could see the light rain drizzling from the overcast sky. Carra Carre sat beside her, an arm's reach away. Her shoulders were slouched, and her eyes were unfocused, sapped of the power of the Gods. The jump must have taken everything. She was bruised all over, slicked with sweat and rain. The top half of her vine mask was torn, revealing a few wisps of short brown hair.

Across the arena, the timekeeper was facing a shouting Verdi. Most of the Vine had broken the discipline of their formation and were crowded behind their Second in support of whatever she was yelling at the timekeeper. The rest had dispersed about the arena grounds, some dancing, some conversing in small groups, some appearing to antagonize the crowd.

The first thing Dirt could make out as her hearing returned was the audience, and their sound was unanimous–outrage. Their deep *boobooooo* of discontent, combined with the lingering buzz in her skull, sounded to Dirt like she'd stuck her head in a beehive.

Finally her ears began working again and Verdi's voice reached her.

"Dirt cannot continue. Na Bow is finished. Speak it!"

The timekeeper had terror in her eyes, but she was still shaking her head, denying Verdi the conclusion she desired.

Then Antie Yaya appeared. Resplendent in a deep gold gown with auburn flower patterns, she walked gingerly across the Grand Temple with her skirt hiked up to keep from dragging in the mud. Ebe followed close behind, holding a palm-leaf umbrella over Antie Yaya's head to block the rain. Trailing behind them was a retinue of at least two dozen Mosquito girls.

Antie Yaya had come to the Grand Temple.

Through her still-foggy mind, Dirt could vaguely remember Antie Yaya mentioning she might come watch the Bow. But it was another thing entirely to see it. Dirt couldn't remember that happening before, had never even heard of it happening. While Antie Yaya was the ultimate judge of what happened in the Grand Temple, she was notoriously uninvolved, preferring to let Bowers handle Bower business.

Without a word, she went over to the Bower's spectator box and took a seat. She was too far away for Dirt to tell what exactly she was looking at, but Dirt could feel the woman's eyes, knew they were watching her most of all.

While Verdi and the Vine and the entire audience were stunned into silence, the timekeeper took the opportunity to speak up.

"It is full sand," she said in a high, tight voice that didn't reach very far in the intensifying rain. She tapped the empty hourglass. Somehow, Dirt saw, time had finished. "But I cannot see who makes who Bow. So–"

"Look at her!" Verdi shouted, pointing at Dirt. "Look at her face! She has na Scarring!"

Everyone on the arena floor froze with their gaze on Dirt. Gradually, those in the audience who heard Verdi whispered her words to those who hadn't, until a hush fell over the entire Temple.

Dirt touched her cheek and brought her fingers before her eyes. No Mud Offer. Her face was bare to the world.

"Sis Dirt is na woman!" Verdi continued. "She cannot Bow! She must go!"

Dirt staggered to her feet. "Go where?" she called back. "To Antie Yaya?" She extended a hand, pointing out that Antie Yaya was in their very midst.

"Y–" Verdi was at a loss. "Yes . . ."

When Antie Yaya rose, the air in the arena changed. They were no longer in the Grand Temple, among the sand and sky, watching a fight. Immediately, it seemed as if they'd all been transported to Antie Yaya's compound, a breeze stirring through the short grass, awaiting Antie Yaya's judgment.

"The Gods have returned to the Isle, children," she said, eyes slowly sweeping the arena. "In the old days, Sis Verdi would be right. But the Gods have chosen their skins and Godskins must

Bow, for all our fates. In the days ahead, you all must choose who you will be when you meet the Mamas and Papas. Today, Dirt is still a sister of the Mud." She gave a small shrug, then sat back on her bench.

"The Bow continues!" the timekeeper called.

The roar of excitement from the crowd was only matched by the roar of pure rage from Verdi. She charged the timekeeper and, too fast for the flimsy girl to react, clamped one of those massive hands around the girl's neck, raising her into the air. The time-keeper's spindly legs kicked, her stick arms slapping against Verdi's fat, powerful ones.

A group of Mud fans in the lower row, all Pusher boys, jumped down to the Grand Temple floor and surrounded Verdi. They were smart enough not to try anything, but their bravery inspired others, until hundreds of Pusher boys and even some Flagga boys stormed the arena floor, a wave of humanity pushing toward the Vine and demanding a restoration of order.

But the Vine only knew violence.

A Vine Sis the size of Webba grabbed a Pusher boy around the waist, hauled him into the air, and slammed him as if he were unbreakable. Except he wasn't. His agonized scream brought others rushing to his aid, several of whom got kicked in their chests by the first wave of charging Vine sisters.

Dirt could only stare as chaos reigned around her. Some Pusher boys from the Creek and Rock were trying to break up the fighting factions. But the Sand sisters had joined on the side of the Mud and they were a battering ram, tearing through any who stood in their way in an attempt to get to Verdi.

It was utter madness, but the sort of madness Dirt had seen all her life at different Bows. Sometimes madness was the only way to restore order.

But when Dirt looked over at the Bibi, she felt otherwise. Nana was frozen, eyes wide. Snore was entirely distant, playing with stones in the sand as if fists weren't flying and bones weren't breaking all around her. They were both damaged, Dirt realized. Each in their own way. Nana was destroyed by violence, fearful of it, paranoid that there was no end to how much worse things could get.

Snore was shaped by it. She'd seen so much at her young age that all the chaos around her was just another pair of pants to wear. She'd make a great Bower someday, that girl. Dimly, Dirt felt proud.

More than that, though, she felt sad.

Dirt turned to look out into the jungle, out to where Webba must have been still sleeping off the tea, hopefully in as little pain as possible. She couldn't see her Sis, but she could hear her encouragement. Feel her confidence. Smell her faith.

"I am brave. I am fat. I am Dirt."

Like that, her mind quieted. The pain in her skull, the watery weakness in her belly, the dull ringing in her ears. All of it vanished.

She ran directly into battle, right into where the two sides clashed. She raised both hands in the air, then brought them down, Slapping the muddy ground. The impact rippled across the arena, rolling out in every direction. The circle of those closest to her was pushed away, stumbling back and falling to the ground. Everyone else stopped as the vibration passed beneath them, covering their eyes as thick mud splashed up and rained down all around.

When Dirt stood upright again, she saw that the fighting had ceased. Everyone stared at her for a moment, and there seemed to be a collective realization that she was a True Godskin, and that if she decided to destroy them, there would be nothing any of them could do to stop her. In a mad dash, the Pusher and Flagga boys stampeded away, spilling over themselves to get back to the safety of the stands. Even the girls of the other Fam retreated.

The only people who remained were the Vine. More than a hundred girls, caught up in bloodlust and suddenly with only one target for their wrath.

The Vine slowly circled around Dirt. The Bibi stayed back, some of them tending to Carra Carre. But the Sis and even the NoBe advanced cautiously in their Bower stances. They each wanted to be the first to land a blow, yet they were also terrified of being the first to catch Dirt's attention.

"Do you not understand, Dirt?" Verdi called out over the rain. It had grown into a full storm, fat drops falling in sheets, a pool of dark gray clouds obscuring the sun overhead. "Na timekeeper cannot save you. Antie Yaya cannot save you. All rules are finished. Only na Gods decide now, and na Gods choose my sister." She paced a slow circle in front of her advancing sisters, spiraling toward Dirt. "Na Mud will be na first to Bow Down, but breathe easy. Other Fam will join. This is not na end. This is na beginning."

"Verdi," Dirt called back. "I make this promise to you. After I punish your sisters, I will break you."

Verdi's violet eyes flashed behind her mask. "You? Na false Godskin?! You are nothing! Even your name knows na truth. You are dirt!"

I am Dirt.

"Na Vine!" Verdi snarled. At her call, they attacked. Not one at a time, but all at once, pounding through the mud to collapse on Dirt.

Dirt didn't wait for them to reach her. She sped into one flank, unleashing a blur of Slaps and Traps and Bows, a cacophony of snapping bones and crippled screams. Here, she smashed two skulls together. There, she kicked out a NoBe's legs and Slapped her across the arena midair. As she devastated one wave, the next poured in. Soon they changed their strategy from hitting her to just slowing her down. One Vine girl after another latched onto her legs, arms, waist, until she was dragging five, then ten, then twenty through the mud.

Then suddenly it seemed that all of them were on her. She couldn't see anything but Vine limbs wrapped around her face and neck and everywhere else, the weight of their entire Fam crushing her down.

It felt like she was standing in an anthill, covered in dozens of bodies.

With a roar, Dirt threw all her limbs outward in an explosion of energy. A dome of Vine bodies burst across the arena, embedding all along the arena walls, crashing into the crowd, flying into the air and coming back down with a heavy, bone-bruising splash.

Dirt remained in the center of the arena, covered in mud. Her head was starting to hurt again. Her lungs were starting to singe again. No girl, not even a Godskin, could hold the power of the Gods in her without eventually being consumed, and Dirt could feel that she was reaching her limit.

She stalked toward Verdi, rain skipping off her skin, mud sucking at every step. Earlier, she'd imagined all the ways she could have hurt the girl, but in this moment her mind was blank. She didn't need to imagine anymore. It was time to act.

Verdi didn't back away. She didn't even lose the smirk in her eyes. She watched Dirt approach like it were any other day. Only when Dirt was just an arm's length away did she raise a protective hand.

Dirt grabbed Verdi's fingers before the girl had a chance to do anything and snapped them like twigs. She screamed out and fell to one knee.

"This is na end," Dirt said. She twisted Verdi's hand, enjoying the crackling of bones as her wrist turned into a corkscrew. "Speak it. For all na Vine. For all na South. Speak it. No more!"

"It is na end," Verdi said, head bowed. When she looked up with as much arrogance in her eyes as ever, Dirt realized something was wrong. "For na Mud."

She flung Verdi's hand aside and turned just in time to dodge Carra Carre's tree-trunk arm. It Slapped by her face, crushing the air it passed through.

Dirt hopped back, falling into her Bowing stance. Her arms were sore, both from use and from a half dozen knots she could now feel.

"You and I," Carra Carre said. "Leave my sister."

"As you leave mine, eh?" Dirt shouted back. "You will suffer for what you do, Carra Carre."

"I am sorry."

Dirt blinked. "Eh."

"Cee Cee!" Verdi screamed, horrified.

"Verdi and I punish na Mud, this is true. Before, I believe we must, but now . . ." She gestured to the arena around them.

Dirt took in the full scope of the damage they'd wreaked. No part of the arena was untouched. Everywhere, groups of Pusher boys were helping free people from rubble. Bonemenders were tending to the injured.

"Na Gods choose us," Carra Carre said. "I do not know why. But it cannot be for this."

Dirt didn't want to agree with her, but it was true. They had brought nothing but destruction.

Still, Dirt wouldn't leave the Grand Temple without getting revenge for Webba and ensuring the future of the Mud. If the whole South had to fall into the sea for that to happen, then so be it.

"You want it to end?" Dirt asked. "Breathe easy, Carra Carre. I will end you."

Carra Carre stared back. "One Bow," she said. "One fair Bow. Strong Bow. And it is finished."

"Cee Cee!" Verdi screamed, her voice raw and frantic. "Na Gods choose *you*! Na First of na First! For na Vine!"

But Carra Carre just shook her head. "There must be another way, my Sis."

Verdi's eyes grew wet for a moment, but Dirt couldn't tell whether she was about to cry or if the rain was getting trapped on her face. Before one answer became clear, Verdi gave her face a shake, clearing the water. Her eyes flared dangerously.

"If you cannot do what must be done," she said. "Then I must do it."

She charged Dirt, not with the technique of a trained Bower but with the mad violence of a starving jungle cat.

"One fair Bow," Dirt said as Verdi drew closer. She nodded. "And it is finished."

Verdi lunged at her from behind. Dirt turned and clapped the girl's head, palms smashing against her ears. Verdi fell back, unable to catch her balance, staggering and sliding and falling into the mud. She raised a hand to her ear and it came away bloody.

"Cee Cee, I cannot hear," she said, too loud. "I cannot hear, Cee Cee!"

Only when Verdi's tears began to flow did Dirt turn back to Carra Carre. "For Webba," she explained.

Carra Carre snarled, and her eyes took on the calm focus of the Gods. Dirt strode forward to meet her.

This was the end of everything.

The fight between Carra Carre and Webba. The fight between the Mud and the Vine. The fight between the Mud and erasure. The winner would be the greatest Bower in all the South. The True Godskin.

I am brave. I am fat. I am Second of na Mud, Sister to Webba and Swoo, Nana and Little Snore. I am na woman. I am enough.

I am Dirt.

And her mind fell silent.

"Final point!" shouted the timekeeper. The next person to score would be the winner. "Bow begin!"

Both girls Rode in, and their collision ripped lightning down from the storm above, washing the arena in a searing wind and a clap of thunder. Carra Carre tried a front Bow. Dirt evaded. Dirt tried a counter. Carra Carre stood firm.

They waged war. Each high-speed clash, each torqued attempt at a counter, each Slap absorbed or given broke them down. Through the quiet of her mind, Dirt's muscles wept, and she knew Carra Carre's did the same. A half dozen times, Carra Carre caught her off guard with a Bow, nearly throwing her to the ground before Dirt was able to catch her balance, legs and thighs screaming from carrying her weight at an impossible angle.

But each time, she did not fall.

Soon, all the Offer from Dirt's Godskin was gone, replaced by spatters of the arena's watery mud and patches of blood from where her skin had been rubbed away. She had knots all over her, several of her toes were broken, and her right shoulder was dislocated from a failed counter. Carra Carre wasn't in any better shape. Her vine lattice was completely ripped away. Chest heaving up and down, her mouth open for air, she moved with a visible limp.

Dirt tried a final Ride, and as Carra Carre dodged, Dirt felt the last of the power of the Gods seep out of her. Carra Carre backed away, eyes wide, and Dirt knew she'd experienced the same. They'd both used as much power as their bodies could handle. The Gods weren't involved anymore. It was just the two of them.

Even exhausted, Carra Carre Rode in lightning-quick. Dirt was too tired to defend, so she just fled, shuffling backwards until she slammed up against a stretch of the arena wall that still stood. Then Carra Carre's arms wrapped around her waist with the squeeze of a python.

Dirt thought of the mud pit. She was in the same position Swoo had her in that day. The two of them exhausted, stuck in thick mud, in a battle for a single Bow. On that day, Dirt had given up. She'd been too weak, too unwilling to suffer the pain she needed to endure to win.

Not again.

She'd had a nearly sleepless night. She'd been slammed from the sky onto her head. She'd fought off the entire Vine Fam by herself. She'd had more power surge through her body than any girl in thousands of years. Even with all that, she refused to give up.

Not again.

Dirt strained until every muscle screamed, until the veins in her skull felt close to bursting. Carra Carre met her strength in kind, but Dirt could see doubt in her eyes. The doubt of whether she was strong enough, the fear that she wasn't worthy of winning, the pain that she was going to disappoint everyone who cared about her.

Finally, Carra Carre's grip broke. Dirt shoved the bigger girl away, sending her reeling and searching for balance.

But Dirt gave her no time to find it. She barreled into Carra Carre with everything she had left. She didn't just put her body's weight into it. She put all the weight of the last several weeks. The weight of Webba's heart and Swoo's rage. The weight of Nana's fear and Little Snore's loss of innocence. The weight of all the people who supported and believed in her—Antie Yaya, Pebble, the Mud boys, and the thousands of fans among the Creek, Rock, and Sand.

Carra Carre was exhausted. She had nothing left but fear. The sweet honey of victory swelled in Dirt's heart as she tripped the First of the Vine backward into the earth . . .

. . . only to be turned to poison as Carra Carre rotated with the terrifying strength and speed of a champion Bower, body surging, muscles bulging from effort, forcing Dirt's back into the sand.

"Counter!" the timekeeper declared. "Carra Carre is na winner!"

The arena was silent but for the falling rain.

All Dirt could feel was her heart, still beating somehow. She was surprised that a heart so broken could still beat. Above, the thick gray clouds continued to rain. Beside her, she heard her opponent's heavy breaths.

"It is finished," Carra Carre said, just loud enough for Dirt to hear. She got to her feet, and Dirt listened to her steps move away.

"Na Vine!" a few voices shouted, but they didn't have the same ferocity.

Fight!

Crush!

Na enemy!

The chant diminished as the Vine gathered their girls and left the arena.

Dirt clapped caked mud from her hands and wiped her palms across her cheeks. She exhaled. She didn't have anything left. She'd given everything.

The Whispers had told her she wasn't good enough. They'd told her she was too scared, too weak. They'd told her that a few weeks of training wouldn't be enough to defeat an elite Bower like Carra Carre.

She should have listened to the Whispers.

Dirt looked out over the audience. They'd believed in her. They'd given her their strength. And she'd paid them back with failure. Shame hit her, as cold and hard and sharp as a knife to the spine.

It hit her again when she saw her sisters approach.

Nana supported a battered Swoo, while Snore walked beside them with Nubbi in her arms. Tears rolled unabashedly down Swoo's cheeks, her face stuck between scowling and crying. Dirt had seen her cry before, of course, but never with such fierceness and freedom. When they reached her, Swoo and Nana extended their hands to help Dirt back to her feet.

"My sisters," Dirt said, taking their hands and pulling herself up. "I am sorry." She found she couldn't look them in the eyes.

"For what?" Swoo asked.

"I . . ." It was hard to say. "I lose."

Through the tears, Swoo's face split in a smile. "My Sis, you fight like Papa 'Duma Himself. You . . ." She was suddenly overcome by emotion, her face contorting for a moment before she jumped forward and wrapped Dirt in a tight hug. Nana and Snore joined in, all of them embracing her.

They stayed like that for a long time, enjoying the feeling of reunion. Then music issued from the crowd, a lone voice sailing across the arena.

"We are na Mud sisters."

Dirt startled and looked into the crowd for the source.

"We fight, oh yes, ooooooh!"

This came from another part of the audience, more voices this time.

"We are na Mud sisters!"

Dirt watched in disbelief as people all around rose to their feet, the song leaping from one section to the next like a harmonious wildfire.

"We never quit, noooooo!"

Swoo led another round of song, howling into the sky from the depths of her lungs.

"WE ARE NA MUD SIIIIISTERRRS!!"

And the entire Grand Temple answered her call, one voice united in the Mud anthem.

Even Antie Yaya was on her feet, standing among the rubble Dirt and Carra Carre had made of the arena, singing with a light smile on her face.

Dirt felt something inside her burst.

She pressed her face into Swoo's shoulder and hugged her sister. The sister who she'd fought with more times than she could remember. The sister who she'd laughed with more times than she could count. The sister who had pushed her, made her a better girl and Bower. The sister who infuriated her, made her boil with rage. The sister who she'd thought had abandoned her and their whole Fam. Dirt hugged Swoo as tightly as she'd ever held anything and sobbed with every part of her body. She cried for all the times she'd felt ashamed of herself or her sisters, for all the times she'd condemned Swoo in the petty turns of her mind, for every memory of failure and self-hate and not trusting that the love her Fam felt for her was anything other than vast and endless.

And she cried for the end of that Fam.

45

The Climb

THE VINE CAMP was ash.

From the lowest platforms and huts, up to all but the tallest trees, fire had swept through, charring everything black. Their network of descending vines was completely burned away, with long, singed chunks floating in the River's current, wrapped around the remaining wooden support pillars, each scorched so badly they'd crumble at a touch.

From the edge of the jungle, Carra Carre stared in disbelief. She'd grown up among the wooden beams and platforms of the Vine camp. Every corner of it held a story from her life, from the day she first met Verdi to her first spar to her Sis promotion ceremony. It was like the last decade of her life had been erased.

And all by one girl. A NoBe, no less.

Jaldi, their young but most promising NoBe, sat on the narrow wooden bridge that stretched into camp from the riverbank. One of her eyes was swollen shut, and deep, dark bruises marred her left arm. As Carra Carre and the other returning Vine sisters walked toward her, she was sniffling and shaking her head, muttering to herself.

"Jaldi," Carra Carre said.

The girl jumped to her feet, hastily ridding her face of emotion.

"Sis Carra Carre," she said, apology in her voice.

With most of the Fam at the Grand Temple, Jaldi had been in charge of the camp. The job was a formality, granted to the NoBe who'd performed best in training that week. Most of the time, the chosen girl would be able to just enjoy some extra sleep and relaxation. On rare occasions, she'd have to protect their food from monkeys. Jaldi couldn't have been prepared for an attack by a madgirl like that Swoo.

Still, duty was duty. And she'd failed to the highest degree.

"Where are the others?" Carra Carre asked. It wasn't just Jaldi. She was in charge of a team of five lower-ranking NoBe.

"I am na one who failed, Sis Carra Carre," she said, lowering her good eye to the ground. It was unlikely that she was solely to blame for whatever had happened, but it was good leadership to protect those beneath her from consequences.

This was normally the sort of thing Verdi handled. No doubt she would have thought of a suitably cruel punishment, one that involved both work around the camp and physical pain.

But wasn't it enough that the girl had to live with her own failure? What punishment could be worse?

Maybe things didn't have to be Verdi's way anymore. If Jaldi could take responsibility, so could Carra Carre.

"Send someone to Antie Yaya," she said. "Your eye will need na Bonemender."

Jaldi looked up, confused. "Yes, Sis Carra Carre." She set off.

"My Sis . . . ," Nuna, their Third, said. She came over and put a hand on Carra Carre's shoulder. "Maybe allow Verdi to do this, eh?"

Carra Carre looked back at Verdi. Her sister still couldn't walk properly. She was supported by a Sis on either side, and she stared blankly at the jungle floor, just as she had for their entire trek home. She hadn't spoken since the Grand Temple.

"It is fine, Nuna. Take na Sis and gather all that you can."

"Eh? Why, my Sis?"

Carra Carre looked out over the camp. It was all her fault. Not just the burning of their home. Everything from the very beginning of the season: breaking Webba's leg, injuring Nat, the attack on the Mud, the riotous mess of the tournament finals, Verdi's damaged hearing.

All of them had happened because Carra Carre had been too scared to lead. None of it had felt right, but she'd let Verdi decide. She shouldn't have. Verdi was only being a good Second, ensuring the First kept ambitious goals for the Fam. It was Carra Carre's job to listen to Verdi's advice and decide whether it was wise. It was Carra Carre's job to preserve not just the future of the Fam but its honor as well.

Now another Fam knew where they lived. The word would spread quickly, no doubt, which meant they would never have privacy there, could never feel safe. That was no way to conduct a Fam, especially with dozens of new recruits soon to join. They needed a fresh start.

"This cannot be our home," she said. "We must go."

Nuna raised an eyebrow. "Go, eh? Go where?"

"Any place," Carra Carre said. "But we cannot stay."

"My First, I respect your wisdom, but . . ." She shrugged, then squinted in a skeptical way. "We should talk with Verdi, eh?"

Carra Carre stared at Nuna, then drew her gaze across the rest of the Fam. Most of them were wounded, many bloodied, from the beating Dirt had given them. They'd been promised a victory over the Mud, the first in a future of triumphs. Instead, they'd been attacked by the boys and girls of the South, their own people.

There was nothing godly about what she'd done in her fight with Dirt. They'd desecrated the Grand Temple. They'd injured dozens of boys and girls, who would pass down stories of how the Vine behaved when they were strong, how they could never be trusted with power again. Was that leadership? Rule by fear rather than respect?

No.

Even if Verdi was right and the Gods were returning and a war was coming and all the Fam of the South needed to be united, fear could not be the way.

Carra Carre had won the Bow. She always won. But in winning, she'd destroyed her Fam.

"My sisters," she said, raising her voice. "I see you are afraid. And I understand." She hated how her voice sounded; she was a girl built for fighting, not speech-giving. "But do not be afraid. Because . . ." Their eyes were blank, their faces as well. They didn't believe her. Verdi was their true leader, the one who had built the Fam into what it was. All Carra Carre had ever done was win on their behalf. But now they saw that all those victories meant little, and her words couldn't do anything to change that.

If the Vine Fam had any hope of surviving and rebuilding, she'd need their trust. She'd need them to have faith that she would lead them as boldly as Verdi had. But she wasn't going to restore their faith with words.

The solution came to her immediately.

Carra Carre went to the center of camp, where the vine of the Climb hovered over an empty circle in the charred wood. Beneath it, the River raged.

She grabbed the vine in one hand, and behind her she heard a murmur from among her sisters. She had their attention.

With a deep breath and a short hop, she wrapped herself around the vine: the Climb had begun.

It was always easy at the beginning. For any girl who'd spent her life in Bower training, ascending five strides was a simple feat. She moved in a steady rhythm, arms first, then legs, each holding her place while the other moved.

But things soon changed. The last time she'd tried the Climb, she was a new NoBe, skinny and made fearless by foolishness. Now she was a full Sis, the biggest girl in the South, with a great big belly and a pair of thick thighs. As strong as her arms were, carrying all that extra weight quickly sapped them of energy. By the time she was halfway up, her arms felt doubled in weight, and sweat trickled into her palms, making it harder to maintain her grip.

She couldn't do it.

Even if she made it to the top, she would lose her strength and fall. At best, she would plummet to a spine-breaking impact against the water below. At worst, hippos and crocodiles would be waiting for her. She was too heavy, too weak, and too afraid. Verdi had done it, but she was no Verdi.

Instinctively, she wanted to quiet her mind, bury her doubts in the silence of the Godskin, fill her aching muscles with the power of the Gods. But she knew she couldn't. She had to prove to them that Carra Carre was fit to be their leader. Not because of the Gods, but because of her own strength of will. Her own fearlessness.

So she took another deep breath and continued her upward rhythm, one hand, then the other, both legs at once. Little by little, the length of green vine above her disappeared, and the treetops grew closer. And she grew sweatier and her palms grew weaker and soon her legs, too, had had enough. Every bone in her body groaned in pain, and all the injuries she'd sustained against Dirt roared in protest.

It was a stupid thing to do, really. The fight with Dirt had nearly broken her, yet here she was, pushing her body to its limit again just hours later.

Maybe na hippo and crocodile can enjoy my body.

That was the thought she had right as she reached the top.

Though her sisters were far below her, their cheers made them sound as if they were up there with her. She could hear them screaming, pounding their feet, urging her on.

"Oos oos, Carra Carre!"

"Oos oos, Carra Carre!"

Against her better judgment, she looked down.

From eighty strides up, her sisters were just tiny, vine-masked dots. Even still, she could tell which was Verdi, not from the tiny dots of purple shining out her mask, but because she was the only one who wasn't cheering. She just stood there, unmoving, watching.

Carra Carre pulled her eyes back up and gritted her teeth. She knew the hard part was still coming. Going down took even more strength and control than going up. She managed her first small descent—legs, then arms this time—but her body soon began to shake.

She was past her limit. If she didn't get back to the ground quickly, her strength would fail and she would plunge into the water.

Verdi's words echoed in her mind. *It is not na test of strength. It is na test of fear.*

Carra Carre closed her eyes, took a breath, and let go of her fear.

She loosened her grip and slid down the vine. Her palms were already slick with sweat, making the descent easier. And faster. She slid with increasing speed, and soon her hands and inner thighs grew hot, burning from the friction.

As she reached the bottom, just ten strides above the earth, she tightened her grip again. Her palms immediately dried out and broke, cutting deep gashes in each. Her blood gushed warm all over the vine, forcing her to tighten her grip even more. She hid the pain from her mind, focused only on stopping herself before she punched into the water below.

Finally, she stopped moving. The world held the heavy iron scent of blood. Her head was light, her body sweaty and exhausted, her spirit weary.

But when she opened her eyes and saw all her sisters on their knees around her, she felt a surge of pride. She'd won them back. She'd earned their trust, proved she could lead them. Not just with strength, but with bravery.

All except one.

Verdi stood, still watching her. She seemed to be taking her in, fully examining what Carra Carre was and what she had done and what it all meant.

"My strongstrong Sis," she said, louder than she'd ever spoken before Dirt had destroyed her ears. She descended on one knee, head bowed. "First of na First."

"'First of na First!'" their sisters repeated, but Verdi didn't hear them. Carra Carre wasn't sure her sister would hear anything ever again.

Carra Carre wasn't convinced she'd fixed all the damage done to her Fam. But it was a start. They were united again. United under a leader who would no longer be too scared to do what was right. The leader they'd always deserved. She would be sixteen soon, then a woman soon after. The Vine would be getting new recruits–new minds, new hearts, and new girls she could bring up in the right way. As long as there was a future, there was always a chance to do better. The recruits were that future.

Only the recruits never came.

46

All Girls Must Choose

"GOODGOOD THAT I bring fire to na Vine," Swoo said, eyes roving the destroyed Mud camp.

On the trek back from the Grand Temple, she'd explained how she'd heard the Vine attack but arrived too late to stop it. So she followed them back to their camp and waited until they left before she struck. Dirt made a vow to never doubt Swoo's allegiance again.

"Bring fire?" Webba said, laid out on her back, hidden among the ruins of the sleep hut.

Swoo nearly jumped out of her skin. She peered at the disheveled pile of wooden scraps. "Sis Webba?"

Before Webba could answer, Swoo was by her side. "My Sis . . . I am sorry." She had tears in her eyes for the second time in just a few hours. "I am sorry I leave, My Sis. I . . . never again. Never will I leave."

"Eh heh?" Webba said. "'What good is na banana tree that does not make banana?' Your heart is as strong as your body, Swoo. Never be sorry for this, eh?"

Swoo nodded, wiped her eyes. Webba looked past her, over to Nana and Snore.

"Tea, eh?" she said with a strained smile. She was scarcely removed from a life-changing injury at Carra Carre's hands. The pain must have been unimaginable, but she hid it.

As the Bibi ran off to prepare the griff root, Dirt moved over to the sleep hut and sat beside Webba, atop a pile of wood.

"And what of you, eh?" Webba asked.

Dirt swallowed. It hurt to repeat. "I lose, my Sis. Carra Carre is na champion."

Webba closed her eyes and took a deep breath. Then she shook her head. "Not win or lose," she said. "Tell me na fight."

"I . . ." Dirt wasn't sure what to say. She didn't know where to begin, which details to leave in or take out, what tone to tell it with. She wasn't much of a storyteller. "I . . . go to na Grand Temple. And I go to na tent and eat. And talk with Nana. Then—"

"Carra Carre tell Sis Dirt to Bow Down," Swoo interjected. "Sis Dirt refuse, but she knows she must save Snore so she is soon to Bow Down when I come like Oduma Himself. '*NA BREEZY CLUCKING CHICKENS!*' I say this and na entire Grand Temple is 'Chaaaiii!!' because I have Bibi Snore. But then that sweaty swine Verdi attack me and Sis Dirt go to mash her but Carra Carre block her, so Sis Dirt say, 'TIMEKEEPER' and na Bow begins."

Swoo retold the story of the Bow, with more detail and drama than Dirt remembered. And more humor. They all laughed at moments that had been terrifying just hours before. Verdi's attack on the timekeeper became a humorous image of a Bower smacking aside a Mosquito girl as if she really were a mosquito. The Vine's assault on Dirt was portrayed as dozens of hapless ants being flicked in every direction. Even Dirt's loss was stated casually, like it was just another fight.

Nana and Snore returned midway through the story to help Webba down a gulp of the tea. It visibly eased her, decreasing the tension in her neck, softening the set of her jaw.

"When it finishes," Swoo continued, "na Vine shakeshake." She mimicked the Vine marching dance, mocking them as thoroughly and succinctly as only Swoo could. "That dirty onion Verdi smiles when they win, but na whole temple sings our song, Sis Webba! Eeeeveryone singing, 'We are na Mud sisters!' We lose, but they see my bigbig Sis Dirt and they know they must sing. Chaaaiii, Sis Webba, if you see how Sis Dirt cry, you will hide from na Gods in shame."

Everyone laughed, then Dirt frowned. "And what of you, eh?"

Swoo waved a dismissive hand. "My eyes have sand."

"Eh heh . . ."

"You do not know my eyes, Sis Dirt."

They talked and laughed for the rest of the day. They didn't bother putting the camp back together. They were all united again, and safe, and there was nothing more important than simply enjoying the inimitable closeness of sisterhood. They prepared a feast from the scraps of their garden, told each other more stories, played the Gekko and the Guava, and ate dish after dish of delicious food, as if they were celebrating a win rather than nursing defeat.

When thirdmeal was finished and the day was done, they put out the fire and talked in the dark beneath the wide sky and winking stars. Dirt remembered Snore falling asleep first, of course, her rumbles echoing through the night. Then she remembered Swoo telling a joke, but hearing only Nana's soft breathing in response. Then, finally, she remembered Swoo mumbling dreamily midway through a story and Webba, in a voice that was still wide awake, saying, "Rest your eyes, my sisters."

Then Dirt drifted away on the tides of sleep and she remembered nothing else.

It was the last night they were all together.

It was New Year's. Recruitment day.

The world held a damp haze from the rains the day before. The sun was hidden on the horizon, auburn light suffusing the jungle canopy with a warm glow. Birds conversed overhead. A band of monkeys barked in the distance.

When Dirt took her first breath, every point of pain in her body suddenly flared to life. She felt as if she'd slept with bees beneath her skin, stung in a thousand and one places.

"She wakes." Webba's voice.

Dirt turned her neck as much as she could. She was the last to wake up, she saw. Swoo and the Bibi were gone.

Despite the pain, Dirt bolted upright, panicked. "They leave already?"

"For food, my Sis," Webba said. "Breathe easy."

Dirt sighed and collapsed back onto the sleep hut floor. She would have been heartbroken if they left without saying goodbye. She winced bitterly at the knowledge that she'd almost done it to them.

"You ripe, eh?" Webba asked softly.

Dirt sighed. "I fail, my Sis. I fail na Fam. Na Mud is no more."

"What will you do?"

There was only one path for her, and it was to go back to Antie Yaya, join the ranks of all the former Bowers before her. It didn't seem as scary a notion anymore. After seeing how much damage she and Carra Carre had done, both to each other and to the Grand Temple, she couldn't imagine ever Bowing again. If she were a Bower at seventeen, when would it end? Eighteen? Twenty? Would she be a woman Antie Yaya's age, still eating and dancing and fighting?

No. She had to move forward. Walk a different path.

"I am na woman. I only come back for my Fam. If my Fam is no more . . ." She shrugged. Even that hurt.

"We will see . . . ," Webba said, biting her lip.

Dirt wasn't sure what that meant. "And what of you?" she asked. "Where will na First of na Mud go?"

Webba smiled. Not her usual grin, but a small and sorrowful smirk. "I am not First, my Sis."

No Mud Fam meant no First of the Mud. It was a sad realization. To Dirt, Webba *was* Bowing. She was an incarnation of the ritual itself, all its highs and lows, the honor and dedication it took. Seeing the end of her Bowing life felt as wrong as seeing the sun rise at midnight.

"You will always be First," Dirt said firmly.

Webba just shook her head. "You do not understand."

Swoo and the Bibi returned with food they'd foraged from the jungle and prepared the firstmeal. Despite the celebration of the night before, breakfast was somber. None of them seemed to know what to say or who to say it to.

They were halfway into the meal before anyone spoke. It was Swoo, of course.

"I will go to na Rock. I and Bibi Snore. Nat can no longer Bow and"–her nostrils flared a bit with strangely bashful pride–"and na Rock need a new Sis."

Webba's face split in a grin. "Chaaaiii! Sis Swoo of na Rock, eh? I will remember you!"

"I will remember you, my Sis," Dirt said, unable to keep a smile from her own face. She had no doubt that Swoo would be the First of the Rock before her time was finished. It was almost unfair that a girl so talented was also so ambitious. The other Sis of the South were going to have their hands full once she finished growing.

"And what of you, Little Snore?" Webba asked. "You will be na Rock Bibi, eh? Are you ready?"

Snore shrugged. Nubbi sat on her shoulder rather than in her lap, like she was a Pusher boy with his Petti. Snore hadn't spoken much since coming back from the Vine. Something had changed within her. Gone was the endless curiosity. Gone was the mad, unfettered laughter. All that remained of the old Snore was the calculating mind, but rather than looking for fun and trouble, she seemed to only seek safety.

"I will go," Snore said simply.

Dirt's heart broke for the end of Snore's innocence. The Rock would be good for her, though. They were the cheeriest girls in the South. Simple, but cheery. If anyone could help Snore find her joy again, it would be them.

"And Nana?" Webba asked.

Nana took a deep breath before speaking. When she did, her voice was clear, confident. She'd changed too. In a different way from Snore, but a change all the same. "I will be na Butterfly girl."

"And do what?" Webba asked, not unkindly. None of them really knew what being a Mosquito girl was like.

"I will be na Adorner. Make adorn for"–she looked around the room at the unenthused faces of her sisters–"everyone."

They sat in silence.

"So na whole Mud is finished, eh? So easy?" Swoo said finally, around a mouthful of pomegranate.

"Who says we must finish?" Dirt countered.

Swoo frowned, confused.

"NoBe–Sis Swoo," she said, and the pleased disbelief on Swoo's face made Dirt's heart pang with yearning for the lovely life she would soon be leaving behind, "and Bibi Snore will go and join na Rock. Bibi Nana will go and be na Mosquito girl."

"Butterfly," Nana said.

"Butterfly," Dirt conceded. "Sis Webba and I will go and make life how women make life." She still didn't know what that was, but whatever her life was going to be, she trusted herself to succeed. "But wherever we will go and whatever we will do, we are sisters. Always. We are na Mud."

She wasn't sure what else to say.

Swoo led the hug. She pushed her food away, grabbed Snore by the hand, and the two of them wrapped around Webba as best they could. Swoo then stretched out a hand and pulled Nana in.

Then they all looked at Dirt.

Dirt moved into their hug, ignoring the pain that skipped through her limbs as she joined her sisters in one long and final embrace. She closed her eyes, storing the feeling in her memory as best she could. The mix of their scents, the soft and hardness of their bodies. Webba's great slow breaths beside Snore's tiny ones.

"We are na Mud sisters!" Swoo crooned in her smoothest and most powerful voice.

"We are na Mud sisters!!" they all responded, giggling to avoid the tears.

We fight, oh yes, ooooooh! We are na Mud sisters!
We are na Mud sisters!
We never quit noooooo!

They squeezed together a final time, then separated.

"We are na Mud sisters!" someone sang.

Dirt looked around, thinking it was one of her sisters, but each of them seemed just as confused as she was.

"We are na Mud sisters!" a host of voices echoed back, clearly coming from the jungle. "We fight, oh yes, ooooooh!"

Swoo, wide-eyed, turned and ran for the tree line. Nana and Snore followed after her. Dirt stood beside Webba, watching the jungle. There was only one way into the Mud camp. The same narrow path Dirt had traveled upon for years, the same one she used to wait at each morning for her sisters to come back from their morning run.

The singing continued. Once they finished the song, they started it over again, growing from faint to loud, a choir on the march.

Then they emerged into view, dozens of girls moving in a single column, winding through the jungle. Most were young, younger than Snore. But many were not. Some were as old as Swoo, bellies already growing. Some were girls who had yet to join a Fam. Some were girls who Dirt recognized from other Fam. Some were Mosquito girls, skinny as falling rain. They marched together, all of them with hope on their faces, walking toward the Mud camp.

Toward Dirt.

At the front of the group, Pebble strode along with her white Bonemender's bag slung across her shoulder, a bigger smile on her face than Dirt had ever seen from her. She led them to a stop in the scattered ring. Many of them eyed Dirt's Scarring, but none of them seemed surprised or disgusted by it. Rather, they stood tall before her, some even elevating onto their toes, each hoping to prove that she was special, each hoping that Dirt would take notice of her.

Then Pebble raised a hand and the singing ceased.

"Na Mud Fam," she said, her voice carrying across the clearing. "For your strength and your bravery, na recruits behind me wish to become Mud. Do you accept?"

Dirt looked to Webba for her answer.

"I am not First, my Sis," Webba said, smiling like the sun after a long, hot day.

Then Dirt understood.

It was strange. She'd never wanted to be First. She'd never thought she could do it. She didn't have Webba's endless hope or Swoo's relentlessness and charisma. Her dream had always been to be at Webba's side. To watch the world recognize her sister's greatness, and do her best to help. Dirt had never wanted to be a leader.

But the Gods had chosen her. The last month, she'd led the Mud as best she could. She'd failed, yes. More than once. And she'd almost lost everything. But in the end, she'd become the Godskin, saved the Fam from the Vine, and ensured that all her sisters were free to live the lives they wanted. Maybe the Vine was right. Maybe something bigger was coming. If so, Dirt had been the one chosen to face it.

"Greatness," Webba said, tears trailing down her cheeks, "is not for she who wins. It is not for she who can punish her enemies. It is not for she who is na most strongstrong Slapper, Rider, Trapper.

"Greatness is for she who can overcome. And overcome. And overcome. Because then na other girls can look and see and *believe*," Webba said. "Greatness is not for she who wins. Greatness is for she who inspires."

Dirt curled her hand over Webba's palm and wiggled her fingers. Webba did the same to her. Then she clasped her hand over Webba's and squeezed.

"I do not accept . . . ," Dirt replied, turning to Pebble.

Pebble seemed hurt, and the group of girls behind her visibly shrunk.

" . . . until I know who they are."

They'd come to her to learn. To be mentored. To be taken in and turned into something better than they were. They'd come to her for the same reasons recruits went to a Fam every year: because she was the greatest Bower in the South.

Some traditions were good to keep.

"Na line," she said, and they all scrambled into rows. Pebble hurried out of the way.

"You think this is na line?!" Swoo stormed over from the edge of the jungle, dragging Snore along, with Nubbi trailing them. She pushed through their ranks, straightening shoulders, tilting chins, setting feet at proper distance. "This is na Mud Fam! Stand ready, you baby goats!"

When she had them all in order, she went back to stand beside Dirt, one hand on Snore's shoulder.

"What of na Rock?" Dirt asked.

Swoo sneered. "And what of them? Na Mud Fam is here. So Swoo is here."

Dirt had her Second.

Then she looked over to the edge of the jungle where Nana stood, a colorful bracelet already around her wrist. She was beside Pebble, and if Dirt didn't know her, she would think they were two Butterfly girls. Nana raised a hand in goodbye. Dirt nodded back, praying for health and safety and a long, beautiful life for her sister. Then Nana and Pebble turned and plunged into the tree line and were gone.

The South's newest recruits–nearly fifty girls in all–stood at attention before Dirt. She let go of Webba's hand and took a step forward. Not just as Dirt, but as the First of the Mud, her sisters behind her as they always had been.

It wasn't exactly her dream. Webba should have been the one standing in her spot. But seeing this many girls in the Mud camp was a version of her dream, one she and her Fam had turned into reality.

"Slap na Water!" Dirt commanded.

Some of them clearly knew a little about Bowing. They churned their arms, though in a wholly silly way. The others stared blankly, then did poor imitations of what they saw around them. They were as bad as any group Dirt had ever seen.

But that was fine. They just needed a coach.

She almost laughed.

A few minutes before, she'd given up Bowing. She'd been ready to find a new path in life.

And here, a new path had found her.

Acknowledgments

I wrote this book, like everything I write, because I owe a debt.

Not financial debt (although, hello, student loans!), but a life debt; there are Black women in my life whom I love very much, and the debt I owe them for raising me, loving me, nurturing me, inspiring me, checking me, and sacrificing so much for me is one I can never repay. All I can do is create a book like this that celebrates the love and sacrifice and boundless joy that they've shown me.

For that reason, I'd like to acknowledge the Dream Nurture Foundation for the work they do in housing, educating, and providing support for indigent girls in Nigeria. I'll be donating a portion of the revenue from this book to help them continue their work. If you'd like to learn more about their incredible mission and make a donation, head over to www.dreamcatchersacademy.org/donation.

As far as individuals I'd like to acknowledge, I have to start with Jim McCarthy, my agent, who accepted an unsolicited manuscript from a writer who was weird and probably overeager and definitely had no market sense. Jim has talked me through so many essential moments of my early career and for that I will be forever thankful. My publishing guardian angel.

Then Reka Simonsen, my editor, who saw potential in this book, championed it from the beginning, and may now somehow have a better ear for the pidgin of the Isle than I do. Thank you for putting up with both my publishing ignorance and my pickiness. Ditto all of this for assistant editor Kristie Choi.

To cover art queen Laylie Frazier: you're a superhero for the work you did on this cover. Its power is palpable.

To art director Greg Stadnyk, managing editor Clare McGlade, production manager Elizabeth Blake-Linn, copy editor Kaitlyn San Miguel, proofreader Stacey Sakal, top boss Justin Chanda, and the entire Atheneum team: You all are incredible. You all took my fever dream and turned it into something real.

Lastly, I'd like to acknowledge you, the readers, my Fam. Writing a novel can be a very slow, very lonely task. From researching various West African martial arts (Bowing is most inspired by *laamb*, or Senegalese wrestling), instruments, and dances to sitting my butt down on the subway seats and writing every day on the chaotic, hour-long rides home, there was a lot of work that went into this project with no guarantee that it would ever pay off. The idea that this novel could entertain–or more, ideally–even one of you made the sacrifice worth it. Thank you from the deepest, thickest mud pit of my heart. Webba thanks you, Swoo thanks you, Nana and Snore thank you, and, most of all, Dirt thanks you. It is your belief and empathy and willingness to share another person's world and hear their story that make this book what it is.